Heart Up for Ransom

'Love From A Boss'
&
'Boo'd Up With A St. Louis Goon'

Spinoff

Taug Jaye

Heart Up For Ransom

TaugJaye

Heart Up For Ransom

Disclaimer

Imagination: noun: the faculty or action of forming new ideas or images or concepts of external objects not present to the senses.

Fantasy: noun: the faculty or activity of imagining things, especially things that are impossible or improbable.

Author TaugJaye's novels are far from typical. She does a fine job of intertwining urban fiction or urban romance with fresh, "fantasy-like" storylines to create one hell of a book you've, nine times out of ten, never read before.

Author TaugJaye believes in no limitations when it comes to her writing, wanting no barrier or possibility to box her in when she's pushing the pen.

This disclaimer is a pleasant forewarning that her novels may not be for you. While she does execute the use of relatable social issues, common day-to-day struggles/battles, and spirituality within her stories, her main focus is to present readers with a page-flipping experience within the urban literary world that you're not used to experiencing.

Google said it best: "A surreal mix of fact and fantasy."

So, with that token in mind, please proceed with caution and fasten your seatbelts. She hopes you enjoy the ride.

Heart Up For Ransom

TaugJaye

*If you haven't read **'Love From A Boss'** or **'Boo'd Up With A St. Louis Goon'** STOP NOW! In order to fully understand how Tiri and Steelo's love affair unravels, it's crucial to read these two novels beforehand. Thank you.*

-Author TaugJaye

Heart Up For Ransom

Taug Jaye

Dedication

Ariel Jackson; Action-Jackson. Boo, thank you for your inspiration and continuous support. You have been my number one fan since middle school when this writing journey of mine first began, and your unwavering dedication to me as an author and a cousin means more than I could ever express with the written word.

Ink Mob, y'all owe Steelo and Tiri's dangerous love affair to my bestie.

She birthed this dope shit.

Sorry for the wait.

Love y'all to pieces.

-TaJ

Heart Up For Ransom

Taug Jaye

Heart Up For Ransom's Track list

Bobby Valentino
"Obsessed"

Cardi B
"Money"

Carl Thomas
"Emotional"
"That's What You Are"

Chris Brown
"Indigo"
"Come Together"
"Girl of My Dreams"
"Sorry Enough"
"Part of the Plan"
"All On Me"

Drake
"Teenage Fever"
"Own It"
"Weston Road Flows"
"Controlla"
"Fire & Desire"
"Faithful"
"Feel No Ways"
"Do Not Disturb"
"From Time"
"Pound Cake"
"Since Way Back"
"U With Me"
"The Real Her"

French Montana
"No Stylist"

Future
"Mask Off"

11

Heart Up For Ransom

"March Madness"

Ginuwine
"Betta Half"
"Love You More"

Jhene Aiko
"Moments"

Kashdoll
"Everybody"

Kehlani
"You Should Be Here"

Kendrick Lamar
"Loyalty"

Lil Baby
"Drip Too Hard"

Lil Wayne
"Mona Lisa"

Migos
"MotorSport"

Nipsey Hussle
"Don't Take Days Off"
"Skurr"
"Racks in the Middle"
"This Plane"

The Notorious B.I.G.
"Notorious Thugs"

PARTYNEXTDOOR
"Recognize"
"Freak In You"

Sinead Harnett
"If You Let Me"

T-Pain

Taug Jaye

"You Got Me"
"Can't Believe It"
"Time Machine"

Yung Bleu
"Warzone"
"Ice On My Baby"
"Know Who You Are"
"Slide Thru"
"Elevatorz"

Heart Up For Ransom

Prelude

Story of a Champion

Like a circle of knives, my thoughts were surrounding me,
Hounding me.
Crashing and burning, steadily fighting with the attempt in
drowning me.
But something holds me back each time reminding me that the
enemy breeds from a broken mental.
So I sober up trying to remind myself that this isn't the most
challenging thing that I've ever been through.
And with these glazed eyes, I can't seem to perfectly visualize,
the things that I'm doing an about-face.
I kept asking myself, was it the hurt or the pain?
That was blinding the way.
But every time I reached out to find a solution, it's like no saving
salvation had ever come.
The darkness stunts my growth.
It hinders my strengths.
And forces me to look down at my hands and my wrists.
And at these feet of mine that are shackled; trapped and caught
up in chains.
While in my mind, I'm fighting to practice the perfect prayer that
will cause all of my troubles to suddenly disengage.
But this wasn't a game.
I was truly going insane.
The neurons in my head are steadily losing their fire.
I'm in and out of consciousness.
All this shit's steadily frying my brain.
But they point hands and fingers in the directions of the
substances that humble me.
The outlets I binge in so hungrily.
Because I'm a slave to the gluttony.

But instead of looking at the bigger picture, they take my sins and
try to huddle me.
Backing me into a corner that triggers an onset of the pain that I
had just forgotten.
All of the yelling and shouting.
The backlash and screams.
All of the temporary yet mentally stammering dreams...
that never really meant a thing.
Because I decided that it was best to cover my own wings...
And for the ladies and gentlemen in the back,
it was in that moment that I (Steelo) suddenly began to realize
that my biggest enemy had always been me...

"We cross paths on the wrong road; your body
is a warzone.
So many trying, so many dying to get your
love.
Somebody call the ambulance.
I been shot through the heart.
I been falsely accusing, departed ways with
you, baby.
Stay with me, baby, yeah.
Have you ever had a dealing with a thug
nigga?"

-Yung Bleu, Warzone

Heart Up For Ransom

Taug Jaye

"I won't say anything...on my life you have my word, but if you don't believe me, then you can just kill me now..."

-Tiri

Heart Up For Ransom

Chapter

1

Growth is the stage or condition in increasing, developing, or maturing.

787 Bayside Terrace was a long distance away from St. Louis, Missouri.

Tiri's hair blew in the wind as she held on tight to the large Gucci duffle bag. Her eyes scanned the ocean shore that was only miles away from her room at the Spellman Hall dormitories. Her chest was heavy. The fall semester came faster than she'd expected it to, and now, she was having second thoughts about being two thousand miles away from home.

"If you scared, sus, we can turn back around right now. I'll go get ya shit like, now."

The sound of her older brother's voice made her smile as she turned around to look at him. Messiah approached her with a smirk before he wrapped his arms around her neck. This was one of the hardest things he'd ever had to do. Killing a nigga was nothing. That shit came easy, but letting his baby girl go was an aspect that was seconds away from bringing him down to his knees.

After their parents died almost four years back, then when their cousin Trudy was murdered at his expense because niggas got to her looking for him, Tiri was all he had family wise. He was a father and a husband now, and yeah, he loved his wife deeply, but the little girl in his arms right now was his heart. He'd go to war with the devil himself on her behalf.

No words were spoken between them after his comment, so in silence, he followed her back up to her dorm. Messiah helped his baby sister with the rest of her belongings before there just stood the two of them, with the silence taking over once again.

"You know I'm only a phone call away if you need anything, and I mean that, Tiri."

Her eyes watered as she stared at her brother. If it weren't for Messiah, Tiri wouldn't be who she was to this very day. It was unbelievable. He may have been ten years older than her, but they were like a large Wingstop fry and cheese cup. You couldn't eat one without the other, so their separation was killing her too.

"I miss you already," she cried as she buried her face in his chest.

Messiah wrapped his arms around her back before he kissed her forehead.

"Chin up, champ. You do yo' thing out here, live yo' fucking life, and keep yo' head in them books. You Dr. Stallion in the making, and if you have any second thoughts about anything? Whether it's yo' major, these lil' hot ass sketchy bitches that you *will* bump into, or if one of these upperclassmen do some shit that you don't like? You already know big bro gon' get shit rocking on a negative or positive note. Long story short though, don't think just because you out here alone that you *are* alone, a'ight?"

She looked up into his eyes.

"Okay. Malama Pono, big brother. I love you. Kiss baby Ashanti and Riley for me, okay?"

"You can kiss us yourself. You thought I was gone? I had to pee. This baby's elbow is sitting right on my damn bladder, and I couldn't hold it."

Tiri turned around when she heard her brother's wife, Riley's, voice. A huge smile appeared on her face when she got a glimpse of her chocolate niece.

"Hey, Shanti Baby! Tee-Tee is gonna miss you soooo much! I promise to be home for Thanksgiving dinner to see you, boo-boo!" She kissed her niece's cheek, who was chowing down on her thumb, fighting the hell out her sleep.

"Be safe, lil' bit, but have the time of your life. Seth, Nas, and the kids send all their wishes, hugs, and kisses too. You know California ain't ready for you girl, so show out."

Tiri giggled as Riley kissed her forehead.

"Thanks, sis. I really appreciate it. I can't wait to meet my next niece too. Messiah, you gon' let my girl rest before you knock her up again? Gosh."

Her brother chuckled as he ran his hands down the sides of his head. He was rocking a braided top knot with a tapered fade.

"Her pussy shouldn't be so damn good, sus. You know how shit go."

"Omg!" She busted out in laughter. "But, y'all be safe too. I'mma hold it down out here. I promise."

Messiah grabbed her hand and kissed the top of it.

"Malama Pono, sus. I love you too."

The door closing behind them felt like the end of the world, but Tiri soon wiped the tears from the creases of her eyes, startled by the sudden knock right after their departure. When she opened the door, she was greeted with a warm smile by one of her three roommates, Abby. Abby was your typical white girl, who'd flown all the way from Maine to attend school at the HBCU.

"Hi, I'm Abby. We've spoken over Facebook a few times."

"Hey, Tiri. Nice to finally meet you. You can come in."

"Thanks. Damn girl, you've got tons of shit. You're gonna be here all day unpacking all of this."

"I know, right!" Tiri exclaimed as she thoroughly glanced around her room.

She hadn't realized how much shit she'd packed until the moving truck arrived. She might've gone a little overboard, so this room arrangement would be one hell of a puzzle to solve for her.

"Have you checked out campus yet?" she asked after turning her attention back to Abby.

"No, not yet. I was actually a little scared to go by myself. I was wondering, if you don't mind, if you would go with me?"

Tiri laughed a lot harder than she should have, causing Abby to laugh as well.

"Why did you choose an HBCU? I have to ask."

Abby smiled.

"I really like Black people."

It was quiet before they both busted out into laughter.

"Okay, *Drumline*," Tiri joked.

Abby giggled.

"Seriously, I really do. Y'all are so open and honest about who y'all are and aren't scared of anything. I wish I was that outgoing. Plus, my big sister has mixed kids. Don't worry, I know what you're thinking. I'm not like that. I promise. I got a full ride here, and I was like well shit. Their medical program is one of the top ten in the country, and I was down."

"That's wassup. You not one of them Vicky from off social media type-chicks, are you? I don't fuck around with the foo-foo shit."

Tiri raised her brow in defense hoping she didn't come off too strong.

"Girl, hell no! I know I'm White! That shit is embarrassing to me, for real. The way she be trying so fucking hard to be 'down' is too much. Like, bitch, you gotta wash your hair everyday just like I do, so chill."

Tiri was bugging up.

"Okay. Cool. Where you going on campus? Is it close to Mason Point? I'm starving, and some Zaxby's is calling my name."

"Yeah. That's exactly where I'm going, actually. I have to get some things figured out in registration and sign some papers. You're a freshman, right? I know some sophomores live in Spellman Hall too."

"Yup. I am. Just let me shower and get out of these clothes that I flew in, then we can make sum' shake."

"Then we can what?"

Tiri laughed.

"St. Louis lingo for we can go/to make it happen."

"Oooooh okay. Girl, you gon' have to bear with me until I get hip, but I'll be in my room. The other girls haven't arrived yet, so my door will be open, and you can come right on in."

"Wait, you gon' be scared to have it open when they get here?" Tiri raised her brow.

One thing she didn't have time for was sketchy bitches.

"I don't mean to say it like that. They just weren't the friendliest when I reached out to them on Facebook. You were super nice when you responded. One of them just ignored me, and the other... wasn't so nice."

Aw, hell nah. I wonder what the fuck this school year is about to be like, Tiri thought as she unzipped her duffle bag.

"Don't let nobody intimidate you. Fuck them. You here for you and your experience. Not making nobody else happy."

Abby smiled.

"Thank you. That means a lot. I'll be in my room once you're ready. Take your time."

"Okay. I should be about thirty minutes."

"Okay."

𝕳𝖀𝕽𝕱

"Get you a straw, nigga. You know this pussy is juicy..."

Tiri stood in the mirror and ran the shade of Silk Indulgent by NYX across her plump lips as that "Motorsport" blared from out of her Beats Pill speaker. It was her favorite song right now even in 2018. She raised her brow as she eyed her appearance following a few squirts of her favorite fragrance, Gloss by Prada.

The high waist, distressed, denim walking shorts with creases above her knees, and the white crop top that hung off her shoulders was flawless against her smooth, silky chocolate skin. Everyone who bumped into her swore she looked just like Justine Sky. She was slim with some wide hips and niggas couldn't resist her beauty.

Her jet-black hair with a neon purple ombre was pulled up into a sloppy bun, high on her head while some Gucci Ace kicks rested underneath her feet. Everywhere she went, she was rocking something Gucci. She was definitely a Gucci Guilty bitch. Of course, Tiri donned Fashion Nova, Gap, and all that good stuff too, but Gucci was the MVP in her book. Her billionaire, drug-dealing brother spoiled her rotten with whatever her heart had desired, so all she knew was top designers.

Tiri could be a firecracker when it was needed, but all around, she had an innocent soul. When she wasn't checking a bitch for coming at her the wrong way or standing her ground, she was nothing but a timid lil' cool chick who sat up with her hand in a bag of popcorn while watching Disney movies. She was a kid at heart, and in November, she'd be a nineteen-year-old young woman who still had her V-Card.

Tiri wasn't like other girls. Yes, she loved to dress and keep her nails done, and she might have gotten high like Smokey from off *Friday*, but she wasn't into all the other shit. That's just who she was, but she knew attending an HBCU would come off as a challenge.

Trinity College was the most popping school in the region. It blew UCLA out the waters. Her school was always cracking. Their football and basketball teams were the top in the nation, parties were always being uploaded on The Shade Room, and their studies was A1.

She couldn't have asked for a more intense adventure. But one thing she promised herself before she left St. Louis was that she wasn't going to lose who she was by getting caught up in all of the hype. That was a promise that she planned on keeping.

"Okay, pretty girl. Time to go."

Tiri cringed a bit when those words came out of her mouth. She pep-talked with her reflection every day and reminded herself that just because she was chocolate, didn't mean that she wasn't beautiful. The more melanin, the better, but it wasn't always that easy until her brother started to drill it into her head that *she* had to love herself first before the world had followed suit. So she did just that.

Tiri was locking the door to her room when two guys entered the hall of their dorm, carrying a big fifty-inch flat screen that no one bothered to cover up or put back in the box. They headed down the hall to the last room on the left.

Them other chicks must be here, she thought as she gave the men that quick little smile you flashed once you made eye contact with a stranger, then went to Abby's room.

"Hey, you ready?"

"Holy shit!" Abby jumped when she heard Tiri's voice over the music. She turned it down and spun around in her computer chair. "You scared the shit out of me, girl. Look at you! You're fine!"

Tiri smiled.

"Thank you. We gon' have to get you blended in here, so you ain't so damn shook whenever somebody comes around."

"Ugh! I know, right. I'm kinda dreading this walk. I'm gonna stick out like a sore thumb," she panicked as she picked up her large-framed, stylish sunglasses.

"Own that shit, Abby. Black niggas love White girls."

Abby was too naive to recognize the shade in her compliment. Tiri didn't mean any harm, and she wasn't racist either. Abby came off like she could be the white girl at the cookout once she loosened up. It was so funny to Tiri. Homegirl heavily resembled Hayden Panettiere from *Bring It On: All Or Nothing* with Solange and seeing her at a HBCU felt like she were reiterating that classic in 2018.

Those light but pleasing winds from the sea blew against them as they headed down the block for Mason Point Millennium. It was the temple of campus where the main dining area was located as well as the registration office, the super gym, a library, and all other kinds of amenities.

Niggas were everywhere. Chocolate ones, light skinned ones, thugs tatted from shoulder to wrist, short ones, fat handsome ones, niggas with locs, fades, jocks, lames; just niggas, niggas, niggas! Tiri was in a fucking Candy Land, and by the way, Abby was secretly pointing them out she could tell she was impressed to. She'd have her a lil' boo thang soon. Tiri could feel it.

After grabbing a bite to eat and showing Abby what seasoned chicken tasted like, they headed up the escalator to the registration hall.

"I won't be long. I just gotta sign a few papers then we can go do whatever you want."

"I'm new here just like you, so this gon' be a journey for us both," Tiri laughed as she took a seat. "I've only been here once for the tour. Maybe we can just walk and look around. I think they have a pep rally planned for today on the football field in like an hour."

"Okay. Sounds like a plan. I'll be right back."

Tiri was scrolling through her phone, while Abby took care of her business when she noticed a woman enter the opened double doors, looking bad as fuck. This woman took Tiri's breath away.

Tiri didn't like girls, but when a bad bitch crossed your path with so much poise, attitude, and a vibe that couldn't be ignored, she couldn't help but to stare at her. She had to be someone of importance.

The black, thin-strapped bodycon dress hugged her curves like something fierce stopping at about calf length. The high split up the side displayed the tattoos along her juicy thigh and the denim red bottoms underneath her pedicured feet.

Kovu Usher held her head high rocking a blunt cut bob that looked as if God himself had cut it; the red lipstick painted along her lips was all the color she needed.

A tall, fair-skinned man rocking a sick ass fade with a top knot high on his head was beside her, along with a mob of five henchmen as they all headed down the left hall and to the back of the office.

Tiri didn't know what had come over her in that moment. The force the unknown woman had brought with her still lingered in the atmosphere even after she'd disappeared.

Damn, what the fuck just happened? She thought with Kovu's wrath still sitting heavily along her chest.

The ice was broken when she finally noticed Abby heading back in her direction with a tall, fine ass chocolate brotha' lingering behind her.

He was smiling too wide from the sight of her ass. Abby was slim, but she was stupid thick as if she used to be the volleyball champ back in high school. He licked his lips as he kept walking while eyeing her before he was out of sight.

"Girl, he would not stop staring at me while I was back there," she whispered in disbelief.

"You gave him yo' number, didn't you?" Tiri joked while turning her lip up.

"Shit, I was afraid not to!" she shrieked.

"Shut the fuck up, Abby!" They were cracking the fuck up. "Uh-uh, you can't be giving yo' number to these niggas out of fear. We gotta prepare you for this—"

At the speed of light, a team of men swarmed into the office running with large choppers aimed, cutting Tiri's sentence short. Bullets started blasting from the direction of the bureau that the woman and her guests from earlier had headed to. Tiri grabbed Abby by the hand, and they ran behind the nearest counter where they ducked off to get out of dodge.

Memories from Tiri's first encounter with ringing gunshots flashed in her head, back when she was seventeen, and she couldn't keep up her tough demeanor. That hood shit still didn't sit right with her stomach even after all of her experiences with that lifestyle. Tears trickled down her face as she screamed into her hand that was holding over her mouth, praying no one could hear her.

The shots were so hollow, so crisp, so close; more men were rolling in. She'd heard too many bullets going off, and her heart couldn't take it. Abby screamed for dear life when the barrel of a Tech was aimed at her. A gunman, who'd looked over the counter and discovered them trying to hide, charged for her quick. They didn't want any witnesses.

"Tiriiiiiii!"

"Abby!"

The man grabbed her by the arm before another one grabbed poor little Tiri as well and pulled her up to her feet.

"Put her down, nigga!"

The voice startled Tiri. Her eyes searched the smoky room until they fell upon the man holding two Desert Eagles in her direction; it was the guy who was with Kovu from earlier. A foreign dialect with such a heavy accent exited the mobster's mouth who was holding the gun up to her head. His pronunciation was so thick that she couldn't understand what he was saying.

The chanting continued, but very briefly before two single rounds were popped from Steelo's guns, then the bullets started blasting again. All Tiri remembered was the man's body hitting the floor who'd had her held up and hers falling on top of his.

She looked over and screamed her head off when she saw Abby laying in cold blood. She'd been shot in the side of the head, and the sight was horrifying.

Tiri scooted on her hands and feet to get far away from the dead bodies when she noticed another armed henchman heading in her direction. Time went slow when she saw his bullet exit the chamber. She could see it flying across the room just before she saw someone jump in front of her.

Steelo leapt forward and threw his body in front of Tiri as a shield with his arms stretched out in the gunman's direction. Bullets exited his chambers, making the gangsta's body shake before he hit the ground.

Steelo threw his hand around Tiri's mouth to muffle her screams as he rolled her over and laid on top of her as if he were a dead corpse. They laid there for a minute before the bullets stopped ringing, but he waited a second longer to make sure the coast was clear.

"Steelo!"

Hearing Kovu's voice meant it was time to shake. When he stood to his feet, he grabbed the unconscious girl by the hand and threw her over his shoulder. She'd blacked out from all of the excitement.

"What you working with? You get what you needed?" he gasped while going behind his suit jacket and removing the bullet from the Kevlar vest that was in his stomach.

"Yeah, I got it, and I got a full clip. I just reloaded. Here."

Kovu tossed him an M4 as she pulled the chamber back on her own. Sadly, they were the only two left to walk out alive when they'd shown up as a group of seven.

"Who the fuck is that?" Kovu questioned.

She was referring to the girl Steelo had over his shoulder as she stood against the wall while peeping out of the doorway. She could see more men swarming up the escalator. They had to get the fuck out of there and fast.

"Like I fucking know, KD! She was just here!"

"Alright, you light skinned, save a hoe ass bitch!" Kovu joked as they broke across the hall with their guns blazing while they ran for the nearest exit. It was a good fifty feet away.

"What's yo' location!" Steelo yelled into his Apple Watch while trying his best to shoot with this left hand, which wasn't his dominant one to handle an M4 with on its own.

"ETA, one minute. Pulling up on the south end of Mason Point's basement," the driver automatically responded.

"I told you not to let this shit get sloppy, KD!" Steelo laughed as they leapt down the steps rushing for the basement level.

It always wowed the fuck out of him how Kovu could manipulate a stiletto as if they were normal tennis shoes.

"I told you that bitch was gon' be on some bullshit! Marius gon' be pissed! We was supposed to be in and out!"

Her heels click-clacked against the gravel until they made it to the sedan with the doors held wide open, awaiting on their arrival. They'd gotten away just seconds before Trinity PD swarmed onto the campus, missing their targets and possible suspects.

Taug Jaye

HUFR

The obnoxious sound of Tiri's phone ringing interrupted her sleep. She felt like she'd been hit by a damn truck as she sat up along the side of the bed and massaged her thumping temples. Looking at her phone, she noticed that it was three o'clock in the morning.

Her mind was so hazy, but first things first; she had to pee. Once her urine had completely exited from out of her body, everything from earlier in the day came rushing back into her mind like a boomerang.

Seeing Abby's eyes rolled to the back of her head made her jump up, clean up, then rush over to her room. It was completely empty: no sheets were on the bed, none of her belongings were there, and even the fresh smell from her Febreze plug-ins was gone. It was like she was never there.

Tiri ran back to her room and grabbed her phone. She searched all over social media hoping to find something on her roommate. There were posts about the shooting, but no witnesses had been found, and there wasn't a single reference made to Abby. Tiri knew she wasn't dreaming.

She knew what she saw! She closed her eyes shut and tried to revisit the madness from earlier once again. Images of the woman in all black flashed in her head. Then there was the image of the man holding the two guns in her direction before he jumped in front of her, saving her life.

Did he take a bullet for me? Did he even know me? Why did he save me? How did I get here safely and not raped? What the fuck is going on?!

She panicked as she slid her feet into a pair of Gucci slides before heading for the door. Nothing was making sense to her. This had to be a dream that she was begging God to wake her up from because it wasn't the least bit funny. This couldn't be real!

When she opened the door to her room, she was greeted to a hand around her throat and the barrel of a gun being shoved into her mouth. The man guided her back inside, then quietly closed the door behind him.

He had a ski mask and gloves on, so Tiri couldn't take a mental photograph of who her killer was. She couldn't even make out his skin complexion behind the shield.

All she knew was he smelled of Armani Gio, was well over six feet tall, and he was seconds away from reuniting her with her mother and father, whom she'd missed dearly since she was fifteen years old. This moment had to have something to do with the shooting from earlier. There was no other explanation to it.

Steelo looked at the tears streaming down her precious little chocolate face. He'd been waiting on her to wake up all fucking day. The Monstrosity had ordered him to get rid of her body just as they did with the White bitch.

Tiri was supposed to have *been* fed to their pack of hyenas, hours ago, but Steelo couldn't bring himself to do it. He killed people for a living; had been since he was sixteen. He could do the shit in his sleep, blind, deaf, and while physically frail.

After he'd hit one hundred bodies, he'd stopped counting. Nothing else had mattered once he realized that this is who he was: a coldhearted and restive assassin. He did the shit and he did it well. After six years of endless, bloody, body sleighing, it had become a fetish.

Now granted, he didn't walk around with his clip blazing just knocking off innocent people, but when it was time to get the game rocking, he was down for whatever with whomever. Gender didn't matter; age, sexuality, class, or none of that shit. A target was a target, and the job wasn't done until his animals were fed.

But, in this moment, Steelo had a personal mutiny on his hands. Tiri was still alive, and she'd remembered enough to have her life taken away from her. But even now he was hesitating to blow her brains out with the suppressor that was shoved down her throat.

His mind kept telling him to look away from her glowing eyes. The eyes he couldn't break free from while she held on to his wrist without putting up a fight.

She just stood there; almost willingly, no matter how afraid she was. The same astonishment that filled him earlier when he had her unconscious body laid out along the mortuary table had taken over once again. The machete in his hand was ready to dismantle her every limb and go on about his day *then*. Twice now, he stood before her defeated.

Every once in a while, affection and passion could get the best of him. Steelo could sense hatred, negativity, betrayal, evil, and vengeance from a mile away. He didn't know how, and he didn't know why. It was a trait he'd honestly had since he was a child, and he never bothered to question it until scarce moments like this occurred, when none of those elements had coined her presence.

Most of his victims were guilty, and some weren't, but nothing had ever stopped him from drawing out an execution. Nor an order like it was doing now. His hand shook as he tightened the grip around her neck, but those eyes... Tiri's dark brown eyes were hypnotizing him. They were turning him into the man that he wasn't: a man of mercy...

Mercy, her flaming eyes kept begging him. *Mercy! Mercy! Mercy!*

Mentally frustrated, he shoved her into the bed and turned to walk away from her.

"I won't-say-any-thing..."

Her cries were barely above a whisper, but they'd gotten his attention. He stopped in his tracks and looked over his shoulder as if he were waiting on her to finish.

"I don't know anything...just please...don't kill me. On my life, you have my word, but if you don't believe me, then you can just go ahead and kill me now."

Steelo inhaled deeply before the room door closed behind him and he got the fuck out of dodge. He may have done the devil's dirty work, but when God told him to fall back, that's exactly what the fuck he did. It was contradicting. It always had been for him, and it always would be.

His actions were sparse tonight, and little Miss Tiri Nyree Stallion better had gotten down on her knees at the very moment. She needed to thank the Lord that the tiny piece of the Holy Spirit concealed within Steelo's tampered heart had, yet again, spared her life.

Heart Up For Ransom

Taug Jaye

"No. What you're doing right now is playing wit' yo' fucking life."

-Steelo

Heart Up For Ransom

Chapter

2

"**M**essiah, I'm okaaaaaaay. Please calm down," Tiri begged while FaceTiming her big brother on her laptop.

She was massaging her temples to refrain from losing her shit as well, but from the looks of Messiah going nuts on her screen, it wasn't likely that she'd be able to hold it in either.

"Fuck that shit, Tiri! I'm coming to get yo' ass! Pack yo' shit!"

"I SAID I WAS OKAY!"

Her screams made him stop pacing the floor. He looked directly into his baby sister's eyes and observed the seriousness that rested within her body language. The shooting had made CNN, and the moment he heard about it, he'd gotten an army ready to go out and get her. Luckily, he called her before he acted upon that shit like he usually did, or else he would've been there.

"They've gotten to the bottom of it. The suspect was taken into custody and we're finally off of lockdown today," she explained while the eyes of her "almost masked killer" flashed in her head. That was four days ago. "You saw the news, Siah. Apparently, the previous owner of the college's wife was salty about her husband's death last year, and she snapped. So, she hired people to shoot up the Mason Point Millennium out of spite, thinking they had something to do with it. You saw her mug shot, and you see that school is starting back up next week. I'm okay, so you should be too."

There was a long pause following her statement. Messiah had pulled the phone away from his ear to stare at the screen, making sure he was talking to the right person. This couldn't have been the scary little Tiri Stallion he watched grow up. It just couldn't be.

"What the fuck you do with my whiny ass lil' sister? How the fuck you get this solid after four days, Tiri? Not to mention that you ain't even call me balling yo' eyes out about it like you don't cry at the drop of a damn hat just for some stupid shit. Like you not being able to find yo' damn phone charger."

Tiri smiled.

"That was one time, and I was only devastated because I was tryna win those tickets to that OVO concert and I didn't wanna miss out on it. Shut the fuck up." They shared a laugh. "And I've been telling you that I've gotta grow up someday. I know you love me and will drop what you're doing to make sure I'm safe, but little sister got this. So, you can just chillax, boss man."

Messiah laughed.

"I guess, Tiri. I'mma still keep my eye on that shit. You said y'all can leave campus and shit now?"

"Yeah. I wanna get out and just relax my damn self. I wish I had my car. I'd just let my top back and let my hair blow in the wind..."

"Why you always do that shit, sus? I can't never surprise yo' lil' ug'lass."

A smile covered Tiri's face.

"Messiah, you sent my car down here?!" she shrieked.

"You know big bro got you. I just sent you the address of the dealership where you can pick it up from. I got it washed, checked out, and all that good shit. I sent you another address where you gon' keep it parked at. It's a rented garage just for you. I took care of the finances already, so you should be straight."

Tiri couldn't believe her ears. Trinity U had strict transportation rules. Due to limited spacing for parking, first-year students couldn't have cars, so this was the best thing she'd had happen to her since that gun was shoved down her throat... she honestly couldn't believe she was still holding that in.

Tiri told her brother everything, but she knew for a fact that the man in her room would come for her before Messiah could handle anything, so she kept quiet like she swore to. But it was a relief to be able to breathe again knowing that she had her car now.

"I love youuuuuuuuu, Messiah!" she beamed with her pearly whites flashing along the screen.

"I love you too. *Call me*, Tiri, a'ight? You gon' be mad if I pop out on yo' ass."

"I will. I will. I promise. Malamo Pono."

"Malamo Pono, sus."

Tiri couldn't jump out of bed fast enough and get dressed. She kept it simple and slid on a black Nike cycling unitard with a black sports bra and matching sun visor. She wore her hair down in voluminous, loose waves that dried from her shower earlier, and black Gucci slides with an accentuating handbag to complete her look.

"We off lock-down?"

Tiri turned around and looked over her shoulder at her roommate, JZ, standing in her best friend's, Hazel E, doorway.

"Did you see the news or get the email?" Tiri retorted.

She tried being cordial with her and Hazel E these last four days. Hazel E wasn't that bad, but they all were simply cut from a different cloth, and she wasn't gonna fake no friendships.

"Should I have watched or checked it?" JZ shot back.

"Who you talking to? Oh, hey, Tiri."

Hazel E stuck her head out the doorway and threw up two fingers in Tiri's direction. She obviously was more cordial than her friend was.

"Wassup, HE, and yeah, you should've, *Javeline*, or else you wouldn't be standing there asking me all of these dumb ass questions."

Tiri hated to tap into that side of her gangsta', but that bitch Javeline was always pushing it, and the last thing she wanted was for people to think that she was the same soft ass Tiri from back home. Being in another state she had to stand her ground with whomever she crossed paths with. There was no more being too timid to speak for herself or holding her tongue. Those days were over.

After locking up her dorm, Tiri threw the deuces up back at them and left. Messiah's comment kept running through her head while her Uber driver took her to her destination. Who was she right now? The old Tiri was quiet, bubbly, and friendly no matter what, yet, she'd been the total opposite ever since *you know what* happened. Maybe it was just a bad case of nerves, but she also knew that it was time to step it up and be a boss bitch like Messiah' always told her she was. But she was sure once she got behind the wheel of her Black Berry that she'd feel ten times better.

HUFR

"Hi, my name is Tiri Stallion. I'm here to pick up my car."

"Hello, Miss Stallion. And which vehicle are you picking up today?" The secretary questioned, a bit query about someone as young as she was, inquiring about a vehicle.

"A black 2018 SL Roadster."

"One moment. *I need an available member to the showroom please. An available member to the showroom,*" the clerk announced over the intercom.

Not even a minute later, a man who Tiri swore looked just like Joe Biden appeared before her. He was casually dressed in Armani slacks and a silk Polo with the Mercedes Benz logo printed along the chest.

"John Wittman. How may I help you, Miss...?"

"Tiri," she smiled as they shook hands.

"A very pretty name to match a pretty girl. Are you interested in a particular vehicle?"

"Yes. Mine. There should be a black SL Roadster here for me that arrived from St. Louis."

He smiled.

"Absolutely. Follow me. Wait, you're Messiah's younger sister, correct?"

"That's me."

"Aww, I see. I've been expecting you. After you, dear."

He held the door open to their loading dock. Tiri thanked him and headed outside, smiling from ear to ear when she laid eyes upon her Black Berry. The glossy paint and shining rims made her heart race.

"Your keys, Miss Tiri. Any issues, questions, or concerns just contact me personally. And make sure you come and get your car washed every Friday morning. It's complimentary for all Mercedes Benz owners here in Trinity."

He handed her his business card as well.

"Thank you, and I sure will. See you in the near future, Mr. Wittman."

"Absolutely."

When Tiri opened the door to her car, a black G-Wagon pulled into the lot and parked right next to her. When the driver exited the vehicle, she felt like all of her insides had fallen out of her body and hit the floor.

Steelo was clean in his simple attire. He donned a black leather Gucci web jacket, black t-shirt, black straight leg Radburn jeans, and custom-made Cole Haan wingtip sneakers. Nothing but a single gold chain and a Rolex on his arm completed his fit. Steelo looked as if he'd just come from the barbershop. His lining and beard were both tapered to perfection.

When he noticed Tiri, time stood still. Her mahogany-colored skin looked succulent and good enough to eat. She was the most beautiful chocolate drop he'd ever seen before with her cute little button nose and high cheekbones. Plus, she had a nice lil' shape on her too, to be so young. The attraction was ironic. He could sit back with a blunt and stare at her beauty all day; admiring the curvature of her nose, her big, brown eyes, her full lips, long legs, and the way her clothes fit her frame perfectly, but instead, he reverted his eyes to Mr. John Wittman, who he then slapped hands with.

"Right on time as always, Mr. Steelo. I'll get your vehicle all together for you. You're still test driving the Vision 6 today as well, correct?"

"As we discussed."

Steelo raised his brow as he put his Gucci shades back on his face.

"Yes, of course. Let me go grab the keys for ya. I've just finished up with a customer. Is everything alright, Miss Stallion?"

Tiri's trance was broken when she heard John's voice addressing her. She hadn't noticed that she was just staring at Steelo as if she were stuck on stupid until she was questioned. With no response, she hopped into her vehicle, connected her phone to the Bluetooth, and let that old school rap blast in the air as she pulled out of the lot. Eazy E's voice always gave her a sense of calm, and that's exactly what she needed at this moment...

Taug Jaye

ℌℭℑℜ

Triple Beam Pizza was one of Tiri's favorite spots in the Sunshine state. The eatery was known for their large portions, and on-lookers kept eyeing the large chicken, spinach, and feta alfredo pizza sitting before the frail girl, wondering where she was about to put it all... well in her stomach, duh! With the way her tummy was growling, she could go for an order of wings too if her favorite spot was near. One thing she wasn't afraid to do was put some shit down no matter who was watching.

The air in California was so much different than in St. Louis. It was crisp and freshening, mind stimulating, and no matter where you were, it felt like you were right on the ocean shore. She could reside at the café and read all day until the sun went down. It was the perfect getaway after being cooped up in her dorm for a week.

Her nose was deep into *Love From A Boss* by Kovu Usher while she shoved another slice of carb happiness into her mouth. She hadn't been able to put the book down since she cracked it open thirty minutes ago, and now she was on Chapter 5, wondering if the characters would make it out of their raided apartment alive.

It wowed her how she could connect with an author's words as if she were there. The novel was picture perfect, and it almost kept her mind off of the man that was dining three tables behind her.

Ten minutes ago, she had her phone in her face for a selfie check when she discovered his rich, silky-smooth butterscotch skin in her camera. It was almost beginning to be too much. Was he following her? Trinity was a huge city, and there was no way in hell that twice now, they'd ended up in the same place at the same time. Tiri had butterflies. She couldn't get his voice out of her head.

For four days now, she'd studied her "almost masked killer's" baritone until she was reunited with it just hours ago when she picked up her car. That's what had her so hexed when she saw him. Tiri was timid, and it was getting the best of her right now, but her alter ego was eager to

44

know why he'd placed her life in his hands. If he could just answer that one question for her, then that would give her the closure she needed to move forward.

Her nerves were running her ragged, and she was seconds away from losing it... so fuck being in public. She lit her Chillum and inhaled deeply as the weed consumed her body. There was a hookah lounge right next door, and she'd caught a few whiffs of marijuana from the entrance each time someone entered while she'd been there. So why not burn one... or maybe even three or four hits to help her mellow out.

When her body loosened up, she inhaled deeply to ease the pain brewing from within from thoughts of addressing this man. Her heart was racing before she'd even gotten up, but her emotions wouldn't let her be.

Tiri did one last selfie check to make sure he was still there. To her surprise, he now had a guest sitting across from him, but that didn't last long. The man in the tailored suit soon made an exit, but little did Tiri know, Steelo was watching her just as much as she'd been watching him. He'd pepped her peaking at him in her camera for a while now and found it a bit amusing.

Steelo might have been The Monstrosity's right-hand man, and one of his only best friends, but one thing he thanked God for his ability to "blend in" with the crowd. He didn't step out on his own much, but when he did, it was always at a low-key spot where he could chill and handle a little business if need be.

It was an advantage for Marius as well. Besides his wife, Steelo was the perfect set of eyes that could roam the streets almost untouchable when the heat wasn't too hot. Steelo was instantaneous. One minute you saw him, and the next, he'd disappear as if he were never there, but the presence of young Tiri couldn't allow him to leave.

It honestly irritated him. Seeing her alive was nothing but physical evidence of the emotions and sentiment that he'd managed to keep veiled and in control of until he came across her. Something about offing this girl had his stomach choppy.

Between the gun at his waistline that his free hand rested upon, and the sniper waiting on the signal to splatter her shit in the distance? She should've *been* dead, and his presence should've *been* absent.

The fuck is going on wit' you, man?

His thoughts were interrupted when she boldly took a seat across from him. Silence consumed the atmosphere. He watched her thumbs twirl back and forth while she stared at the table, fighting herself to avoid making eye contact with her "Superman."

On the bright side, Tiri's glow was irresistible. Steelo was caught up in yet another spell, just as he was earlier, while her vibrant hair blew in the wind. Eccentrically, he was seconds away from vocally admiring her beauty, but that thought was short lived. Instantly, he contained his composure and checked himself. He'd found himself having to do that shit too often while in her presence.

"I see you like playing with fire," he affirmed while downing the rest of the Virginia Black in his glass that he went nowhere without.

Most people couldn't swallow a sip without the fumes from the high ratio of alcohol burning their throat, but all he'd known was pain. The drink traveled through his passageway with ease.

"Umm… why did you save me?" she innocently retorted, finally building up the courage to look him in the eye.

His face was gorgeous…yes, fucking gorgeous. The man was so fine, and his skin was so clear she swore the nigga was wearing a full face of Fenty Beauty. His full pink lips, quirky though cute, thick eyebrows, and his panty-dropping, low beard made her feel like she was watching that video of Diddy recording his stepson, Quincy Brown, while admiring his looks himself. She was mesmerized.

His cocky shoulders, the lean, yet, muscular structure on his six-foot-three frame, his aura, and the scent of his signature Armani cologne had the insides of her virgin thighs tingling. She'd never been so aroused by a man's presence, who wasn't her faithful man crush Monday, Dez Bryant.

Tiri didn't like light skinned men to be honest. The 6 God was an exception because she loved his music, but that was it. Steelo had an effect on her that she couldn't understand, and she wanted to get to the bottom of it.

"The only thing that should be on your mind is that you're alive."

His words were vile, and the average girl would've been offended. Tiri might've been young, but she was very hip to game. Steelo's presence alone had put together the perfect visual for her to see that he was a man of importance in this town.

He merged well, but one thing he honestly couldn't do was refrain from drawing an attraction to himself no matter how hard he tried, and it impressed her. A well respected though highly feared and intimidating man was all she'd known being raised by a kingpin. Steelo's ability to possess such dominance yet, obtain ordinance in his city had said a lot about his character.

"Excuse me for being concerned about my welfare," she snapped while looking back into his eyes.

"No. What you're doing right now is playing wit' yo' fucking life. Now go on about your business before I walk away, this time doing what I *should've* done four days ago... you understand *that*?"

Those words were like ice; *those* words had cut her deep. How could he be so melancholy when he'd saved her life? That shit wasn't normal. He obviously had to care enough if he kept giving her chance after chance to save herself, but nothing about him in that moment gave her any sense of optimism.

Heartbroken with tears falling down her cheeks, Tiri stood to her feet, retrieved her belongings, and ran for her vehicle. She'd gotten his message loud and clear that go around. No matter how much her conscious would fight with her about a stranger saving her life, it was an L that she was willing to take if it would allow her to never cross paths with this man ever again.

Heart Up For Ransom

Taug Jaye

"Why did you save me?"

-Tiri

Heart Up For Ransom

Chapter

3

One Week Later

Sweat trickled down Steelo's forehead, arms, chest, and back as he forced himself to continue with his last set of pull-up variations.

He cringed from the burning sensations as he bit his bottom lip, fighting to pull through.

Three, two, one...

He hopped off, landing down to the floor with his elbows resting along his knees. Steelo's breathing was heavy; too heavy. He'd been overexerting himself for hours before he finally decided to call it quits. Heading to the sauna, he made sure he had his gun before he took a seat and inhaled deeply to slow down his heart rate.

Steelo removed his hair from the bun and let it fall in his face while lowering his head. He simply couldn't think. For a week now, he'd been unable to get Tiri's beautiful face from out of his head. She was so precious, and he couldn't believe how frazzled she had him. It's not like he'd fucked her, it's not like they'd been communicating, or even had a real conversation.

The man had hardly known her, but the constant desire to *want to get to know her* is what was driving him out of his mind. The other killer part was that his arrogance wouldn't give him the permission to admit that she'd made an impression on him from their brief encounters.

But how when it was *him* who saved *her*? *He* jumped in front of that bullet, *and* he left her alive after Marius told him not to. Tiri didn't understand how her presence on this earth had said a lot about him as a man. Steelo was convinced years ago that him, love, relationships, and all of the sentimental shit just weren't compatible.

Ever since his father walked out on him when he was a newborn, then when his stepmother overdosed in front of him at the age of five, he had no desire to channel those emotions. He and Marius understood one another greatly because they'd faced the same struggles no matter how much time laid between their age difference.

Pain was pain no matter when, where, or how you felt it. On one hand, Steelo was cool with being a bachelor. No commitment; every man's weakness. But after damn near living up under Marius and Kovu's ole' in love asses, and watching them raise their kids, it left him torn.

Steelo was only twenty-five. He still had a long life ahead of him to live, and he honestly couldn't fathom harboring so much unnecessary vengeance and hatred, outside of when he was killing niggas, until he was thirty. He'd lose his shit.

The major difference between him and Marius was that he wasn't afraid to love. If anything, he was more afraid of himself and who he'd turn into without it. When he was appointed to be Kovu's bodyguard, that situation showed him aspects about himself that he didn't know had still existed. He loved KD. Sincerely. She was his big sister, and blood was the only thing that separated them.

Taking to her, riding for her, placing her, and now, little Aubrey and Jayce into his heart was some relief. It was uncanny. No matter how many guilty souls he'd slayed, he found the most injustice within the man in the mirror. He was a killer, and he took to what he did as if it wasn't unruly, due to the thirst he had for the pain that he'd become so accustomed to...

His mind would endlessly race about the unfortunate turn of events that he now called his life if he allowed it to, so he showered, got dressed, and headed on about his day to keep his heart from being so heavy.

HUFR

"Hi, Ste-Ste!"

"Wassup, boo!"

Steelo swept Aubrey up into his arms and kissed her cheek. She was sixteen months now, and he never knew how a child who wasn't his own, could hold so much of his weary heart with an unconditional barrier, within the palms of her tiny little hands.

"What you up to, pretty girl? Chilling?"

Aubrey clapped her hands in excitement following his comment before she wrapped her arms around his neck.

"Where yo' brother at?" Steelo asked as he took a seat on the couch.

They were in the second living room at Marius and Kovu's new twenty thousand square foot home that he'd just arrived to, making sure that everything was everything. Toys, two cribs, and baby gear was laid out everywhere.

"Say hi to your uncle Steelo, Jayce," Reba Koi cooed as she entered the TV room from changing him at his diaper station.

"How you doing, sweetheart?"

Steelo stood to his feet, threw his free arm around Reba Koi's shoulders, and kissed her forehead. She was Chef Koi's wife and the kids' nanny.

"I'm good, baby. How are you?"

"I'm straight. It's almost nap time for them, ain't it? This one wired," he referred to the jolly Aubrey singing her ABC's with the television.

Steelo glanced down at his Richard Millie, seeing that it was a quarter after three.

"That one just woke up at noon. I'll be lucky if she goes back to sleep." Reba Koi smiled brightly before sticking her tongue out at Aubrey.

"You see that? She stuck her tongue out right back at you, Miss Lady. Acting like her momma," Steelo chuckled. "Speaking of, let me see if she answers."

He placed a Facetime call to Kovu, who picked up sooner than he expected her to.

"Hi, pretty girl! Is that mommy's baby?! I was just about to call and check up on you two. Mommy misses y'all so much!"

"Hi, mommy!" Aubrey cheered.

"Hi, baby! Are you being good for Reba Koi, you little stinker?"

Aubrey scrunched up her face in response to her mother's question.

"See, that's the look of deviousness right there, sus," Steelo joked as he blew in her ear, causing his princess to giggle.

"Wassup, light skinned?"

He laughed.

"Wassup wit' it?" Steelo put little Aubrey down in her playpen and handed her the sippy cup he retrieved from Reba Koi. "Y'all straight?" He questioned.

"Yes. This break was surely needed. We'll be back in a few days. Is Jayce asleep?"

"Yeah, she just laid him down."

Kovu blew kisses into the camera at her slumbering son before thanking Reba for watching the kids while she and her husband were away. After their brief convo, Steelo left the room so the two of them could talk.

"How are you? Everything's all good?" KD questioned.

"'Sal good, shorty. Everything in line, everybody on watch, and I'm just chilling," he confirmed as he opened the patio door while pulling the Backwoods from behind his ear.

He let the gas burn while he took in the scenery from the ocean view behind their home.

"What's on yo' mind, potna?"

Steelo chuckled. To this day it still fucked him up how well Kovu had known him.

"Ain't shit on my mind, bruh," he smiled.

"Lie again," KD threatened with the barrel of her .45 in the camera.

"Yo', sus, after two kids you gotta retire. Bad enough you was getting shit cracking the other day," he joked.

"I know, right? I'm getting old. It might be a third mini Usher if Marius don't leave me the hell alone. I'm putting a lock on my shit. I need a break from being pregnant. I dun' had them back to back. I'm is tired, Steelo, bruh."

He was cracking up.

"You wild, KD."

"And you thinking about that girl, ain't you?" she blurted, already knowing his dilemma.

Steelo's heart raced thinking about Tiri. It was sickening. Visions of the tears falling down her face due to his mean and rude ass being ignorant with her, when all she did was ask him a simple question, was really starting to fuck with him.

"So, go and talk to her," Kovu asserted.

He inhaled deeply from the blunt.

"I'm tryna forget about it."

"But you haven't. She's not even supposed to be alive, bro. Baby girl must got the juice if yo' mean ass is capping. You saw her again, didn't you? That's why you tripping."

"Aye, shut the fuck up, KD. It ain't even like that."

They shared a laugh.

"Real shit though, *you're* the one who needs to relax and clear your head, Steelo the Deelo. The kids are okay; me and Marius are straight. Do something for yourself besides fucking all of these dead-end ass bitches that you can't even lay up and chill with, even if you wanted to.

Hell, I don't even know why you saved the girl in the first place. Now its got you feeling a way. But never will I judge you; I understand all too well. You see how me and Marius met. That saving strangers shit places a hold on ya heart. It's not normal."

"Yeah, sus, that made you captain save a ho—looking ass."

"Aye—well… you got me that time. I'll give you that. Lil' light skinned muthafucka."

He laughed.

"Enjoy the islands, sus. I'mma find something to get into."

"Alright. Love you, brother. Marius said he'll holla at you later on tonight, but don't forget what I said either. Make sure she's worth this headache and if not, kill her and move on."

He rubbed the back of his head with the blunt hanging out the side of his mouth.

"Love you too."

ḢUFR

One week into school and the professors had already begun piling work on top of their students. Tiri stared at her Trigonometry textbook, Biology textbook, and English prompts thinking to herself that this shit wasn't getting done tonight. Maybe tomorrow, but not on a Friday night. She reached for her Gucci fanny pack, filled it with her favorite Brightside Skittles, some 'Woods, and her weed before she left the dorm hall.

"Wassup, Lil' St. Louis?"

She smiled at her classmate, Rodrick, who was chilling with his boys. They were waiting on some of the girls that lived in her hall to come outside.

"Hey, wassup. Y'all partying tonight?" she asked, peeping how fly they all were.

"Damn right. The upperclassmen throwing a filthy ass kickback at Black Lava Apartments," he answered.

"You should come through, mama," his potna, Montrell, chimed in.

He'd had his eye on Tiri since the first day of their Trigonometry class. She walked in looking like a bad and bougie chocolate Barbie doll. Her silky brown skin was the center of attention, and ever since, he's wanted her bad.

"Not tonight. I'mma catch this sunset before it gets dark. Y'all be safe though."

"You should burn one with us when we make it back then," he insisted.

She had to give it to him. Montrell was handsome in his own kind of weird way, and he was a sweetheart. He favored Quavo from The Migos. He was fly too, and that's what made him attractive. Hell, the bitches loved him. Tiri knew he had groupies already, but she'd only looked at him as a friend anyway. She knew it was nothing there for her.

"If I'm awake when y'all pop back out then bet." She smiled before she walked off, headed for the shore.

Tiri spotted the beach guard with a hundred dollar bill once she arrived to keep his nerdy ass quiet like she'd been doing since her first night there, so she could smoke her weed in peace. She found the perfect spot not too far from the water before she unfolded the beach chair and kicked back. She'd never seen anything so beautiful. The color formation was so exotic-looking with deep blues, pinks, and yellows, that Tiri just had to take a few flicks for the 'Gram.

"I made it through my first week of college, ma and dad, and it didn't kill me," she giggled as she took a long pull from the blunt.

A day didn't go by when she didn't think of her risen angels. It was bittersweet, but now that it was almost four years later, she could handle their departure without so many tears. Tiri smoked three Backwoods before she called it a wrap. She was floating with the clouds, had a hard case of the munchies, and some Pizza Hut was right up her alley. She couldn't wait for her order to arrive.

When she made it back to the dorm, a clean and flashy Maybach limousine was parked out front.

Somebody's got some company, she thought in excitement as she headed for the entrance.

"Excuse me, ma?"

Tiri turned around with her mace ready when the obscure man tried to get her attention. The large black goon, looking like the hefty version of Rick Ross, chuckled from her actions.

"I don't mean you no harm, mama. You're Tiri, right?"

"Who's asking?" she raised her brow.

When the back window lowered only halfway, her poor heart almost jumped out of her chest. It was Steelo. She couldn't believe it. Her mind kept telling her not to walk over to his door, but her feet wouldn't listen.

"Get in," he ordered.

Oh no. He really is gonna kill me, she panicked, not knowing what the fuck to do.

"I'm not gon' tell you again," he asserted with a raise of an eyebrow before the window closed.

Tiri gazed over at the guard holding the door open for her. She was too high for this shit, but her stubborn ass feet still weren't listening. They went against her wishes when she found herself in the backseat

57

along with the man whom she begged God to never see again. She remained quiet as the driver pulled off. Her school was now miles behind her, and the only thing she could think of was this being her last moment alive before the kill.

"I swore that I wouldn't say anything, and that was my word. I haven't said anything to anyone," she pleaded with a tremble in her voice.

Unable to keep a straight face, Steelo laughed at her actions. Kovu could drive him all day long about that light skinned, pretty boy shit. He knew he had more than enough darkness within his soul to make some shit shake. She just liked to talk shit like he and Marius weren't the same skin complexion.

"You would've been dead, Tiri. You and I both know that," he chuckled.

Steelo looked good when he wore a blank face, channeling his inner boss and swag. But he consumed a level of endless happiness and serenity when he took the time out to smile. Tiri was filled with so much ambivalence that it was making her feel trippy.

"Now, wait a got damn minute," she screeched, trying to get everything in order. "What the fuck do you think you're doing?"

She was so high the weed she'd smoked had engulfed his cologne in the atmosphere, making him higher than he already was. Tiri was so confused it was cute.

"Let's save all of the questions for the dinner table, mama."

"Dinner? Do I look like I'm dressed for dinner? And, first of all, *Mr. Steelo*, why did you save me? Why can't you just answer me? It's a simple, yet critical inquiry that I need answered," she protested.

Steelo could see it now that he'd have to break Miss Twenty-One Questions in real quick before she started to irritate him.

"Do what I said and save all them fucking questions for later. Now, go inside and hurry the fuck up, so we don't miss our reservations. I've already waited on you longer than I expected to."

She hadn't noticed that they'd arrived and were parked in front of **the** Trinity Galleria shopping mall until he pointed it out.

"Tiri."

The baritone in his voice made her jump out the car not being able to handle being around him in that moment. His aura was overbearing, and her racing heart couldn't take it. Twenty minutes later, after his team was finished with her, she exited the mall in the more appropriate attire for their evening.

The thin-strapped, soft gold maxi dress hugged her slim waist and hips phenomenally. The hairstylist had picked her Bantu knots out, so the results ended with her rocking a voluminous and bouncy style parted down the middle. Almost identical to Beyoncé's look in her "Freakum Dress" video.

Tiri thanked God that one of the heel selections she had to choose from were platforms. Nervously, she continued to pray that the Yves Saint Laurent sandals would be nice to her and not embarrass her in front of this man. She'd just learned how to walk in heels comfortably back during prom season. With him being so got-damn impatient, she could barely get a catwalk going to break them in, even if it were brief. This night was surely going to be interesting.

Steelo removed the glass from his lips when she entered the limousine. He was already out of his mind for being so indecisive over a girl who'd only be nineteen in November, but when she was so beautiful and possessed an allure that he couldn't resist, how could he not be?

When they finally made it to their destination, Tiri hesitated to get out of the car. Was this right? Should she be here? Her stomach was choppy, and she could've puked at the drop of a hat.

So many thoughts were going through her head that it startled her when Steelo opened her door. As he held his hand out, she softened up. Tiri placed her hand into his while he helped her make an exit.

Their bodies were meters away once she stood to her feet. Tiri looked up into his eyes and felt all of her troubles just suddenly vanish. Clearly, she was dealing with a grown ass man, so she couldn't be on any bullshit tonight. But shit, for his fine ass donning the all-black Tom Ford suit with the undershirt and tie to match, she could fix that and keep herself in check.

"You look beautiful," he complimented with the raise of an eyebrow.

Her smile was magnetic to his comment. Hearing those words come out of a man's mouth like *his* had her floating on cloud nine. The weed was simply a bonus compared to him.

"Thank you. That really means a lot to me. You look good as well, Steelo."

He chuckled as he grabbed her by the hand and led her to the entrance with their guard leading the way. Tiri's innocence is what had him so captivated. He hoped her conversation could keep him just as focused, or all of this would've been a waste of time. Something he hated to do when he could've been running in and out of some slippery, wet pussy. Hell, he was a man, and it was the truth.

Tiri had never heard of Indigo Seafood and Steakhouse before. By the way the staff catered to her alpha male company, she guessed that it was a franchise he'd owned. They were escorted to a private room with a table, an open grill, a chef, and dining staff all waiting on their arrival.

"Good evening, Mr. Steelo, and his gorgeous guest. May I start you two off with any drinks?" The waiter greeted.

"Virginia Black," Steelo replied.

"Yes, of course. And for you, ma'am?"

"Hi, and thanks for your compliment. Do you have any sweet Riesling?"

"Yes, ma'am. American or German?"

"German, please."

"Of course. I'll be back momentarily."

Steelo raised his brow at Tiri. He was just waiting on her to say something more on the lines of water or some sort of soft drink, but this girl dun' jumped the gun and started speaking wine language on him. She looked into his eyes after placing her serviette along her lap, then giggled.

"What?" she innocently asked.

"The fuck you know about Riesling?"

Tiri held her face in her hands from blushing. Now she was herself. Now her true personality had come to surface after two weeks of being away from home. It was in his welcoming presence that she felt like she could just be her.

"Don't judge me," she blushed.

"Judge you, no, but study you, yes. You fold under that kind of pressure?" he questioned with suspicion.

"Absolutely not. My brother is part owner of the biggest and most prestigious black-owned winery in the Midwest. Our family was damn near raised on wine. I know how old I am, and I'm also very aware of the age limit on drinking. I might not have been carded because of your stature, but the only person in this room who knows or even suspects that I'm a minor is *you*."

"Your wine, ma'am."

"Thank you very much."

"And your bottle, sir."

The server poured Steelo a glass before he gave them a few more minutes to look over the menu. Hey, the man could admit that he was impressed. Like a gentleman, Steelo raised his glass to Tiri's response. She managed to do something that no other woman in his life had ever done, and that had shut him the fuck up. He was reverent of her ability to stand her ground. Steelo guessed age wasn't anything but a number as long you had some common sense.

"Ewww, it's moving. It's raw. I don't want that," Tiri cringed as the legs on the calamari continued to dance from the cooking solution the chef had sprinkled it with, seconds ago. "Is it alive?!" her eyes dilated as the arms of the creature climbed over the edge of the bowl. "Ew, Steelo, get it," she squirmed in her seat while holding the serviette up to her face, shielding her eyes.

Endless laughter escaped his lips as well as the chef's before he removed the dish and replaced it with something that was more suitable for her liking.

"You're fucking with me." She beamed with a smile so beautiful that it could've made Steelo's heart stop. She was adorable.

"You loose yet?" he questioned with a smile in return.

He'd felt so bad about the last time he saw her. His only mission tonight was to make her smile without coming off too much like the asshole he truly was.

Tiri held the wine glass up to her lips and unknowingly devoured it all.

"You're going to give me a damn heart attack. I hate anything that crawls. What's this?"

She used the chopsticks to fish for the lightly breaded and fried appetizer sitting before them. Loads of flavor burst into her mouth following the first bite. The texture was a bit odd, but all around, it was tasty.

"A fried version of your little friend that was just removed from the table."

Her face flushed to a tan shade as she swallowed the remains in her mouth, causing him to double over in laughter.

"I don't fucking like you. You *are* trying to kill me. What kind of deranged ass psychopath are you, Steelo?"

He shook his head.

"It's good though," he insisted.

Tiri would rather do anything in that moment than to agree with him, but she answered his question when she reached for another piece.

"If I get sick, I'm coming for your light-bright ass with my chopper fully loaded," she smiled.

"That's cute. I almost responded in awe."

"Don't let the age fool you. I'm 'bout that life."

Due to the look he shot her, mixed with how quickly his left eyebrow raised in the air, she couldn't help but laugh.

"That's what the fuck I thought," he chuckled. "What are you studying?" he then inquired, referring to her schooling.

"Biology. The goal is to become an Emergency Medicine Specialist."

"So you like blood and all the hype?"

"Yup. My mom was a nurse in the ER. Plus, I figured if I was going to college that I might as well do something that I was gonna earn six figures doing and make all of the money my brother is dropping worth it. School is so fucking expensive; it's almost not beneficial to go in the end. My scholarships did not cover everything, which is some bullshit."

"On me."

"And what do you do?"

Tiri almost felt uncomfortable asking him about his "occupation," but he just didn't seem like the kingpin type. She doubted that he'd be honest with her, but his condescending though mystique aura sent chills down her spine, giving her the thirst to want to know more.

"I'm not the captain of the ship, but I run this town. Let's leave it at that for right now."

Leaving the question alone, Tiri's eyes changed to the server who placed her meal before her. Her eyes glowed from the giant king crab claws and pound of crab legs that were pre-cracked, the two lobster tails already removed from the shell, the jumbo shrimp kabobs lathered in a shrimp scampi butter sauce, mussels, oysters, scallops, and her side of fettuccini pasta.

She glanced across the table and noticed that Steelo was dining with the same meal except he'd have to de-shell his food, not to mention the T-Bone steak and arugula salad he had on the side.

"Why'd you have to get your hands dirty?" she questioned before inserting the kabob into her mouth, removing two of the shrimps.

Everything was so delicious she could've slapped the nigga's momma.

"I prefer to get my hands dirty, mama. What type of man would I be to sit and watch you struggle to get that shit open? I'd do it myself, but then my food would get cold. This way, we both win."

Tiri smiled. His mean ass did have a dash of some mannerisms and sincerity stored within his character after all.

"So, you know that you have to be nice to me from this day forward, right?"

He chuckled from her response.

"I can't make no promises on all occasions, mama."

Her ass started to blurt out, "On what occasions, nigga!" but she caught herself and instead, replied with, "That's understandable... Yet, to clear the air, I don't wanna know all of your secrets, Steelo, but I do wanna get to know you."

He stared her in the eye as he cracked the crab-claw in half. Tiri was gonna give him a run for his fucking money. He could already see it, and it made him wonder if he was down for the cause. Thoughts of possession were different than ownership. Contemplation was harmless but embarking on the journey towards a desire is where the challenge lied. Steelo could admit wholeheartedly that, that was a tough decision to make.

"What do you wanna know?" he questioned as he sipped his drink.

"Why did you save me?" She didn't hesitate. "I don't wanna irritate you with that question, but it just... it keeps me up at night not knowing why. But, if it's nothing, and if I'm blowing it out of proportion then, I won't ask you anymore. It's just not every day when someone jumps in front of a bullet for you, then spares you more than once when you barely even know them. That's all..."

"Are you speaking to me, or the food that's on your plate... well, barely."

Tiri looked up at him with a smile. She'd knocked off half of her food in minutes from the THC and now the wine that was doing the water Olympics in her blood. It's almost like, every time she felt herself sinking in his presence, he rescued her out of the trenches, and she admired it.

"I'mma answer that question for you soon, a'ight? It's a time and a place for everything, Tiri. That's one thing you need to learn about me and take heed to, a'ight?"

Tiri couldn't place an understanding on it right now, but strangely, she enjoyed submitting to Steelo. He sparked a flame for her with a wrath that she couldn't fight. Also without making her feel foolish.

Her brother was a dominate man, and she always eyed Riley sideways behind closed doors from the way she yielded to Messiah's stature. That is, until Steelo made her see things from a *woman's* point of view and not a little girl's.

Short of the dick or the crazy tongue tricks that she'd overheard countless stories about that came along with dealing with niggas with power, Tiri's callow mind was already hooked. She could already taste on the tip of her tongue, the sweetest taste of sin that she knew was to come from dealing with the man sitting tall before her.

Taug Jaye

Heart Up For Ransom

"I know bullshit when I hear it, Steelo,"

-Tiri

Taug Jaye

Chapter

4

It was rare when The Monstrosity made a public appearance. Most people only lived to hear the stories behind the malice and endless racketeering he engaged in throughout town, but today was a new day. Today was one of the few times when the city would be blessed to see their king in person opposed to being in handcuffs on Trinity news.

Trinity National Park was filled from one corner to another with thousands of children, young adults, elders, parents, and family members enjoying the festivities. The Monstrosity did a fine job at getting himself into some bullshit with the laws.

It was all a cat and mouse game that he'd honestly enjoy until the day he died, there was no doubt about that. But there comes a time when a man's rib changed his focal point and allowed him to tap into his inner peace.

The large eighteen-wheeler blew its horn, announcing its arrival while the driver backed into the grass. A fellow colleague directed the vehicle until it was parked perfectly for the unloading process. The crowd had become mute as two mobsters dressed in all black unhooked the latches along the door. The anticipation was eating away at their insides as the seconds continued to pass by, almost drowning them in fear as if the whole orchestration were a setup.

"STRO-SI-TY! STRO-SI-TY! STRO-SI-TY!"

The crowd blared his name in unison until the door slowly raised, and The Monstrosity showed his face. Applause immediately erupted when he flashed his white million-dollar smile in return. Marius was a celebrity in his town.

Most people saw him as Trinity's Gangsta, and they loved that shit. The dope boys wanted to be him, every woman still broke their necks in an attempt to have five minutes of fame with the man even though he was married, and the old heads now respected him.

Sure, being a crook and causing havoc wasn't the jack of all trades, but who wouldn't advocate for the black man who had the laws dangling by their dicks? At first Marius was simply greedy, and just hateful, and shared his success with no one, but he earned himself a better reputation with the Back to School drives he held, the homeless he fed, and the new homeless shelter he funded to build when Trinity shut the main institution down.

This would be the second year around Thanksgiving and Christmas when he gifted families in the holiday spirit with hams, turkeys, and full-course meals. He even created the Usher Scholarship, where he granted two graduating high school students with full rides to the college of their choices. KD got inside of the man's head and she rekindled his gracious spirit.

Yeah, he still tore shit up. Don't let the present event fool ya; he wouldn't be himself if he didn't shed any blood or remind niggas how he got his name. Marius was the kind of man that you couldn't easily tip the scale on, and that's just the way he liked it.

"Good evening, ladies and gentlemen, boys and girls. Are y'all enjoying the festivities today?" His voice was joyous and welcoming as he spoke into the microphone.

Everyone roared, waving their snow cones, cotton candy, Barbecued goodies, balloons, flags, and other arts and crafts in the air, showing appreciation for the block party he'd thrown. After last year's turnout, he realized that he'd need to rent out the entire southern half of the park due to the number of people in town who were estimated to show up again.

"We love you, Monstrosityyyyyy!" a drunken college girl yelled out with a Corona in hand.

Marius chuckled.

"I love y'all too. I'mma keep this short and sweet. I appreciate y'all all for coming out. Get as much as y'all can to eat and drink, enjoy everything, and be safe. Remember, this is a violence-free zone, and my man's here at the truck will be more than happy to help divvy out uniforms and school supplies for the kiddos and students. Peace, love, and happiness, everybody. Stay up..."

ℌ𝔘𝔉ℜ

"Soooo, who the fuck is the fine ass Drake look-alike? What they call him? 'Strosity?" Tiri questioned as she bit into the barbequed turkey ribs. They were to die for, and she just couldn't get enough.

"That's *The Monstrosity*. Have you ever seen *American Gangster?*"

"Yeah."

"Well, bitch, that's Frank Lucas. He runs Trinity. Don't let this shit fool you. That nigga right there is responsible for every drop of blood that runs along the streets. He's a crime boss, baby girl. *The* crime boss and most legendary Taker to ever run this town. His clout holds ranks over the Irish Mob who used to run the town for like, ever.

Trinity PD has been trying to shut this man down for seven years now, and he always wins. He's every hood nigga's inspiration and every bitch's favorite wet dream. I never thought I'd see the day when he'd evolve into this kind of G, though. The nigga is unruly, but it's sexy as hell."

Tiri sipped her Corona while her new roommate's words were all stored within her brain. Caesar, aka Ceas, was this cool lil' around the way chick from North-East county. She reminded Tiri of Tia Mowry by the looks and her build.

She was a sweetheart too, but mommy had an edge that Tiri was drawn to. Caesar was a physical recap of Tiri's own gangsta'. She was all smiles and rainbows until somebody pissed her off.

Attitudinal ass JZ learned that shit the hard way when she tried to tell Ceas she couldn't move into the available dorm because she used it as storage. Caesar didn't know who the fuck she thought she was tryna step to her. She put JZ and her dick-riding ass friend in check real quick. Hazel E was there tryna back her girl up, and she caught some of her fade too.

Ceas thought Tiri would be full of herself as well when they met, considering her first run-in with the banshee crew. Plus, name-brand merchandise would label anyone as bougie if you didn't already know them personally.

That's just how the game goes, but surprisingly they clicked, and Tiri made her first week of college a lot smoother. Ceas was a freshman as well studying biology and chemistry with hopes to work at NASA, so their schedule lined up on most days and it was cool to have a friend to kick it with.

"Bae, you want some of these wings?"

Both girls turned around when they heard the deep voice. It was Caesar's man candy, Glenn. He was a fine ass brown skin with tats all over his body, deep waves, and a mouth filled with golds. He was a sophomore, but him and Caesar had been dating since she was sixteen.

"Those look so fire. Tiri, you want one?" she offered.

"One? Where you get them from, Glenn? I need a whole damn basket! Don't tease me like that!" she beamed.

Glenn laughed.

"Here, y'all can take these. I'mma go get me some more."

"Negative. We'll get our own. I will take another one for the road though," Ceas giggled as her man smacked her butt in the coochie-cut denim shorts before they headed over to the food truck.

"So this is how the crime lords do it here in Trinity? My brother and his best friend's ole' mean asses wouldn't dare," Tiri joked.

Messiah wasn't that bad, but she honestly couldn't see him and Seth pulling something like this off.

"Girl, this is all new to us too," Ceas explained while sucking her fingertips clean. "Ever since he's gotten married, he's turned into *this*. You'll see him on the news soon for some kind of trial against the state. I'm positive."

Tiri laughed.

"They say a woman's touch is what tames the lion."

"Damn right it does because most of them are either too damn hotheaded for their own good, and the other half just says stupid shit, and you can't even reason with their dumb asses. And you see him right there? The light skinned man with the top knot?"

Tiri damn near snapped her neck turning around so fast when Caesar pointed the man out.

"That's Steelo. The Monstrosity's right-hand man. Don't let the looks fool you. Word on the block is he's just as cutthroat as Marius. If you see him coming, bitch, run. You'll never live through the man's gunplay. He used to be a hitman before he started working with Marius.

Now, this is just between me and you. My father lives in Vegas, and he does some loan shark and gambling business out there. I remember seeing him one night, when I stayed for the week on my spring break, dismantle a whole fucking body, Tiri, with nothing but an ax and a blade. The sickest shit I've ever seen in my life.

My daddy caught me eavesdropping and made me watch the whole thing until it was over since I was down in his den when I knew I wasn't supposed to be. It traumatized me. When I see him, I don't even speak. I keep walking like I never knew him. Those light skinned niggas are the devil. I swear."

This was surely all news to Tiri's ears. It had been a week since she'd last seen him on their date. He'd given her his number and told her to hit him up whenever she felt like it, but that's all it was.

From sunup to sundown, she'd stare at her phone contemplating on texting him. Tiri swore the memories from their date are what got her through the week because she'd been dying to see him. He'd made a good impression once he put his guards down.

His smile and the sound of his voice gave her butterflies. Tiri's never been so googly-eyed over a man before, and it made her feel stupid. Steelo just had to go all high and mighty, take her out, and get her caught up in his whim, just to not hear from him. No, he didn't have her number, but that wasn't fair. Why did she have to make the first move?

Steelo always managed to make sure that the ball ended up in her court, and that's just not how she operated. Tiri honestly didn't know how she operated when it came to the opposite sex. She was always the "homegirl" or "hella cool."

Niggas didn't take her serious back in St. Louis. They saw her athletic gear that she loved to rock, that long hair of hers pulled back in a ponytail and dapped her up before they ever blinked twice to thoroughly look her over and give her a compliment.

Tiri was out of her shell now after taking the way she dressed to a whole 'nother level, but she was still that timid teenager. It was in her blood. One minute she gathered up the strength to text Steelo "hey" after swearing that she'd pass out before the word appeared after her cursor, but she didn't have the nuts to hit send.

Steelo intimidated her. Tremendously. Their conversation flowed well, but she had to give him all the credit. You could ask Tiri a million questions, and she'd respond like clockwork but leaving her to do all of the dirty work was another story. Maybe that's why he'd given her *his* number: to test her maturity, and it was very obvious that she'd failed.

In her defense, Steelo knew where to find her. He'd done it before, so what else could possibly be holding him back other than him simply not being interested? The thought broke her heart.

Just as she was about to turn away from staring at his fine ass sipping on a Corona himself, they made eye contact. For a moment, it felt unreal. Was he staring at her? Could he really recognize her amongst every other female in the crowd? He was standing along the back of the moving truck above eye level, so she knew he must've had a good view of her.

Tiri forced her lips to form into a half-smile after another long and grueling thirty seconds of a stare down, but in return, he slid his shades on and hopped from off the truck, following behind Mr. Monstrosity.

He's so fucking rude. I don't know what the fuck I see in his pretty boy ass anyway. Fake ass wanna be gangsta. Fuck him.

She rolled her eyes in disgust as she turned her attention back to Ceas, who was handing her over a basket of wings.

"Come on. Let's go chill back at the car where we can sit and eat these comfortably. These Coronas are nasty as hell, but I think I'm starting to like them."

Tiri laughed at Caesar's comment while downing the rest of her own drink. Back to the car is where she needed to head. Puffing on a fat ass blunt would definitely take her mind off the nigga who wasn't fucking with her all because she didn't *fuck him* that night he'd dropped her off, and sis was one hundred percent convinced.

HUFR

"All this fucking ruckus. Who the fuck does this nigga think he is? Frank Lucas? I can't believe Trinity PD is letting this motherfucker pull this shit off like he doesn't lead ninety percent of the crime in this city, but they rode our dicks? Disturbing my fucking peace with all of these people running around and shit; limited customers, and placing caps on the growth of my business? We've gotta put an end to this motherfucker. I'm tired of this shit."

The owner of Irish Pub had an unwelcoming mug along his face as he ran the small hand comb through his hair. A few members of his mob sat around him, all downing the finest Irish Whiskey anyone in Trinity could get their hands on. Mr. Conner O'Sullivan never saw The Monstrosity and his wrath as a threat until he'd become personally affected.

He owned four bars in town, and his gang was well respected. He'd been making a killing in Trinity for over fifteen years, and even though Marius rose to power seven years ago, he managed to stay out of his path thinking that he wasn't dumb enough to go heads up with a real gangster.

But times had changed. People were disrespecting the O'Sullivans like there wasn't a point in time when they reigned supreme. So now, Conner had to step up and show niggas how his family got down. The man was more than an Irish gangster. He was involved in Ireland's export trade with the United States as well. The US purchased billions of dollars' worth of pharmaceuticals from his country. His family had been involved in the trade for eight years and counting.

In Ireland, he owned the largest pharmaceutical facility in the country and had plans on opening a second location on US soil. The only issue was the rise of the Elixir Pharm. Mr. Cartwright knew dozens of government officials who'd shut him down a number of times when he attempted to get licensed for his business. Conner still made a killing overseas, but in his own city progression was stagnant.

He was almost sure that Elixir would fall through in a matter of years, but with The Monstrosity's involvement and criminal tactics, it surpassed regional standards, was one of the top pharmaceutical companies in the country, and that was an issue for him.

"Fuck it, boss. It's gonna be bloody. It'll get filthy. The war will be brutal, but I'm tired of this nigger. He wants smoke? Let's bring it to him. I'm tired of creeping around like this hasn't been our town."

Conner eyed his only son following his comment. Geni was ahead of the physical aspects their gang handled. He was his muscle: lethal and lawless. He'd just gotten out of the pin two weeks ago and was war ready the moment he made it back in town. Geni respected Conner.

He was old and didn't like to be personally involved with the violence, so he honored his father's wishes. Geni was locked up on a murder charge that the family lawyer had finally gotten him out of. Now, he was prepared to pick up where he left off at two years back.

Conner inhaled from the cigar deeply with a head nod. His son was right. It was time to put this shit in motion and reclaim their territory.

"Round up the board members. I want everyone at my house tonight at 6 pm sharp, and not a fucking minute later," he instructed.

Geni chuckled as he threw the last shot of whiskey back before he rose to his feet. His two right hand men and best friends, Looney and O'Leary, stood with him.

"I'll take care of it. Lock up shop for the day; on all properties. We've got shit to do — more important shit. A car for you should be here in fifteen minutes. Get the fuck out of dodge with this nigger's mob so heavy on the streets right now. Don't worry, Papa, they'll be hearing from us and soon."

Geni and his crew exited the building through the back door without any further discussions. By the grace of God, Conner managed to keep his son's wrath content for seven years now. Prison was the cause for the last two, but he'd known for sure that Geni wouldn't stop until The Monstrosity's blood was on his own hands.

"You heard him. Lock up," Conner affirmed, ready to be in the comfort of his home so he could clear his mind and mentally prepare for the war that was soon to come.

One of his mobsters headed to the door to seal the bars closed, but the impact of a bullet from a suppressor went through his head. The shot splashed the wall with his brains while his lifeless body dropped to the ground. Steelo entered the door with a blunt hanging out the side of his mouth and a squad behind him.

"O'Sullivan," he chuckled while approaching the owner, who'd pulled out a revolver from his waistline.

"Don't shoot!" Conner hollered to his mob, knowing the gunshots would cause too much attention with the event going on. He was surely unprepared for Steelo's visit.

Conner's chest was heavy. Beads of sweat immediately appeared along his forehead as his mind raced. He had a team of four men with him, but it was no match for the fifteen henchmen accompanying Steelo.

To the public, their appearance was unquestionable. They weren't dressed in their normal black threads, so it appeared as if the Irish Pub had finally received some business to help with their slow day.

"Mr. Steelo," O'Sullivan chuckled in return, trying his damndest to appear unbothered. "What a surprise. Drink, my good man? First rounds on me, eh?"

Steelo removed the blunt from his lips, offended by this nigga's humor. But instead, he smiled. Everything was all good.

"I'll pass. I'm just here to deliver a message."

Four hidden men appeared from the back of the building and held his small army up in chokeholds, causing them all to drop their weapons. Bullets then pierced three of the four members in the head, leaving one witness alive.

"So when this gets back to Geni, he'll have a survivor to tell him exactly what happened to his Papa," Steelo chuckled before he threw the blade that was in his free hand. With precise aim, it hit Conner right in the eye. His body dropped down to his knees instantly with blood dripping down his face. Steelo wanted this shit to be dirty. He wanted the O'Sullivan family to turn beet red in the faces and shed tears from the images of him killing their loved one. He wanted permanent, bloody memories of him decapitating his body with a blade and his bare hands to haunt them forever. "Here, bruh. This for you."

Steelo tossed the amputated skull at the last Irish man standing. He was shedding endless tears from the sight and disrespect inflicted upon their mob.

"Here's the surveillance tape."

Steelo looked over his shoulder as one of his boys handed it to him along with a briefcase full of the ownership deeds for the bars Conner owned.

"Bet." *Whomp!* The Irish Mobster instantly went to sleep once Steelo's fist came in contact with his mouth. "Get the bodies, and make the fire look good. I want the disappearance of this establishment to look as natural as possible for the news. So figure that shit out and call me once y'all make it out to the Safari lodge. I'll take care of the care package myself. And make sure this nigga is on time for their meeting tonight. I wanna make sure they got the message loud *and* clear."

𝕳𝖀𝕱𝕽

With his feet kicked up and Kwan's national bestselling novel *Animal* in hand, Steelo was chilling in the comfort of his quiet home. It was ten that night. Even though his body ached, and his mind wanted relaxation, he couldn't sleep. After a while, the author's words were running together, and he found himself flipping through the pages without obtaining any understanding from the current content. He rubbed his eyes and let out a yawn before he put his feet down.

"Damn man," he mumbled as he closed the book and headed to the bathroom.

With his hands planted along the edge of the sink, he stared in the mirror at himself with the rise of a brow. His stare-down went on for minutes before he received a notification on his phone.

314-555-6535: So I guess you don't know me now? *rolling eye emoji* Read: 10:07 P.M.

Steelo chuckled before he picked up the phone and responded, already knowing who the message was from and what she was referring to.

Steelo: Who had who's number? *thinking face emoji* Read: 10:08 P.M.

314-555-6535: Whatever. You're so fucking rude. Read: 10:09 P.M.

Steelo: *oh well emoji* Read: 10:10 P.M.

314-555-6535: *fuck you emoji* Read: 10:11 P.M.

Steelo: *laughing emoji* You should be mad at yo' self. Read: 10:12 P.M.

Steelo: Thinking of a reaction still? *thinking face emoji* Read: 10:20 P.M.

𝕳𝖀𝕱𝕽

Tiri cut her phone on Do Not Disturb and hopped out of bed with an attitude. She didn't know who the fuck Steelo thought he was, but he had her fucked up. She didn't care how hard things got; she wasn't chasing after no nigga.

"Fuck that nigga like I said before. I'm not doing this shit with him."

The smell of weed that crept underneath Tiri's door made her smile. JZ and Hazel E always fired up when they knew their RA, Heiress, was in the building. She didn't give a fuck what they did, and that was the perfect signal that Tiri could sit back and get a little reading done in great comfort. Ten minutes into *Arabian Nights* and working on finishing her first blunt, there was a knock at her door.

"What these bitches want now? I know they ain't smoke up all that weed that fast," she mumbled as she climbed out of bed.

Hazel stayed buying gas from Tiri. The connect she got from her brother's Los Angeles distribution was the truth. It was a nice lil' hustle for Tiri even though she knew she wasn't hurting for the money. Messiah stayed wiring her cash, so she was always stacked, but she kept her shit classy.

She only sold it on weekends, not after certain hours, and you could only get in contact with her via Ceas. People couldn't get in touch with her by any means necessary. That was one thing she drew the line at. Plus, she slid her girl a nice profit for holding it down. Being the plug wasn't her focus, and she made that shit known.

"Who is it?" she called out while standing on her tippy toes to look out the peephole, but she didn't see anyone. Shrugging her shoulders, Tiri turned to walk away, but then there was another knock. "Look, who the fuck—"

Tiri stopped dead in her tracks once she swung the door open and was face to face with Steelo. She was so shocked to see him that she could only stand there with her mouth wide open and her eyes dilated as if she had seen a ghost.

"Still thinking of a reaction?" He countered as he grabbed her by the waist and moved her out of the doorway before he closed the door behind him.

"Sure, just pop up on me whenever the fuck you feel like it after a week of ignoring me," she sassed while turning to face him.

"*Arabian Nights*. Good read," he complimented as he took a seat along her bed.

Steelo put his car keys, his cell phone, and his trusty Desert Eagle down on her nightstand before he looked up at her. Tiri had the evilest glare along her face with the blunt up to her lips. Her weight was shifted to her left hip, her hair hung down her back in loose waves, and all she wore was a red bandeau and shorts set that looked painted on. Tiri had average breasts and butt for her slim frame. Her hips were her greatest curves, but she had a sex appeal that tripped Steelo up for sure.

"Drop the attitude, Tiri. I don't wanna hear it. You could've done this way before tonight, so save that shit," he implored as he laid back on his elbow.

"Whatever, Steelo. You here now, ain't you?" she waved him off as she walked over to the nightstand and ashed her blunt.

Steelo sat up, grabbed her by the elbow, and pulled her between his legs as he sat back down.

"You lucky I missed you or I wouldn't have shown up. I knew you was gon' be on bullshit."

He looked her in those beautiful brown eyes and instantly got lost.

"Sure, you missed me," Tiri laughed while rolling her neck.

"Ain't that what you wanna hear?"

"You funny."

"And you petty. Yo' issue ain't with me. You been mad all week for nothing and tripping because the shit ain't fazing me. I've told you, Tiri, that a lot of shit don't bother me. I just be chilling. You thought you was ready, huh? You'll be arguing wit' yo' self fucking around with me. I don't waste unnecessary energy."

She didn't want to, but she laughed.

"You're the man. You're supposed to do all of the courting." Her voice was soft.

"Have I not done that?"

His tone made her bite her bottom lip. He was looking so damn good she had to get it together. She never thought that a nigga with a man bun would drive her so wild.

"Yes, you have," Tiri agreed.

"Then be a woman and play yo' position, and if you don't know something, then ask."

"How old are you?"

"Twenty-five."

"Are you from Trinity?"

"Born and raised... myself."

"What's your favorite color?"

"Black. What's with all the petty inquiries?" he questioned.

"I'm asking about what I don't know. We did so much talking about me at dinner that I could barely ask you about you."

"You was too scared to ask me about me. Keep it a hunnid."

They shared a laugh.

"Well, if you weren't so fucking rude, then I wouldn't be trying so hard *not* to offend your grumpy ass every time I opened my mouth."

He chuckled. She had a point there, and that was something he'd clean his act up on whenever they spoke.

"How was school this week?"

Tiri took a pull from the blunt that she felt like had been burning forever before saying, "It was cool. This biology class ain't no joke. Our first test is in two weeks. I know the work; it's just a lot of content."

"Maybe if you wasn't stressing out over me then you'd be more content and positive about yo' studies."

She playfully pushed him in the chest.

"I was not stressed off you."

He raised his brow like *yeah right*.

"What's your real name? I know it's not Steelo," she smiled.

"Nuri P. That shit don't leave this room."

"No shit? My middle name is Nyree."

"I'm hip."

Steelo leaned back along his elbow once again.

"Why are you single, 'Mr. P'?"

"Why are you?"

"Because before I started dressing cuter, niggas only saw me as the 'homegirl.' Plus, have you ever been to St. Louis? It's nothing but a city full of ain't shit, community dick slinging ass niggas. And you said you were single why, Mr. Sir?"

Steelo was now leaning back against both of his elbows. He reached for the blunt behind his ear, fired it up, then answered her question.

"I'm like a thief in the night, ma. I move too discreet for a relationship."

"Excuses. You gon' be where you wanna be, whenever you wanna be there. Save that shit for them other bitches."

"Whoa, now. You had some soul in that shit, mama. You call yo' self tryna check me?"

"I know bullshit when I hear it, Steelo."

"No, you assume it's bullshit because it's not what you wanna hear. The way I move? You'd really be capping if you was my girl. You'd damn near have to live with me to keep up with me."

"Well then, nigga, what's the address? Looks like I'm moving in." They shared a laugh. "Honestly, Steelo, it just sounds like you're gonna have to work me into this busy ass schedule of yours. If you know my middle name, then I'm sure you know what kind of family I come from. This ain't my first rodeo."

He handed her the blunt but pulled back when she tried to grab it.

"710," he warned.

Tiri grabbed it from him and inhaled deeply while staring into his eyes. Steelo might've been a boss, but he had a soft side that he couldn't hide. Or maybe she just had the sauce and had this nigga dancing to her every beat? Either way it goes, both scenarios sounded pretty damn good to her in this moment.

"I'mma big girl," she whispered as smoke released through her nose. "I know what 710 is, and I've smoked it before."

"Yeah, alright, ma. You ain't nothing but a big ass kid. Is you legit watching *Jumanji* right now?"

Tiri laughed so hard she had to wipe her eyes.

"You know what? I'll second that. Ninety percent of my DVD collection is Pixar and Disney movies."

"This girl said DVD collection like it's not 2018."

"Don't do me," she shrieked before inhaling deeply.

Using her index finger, she motioned for him to come here. When he sat up, she positioned her lips just meters away from his before blowing the smoke into his mouth. Being so close to him, Tiri couldn't help but kiss him. She loved how his full lips felt covering hers, and it sent a chill down her spine.

"If that's what you wanted, all you had to do was ask," he mumbled as he smacked her butt.

Tiri blushed.

"You make it all sound so simple. You can't be mean and easy-going at the same time, Steelo. Make it make sense and pick a side."

"How I act towards you is based off of your actions, and don't make me repeat myself again."

"Yes, sir," she jokingly saluted with a hand gesture before her phone rang. Looking down at it on her nightstand, she saw that it was Caesar. "Wassup, boo?"

"Hey, girlfriend. You busy? You wanna go for a ride with me, Glenn, and the boys?"

Tiri let the smoke release through her nose before saying, "I'mma sit this one out. Let's link up tomorrow. Go ahead and chill wit'cha man. I'm straight tonight."

"Party pooper." They shared a laugh. "Alrighty then, and you better be blowing me off for some dick instead of just sitting there being a loner, turtle."

Tiri blushed so hard from her comment that she tried to turn around and hide her face, knowing Steelo had heard her. But he grabbed her by the waist and made her straddle him.

"Bye, Ceas!" she shrieked.

"Oh, yeah, we'll definitely talk tomorrow when I make it back. See you later."

"Okay. Be safe, girlie."

"I will."

Click.

Steelo grabbed the blunt from her as her free hand rubbed the back of his fade. She was bobbing her head to an imaginary beat, feeling the wax take over her system almost instantly. It gave her an excellent high, making her reach altitudes airplanes couldn't even exceed.

"Can I play some music?" she asked softly.

"You can do whatever you want. I'm in the comfort of your zone, ma."

Tiri smiled as she turned her speaker on via her phone and found the track that was on repeat in her head.

"This is my song, so I don't wanna hear no moaning and groaning. Let me be in my happy place for like, four minutes," she countered as Sinead's voice filled the air.

Steelo chuckled.

"Little do you know, I fucks with Sinead."

"Really?" she beamed as she looked him in the eye.

"Do what the fuck you wanna do and quit being timid, ma."

Every time she tried to reach for him, touch him, or put her arms around him, she hesitated. Steelo may have been hard up, but he didn't want her to be uncomfortable whenever he came around.

Tiri rested her arms along his neck and swung her head back and forth to the beat. Her heart was thumping so hard it was matching the bass in the background.

"I've never been this intimate with a...man before," she confessed.

"I believe it."

"Steelo, I'm serious," she giggled.

"And so am I."

In one swift motion, he rolled Tiri over on her back and held himself over her. He let her take one last pull from the blunt before he put it out and removed his shirt. Tiri ran her pastel purple full-set up and down

83

his muscular arms as she stared into his eyes. She then grabbed him by the face and pulled him close so she could kiss his lips.

Tiri loved to kiss. It made her insides all hot and tingly, and if she had to be honest, he was the only person she'd want to share this moment with. But, when he reached for her shorts, she quickly broke their caress and felt her heart skip a beat.

"Steelo," she whispered.

"What, ma?" he questioned between soft pecks to her lips.

"I've never done this before. I'm... a virgin..."

Her heart damn near exploded.

"Who said I was about to fuck you?"

Her breaths got deeper when he removed her bottoms.

"But I didn't shave," she panicked.

"Don't nobody give a fuck about no damn hair. It ain't even that long, now be quiet, motor mouth."

Oh my God, she thought in disbelief. *Is this really about to happen?!*

Tiri's pussy was pink like a Starburst, and Steelo was about to get this shit rocking. Hearing she was a virgin made this moment ten times better. Since she'd never been intimate with a man before, he was gon' turn this pussy out just the way he liked it.

Her back arched when his tongue traveled from her slit and all the way up her middle until he reached her clit. Now traveling backwards, his tongue glided slowly until he reached her butt. Tiri's body trembled as she clenched the sheets with both of her hands. The fluttering against her love button was intense, and she couldn't stand it.

"Oh! Steelo!"

So that's yo' spot, huh? He thought as he continued to lick along the area that had her squirming like a fish.

"Steelo, shit! Oooooh my gawd! This isn't happening...yeeeees!"

He chuckled as he inserted one finger into her tight slit. She was tighter than a pair of Fashion Nova jeans on Tammy Rivera's juicy round ass and thick thighs. Slowly, his finger went in and out of her, curving each time he dug inside, making sure he stimulated her vagina while he licked on her clit. One finger then turned into two, and before he knew it, she was moving her hips forward and back going with the flow.

84

"You like that, sweetie? Hmmm," he mumbled while watching her make all kinds of sexy faces.

"Steelo, baby, yeeeeees! Oh, I think I'm about to—cuuuuuuuuuum! Aaaah! Yeeeeeees!"

She couldn't resist his tongue flickering over her spot. Tiri thought he'd give her the chance to catch her breath, inhale once more from the blunt, take a sip of water; hell, get on her knees and pray or something to prepare for the next round, but was she wrong.

His hands reached up and freed her breasts from her top while his mouth kept going to work. The sensation of his fingers pinching and toying with her nipples while his head shook from side to side had her cumming a second time almost instantly.

Tiri was seeing stars she came so damn hard, and still, this man wouldn't quit. He laid on his back and positioned her on his face from behind. His hands gripped her butt while his mouth continued to torment her silky abyss. She tasted so sweet and Steelo didn't want to stop.

Tiri reached in between her legs and rubbed on her clit for a while before she put her fingers in her mouth. She was a master at self-pleasure and loved how her pussy tasted after she came from the assistance of her vibrator. That was her little secret and she wasn't ashamed of it. Curiosity got the cat when she noticed the bulge in Steelo's basketball shorts.

Should I touch it? she pondered, terrified though eager to see what he was working with.

The moment she reached for his pants, she stopped and hollered at the top of her lungs. His tongue was drilling in and out of her slit, and his thumb was doing the same to her butt. The tight feeling along her backside made her cringe a bit, but as he continued, she was growing to accept it.

"What are you doing to me?" she cried as she ran her fingers through her hair, feeling her juices trickling out of her body and on to his tongue.

The power of 710 had her out of her element. She started grinding along his mouth and groping her breasts while the other hand rubbed on her clit again. His tongue was twirling in her butt and she was in pure ecstasy.

"Oh my gawd," she gasped when she pulled his dick out.

Tiri needed a ruler because her virgin eyes didn't know dick measurements right off the top of her head yet. All she knew was that baby was long and thick, and it made her body shutter just staring at it. She grabbed hold of it and giggled through moans when it jumped from her touch.

Slowly she rubbed on it like she'd seen on Pornhub. All of this shit was new to her and if she were sober, she knew none of this would be happening, but she wasn't sober, was she? *Smiles like the Grinch on the inside* Working up enough spit, she got a nice load ready for when she'd let it drip down his shaft. Her stroke felt better against his throbbing meat now.

"I don't know what the fuck I'm doing, but here goes nothing," she whispered before her tongue twirled around his tip.

Sucking dick wouldn't be that hard, could it? It was like eating a Bomb Pop, right?

"Watch yo' teeth," Steelo groaned, coming up for air.

Tiri released him and laughed out loud. How fucking embarrassing was that!

"Can we watch a porn or something? I'm a beginner here," she squealed while both of her hands stroked his long dick.

"Suck on the tip while you doing that," he groaned while smacking her butt.

"Like this?" she innocently asked before taking him in her mouth.

"Yeah...like that. That's better. Take ya' time, this ain't no race. This only day one, remember..."

She smiled as her head bobbed up and down. He flinched a bit, feeling her canine take a slight jab at him.

I gotta get me a dildo so I can practice this shit, she thought in embarrassment.

"It's so thick, Steelo... I'm sorry," she whined.

He chuckled.

"It's a'ight, ma. I'll let you off with an E for effort this time."

"Whatever!" she giggled.

Tiri climbed from off his face and mounted him the right way. She looked down at his dick peeking between her legs and thought of something. She started grinding against him, back and forth, getting his manhood all sticky with her honey.

Steelo held on to her thighs and helped her rock against him until she got a hang of the pressure he liked. It even helped with the tickle of her pearl, and from the look on his face, she could tell he liked the feeling too.

"I want you to do it to me, Steelo."

He laughed at her innocence and how tender her voice was. He didn't know why that shit turned him on so much, but it did, and he could fuck with it. Tiri wasn't one of those hardcore ass women who felt like she had to be overly aggressive to get a man's attention. He could tell she was grounded to the woman she was becoming, but her soul was so pure that it made her stand out in a way no man could ignore.

"I might hurt you, mama. This dick ain't little, and I know you not ready for this," he warned.

"I can see *and* feel that *very* clear," she groaned while steadily grinding on top of it.

Tiri bit her bottom lip hypnotized by the way it felt against her. The shit was sensational, and she wanted to soak all of this up before the storm. Steelo sat up and held her body close as he rolled over and laid her on her back.

"Oh my gawd, Steelo. This is about to huuuuurt!" she shrieked while her heart rate increased.

No matter how much she wanted this moment to happen, Tiri didn't think that she could ever be prepared for it.

Steelo chuckled as he pushed her right leg back, creating a nice opening for him to slide inside.

"When I say breathe in, do it, a'ight?"

Nervously, Tiri shook her head up and down. Ever since she was a little girl, she pictured her first time going so different. In her head, there were rose petals amongst the sheets and floors, candles were burning, soft music was playing in the background, and a dreamy chocolate stallion of a man was hovering over her body. Romantically telling her how much he loved her and how he was gonna plant endless babies in her vagina...

The twin-sized bed they were on, alone, was enough for her to pull the plug on this moment, but she was so high, and even though Steelo was damn near white in complexion, she wouldn't trade it for the world. Her music was still going as well, and with the way he continued to kiss on her neck and let his tongue glide all over her flesh, there were enough emotions flaring around to make this shit worth it.

"Gimme a kiss," he mumbled.

She removed her hands from her eyes and stared at him with the most precious smile on her face before their lips met. Their tongues overlapped wildly, and the sensation drove Tiri nuts.

"One... two... breathe in..."

Her back arched as she inhaled deeply. Steelo's dick was so thick it took a number of times before he finally forced it inside of her since the subtle approach damn near made his dick flop. Tiri dug her nails into his back and bit his neck when she felt his soldier break her slit and dig further inside.

"This is noooooot how everybody in middle school said this shit would be!" She screamed while holding on to the back of his head.

Steelo chuckled as he continued to move his hips forward and back. The tight feeling around his dick took him back to when he lost his own virginity. You'd think the man had never been inside of pussy before the way Tiri's walls cast a spell upon him.

"Breathe, Tiri," he groaned while kissing her neck.

"I'm trying... Steelo. Baby, I swear I'm trying, but it hurts..."

"You want me to stop?"

His motions came to a halt as he looked her in the eye.

"Just kiss me," she demanded.

Steelo smirked before their lips locked together again and he continued to stroke her with easy, deep thrusts.

"This thang nice and wet, girl... what got you dripping like this?"

Tiri giggled, admiring that he was trying to make the moment more comfortable for her.

"Am I really that wet?"

"Do I look like I'm the type of man that would— uummm, lie to you, Tiri?"

Hearing him groan made her eyes cross. It was so sexy.

"You're making me wet like that, baby."

"Aw yeah?"

"Umm hmm."

"Just wait, mama. Once I break this pussy in, I'mma make you feel a way no other man will ever be able to accomplish. Just watch."

Tiri kissed his lips while her nails created a new layer of scratches along his back from each stroke.

"You've already done that, Steelo. I've felt a way about you since the day you saved my life, so I know the future holds so much more than I can even wrap my head around in this moment."

Heart Up For Ransom

"Just tell me what all you want, and Papi gon' make it happen. That's my promise..."

-Marius

Taug Jaye

Chapter

5

The sound of heels click-clacking against the kitchen floor was an audible signal that Marius' beautiful wife had just made it home. He sat along the couch with his feet up and his sleeping daughter lying across his lap while he held his son along his shoulder. He never saw this day coming. Not even in a million years could he envision a living room filled with endless merchandise from Babies R Us. Nor, the tattoo of a giant K in Old English along his ring finger until he could add a wedding band to complete the combo that symbolized their marriage.

He listened to KD rummage around in the kitchen until she appeared in the doorway with a gorgeous smile along her face from the beautiful sight of her family. After two kids, his woman was still snatched. He loved her tenacity and determination to keep her body in shape at the healthy size 16 she was on her 5'7 frame.

The lace, neon green bodysuit hugged her curves perfectly while she was back rocking her neon pink lace front for the night. Kovu tip-toed across the floor until her heels made one with the rug to avoid waking the kids.

"Hey, babe," she whispered as she stood behind the couch and leaned over Marius' shoulder. Holding on to the side of his face, their lips met briefly before their tongues took control. They shared a caress that sent chills down Kovu's spine. "They didn't give you too much trouble, did they?" she finally asked once their steamy French kiss was broken.

"Not too much. Our lil' pistol finally tapped out on me."

"Who? Jayce?"

"Nah, this damn Aubrey."

The happy couple shared a laugh as KD reached for the TV remote, already knowing that her husband could only take so much of *The Daddy Finger* before he lost his mind.

"How was the show?" Marius questioned as he watched her sit down next to him.

"Man, babe, it was so good! All the ladies really enjoyed themselves, everybody left so tipsy, and it was just so much fun. You know I got all kinds of pictures and videos to show you too. I think this is a hit, Mr. Usher. I'mma gon' head, put a trademark on it, and quit playing. I'm even thinking about setting one up in St. Louis too since it's such a big hit."

"It's already done."

Kovu's eyes bucked in disbelief from his statement.

"What you talm' 'bout Willis?" she shot with the raise of a brow.

Marius laughed as he handed her his phone. His wife's eyes lit up when she read the official ownership rights paperwork for her Women's Autonomy Poetry Slam.

"Woven Ink Presents *Pink Seduction* by Kovu Usher..." she read aloud with tears in her eyes.

Kovu's success was rocking. She was a New York Times bestselling author of thirty urban novels, five erotic novellas, and an erotic/romance poetry book. Poetry was her first love, so to keep in touch with her rhymes, she created a female organization where women from all different walks of life came together and shared their poems at an open mic session.

It was a moment for women to exercise their autonomy without being judged, frowned upon, or discouraged. They wore sexy clothing, danced, played games, made sister meeting goals, and she was growing to love the community of women that was slowly yet surely growing beyond what she ever could've imagined. Every night they met, she was blown away by the turnout, leaving her beyond excited for the next event to come the following month.

Being a new mother was a lot on Kovu. Especially after Jayce was born. So she had to do something to keep herself mentally healthy *and* maintain her self-care while also doing for their family, but she was a little hesitant to take on another role. Kovu knew she had a lot on her plate already with her publishing company and signing two new authors to help their dreams come true as well, but with a man like hers, she knew she'd have enough support to make anything happen.

"Marius... wow..." She looked up into his eyes before she kissed his lips again. "I've been so skeptical about this. You really believe in it?" she questioned as she crossed her legs Indian style on the couch after kicking off her shoes.

"I believe in anything that you put your mind to, ma. You know that. I told you I want you to be more than Mrs. Usher. I don't ever want you to feel like you don't have your own sense of self or place in this world. You do this shit and you go hard with it. You're young; you're Black, and beautiful as fuck. Give these girls something to look up to. I'm proud of you, youngin'."

KD laid her head along his shoulder while she slid her arm inside of his and held him tight.

"Thanks, baby. I swear nobody does it for me with the words of encouragement and support like you do. I *am* gon' go harder. They ain't seen nothing yet. I'm just waiting to hear back from Netflix then we on a roll with this *Love From A Boss* movie, baby, I'm telling you."

"That's that shit I like to hear. The world is yours, ma. Live and trust that shit."

Marius kissed her lips.

"I do, babe. I do…Check you out though. *Both* of the kiddos are asleep? What, Mr. Usher? You're getting pretty good at this."

He chuckled.

"See, me and Jayce, we got us an understanding, but this one right here? She gets all organic. No more snacks or nothing for her hype ass. She just fell asleep not even thirty minutes ago."

Kovu giggled as she pulled the blanket up over their daughter.

"You got this, pimp. No sweat... Soooooooo," she began as she looked up at him.

"Sooooo, what?" he questioned with a smirk.

"It's September," she urged.

"And?"

"Annnnnd, that means that it's only five more months until we tie the knot for real-for real, Mr. Monstrosity. You still fucking with me?"

He laughed.

"I don't really have a choice now, do I?"

Kovu raised her eyebrow.

"No, you don't, but you *can* put a lil' more pep in your tone though. Don't be acting like you ain't excited for our wedding."

Marius and Kovu had been together for a little over two years now. It seemed like it was just yesterday when he discovered her behind that bar at club Knock Out. And now they had a date saved for Valentine's Day 2019 to make it official despite them already being married on paper. Days he woke up and he couldn't believe this was his life. He loved every moment of it, but it was still brand new considering how long he'd lived in seclusion. Those days were officially over.

"Don't start, KD."

"What!" she gasped.

"You know what."

"No, I don't. And can you start pulling out when we get real freak nasty *at least* until, like, January? I don't wanna be fat in my wedding dress."

Marius laughed.

"I can't make them kinda promises, ma. That pussy too tight and drips unrelentingly."

"Ok, Mr. Dictionary. And yes, the fuck you can, or you won't be getting no pussy until our honeymoon."

"Who you think you talking to?"

"My baby daddy," she sassed.

"Yeah, alright, Kovu. You dun' got too comfortable."

"YoU dUN GOt tOo cUmforTabLe. Shut up," she mimicked as she pulled her wig off and let her head breath.

"Queen Latifah. Get yo' uuuuuh, *Set It Off* looking ass—"

"Boy, fuck you!"

The sound of her mother's voice made Aubrey spring up into action.

"Mommy?" her baby groaned as she rolled over and wiped her eyes.

"Hi, baby. Did you miss me?"

Her little princess crawled into her lap and laid her head on Kovu's chest in hopes to go right back into baby dreamland, now within the comfort of her mother's arms.

"You gon' invite Tammy to the wedding?"

Marius' question threw his wife all the way off. It took her a while to respond before she said, "I don't know. You know she's been extra fucked up in the head ever since Eric so-called 'killed Amber'."

Her words were faint.

Killing her own sister was easy in the moment, but sometimes that shit haunted her. It was contradicting. Amber tried to kill her first and would've succeeded hadn't Marius taught her how to survive, but at the end of the day, she was still her sister, and Tammy was still her mother. They hadn't seen nor heard from one another since Amber's funeral, and despite what happened in the past, she honestly missed Tammy.

Traveling down memory lane made Kovu stand to her feet and leave, heading for their bedroom.

She rocked Aubrey back and forth with tears falling down her face trying to gather her composure, but sometimes it got the best of her. Kovu couldn't help it that Tammy was truly convinced that Eric did kill Amber before he "killed himself" like the suicidal police report said. According to the state, he really *was* mentally deranged, and he had medical paperwork to back it up. But, Kovu still knew the truth.

She never told her mother about the gas hack at her father's home to avoid Tammy putting the pieces together; plus, it left her with a piece of her own sanity. To this day, she didn't understand how Marius could still be so cold yet have a heart of gold. It was uncanny, and maybe that's why he was the boss.

After making sure her princess was nice and tucked in her crib, she ran the shower in hopes to clear her head. Bobby Valentino's sexy hit "Obsessed" filled the air as Kovu stood underneath the water pouring down from the LED rain shower, ceiling mount. The pink lights were the only glare in the room.

One thing Kovu could admit was that Marius stopped at nothing to make her happy. Little things such as her "shower goals" warmed her heart and made all of her L's so worth it.

Most of the time.

Her naturally, long hair that was now free from the protective braids, curled up after coming in contact with the steaming hot water. She ran her hands over her shoulders feeling the melodies from the music within the depths of her soul.

The sudden cool draft made KD turn around. Her husband had joined her.

Together they stood underneath the water staring into each other's eyes before Marius grabbed her by the waist and pulled her close. His mouth caressed her neck with light, passionate kisses while his hands roamed her butt. He hated when she cried. Her tears reminded him of the moment when she found out he'd offed Collins and how she reacted. Her pain was his weakness... one of his weaknesses.

To this day he still blamed himself for any sorrow that ever entered her heart. He knew her mother was a sensitive subject, but the man he was today didn't want her to feel any hate for Tammy. He wanted her to work things out with her mother because he knew how much she really did love her. He couldn't call himself her husband if he allowed her to leave that void empty. But he knew that now wasn't the time to discuss that.

So Marius lifted Kovu off her feet and wrapped her legs around his waist while he slid his rigid soldier inside of her walls. With her back and the palms of both of his hands pressed along its surface, he kissed her lips as he moved his hips forward and back to the pace of the music.

A lot of their intimate times were spare of the moment, but if not, then KD always had some kind of playlist going for them to go round for round with. It was something Marius had grown to love. It gave them a connection, unlike no other and he lived for it.

"I love you," he whispered in her ear as she clenched her legs tighter when he hit her g-spot.

"I love you too, Marius..." she groaned before biting his ear and digging her nails into his back.

"And *I am* excited about our wedding, mama... you hear me? Just tell me what all you want...and Papi gon' make it happen...that's my promise..."

Kovu looked Marius deeply in the eye following his comment. The water pouring down on them like a beautiful rainfall from the ceiling up above was so romantic, it made her smile.

"I want you to make love to me, Marius."

He silenced her with a kiss to the lips. Kovu wrapped her arms around his neck as he held her by the waist, now thrusting his dick inside of her.

97

Dick wasn't supposed to be so sinful, so addicting and whimsical. KD's body shook when he shoved himself so deep, that he touched base, causing her chest to tighten before he removed her back from the wall. She couldn't resist him when he shifted her legs to where he gripped her ass from underneath with her thighs resting along the crease of his arms. Marius didn't give Kovu the chance to ride his dick on her own whim. He held her body firm and stroked her pussy to such an intense rate that a clapping noise filled the air.

KD still had an ass as big as the sun and fluffy irresistible thighs that he never wanted her to lose. Until the day he died, he'd retain his strength to handle his wife's curvy body with no remorse while his pleasing lips induced the tender love and care that she simultaneously yearned for.

Kovu hummed in excitement via each kiss due to her husband's thrusts. That massive dick of his was rearranging her insides. An average woman would've been running with the way he forcefully wedged a path through her walls, but a big dick had always been her type.

Marius sat KD on the edge of the black marble shower bench, forcing her to hold onto the edge with both hands while he gripped her thighs and continued to beat the lining out of her pussy. Kovu bit her bottom lip watching his dick glide in and out of her before she threw her head back and called out at the top of her lungs.

Her husband was strategic about everything he did. His dick was always hitting the right angles. Marius knew no such thing as selfless love when it came to her, Aubrey, and Jayce. Everything he participated in yielded an asset for his family, whether it be him tearing up the streets or tearing up Kovu's hidden valley that still had a grip just as sinful as the first time he entered her over two and a half years ago.

Marius caught one of her bouncing breasts in his mouth and inhaled her hard nipple with his lips and tongue. Thank God she was no longer breastfeeding, and her girls were back to normal. Jayce wasn't the only one in need of her bosom.

Their bodies were slippery as they grazed against one another with the warm water cascading down their melanin skin. Marius' panting was getting deeper, forcing him to work Kovu's middle as his hips moved in a circular motion to hold back that nut. Knowing what his movements meant, she pushed him off of her. Marius ran his hand down his face, removing the water from his eyes once he stood to his feet. Kovu didn't hesitate to slip him inside of her warm mouth, cleaning every ounce of her sweet cream from around his shaft with the bob of her head. She loved making eye contact with him each time his dick was down her throat.

The way he stifled those potential outbursts by holding his fist up to his mouth or biting his bottom lip empowered her. Marius might've been the boss, but he knew with the way she cunningly slurped and sucked him off, she nimbly transformed him into a pawn in her own chess game. His ten fingertips lightly massaged her scalp while he intently pulled her hair up then held it firm like a sack of money by one hand to keep it from interfering with her technique. She was like a vacuum on his rigid soldier, humming against and stroking his base, intensifying the unbearable sensation that stammered his balance.

He looked down at her pretty, slutty ass swallowing every inch of him while her hands massaged his nuts. The way she strategically interchanged from pumping his wood to using no hands while a few strands of her wet hair hung down the sides of her face, Marius was releasing his load, her mouth like a cozy and bottomless fissure that showed him not once ounce of mercy.

KD stroked every last drop into her mouth, lapping up the spillage that trickled down her plump bottom lip, leaving no aftermath. Without delay, Marius got down to his knees, curling one of her legs around his neck and held her other one spread open. He ate his wife's pussy so long and passionately that tears emerged from the creases of her eyes. Each time she thought he was finished, Marius' head rotated in circles with his tongue doing donuts around her pearl before it was once again encompassed by his lips, and he was whisking her away with yet another sensual orgasm.

Making love to her was an understatement. Marius sexed, flipped, pounded, and licked her in a plethora of positions until their bodies were pruney and drained. Kovu hardly remembered drifting off to sleep since they laid down for bed. Her rest was sound until Jayce's hungry cries around 3 A.M. interrupted her slumber. When she rolled over and attempted to force Marius to attend to his son, that's when she realized that his side of the bed was empty. Aubrey was sound asleep, so after sliding into one of her man's t-shirts, Kovu grabbed her son and rocked him on the way down to the kitchen. Once Jayce was settled with his warm rice milk mixed with a little cereal to keep him nice and full, she pulled up the live feed from the security monitor on her phone and saw that Mr. Monstrosity was downstairs in their sutajio **studio.**

Marius' bare chest was drenched in sweat, but he couldn't put the Samurai sword down. He was light on his feet with each move, swiftly swinging the razor-sharp blade equipped with no rattle or wiggle of the steel due to its excellent and grade A grip. Those sleepless nights had decreased in great number over the years for sure, but tonight, his troubles were unbearable. After plunging into Kovu until he made her cum back to back to help her rest, then sitting up for an hour watching their children peacefully sleep, mounds of guilt, greed, and animalistic gluttony filled him. Sixteen years later, he was still caught up and captivated; shit, maybe even obsessed with raising hell in Trinity.

Ordering Steelo to whack Conner O'Sullivan was no subtle offense. Nothing in this world had the ability to rattle his peace until tonight. Slowly yet surely, his anxiety was reaching a peak knowing that a war with the possibility to spark a State of Emergency was due to rise any day now. In the past, this shit was like exercise to him.

A hunt.

A challenge.

It got his dick hard to show these muthafuckas how he was *that* nigga, *that* unstoppable outlaw. Arrogantly taunting the law enforcement with his boastful reign and finesse until he got the chair, but now that shit seemed pointless. The more his wife and kids pumped adoration into his heart, the more he yearned to provide them with a regular life. A sense of normality where they all could walk the urban streets of their city unarmed; no guards, no enemies, and simply enjoy a day at the park.

He didn't want Jayce to be him. To hurt like him. To hate like him. To kill, manipulate, violate, and regulate in a state of mind that would silently bury him alive. He wanted to drop his baby girl off at ballet lessons without the company of the national guard. He sought to cheer his wife on at her every event not feeling like they too were targets; casualties of war due to the association of being an Usher. Being an outlaw was all the satisfaction he'd ever needed until he fell in love with an angel and their heirs; *they* should've been his main focus.

His *only* focus.

Taug Jaye

Dying was never a fear until the days came where he'd be leaving behind something too precious to walk this earth without him. He wasn't ready to enter hell yet. After all of the chaos he'd orchestrated, the miles of bloodshed on these streets that were permanently stained along the palms of his hands, the innocent lives he'd taken, and the destruction he'd caused the city of Trinity, no matter how optimistic his wife encouraged him to be, he knew there was no place in heaven for such an acrimonious spirit that had coined him.

Any day could've been his last, so now, he was faced with an onerous challenge; the most onerous challenge yet, and that was righting all of his wrongs so his family could bask in the ambiance of freedom. But where would he begin?

Kovu's reflexes were quick. She managed to dodge the shiv Marius threw in her direction that hit the wall in the hallway like a dart once he sensed the sliding bamboo door being whisked ajar. By now, his behavior was no surprise. Being "The Monstrosity" came with the "perks" of consuming 24/7 prudence; even in your own home. Pumped and ready for some real entertainment now, Marius quickly threw a sword at Kovu before charging in her direction; fucking ambushing her with no sorrow in his eyes. The tsuba **guard** holding the sword went flying in the air when she withdrew the weapon to counteract with his swing. The sound of steel clashing filled the air as they maneuvered around the studio. Kovu didn't expect to break a sweat while going to check up on him, but this is Marius Lionel "The Monstrosity" Usher we're also talking about.

He was impressed with her agility, improvement, and overall satisfactory performance. Self-control and discipline didn't come easy, and to this day Marius continued to push Kovu to master her energy and frequency on a level that would properly enhance that extremity.

KD ducked when he made an attempt at her head for the thousandth time. Her body bent over backwards with ease before she twisted her frame to where she was able to stoop down low and use one of her legs to sweep him off his feet and onto his ass, causing him to drop his weapon. Seeing that he was down longer than she expected, Kovu swiftly climbed on top of him and held the blade just inches away from his neck, noticing the few cuts she innocently managed to implement upon his steel-cut arms. He always pressed her to perform as if she were trying to kill him, and if she didn't then, he'd simply go harder on her until she took him for his word and gave it her all. It sounded brute, but it modestly helped him exercise his own bouts of discipline that assisted to balance out his temperance.

Defeated, Marius threw his head back and collapsed with his chest heaving up and down. Kovu soon dropped the blade at her side then laid on his chest, burying her head in the crook of his neck while reaching underneath him and latched onto his shoulders. She hated that her husband could still hurt so much. That he could still harbor the pains that tried to force him to believe that he truly was a fucked-up person. She prayed for him endlessly; numerous of times throughout her day, talking to God and hoping that he'd bless Marius with the peace that he didn't have to sacrifice for no matter how happy they were. He put so much pressure and angst upon himself that she could hardly stand it, and even though they hadn't stood under the Lord in union just yet, she promised with all of her heart to remain by his side and be the strength that he needed when he verbally refused to admit it. This love shit between them was a forever thing...

Their panting filled the air; Marius' arms were wrapped securely around her waist, and his mind now one hundred percent made up. He knew what he had to do. He knew what decisions had to be made, and while he still had the opportunity to buy his way out, that's exactly what he would do when the time permits.

"I'mma stop being selfish and get right, Kovu...I promise."

Taug Jaye

"You know you fucked up, right?"

-Steelo

Heart Up For Ransom

Chapter

6

"Tiri, you did not lose your virginity last night," Caesar shrieked as she slapped her on the thigh. Tiri couldn't hold it in. She had to tell somebody.

"Girl..."

She rested her head along the seat of the car and closed her eyes, daydreaming about falling asleep in Steelo's arms. It took everything in her not to beg him to stay that morning, but she knew he had to go out and be the boss he was.

"I'mma be honest, Ceas, the head was so fucking clutch, but the sex? Bitches was lying all throughout middle and high school talking some, that shit was fire on their first round! Talk about a pissed bitch!"

Their laughter filled the air as Caesar pulled her SS Camaro into the parking lot at Trinity Galleria. After a nice patio breakfast and an exclusive mani/pedi with wax and hot rocks, the girls were ready to do a little shopping.

"I swear that's how it was when I lost my virginity to Glenn in the 10th grade, and I'mma be honest. Glenn's dick isn't super long. He's got a nice six inches with some good girth and beats this shit up better than the Mandingo dick that I've had before."

"I thought Glenn was the only guy you've been in a relationship with?" Tiri asked.

"Oh, he is. My senior year of high school, he fucked my cousin, claiming he was gone off some syrup. And did I cry? Hell no. I fucked his best friend and asked him how it felt. The nigga's been in check ever since. How about them motherfucking apples, bitch."

"We are not bringing that phrase back, girl! Stop it!" They shared a laugh. "Okay, Ceas, with your trill ass. My crybaby ass would've been somewhere drowning in tears. Your cousin, though?"

"Ugh. I know, right? Straight rat. I knew she wanted him the way she used to always low-key ask about him and shit. Trust and believe him and her both got their asses beat too. Glenn pursued me for six months until I forgave his ass and I haven't heard nor seen another birth following that shit. You wanna see the video?"

"You do not have the video."

"Uploaded on Instagram, Facebook, and saved in my Apple storage. Yes, I'm *that* bitch. So, who is this mystery man? You've been dodging my question all morning."

Tiri's heart skipped a beat as they entered the doors of the mall. The malls back home didn't have shit on this California luxury.

"Stop it! They have a Fashion Nova in here! I did not notice that when I first came here."

"Tiri," Caesar retorted, fed up with the bullshit.

"Can you keep a secret?" she responded, turning around quickly to look her friend in the eye.

"What kind of silly ass question is that, Ri?"

"Ceas, I'm serious," Tiri whined.

Caesar held her pinky finger out before they locked them together and placed their foreheads against their hands. It was crazy how close they'd grown to one another. They honestly were inseparable.

"I'm not even gonna respond. I'm just gonna casually nod my head and say okay."

Yeah right.

Tiri knew better than that. All that shit was going out the window once she told her who it was. Inhaling deeply, she looked her friend in the eye and whispered, "It's Steelo."

Caesar's eyes bucked so wide she couldn't help it when she screamed at the top of her lungs and threw her arms around Tiri's neck.

"Don't worry! There's nothing to see here! It's alright! Y'all can quit staring and mind ya damn business!" she beamed, never letting go of Tiri while shoppers continued to stare in their direction.

"Do you know I thought you were getting ready to say Trell's name?!"

"Lil' Quavo! Ugh, hell no!"

Their laughter filled the air.

"Was it big?" Caesar was cheesing from ear to ear, too happy for her girl.

"Big as fuck! Why do you think that shit hurt so bad? I'd never seen a dick that big in person!"

"Oh my God! Not killer ass Steelo. How the fuck did you bag him? Bitches break their necks tryna jump on his dick! He's mean as hell."

"He really is if you don't know him, but he's a sweetheart. I won't even front. That's bae, girl," Tiri blushed.

"How long have y'all been talking?"

"Off and on for like a month."

"Damn. Okay, lil' momma. I fucked Glenn the first time I ever chilled with him."

"OMG, Ceas!"

"Whaaaaaat! I wanted the dick! I can't lie!"

Tiri and her girl strutted up and down the mall for hours shopping like they were spending with no limits. They came across so much merchandise that caught their eyes that they couldn't help but to swipe, swipe, swipe away with the black cards given to them by their families.

Ceas was now in the dressing room at the Chanel store trying on this bad ass jumpsuit that she just had to have. Tiri sat in the lobby chilling on the velvet loveseat while sipping a glass of the complimentary champagne the staff was passing around. She stopped for a minute to look up from her phone, silently drowning in mounds of anxiety, to glance at the entrance. She was a nervous wreck after not hearing from Steelo since she kissed his lips goodbye hours ago before the sun came up.

Was her pussy wack? Did all he really wanna do was fuck, and now he was gone? You didn't just take a girl's chastity, then not communicate with her. That was law! Fed up with the bullshit, Tiri was a push away from calling him when he walked past the store with a bright skinned baby in his arms and a woman beside him in a blunt cut bob wig, pushing a stroller.

Tiri's...heart...STOPPED!

She did not just see what she think she saw.

So he fucks with that bitch? He has a whole fucking family?! she panicked as she ran for the door.

Tiri zoned in on her camera and snapped pictures of him laughing and congregating with her as they entered the Diamond Shoppe. She didn't have the nuts to confront him in public. She was too heartbroken. Instead, Tiri ran back over to the loveseat, grabbed her belongings, and headed to the dressing room. She banged on Caesar's door uncontrollably until it opened.

"Tiri, what's wrong?!"

"Give me your keys! I'm going to the car!"

"Tiri, what? What happened that fast!"

"Ceas, just please!"

The tears in Tiri's eyes let Caesar know that something big had popped off. She rumbled through her purse and handed them over, letting her know that she'd be out soon.

With her hands in her head, Tiri sat doubled over in the car crying her eyes out. How could she be so stupid to trust Steelo, let alone give him her body when she should've recognized what he was doing all along? Her crying didn't come to a halt until he heard the back door open and Caesar loading the car with her bags.

"Now what the fuck is up, Tiri?" she puffed out of breath. She damn near ran the whole way to the parking lot to make sure that her girl was okay.

Tiri could hardly speak. She handed Caesar her phone while she started back up with the tears like her heart had been ripped out of socket.

"Umm, don't get mad, but what should I be looking for in these pictures?"

"He's with another bitch, Ceas! The nigga has a whole fucking family, but he was just laying up all night with me!"

"You idiota!" Caesar pushed her in the shoulder. "Tiri, this is Kovu! The Monstrosity's wife, and those are their kids! Did you send these to him? Lord, this bitch dun' already sent the damn pictures and went off."

Tiri shot her head in the air as she wiped her face.

"What?" she sobbed.

"*What*," Ceas mimicked. She couldn't hold her laughter. "You should've told me what was up right then and there, and I would've cleared all of that up. Look, baby girl, we've gotta get your emotions in check. This is crazy. Has he responded yet?"

Tiri shook her head feeling ten times as worse.

"Kovu as is Kovu Usher? The author? Ceas, please tell me you're lying," she prayed, her voice barely above a whisper.

"No, boo. Next time, when I ask, just fill me in before you go and do something stupid. He is not gonna like this."

"I fucked up."

"That you did."

Tiri looked Ceas in the eye before they shared a small laugh.

"Girl, your phone! He's calling!"

"Oh my God, Ceas, noooo!" Tiri's stomach hit the floor when she grabbed her phone. It's like time stood still when she put it up to her hear, not ready for the outcome. "Steelo, I'm—"

"What I tell you about that shit, Tiri? I don't have time for this shit. You know you fucked up, right? Find you a nigga that's gon' go 'round for round with' you because he ain't me."

Before she could get another word out, the call was disconnected. Caesar had overheard his every word, so she kept her comments to herself while she pulled out of the parking lot.

Tiri was speechless.

With her arms folded underneath her breasts, they rode in silence, both knowing she was too embarrassed to discuss it.

𝔥𝔘𝔉ℝ

Tiri wanted to die. She just wanted to wither away while lying in her bed with a face full of tears, wishing that she never came to Trinity in the first damn place. How could she be so stupid? Why did she jump to conclusions when all she should've done was brushed seeing him with Kovu off until she was able to question it with a level head? Now, she'd fucked herself hard in the ass with no lube and knew that Steelo would never speak to her again.

Her world was ending.

Knock-knock-knock.

"Go away!" Tiri screamed through tears as she rolled over and turned her back to the door.

"Tiri, it's H.E."

"I said go away!" Her heart was pumping so fast it was starting to make her tremble.

"Come on, Tiri, don't be like that. I really need to talk to you."

Frustrated that this bitch wouldn't leave, Tiri rolled out of bed and stomped the entire way over to the door until she swung it open.

"What the fuck, Hazel! What the hell happened to you?!"

Tiri pulled her inside quicker than she realized, causing Hazel to trip over the welcome mat. Her nose was busted open and blood was stained all over her clothes.

"What kind of a nigga would put his hands on a female?" Hazel E was hysterical. She was so distraught, she plopped down in the middle of the floor and cried her eyes out.

"Who did this to you? Kennan?!" Tiri shrieked as she grabbed a washcloth, wet it, then popped it in the microwave.

Kennan was the upperclassman that Hazel had been fucking for weeks now. He was the quarterback of their football team and all the hoes went crazy over his ass, but his status and popularity didn't mean shit judging the sight of Hazel's face.

Tiri had her cleaned up in no time. Hazel sat on the edge of her bed explaining how he jumped on her because she didn't want to get down with a train and Tiri was disgusted. No, neither of them weren't super cool with each other, but she felt for her in this moment. Domestic violence was intolerable on even the smallest level or first occurrence.

"Thank God you got out of there safe. His ole' insecure, bitch ass gon' get mad at something like that and put his hands on you? I hate these niggas, Hazel, I swear."

She nodded her head in agreement to Tiri's comment.

"I actually thought he liked me...I guess not."

"Girl, fuck him. Don't waste another tear on that bitch ass nigga. He's definitely not worth it with his lame ass. He's a bitch. On to the next. Look around you. We're at Trinity U; nigga Candyland, and there's thousands of other niggas that look better than his lopsided head ass anyway. Plies looking ass nigga."

Hazel E managed to laugh.

"He looks more like Kirk Franklin now that you mention it. Yuck, what was I thinking?" Their laughter filled the air. "Thanks, girl. I know I can come off a little strong; me and my best friend, who shook on me for some dick, can be some bitches, but I'm not that bad. We all have our ways."

Tiri smiled.

"The universe sends the vibes you give out. Not saying you deserved this at all because this was some bullshit. No one deserves to be treated like this, but you do gotta watch who you surround yourself with. Now that's a hunnid."

"No, that's a thousand," she agreed. "It looks like it's just me and you tonight. I see Caesar is gone and Jay-Z will be with Iman all weekend. I don't know about you, but I'm not staying in on a Saturday night. Let me check the 'Gram and see what's popping."

About an hour later, they were dressed up in the latest Fashion Nova fashions and throwing back shots of Cîroc at an upperclassmen's loft in the Black Lava Apartments. They both needed to clear their heads, and a party was the best way to do so. Tiri wasn't a pro at throwing back shots like her acquaintance, so not only did she gag with each shot, plus need half a cup of a chaser to follow them, but she'd transitioned into a drunken state sooner than she expected.

She'd gotten a little tipsy off of a few glasses of wine before, but never had she crossed over to the dark side until tonight. Tiri tried her hardest not to stumble as she and Hazel continued to get it cracking in the middle of the dance floor, swaying their hips to the latest mumble rap trending on the radio. Everything was moving in slow motion, her body temperature was increasing, and she hadn't noticed how aroused she was until she felt a lightning bolt shoot up her center.

Does liquor really make you feel like this...

Tiri's mind was trapped in a maze as she puffed on the third blunt she'd brought along their adventure for them to enjoy.

Smoking was more of her thing, but tonight she was being a college student. Drinking and smoking was the theme, so why not live a little since sober her was still in shambles over what happened earlier in her day.

She and Hazel E were mouthing the words to Kash Doll's "Everybody" back and forth at one another until the opened front door caught their attention. When Kennan walked in, by default, Hazel's entire demeanor changed. Tiri warned her not to keep chugging the cups of jungle juice everyone was passing around, but she too was having a crisis. She didn't know whether to be mad from seeing him or to go suck his dick since the liquor had her ready to fuck.

Hazel didn't get much time to weigh her options before Mr. Quarterback found his way over to her and immediately reached for her juicy ass in her dress. Tiri just knew this dumb hoe was not about to fall for that shit. She just knew it...but that thought was short lived. When Hazel whispered in her ear, informing her that she'd be right back in the midst of him trying to pull her in the direction of the bathroom, the game had suddenly changed.

"Hazel, do you really think that's a good idea? You're not in the right headspace right now," Tiri tried to reason with her, but Hazel insisted.

"Girl, I drink all the time. You the newbie. Look, hold this then. I won't be long. I promise."

Tiri took the half-empty cup of the mind-altering concoction from her hands and felt her heart stop. With the blow of the wind she went into panic mode. Other than Hazel she didn't know anyone else at the party, so now she was trembling in double time from both the fright and the amount of liquor she'd consumed.

Did this bitch really just leave me? Aw, hell nah! It's time to go!
"Wassup, ma."

Tiri jumped when she felt someone's intersection against her butt. She turned around and was face to face with a light skinned dread head rocking a letterman jacket.

"Hi."

Her tone was not only condescending, but Tiri could've sworn the word UNINTERESTED was written across her forehead clear as day due to the ugly scowl that was on her face, yet the jock insisted.

"Relax, ma. I ain't gon' hurt you." He grabbed her by the waist and pulled her close. "Not unless you want me to. I been watching yo' chocolate ass for weeks now. I know it's a prize between them thighs. I can smell yo' virginity coming out yo' pores, ma. Let me have that."

"Can you get off of me!" she yelled as he held her tight, but the bass in the speakers did nothing but drown her cries out.

"Don't fight it, baby. I'm finna change yo' life. I been seeing you shaking that ass in this skirt for the past hour, and I'm about to give you what you been asking for."

Tiri tried to fight his drunk ass off, but she was no match for the linebacker. The loft was packed beyond reason, so no one noticed him pulling her away and shoving her into an empty room...Or so she thought.

Her heart rate immensely slowed down as if she'd seen her life flash before her eyes. Tiri didn't want to believe that there were four other guys in the room, each of them with their eyes locked and loaded on her as if they were only seconds away from pouncing on her. No, this couldn't be real.

"Come mur', lil' red skirt. What's up under this?" A guy licked his lips as he pulled her close. "Aaaah, shit bitch!"

She was quick when she pulled the mini can of mace out her cleavage after remembering she had it and squirted every last drop in his eyes. Two more guys grabbed her by her arms and tried to hold her still since she wasn't too fond of their little get together and wanted to fight.

"Somebody! Help me!" she cried as they hemmed her up against the wall.

"Nah, bitch, this what you want!" The muscular guy who lured her into the room screamed as he unbuckled his jeans.

Tiri couldn't describe the terror that swept over her. Words couldn't properly be aligned in a sentence to express the mounds of horror that were currently drowning her, but she also knew that her fear wouldn't save her. Some way, somehow, she managed to slide out of her shirt. By the grace of God, she was able to fight her way through their hands grabbing at her and break free as she ran for the back of the room. Finding refuge in a bathroom, she quickly locked the door and used the decorative ladder that was designated as a towel rack to wedge underneath the lock.

Tiri held onto the top of her head as she curled up in the bathtub and prayed to God that He saved her. Hearing their feet ram against the door made her scream and cry even louder, pumping her with mounds of devastation rather than faith. Who could possibly come to her rescue? Who would've known where to find her since she left without telling Ceas that she was stepping out for the night for her safety? The Lord Himself would have to peel her eyelids open because once they made their way through that door, there was no way she'd be able to be her own witness to what was soon to come.

HUFR

Steelo was riding around with the top down on his Bugatti, vibing to some Yung Bleu debating if he should pull up into Trinity University and handle Tiri's little ass. That shit from earlier had him so disgruntled he could hardly enjoy his day. He liked Tiri; honestly, but the assuming, texting him like she'd lost her fucking mind/ disrespecting his stature, and the childlike behavior wasn't what he signed up for. He didn't need those kinds of problems when the life he ran was enough, but ever since day one, there was something about this girl steadily screaming, *"Steelo, please have mercy on my soul."*

Inevitably, she forced him to open doors that he prayed to keep closed since he'd thrown away the key with hopes of never going back. Yet, here he was, all out of character and shit again as he pulled up to her dorm. The incoming call from her was surprising, but he was still so pissed off, he answered with an aggressive approach.

"Bring yo' ass outside, Tiri."

"OH MY GOD, STEELO, BABY, THANK YOU FOR ANSWERING! PLEASE HELP ME! THEY'RE TRYNA KICK THE DOOR DOWN AND RAPE ME! STEELO, PLLLLLLLEASE!"

All he needed to hear was the tremble in her voice before his persona switched into assassin mode. Steelo pulled out his second phone and instantly got a location on her. The tires screeched as he busted a U-turn and cut the five minute arrival time into one after wildly maneuvering throughout the campus. He pulled up in front of the building where her Apple Watch said she was located after sending out an alert for a small squad to meet him there ASAP.

Steelo hopped out the car with the Heckler UMP .45 Caliber machine gun in hand and a set of Desert Eagles in his waistline, for back up, as he entered the apartment building. Fucking with these wannabe hardcore college students, Steelo had to come armed and ready. He shot up the steps and followed the tracking device application until he made it to his destination.

A cloud of smoke smacked him in the face when he entered the door with his gun raised. People were everywhere spilling drinks, popping pills, sniffing cocaine, getting or giving head, and having a good fucking time until the music was abruptly cut due to his appearance.

He hated to interrupt on these terms and conditions, but these niggas had his bitch fucked up. Nor did he give a damn about the niggas recording him. Who'd convict him? Who'd testify against him? Whose lawyer had shit on the nigga that represented him and Marius?

That was the same thing running through his head too.

Like the Red Sea people started parting to provide a walking path, no one being tough enough to go up against him. They all knew who Steelo was and how a gun battle could've easily broken out, but none of them would live to see the next day, so they remained quiet while he proceeded to look around for who he'd come for. His blood was boiling when he kicked in lucky door number one where he found four niggas all banging at the bathroom entrance trying to get inside. Tiri had the knob secure for the time being.

"The fuck you doing in here, nigga?! You miss the do not disturb sign when my muthafucking door was lock—"

Steelo rocked that nigga to sleep before the other three lame ass niggas came for him. These lil' niggas didn't know they were fucking with a hard hitta. The moment these youngins got the smallest dose of liquor or dope inside their system they thought they were invincible. Shit was funny. The only thing that stopped him from killing them niggas was the fact that he didn't have the time to clean this shit up for the press while him and Marius were already battling the heat with the Irish Mob, or else there'd be some pretty upset mammies crying over their nasty ass sons all savagely trying to attack an eighteen year-old-girl.

His only mission was to get Tiri out safely, and after receiving confirmation that his squad was on the territory, that could be done without a hassle.

If he would've arrived even a second later, it would've been too late. The door had finally been kicked in, and he wouldn't have forgiven himself if them niggas had succeeded at running her.

"Oh my God! Steelo! How did you find me! How did you get here so fast!" Tiri cried as she jumped up to her feet.

Steelo was seeing red when he saw her shirtless before she threw her arms around his neck. Her cries were hysterical as he held her close with his arms around her waist, thanking God this shit didn't fall through. Too many young girls are victimized at these college parties for wanting to fit in, and he was grateful that she wasn't one of them.

In one swift motion, Steelo cradled her body. He made a mental note of the niggas all laid out along the floor on their way out.

Taug Jaye

Heart Up For Ransom

"Don't go,"

-Tiri

Taug Jaye

Chapter

7

Tiri sat balled up into a fetal position inside of the bathtub at Steelo's beach house crying her eyes out for an hour now. She begged him to be alone so she could attempt to get herself together after all that occurred that night, and he respected her wishes until he entered his bedroom hearing the same cries escaping her lips since he'd left.

Steelo took a sip of the Virginia Whiskey as he made his way to the tub. Feeling his presence in the room, Tiri's head rose from her hands to greet him with her bloodshot red eyes. She was distraught by all means and his heart couldn't take it.

"I'm sorry. I was just about to get out..."

Her voice was barely above a whisper as she choked back the tears that wouldn't cease to fall.

Steelo looked into her eyes as he lathered her dry washcloth with soap. Their gaze went on for miles as he attempted to wash the remnants of her haunting experience away. His touch was gentle. Tiri didn't understand how some men could be so disgusting, brute, and infringed, but then, there was him.

The man who patted her body down before he cradled her in his arms and led her to his bed. The boss who'd been saving her life since the day she'd met him. The regal running his fingers through her damp hair hanging down her back after he helped her change into one of his white t-shirts.

There was a sense of peace that swept over her as she merged with his memory foam mattress. Steelo pulled the sheets up over her shoulder before he stood to his feet with his eyes never leaving her.

"Don't go," she pleaded.

"I won't. I'mma be sitting right here," he assured as he nodded to the black suede loveseat next to the bed.

"Lay with me. Please?"

Unable to resist her solicitation, Steelo kicked his slides off after downing the rest of his drink and climbed in bed with her. Tiri grabbed her phone from off the nightstand and searched for her Yung Bleu playlist until she found her favorite track "Warzone." It was something about the way the melodies serenaded peace in her ears that made her soul feel free, and she needed that type of energy.

Steelo wrapped his top arm around her waist after sliding the left underneath her so she could rest her head on his shoulder. He made her feel safe. So secure. Tiri had never trusted a soul with her life who wasn't her brother or Uncle Seth following the death of her parents, but everything with the man locking her in his embrace felt like all the safety she'd ever need from this day forward.

Steelo didn't understand what he was doing to her heart. He didn't understand the faith she'd bestowed within him, nor the serenity that consumed her when he crossed her mind.

Or maybe he did?

The lyrics on repeat had their hearts in sync, but this time around, Steelo couldn't ask God why he kept coming to this girl's rescue. In that moment, he willfully came to terms with the fact that he had to protect Tiri from the world that wanted a piece of her because she was a Stallion. She didn't understand how her name itself had premeditated the besiege that the enemies had plotted against her. She was so frank, so oblivious, and even blindsided to the way the world went 'round, but that was nothing that a little prep and guidance couldn't take care of.

A lot of men hated a woman they had to coach, instruct, and physically walk through the trials of life with. It wasn't innate to their masculinity, but if men really took the time to peel back the layers of that statement, what was a woman without his touch? Without his influence? Without his mark? Steelo didn't want to hound Tiri and make a puppet out of her. He wanted to educate her and prepare her for the life she'd soon be living while being on his arm.

What man wanted a woman who didn't know how to merge with or lead his lifestyle if the opportunity permits itself? She could reach for her dreams, she could dive headfirst into her every aspiration, she could be the next President, or even fight to change the world. He'd never deprive her of wanting the things in life that her heart has always desired.

Yes, embarking upon relationships and compassion were simply a new journey for a secluded man like Steelo, but he'd never reduce Tiri as a woman to make himself feel whole. An emotionless assassin he may have been, but his heart didn't house that type of selfishness. Not for someone that he wanted to protect. Not for someone that he would possibly... one day love.

The energy she gave Steelo filled him up to a height he'd never reached with another woman. And whenever he had her in his arms, she somehow erased all of his physical pain. All of the stress, the demons that haunted him, and the darkness he swore he'd never break free from; it all vanished when he was with Tiri.

That's why he was willing to protect her.

Tiri kissed his hand before she noticed the purple bruise along his arm; one he couldn't hide due to his fair complexion. Her eyes scanned up his body until she reached his shoulder and found another with deep green traces blended as well. Sitting up, she turned and faced him. He changed his position and laid on his back with his head against the pillow, instantly knowing why she was giving him the side-eye.

"The job I do comes with a lot of 'perks,' and this is one of them. Rule number one: don't die. It's kill or be killed. A gun ain't the only thing that leaves a graze," he mumbled as she ran her hand along his arm.

"Turn over."

Steelo did as he was told and laid prone while resting his head along his folded arms. The sight of the large purple bruises along his shoulder blades shot a dagger through her heart. Who could possibly ever want to harm this man? Tiri couldn't stomach the trauma he went through as a hitta, but then again, she'd never question his position.

"Don't move."

Minutes later, Tiri returned from the bathroom and climbed on top of him. The bottle of coconut oil she left soaking in the sink was still warm as she squeezed a heaping amount into her tiny hands. The sight of his muscular frame was making her hot and heavy as the palms of her hands glided against his flesh. With each motion, she could physically feel how stressed and uptight this man was.

Steelo was missing a woman's touch. He was missing her caress, her ability to take all of his troubles and make them that much easier to cope with as long as she was around as a scapegoat. And Tiri wanted to be that for him. She wanted to be his peace. The reason why he smiled. The one to ignite his laughs. To introduce him to love and forever lasting sentiments that he'd always cherish and one day wouldn't be able to live without. She wanted to be his.

"You want me to change the song?" she whispered in his ear as her thumbs dug into the muscles right below his neck.

"Nah."

Tiri smiled. He could be so romantic and easygoing when he wanted, and it put her at ease. With her hands slowly running up and down both of his arms, she planted soft kisses to the side of his neck. Trailing them back and forth from one side of his face to the other until she came in contact with his earlobe.

She was easing pressure points Steelo wasn't aware that he had until her touch left behind a soothing sensation that his body's been craving. He was floating on a cloud that his mind didn't want to come down from, and even though he may have had a few drinks, his intoxication made no difference to the way he was feeling right now. She'd been on his mind for hours, and her presence was sealing him within an envelope that he never wanted to escape from.

"Turn over," she whispered before she stood to her feet to allow him to move. When their eyes met, she sat on her knees and pulled the string on his joggers. "I wanna make you feel good, Steelo," escaped through her lips as she released him.

Tiri closed her eyes as she mounted herself atop of his manhood. Her poor pussy was still sore from last night's erotic journey and the three rounds he'd turned her into a woman, but none of her pain nor dilemmas had mattered anymore. Only his satisfaction. Tiri bit down on her bottom lip as she allowed all of him to fill her before she opened her eyes.

Slowly, she rotated her hips just like Caesar coached her earlier to prepare for their next encounter. Steelo ran his hands up and down Tiri's thighs until he wrapped them around her waist. She began to move her body to the perfect rhythm; a rhythm that manipulated each depth of his width until she took off in a steady stride that made his toes curl.

"Damn, ma," he uttered in surprise.

Steelo couldn't tell if he were more so impressed or caught up in the moment from the way she felt around him. The numbers were running neck in neck as he watched her breasts bounce up and down that he could see through the fabric due to her mahogany-colored melanin shining through.

He sat up and ran his fingers through her hair as their tongues hungrily overlapped. Tiri threw her head back once his tongue traveled to her neck and began to mark her silky-smooth skin with passion marks. Her body trembled. She squirmed on top of him falling deeply in love with the zest and arousal his lips triggered each time she felt him plant a myriad of kisses along her flesh.

"Ummmm...Steelo..."

He loved the way she said his name. The way it pierced his ears and exploded like fireworks. The way it made his dick throb, his heart heavy, and his body yearn for her. It did something to him that he couldn't and didn't want to control.

"Steeeeeeelo," she groaned again as the pressure against her love button began to increase.

The angle Tiri was rocking her body was magical in correspondence with her female parts, and she couldn't hold back.

"That feel good?" he groaned between the kisses he planted against her lips.

"Umm hmm..."

Steelo lifted her from of him and changed positions once he slid his pants off. After stuffing a pillow underneath her stomach, he raised her ass in the air with an arch so perfect; he didn't hesitate to taste her before proceeding to the next position.

He swore he only wanted a sample, but Tiri's milky secretions birthed an endless hunger that he couldn't get full from. The way Steelo was eating her pussy, Tiri was turned out and swore on everything she loved that he'd have to put his tongue to work on the daily. His mouth attacking her clit from behind felt like a sin. Each stroke over her g-spot had Tiri's body turning like the exorcist. She was catching convulsions. She couldn't refrain from calling out his name and clawing at the sheets. Steelo had complete control over her body, and she couldn't fight it.

"Cum for me, Tiri," he commanded between his lips and tongue wavering over her flesh.

Her orgasm rolled over in a rippling effect. Her backside bucked against his face while she came so long and hard that it drained every ounce of energy she had left. Tiri was now under the impression that this man had a voodoo doll of her concealed like a shrine because there was no way he could make her feel the bliss that was consuming her.

Tiri's deep panting filled the air as he slowly trailed kisses over the arch of her butt and up her spine until she felt him enter her. Her pussy was so wet, Steelo found himself increasing his speed as he plunged down directly into her g-spot after pinning his chest against her back. Another rush was brewing between Tiri's legs, and she almost couldn't take it. This is why women turned bat-shit crazy overnight. This is why they'd call a nigga's phone twenty-seven times back to back until he answered.

Steelo couldn't possibly think that he'd be able to get away with the miscommunication from this day forward after making sweet love to her body like this. This was that 'cut a nigga's dick off and save it for later' type of sex. Tiri needed to purchase a glass box so she'd have that baby everywhere she went!

She screamed for the high heavens as her body trembled the moment another explosive orgasm was induced from his knocking on her sacred spot. His name spilled from her lips as his seeds spilled into her platinum-coated cavity. Steelo was unable to contain himself. His body shook as he continued to stroke the feeling of his nut away while panting in her ear until his body collapsed onto the bed.

"Damn...Tiri..." his words were faint as he planted kisses to her neck while holding her in his arms.

"I don't... give a fuck...what you say, Steelo..." she panted, trying to catch her breath. "You're mine now...fight me," she dared.

"There's no need to when we already on the same page, ma..."

𝕳𝖀𝕱𝕽

"Still no word?" Steelo questioned after lighting a blunt.

Marius stood over the pool table, easing the stick in and out of his hand before the cue ball rearranged the billiards.

"Solids," he stated his claim before responding to Steelo's question. "They'll react. Trust me. Lil' Geni ain't gon' let us off with killing his pappy. These muthafuckas keep testing me like I won't mail his whole fucking family in Ireland to his front door."

The Monstrosity was highly irritated with the O'Sullivan's steadily pushing to get the Feds to intercept how he ran his business. They were running around "attempting" to coerce legislators, like bitches, to get their foot in the door with the pharmaceutical trade in Trinity, and he wasn't having it.

This was his territory, and if the man had to ignite an Irish genocide to get his point across, then so be it. He slaughtered niggas like he was shipping them off in trucks to be distributed in grocery stores. It's what he did, and well.

Marius could see that his charity events had niggas walking around thinking he was soft. His wrath would always be a dangerous game, and he sees he had to send out a friendly reminder of why he was the one to never be fucked with nor underestimated.

"You tighten up on that security?"

Click—Pop!

Steelo landed the 11 ball in the side pocket before saying, "Twenty-four hour surveillance, twelve-hour shift rotations, and two teams on standby."

"That's what I like to hear. The ball is in their court now, so..." Marius luckily knocked two billiards in separate pockets before finishing. "All we do now is wait. Where is this girl?"

Steelo chuckled when Marius shot him that look.

"Don't look at me like that, man. She's downstairs in the guest room getting ready."

"What?" he chuckled. "Tell her don't be shy, now. I knew this day was coming the moment yo' ass couldn't pull a trigger."

"You capping. Do you not remember that night at Club Knockout two years ago?"

The gentlemen shared a laugh as they slapped hands.

"You know that's gon' cause some static, right? That nigga Messiah pretty hot-headed. Especially about his baby sister."

"I ain't worried about it. Nigga ain't stupid, you feel me?"

"Yeeeah, I'm prepared for them niggas to try to come and rescue lil' Tiri. I give it about another day or two," Marius had laughter in his smile, but he was as serious as a heartbeat, and Steelo felt that.

He'd done his homework about the Platinum Cartel after they'd bought the cocaine trade from BTG back in 2016. Steelo knew all there was to know about Mr. Messiah Omari Stallion; lethal that nigga may have been, but no man put fear in him. Tiri was old enough to make her own decisions, and if fucking with him is what she wanted, then why interfere when they shared mutual feelings, all for her weary and pressed ass brother? Maybe it was the fact that Steelo never had the opportunity to know what that brotherly love felt like.

KD was an exception. Marius would kill her ass before he ever allowed her to be with another man because he knew his potna was bananas like that, so he couldn't use his position with her to add up to the guard that Messiah had around Tiri. Steelo was sure he'd hear from the nigga soon, but until then, and even after it'd happened, he'd be chilling like a penguin in the North Pole.

Let another nigga rattle him for what?

"Here, babe."

Steelo turned his head when he heard Kovu's voice. She looked phenomenal in her metallic pink bikini with a black mesh skirt tied around her waist. Her hair was styled in its natural state, thick and full of volume, donning a silk press, that reached the nape of her back with a part down the middle. Her thick mink lashes, VVS diamond earrings, and egg white full-set matching her pedicured toes was the perfect look for their outing.

"I thought I heard some loud sounds of ass from behind me."

"Boy, fuck you, Steelo. Bitch, I hope you get sunburned witcho' light skinned ass," she teased as she handed her husband a mojito.

"Damn, girl. You tryna kill me?" Marius joked after downing the strong drink.

"Did I make 'em too strong? I left my damn glasses at home, so I couldn't see the serving sizes too good." She sipped her drink to get a taste herself. "Woooo. This baby-making alcohol content right here, now. I low-key was just pouring shit. It's good though. Does Tiri drink, Steelo? I ain't even gon' stunt, I been drinking since I was eighteen my damn self."

Marius smacked her on the ass after pulling her close.

"Be nice. She didn't know," he referred to Tiri accusing her of sleeping with Steelo.

"What?" Kovu giggled. "I know that. You really think I'm tripping off that? I just ain't never seen Steelo geeked over nobody before. That's all, and I'm always nice. *You* be nice, Mr. Monstrosity."

Steelo chuckled as he headed to get his girl while they got all boo'd up in his absence.

Tiri glanced in the mirror shaking like a damn stripper. Steelo had invited her out for brunch the next afternoon aboard Marius' yacht, and she was a nervous wreck. She'd always been the youngest body to have a seat at the table, and it was making her second guess her entire relationship with Steelo. Sure she'd be nineteen in a few months but come on.

Steelo and The Monstrosity were regals. Marius' bitch was Queen B in this city, and little did Tiri know, Kovu's name held weight back in St. Louis as well. She was surrounded by royalty, and here she was, a lonely little solitary peasant begging to be inducted into their throne as if she hadn't come from a prestigious background herself. God, she needed strength and confidence.

She goes from being a normal though, introverted high school student to sleeping with one of the tops dawgs who ran the most lucrative crime mob in the city, and that was a lot to digest. Her poor hands were shaky, her mind was running a mile a minute, the beads of sweat along her forehead wouldn't cease to stop forming, and at this point, she was ready to have Steelo send her back to the boat dock on a dingy.

Tiri, what are you doing? Do you really think you can pull this shit off? You're still a fucking kid at heart.

She placed her hands on her head and let out an exasperated breath, knowing she was being too hard on herself. Obviously, there was something about her that attracted Steelo and kept his attention if she'd made it this far; if he was claiming her as his woman. If she were on the very boat that the college girls at her school would all kill to be on! She felt it in her stomach that everything was about to change once the world found out that she was dating the infamous Nuri "Steelo" P. Oh, and the thoughts of her brother finding out?

Tiri had to fan herself to calm her nerves just as there was a knock on the door.

"C-come in."

Steelo entered the room with two drinks in hand, donning nothing but Givenchy from the white button-down left open to display his defined chest, to the boxer briefs that the matching shorts slightly hanging off his waist showed, and slides.

"You look like you about to pass out," he chuckled.

"That's because I am...oooh shit." Tiri made a sour face. "Okay, bartender. I see how we setting the tempo for this afternoon."

They shared a laugh.

"Sis went a lil' overboard on the pouring. She ain't making the next round. Trust. Tryna get us all fucked up and shit."

"Steelo, what if—"

"Umm-umm," he countered as he downed the entire glass. "Come on. You gon' be straight. KD ain't what you thinking. She a big ass kid her damn self, so lighten up..." he momentarily got caught up in the way the white bikini and long sleeved, colorful mesh coverup fit perfect on her frame. Slim thang she might've been, but those baby making hips were his weakness. Her full hair hanging down her back in deep waves after drying from her shower was the perfect touch to her appearance. "Come 'mur."

With a bratty smile, she walked up on him and buried her chin his chest. Tiri innocently looked up into his eyes before their lips met. That easily, most of her anxiety had vanished, forcing her to feel a million times better.

"God gave you the magic touch," she smiled with a soft voice.

"He sent me the right gal. I can't argue against my affection when I've got what I need in you to display those actions, mama. You alright with that, or you want me to get you something else?" he referred to her drink.

Who said gangstas couldn't be romantic? Because Steelo never hesitated to show her some thug passion and it had Tiri head over hills.

"I'm good. I appreciate it though."

"Yeah, a'ight. Don't have me carrying yo' hungover ass back to the dorm and you be slumped until class in the morning."

"I know my limits. Now, come on before my scary ass chickens out, and I end up hiding down here until we make it back to the dock."

Hand in hand, they made their way up to the deck where the melodies from Aaliyah's "Rock the Boat" filled the air. The Monstrosity's reputation throughout the city was the polar opposite of what young Tiri was presently witnessing. She didn't see a ruthless killer, a public known sociopath, a narcissistic bastard, the present-day Grim Reaper, or an overindulging theft. She saw a man who truly loved his wife. A man smiling and stepping to the rhythm of Kovu throwing her ass against his intersection with his arm wrapped around her waist. They flowed beautifully with the wind; moving in sync, blessing she and Steelo with an image of unconditional adoration and future aspirations for themselves to look forward to together.

At least that's what Tiri was thinking. She rested her head along her man's shoulder and sipped her drink in complete awe until Marius and Kovu noticed their appearance. The diamond on KD's ring finger blinded Tiri from its reflection in the sun as the couple soon approached them. She swallowed the lump in her throat with a larger gulp of the minty concoction before returning the same beautiful smile that Kovu greeted her with.

"Hey, you must be Tiri. It's nice to meet you. I'm Kovu, Marius' wife."

"Hey! Oh my God, I can't believe I'm meeting you. You are my favorite author now. I love all of your books. I literally just finished binge-reading your catalog. It's so nice to meet you, too."

"Thank you so much. I'm so glad you enjoyed them. This is my husband."

Tiri shook Marius' smooth, manicured hand after she and Kovu embraced. The man bore an energy so dominant and intensifying, she knew based off of that aspect alone to kiss the ring and respect his regality.

Brunch was amazing. Tiri and Kovu both got fucked up off mimosas while conversation ranged from art to sports and traveling. It seems they all had a few trips lined up to take with a man named Terrell, and his wife Asia as well; previously planned before Tiri's arrival, who was now more than welcome to attend since she'd been rewarded with the title of being Steelo's beaux.

It wasn't long before the ladies were sitting back tanning along the dock while their men were out on the waters enjoying their view on the jet skis. Tiri was rolling up a Backwoods when Kovu turned over and faced her to start conversation.

"Okay, Ms. Tiri, let's get something out of the way."

Her stomach dropped as she sealed the blunt, but she gave KD a head nod to indicate that she was all ears.

"I ain't got no beef with you, okay? I know how it looked when you saw me out with Steelo. People mistake us being in a relationship all the time, so I understand. Steelo is my brother. He's been holding me down in Marius' absence for the last few years, and it's been a real blessing to have him in my life. I have a brother locked up right now who keeps getting his court date pushed back because Missouri got one of the most fucked up judicial systems in this bullshit ass country. Losing Gerald, that's my brother, hit me so fucking hard, and then when I lost Collins…" Kovu sat up and fanned herself. Sometimes it felt like yesterday when she got that fucked up ass picture mail sent to her phone, and the pain still ran deep. "I'm sorry. I don't mean to tear up like this. It still just hits home for me. You've read *Love From A Boss,* right?"

"Umm-hmm." Tiri took a puff of the blunt before passing it.

"I tweaked the story hellas so that I didn't put Marius' business out there like that, but Tiri, that shit was written based off of the same crazy ass and off the wall ass shit that I went through. Marius really did kill my best friend like Monsta did with Zoie. In the book, I made it that he killed a girl who was married to a kingpin, but I'm sure you get what I'm saying. Moving along…Granted, that shit with Collins happened before he and I even met, but it was still a hard hit—let me say this first though. Shit, I'm all over the place. Please forgive me…Ok. The fact that you are here right now says *a lot.* Steelo is a mini Marius, and he doesn't trust anyone.

My brother has been through a lot, and if you don't know, then you'll soon find out because he is really feeling you. I'm not as hard up as they are. They have every reason to be, and I'd never judge them for that, but I don't pass that same judgment on people as hard as they do. Am I naïve or gullible? Fuck no. I'm Kovu Daniels-Usher. A boss ass bitch and I was solid before my husband put a ring on it. But what I'm tryna say is, I don't get a bad vibe from you at all, and with that being said, because Steelo trusts you, then I do too.

Marius always has his guards up. He can come off a little brass sometimes, but don't pay him no mind. You'll grow to love his crazy ass.

But meeting Steelo saved me from going crazy myself. At least you come from a family of killers. This shit was all new to me. The guns, the thrill, killing niggas, chopping off heads, and the heat of seeing so many people hate and wish death on my man was a fucking battle at first. It's hard being his woman. Do not let me make it look like it's easy because it's not. Steelo talked to me and got me through a lot of that shit. I cherish the bond we have. A big killa' he might be, but that man's heart has so much love to give. So when he told me that he couldn't kill you that day we raided Trinity University, know that he didn't just do that shit for kisses and giggles.

He fucks with your pretty ass. I've never seen *anyone* besides me, and the kids make him smile like that, so you walk tall, and you have confidence in yourself and yo' nigga. Tiri, this is real life. Marius and Steelo don't play with bitches, snitches, kids, mammies, grannies, or none of that shit. He's not gonna step out on you, believe it or not. Before me, him and Marius both were paying bitches to disappear, or else they got kilt. No in between, no callbacks, ain't no other rounds, or second chances. So know that you being on his arm ain't just something to do...I mean you no harm though, girl. My best friends live in St. Louis, so it's actually nice not to be the only woman around to deal with them two locos anymore. Terrell's wife, Asia, is a Geologist, and they're almost *never* home with the way she's always around the world, so it just be me stuck to deal with they ass and the kids."

Tiri laughed a bit as she took the blunt from Kovu.

"I really appreciate that, KD. Trust me, I felt so fucking stupid after I did that shit once my girl Ceas gave me the rundown on y'all. Like, when she said your name, it automatically clicked in my head. Like bitch, I know you not talking about Kovu Usher, the author. I literally got hip on you a week after that shit popped off at TU, so I didn't recognize or know who you were when I first saw you. When we were at the mall, and all I saw was the back of you and some babies I ran with that shit. I owe you an apology. I really do. I jumped ahead of myself and trust me, Steelo got me together, quick."

They shared a laugh.

"I'm only eighteen, and I don't say that to justify what I did, but I'mma keep it one hundred with you too. I'm a late bloomer. I was only seventeen being a witness to the life my brother lives, and when niggas

132

raided our house, killing everything in their path that was moving, including my big cousin who I miss so fucking much? That shit was a pill to swallow. I played naïve to this shit for as long as I could and got a wake-up call that really put my ass in check. And you're right; it is a lot to take on. Steelo isn't an ordinary nigga and trust me, I can see that. The shit still baffles me how and why he's saved me on numerous occasions. He took my virginity the night before I saw y'all at the mall, so if anything, my dick whipped and sprung ass just lost it like, *Uh-uhh! Nigga I knoooooow!*"

They each fell out in laughter, knowing all too well how that shit goes.

"Noooooooow it makes sense. Hell, I would've done the same shit had I seen Marius with a bitch after the first time we fucked too. A man will never understand what that means when a girl loses that token. I brushed and laughed it off when he first told me, but trust me, you surely get a pass after that. Yeah, I kinda felt some type of way when I heard he was seeing you, but that's only me being concerned about his welfare. It ain't me throwing shots at you at all."

Tiri was relieved. Kovu didn't come off as a hater nor a bitch, and she was grateful that they were able to smooth that hazy little situation over.

"So, how old are you, Kovu, if you don't mind me asking?"

"Girl, you good. I'm turning twenty-seven in October."

"Damn, I'm a baby," Tiri shrieked.

"You building a strong mental though. That's the shit that cashes the check. If Steelo thought you were out of his league, then you wouldn't be here. You got an innocence about you that turns him on. I know my brother. Yo' personality isn't a façade, and for that, he fucks with you. We fucks with you. I know for a fact that Marius' antennas still gon' be up until time passes by. This is a lucrative crime family, so don't take that personal."

"No, I understand. Trust me. No offense at all."

"Good. I'm glad that's settled. I just didn't want you to get a bad vibe about me," Kovu smiled.

"Nope, I don't. We're good. Thanks for accepting me. Y'all are really cool peoples."

"Back at you, boo. On another note though, I know Marius' ole' big kid ass needs to park that damn jet ski and come let me ride his dick. I'm horny as fuck."

Tiri busted out in laughter. Kovu was such a free spirit, she always spoke what was on her mind, and she admired that about her.

"My bad, girl. Them mimosas and Patron got me feeling good as fuck!"

"I swear I thought it was just me! I mean, I know me and Steelo have only had sex enough times to count on one hand, but that man's aura talks to me in ways that I can't seem to control. My pussy has a mind of its own when it comes to him."

Kovu took a gulp from the fifth of Patron sitting right next to her before saying, "That means he be beating the lining out yo' shit and does that pussy right. And he got some in-house now? Giiiiiiirl! Yo' ass gon' be a pro by next week. Mark my words."

Tiri couldn't believe the day had come when a dick got her wilding out. For years she'd been timid and uneasy about sharing her body with someone else, but her baby Steelo was the truth and could get it whenever he wanted. Considering the way he always brought her to ecstasy and made her pussy cum all over him each time he ventured within her deepest crevice, it motivated her to get her sex game up so she could please him just as much as he pleased her.

She and Kovu talked and took a few more shots until the boat reached the Trinity dock. Their bond was surprisingly magnetic. In these days, it was a battle for women to click due to hate and animosity, but Kovu was cool people, and Tiri looked forward to kicking it with them.

When the couples went their separate ways, Tiri expected Steelo to take her back to the dorms, but instead, he headed in the direction of his spot so they could spend the rest of the evening together. Steelo didn't want to see her leave so soon, and Tiri happily obliged. The weed and liquor had her in an element that she was growing to love. By no means was she a pro yet with seducing Steelo, but he could honestly admit that she was catching on quickly.

The mimosas and shots had shorty on her level. She'd awakened a weakness of his that he once used to crave by sucking on his neck during the ride home, and it had his dick bulging through his shorts. Tiri's little tipsy ass had her hands down his pants, stroking his wood with deep pulls, loving when the pre-cum oozed from the tip and saturated her fingers. When Steelo pulled up in his driveway, he couldn't hold back. He reclined his seat and instructed her to mount the dick that she obviously couldn't get enough of.

Tiri followed his command, lifted her coverup, and removed her bottoms, but she sat on him from behind, rotating her hips as she felt him reach her cervix. She held onto the steering wheel of his Bugatti and bounced her ass up and down his pole, loving how she gripped his shaft and the delectable pleasure it was to work all of him with ease. Tiri had Steelo in trouble. He didn't know if it was her scent, her infatuation with his mean ass, or the way he struck gold whenever he was in the pussy, but her tight and wet grip was A1, *and* it was his.

Tiri called out when he pulled her back and pinned her against his chest. His mouth caressed her neck, one hand groped her breast, and the other was stroking her clit in the precise motion. She glided along Steelo's thick and long dick, one hand holding onto the door and the other one planted along the back of his head as he brought her to a climax that caused drool to seep out the corners of her mouth. But her man was far from being finished.

After exiting the car, he bent her over the hood of his Aston Martin that was parked beside them and dug deep into that sweet pussy while holding onto her ankles. Fucking Tiri was so blissful it made up for the intervals between getting down with a one-night stand. Never was he hard up, but the privilege of fucking a woman whenever his dick got hard and with her being an asset versus an emotionally detached liability, it brought him that much more peace. There was no more scoping bitches out when him, Marius, and Terrell went out for a drink.

At the end of the day, Marius and Terrell both had wives to go home to. They had daily closure. Children. A family. Love. And for years, he'd been wasting money and threatening groupie hoes whose pussy didn't even add up to the chocolate goddess he was slowly yet surely growing addicted to. Steelo wanted that same privilege. Those experiences. That special and loyal woman, and no matter how much those corny and cheesy thoughts frightened him when Tiri was still a fresh start in his life, he knew that those experiences were supposed to be shared with her.

When he felt his nut coming near, Steelo flipped his baby over and pulled her pelvis to the edge of the car before reentering her. The shit blew him how she always held him close, the way she passionately kissed him and begged him to fuck her with no remorse like she wasn't new to this. Lil' baby was a winner for sure. The moment Steelo felt her honey saturate him once again, he increased his speed and came with her, knowing that he'd released his seeds inside of little Tiri one time too many for their spirits not to be connected. She was now a product of Nuri P.

Taug Jaye

Heart Up For Ransom

"If you think she in trouble then let's go shut that shit down.,"

-Seth

Taug Jaye

Chapter

8

"Nasir Platinum!"

Minutes went by with Seth waiting on a reply from his wife, but silence continued to consume the air, forcing him to get up and go after her. Ariel was clinging onto his shoulder with a death grip in the middle of her sleep, so to avoid disgruntling his little princess, who already had an attitude just as bad as he did, he kept his arm wrapped around her legs as he headed inside of Nasir's massive walk-in closet that she and the kids spent a lot of their days in.

The aroma of the lemon-mint Bath & Body Works three wick candles infiltrated his nose as he bypassed her 700 square foot shoe section, alone, and headed to her wardrobe sector. There she stood off to the side in front of the ceiling high mirror checking out her angles in the Saint Laurent denim shorts that hugged her hips, ass, and thighs like a glove. Paired with a white crop top and her favorite YSL bubble gum pink platform sandals, her simple yet chic attire looked amazing on her, and now Seth's dick was hard. You know how it goes when it comes to Seth and her voluptuous frame. Ain't shit changed but the weather, baby.

"You hear me calling you," he uttered while bending his head a bit to enjoy the view of her reaching over to adjust the strap around her left ankle. "NASIR."

"Isn't my daughter right there on your arm sleeping?" she snapped.

"Aye, what the fuck is wrong wit' you, Nasir?" Seth didn't have time for the attitude shit.

"The same thing that's fucking wrong with you. I'm so sick of your got damn mouth! One of these days I'm gonna punch your ass square in the face, then just *maybe* you'll realize how you *should* and *should not* fucking address me!"

Ariel stirred in her sleep due to the piercing pitch projecting from her mother's mouth, so Seth took her back out to the bedroom and got her comfortable before returning back to handle Nasir's attitudinal ass.

"See man, this that shit I be talking about, Nas. What is you crying for?"

"Bitch, ain't nobody crying!"

Seth couldn't stifle his laughter as she used a tissue to wipe the tears from her eyes, careful not to mess up her makeup.

"Come here, Nas."

"Get away from me, Seth. You always do this shit and I really don't have time for your mood swings today. I'll be back later." Nasir grabbed her color-coordinated, Top Handle Balenciaga tote and tried to leave him standing there looking stuck on stupid, but of course Seth manhandled her and held her secure in his arms. She refrained from arguing against him as he planted deep, juicy kisses to her neckline that were disguised as a sorry ass apology. He's the one who woke up on the wrong side of the bed this morning in a shitty ass mood that he had no supportive evidence to justify, and she was tired of being the target. "Seth, you really need to get your anger issues under control. That shit is not healthy. I'm not gon' take too much more of this shit from you, you hear me? This 'just being who you are' shit ain't no fucking excuse, and either you fix that shit or else—"

"Or else what?" He interrupted with a soft tone before inhaling her skin and sucking so hard that it made her body squirm in his arms. "You gon' leave me? You gon' divorce the love of yo' life?"

Nasir rolled her eyes.

"Shut up, asshole. I know what you're doing, and at this rate, I just might have to file for one. I can't stand your ass."

"Well, you can't."

"Says fucking who?"

Instead of replying, Seth swiftly turned her around, got her shorts down like it was nothing, and bent her over before putting his face in her pussy. He honestly *was* sorry. Akil's birthday was slowly yet surely approaching in November, and even with it being a few months away and two years since his murder, the pain was still carved deep and fresh as day on his chest. He knew his wife didn't deserve the continuous fluctuation of his emotions that he threw at her like wild cards. He tried his best to cope with it, but this was something that he wasn't strong enough to handle, no matter how much time went by.

"I'm sorry, mama," he whispered while taking a nice look at her pink flesh from behind before his tongue went back to work, churning that sweet cream until it formed into butter and started dripping down his chin chair. Nasir's legs were shaking as she held onto her ankles, forcefully biting her bottom lip, fighting hard not to moan or call out his name, just to trump his ego. His mean ass really needed to get a grip and eating her pussy until she was no longer mad at him wouldn't be acceptable after this time around! She put that on everything!

"So that don't feel good, Nas? Huh?" Seth asked with a soft voice while two of his fingers moved in and out of her chamber in a circular motion.

A fuse went off in his head as she continued to ignore him. The man was already short-tempered and yet she did shit like this. Trying to get even, modestly forcing him to tread on open grounds that he knew she wouldn't be able to withstand.

"OH, FUCK!"

Seth wore a sinister grin etched across his face once he stood up and shoved that dick so far up her pussy it forced the words out of her mouth. With one hand pinned into the small of her back, he smacked her ass before grabbing her by the waist and pounded away, slightly bending his knees to keep his balance and simultaneously dig up in that gooey abyss even deeper.

"What you say, Nasir? Huh? You gon' divorce who?"

"Bitch, youuuuuu!" she teased, knowing he hated it when she used that word with him.

Smack!

That big yellow ass of hers turned red upon impact with a single slap. They'd only been married a month, Seth being too impatient to wait another year to make her a Platinum. A week after his proposal, they stood before a reverend in his mother's back yard, just the two of them with their mothers and their sleeping children, and they were secretly

142

wedded. He was sure that Messiah and Riley both would cuss them out once the jig was up after discovering that they were left out from such an important phase in their lives.

They were away in California taking a tour of Tiri's new home in the city of Trinity, and again, Seth couldn't wait. The nigga didn't even hit Prodigy up and let him know what had went down. As long as Nasir didn't go running her big mouth before the wedding came then, they were straight in his eyes, and he'd be free of an ass whooping for pulling some sneaky ass shit like that off.

"Call me a bitch again, hear?"

Nas' chest was caving in with every hard and powerful thrust while the dick rammed in and out of her walls. She was so wet, her silk was dripping down her thighs, and Seth's name was propelling through her lips the moment she came in record timing. The temperature in her dressing room had increased by a good six degrees once they were done talking shit and fucking each other like they didn't have three kids who needed them. Luckily, Ariel was still sleeping, SJ was lying in bed next to her watching *My Baby First TV* with his sippy cup in hand, and Asim was with Falcon at the mansion for the morning.

"Where you going?" Seth asked while redoing his top knot that unraveled in the midst of him getting her ass together.

"Out."

He raised his brow.

"You said you forgave me."

"That was sex talk."

"Damn, I can't get no kiss goodbye though? Some fucking wife you claim to be."

Nasir playfully mushed him in the head after he climbed in bed, kissed SJ, blew Aerie a kiss, then headed out the door. The Nordstrom Bistro was calling her name to go grab lunch for her and her mother to enjoy over some homemade peach mimosas at her condo.

Catori's afternoon yoga session wasn't so pleasant today. She was harvesting an energy that got harder to conceal as the years went by, and it was beginning to drive her insane. Her frequency was vibrating on uneven channels, merely intercepting her ability to strike even the simplest pose, and she could feel her temperature rising from the frustration.

Catori wanted to scream.

Decades have gone by, and she was still chained to the same demons and spirits that hindered her womanhood, her motherhood, her ability to sustain a stable relationship with every man she gave that chance to, and any day now, she'd break down. Much worse than her outburst last week while she was on her lunch break at work.

The sound of her daughter's voice calling out for her forced Catori to hold her composure as she stood to her feet. Saying fuck it on the yoga, she removed the cork from the bottle of Malbec wine and filled her glass centimeters away from the edge.

"Hey, mommy. I brought lunch; did you forget? What's wrong? Are you okay?"

Catori guzzled down the wine as if she'd been dying of thirst, loving the dry bite rippling down her throat on the way to her empty stomach. Nas stood observing her fiercely indulge in the drink until the bottom of the glass was empty. She'd come to visit her mother every single day since the afternoon one of her coworkers at *Neiman* called her about her mother's inconsolable hysterics and she had to leave work to pick her up. Her mother was silently fighting a brute battle and refused to let her in on the secret, modestly crushing her daughter's spirits.

Nasir and her mother shared a sacred bond. No conversation had ever been too difficult, embarrassing, or horrifying that they couldn't sit down and duke it out as a team. So she felt offended; hurt and deceived that it was a week later and Catori still insisted on remaining mute. Not to mention, her being oblivious to the fact that she'd suffered from a seventy-two hour psych visit at the hospital before Nas could take her home.

"Ma, you need to talk to me. Give me this."

"No, Nasir."

"Momma!"

She snatched the bottle from her mother's hand, spilling majority of it along her sunroom floor, but Nas didn't care. Catori's mental health was more important, but for the life of her, they didn't seem to be on the same page.

"Nasir, I don't want to put my hands on you, so can you please just fucking leave me alone and stop badgering me! I'm a grown ass woman; I can handle this shit by myself!"

"Obviously you can't or else we wouldn't be here right now, and you wouldn't be on FMLA until a psychiatrist gives you the permission to return! And I'm not a little girl anymore so don't you ever threaten me, especially with physical behavior, nor talk to me like that when all I'm trying to do is help you!"

"You're shrinking me, Nas!"

Catori stormed off and made her way to the kitchen to avoid facing her daughter, who was doing nothing but telling her the exact things that she needed to hear.

"What the fuck ever to get the job done, momma!" Nasir went after her. She'd never used such language with her mother, but this shit has gone on for entirely too long. Seth nor Catori were going to drive her out her mind with their boastful behavior, so they better had confessed the hell up and quick so she could help them rid the angst that was weighing them down. Starting with her unstable ass, ignorant acting momma. "Ma, please talk to me. I shouldn't have to beg you to communicate with me," Nas pleaded with glossy eyes.

Catori turned around with a look on her face that Nasir couldn't recognize. Her eyes were cold. Forehead wrinkled. Skin emerging into a shade of red that eliminated her normal complexion. Tension was present in each of her jawlines. Brows furrowed. Lips curled. Her lean and sculpted arm muscles started to bulge with the tight clenching of her fists, and had Nas made one further wrong move, gesture, or statement, then the story would never be able to be erased after the moment the ball was dropped. Taking her mother's appearance as a forewarning, Nasir finally complied by backing down and headed for the exit.

When the front door closed behind her daughter, Catori released an exasperated breath. She was trembling; her mind, body, and soul vibrating out of control, and she couldn't take it anymore. Her bare, French manicured feet ravened against the finished wooden surface in search of the hall closet. A plethora of shoeboxes were neatly stacked to the ceiling on the top shelf, but soon came crashing down and onto the floor as she threw them one by one until a black lockbox finally fell at her feet. Her hands were so shaky she could hardly turn the dial to unlock it until that magic click finally went off in her ear. She swung the door open and dozens of Polaroid pictures along with a .357 Magnum came spilling out.

Anger filled up her body past its breaking point as she struggled to load the revolver with six golden bullets. The smiles in the pictures, the proof of a time of her life that she tried to convince herself had never happened were like daggers repeatedly being thrown at her eyes. Everyone said Catori was crazy. Everyone manipulated her to believe that those moments were all hallucinations. Figments of her imagination. Discombobulation. Speculation. Remnants of a sick woman who'd been drugged and cleansed for three hundred and sixty-five long, tiring, devastating, and inhumane days until she too fell submissive and decided to believe their lies to save her soul. Hadn't it been for that old memory box that she swore she lost in the fire back when Nas and Ali were little, then this day would never have come.

After closing the revolver shut, her eyes landed upon one picture in particular. She dropped the gun and reached for it, bringing it up to eye level and the tears beginning to trickle down her stone face almost instantly.

His arm was lovingly wrapped around her tiny though protruding waist that her gown luckily hid. Her frame covered in the most stunning white, velour wedding dress and a floral print veil draped over her face, hiding the makeup that she remembered hating because the artist in 1993 had no proper knowledge of contour to hide her round features. Hezekiah Valentine aka Jamie-O stood hovering over her with his once soft and loving lips pressed against the top of her head while holding hands with the most beautiful fair-skinned, long-haired, baby girl. Ali was holding onto Catori's other hand, smiling for the camera with a few of his front teeth missing in his wide grin.

Time stood still for a good six seconds before Catori snapped.

She started screaming at the top of her lungs while going ballistic; kicking and throwing more boxes, pictures going up in the air like scattering dollar bills at the strip joint. She went on a rage for what seemed like forever until her eyes landed on the gun again. She lunged for it yet was immediately alarmed when she felt someone grab her by the hand. It was Nasir. Had she not forgotten her phone on the kitchen counter, there was no telling what she would've walked into the next morning when she decided to try this approach with her mother once again. They both struggled over the gun, both of their arms held high in the air until shots started ringing throughout the condo.

Pow...Pow...Pow!

"MOMMY, STOP! PLEASE!"

Nas was hysterical. Tears were running down her cheeks, and she tried her best to pry the gun from out of her mother's hands, yet she continued to put up a fight.

"NO! I DON'T WANT TO LIVE WITH THIS ANYMORE! HE RUINED MY FUCKING LIFE!!!"

Pow!

"FUCK YOU, HEZEKIAH!"

Pow!

"FUCK YOU! I HOPE YOU'RE ROTTING IN HELL, YOU SON OF A BIIIIIIIIIIIIIITCH!"

Pow! Clink! Clink! Clink!

Catori's knees finally gave in, causing her to fall to the floor with her daughter collapsing right on top of her. Nasir threw the empty gun before wrapping her arms around her distraught mother, who was still relentlessly crying and screaming at the top of her lungs. She rocked her back and forth, begging God to rid her mother of these demons that wouldn't cease to stop haunting her before it was too late.

HUFR

It was about time another Black man dropped a high-end fashion label that spoke volumes in the designer industry; one just as sound as popular brands such as Tom Ford, Fendi, and Givenchy. *Stallion* was hitting heavy as a commercial enterprise. After St. Louis rapper Lil' Redd was seen on the red carpet in one of Messiah's custom made and tailored suits, and when the high-fashion model/actress Sweetie Johnson repped a gown from his women's line at the Met Gala, bringing him nothing but business in surplus, S's were a symbol that people were rocking like LV's.

Messiah expected his line to make some noise, but at the rate his designs were blowing up overnight, ninety percent of his merchandise online was already sold out, and they had loads of products on backorder. He was just now leaving from a meeting with his marketing team, preparing for the Spring of 2019 collection that would really put the game in the palms of his hands.

One thing he hated about this rise to fame shit though was the paparazzi. With him and Seth still heavy in the streets, it took excessive effort to keep them under the radar. A few soldiers had to be appointed as frontline men to pose as the faces of the states while they appeared to the public as two businessmen outside of that league.

His Audemars wristwatch reflected in the flashes from the paparazzi cameras snapping pictures of him as he held his phone up to ear, now dialing his baby sister's number for the umpteenth time in two days. His jaw clenched when her sweet and chaste voicemail picked up, causing him to plop down in the backseat of the Escalade in frustration.

"Where to, Mr. Stallion?" the fifty-year-old driver asked in a cheerful tone, lightly tapping his fingers along the steering wheel to the Marvin Gaye playing low in the background.

"Vin De Set Bistro."

"Yes, sir."

Messiah's eyes were glued to his phone the entire car ride to his destination. Nonstop calls were coming in, emails were chirping every other minute, and his assistant, Blanca, was lighting their personal line up with text messages regarding further information on promo, advertisements, photoshoots, and other miscellaneous details for their Spring line.

Damn. Had I known shit would be this fucking hectic, I never would've launched this shit.

The blunt burning as they pulled along the curve before the bistro instantly lowered his angst. It's just what he needed. That, and some pussy from his emotional ass wife who'd been holding out on him since business "seemed" to be more important than his family.

"Yo', B," he spoke into the phone after him, and Blanca's call connected.

"Wassup?"

"Schedule my wife and I a spa day at the Four Seasons Resort in Santa Barbara for tomorrow afternoon. Nah, scratch that. Make it for this weekend. She's been dying to go back."

"Do you want me to cancel your 9:00 o'clock meeting with the relator in Paris for the virtual store tour on Saturday morning?"

"Fuck," he uttered, knowing something important had slipped his mind. "What's the schedule looking like on Friday?"

"Let's see...you have a billboard meeting at 11 A.M. and..." he could hear her mouse hurriedly clicking in the background, knowing she was maneuvering back and forth between three different monitors. "That's it. Damn, that's surprising. Your Friday's are usually all booked up."

"I'm hip. Send his secretary over an email and see if we can reschedule it for 9 A.M. Friday morning."

"I'm making a note now. Anything else?"

"Forward all my calls for the rest of the day. If it's not an emergency or something that can't be handled in the morning, then I don't wanna hear about it."

"I got you. Talk to you later. Enjoy your time with your family."

"A'ight. You too."

Messiah hung up the phone relieved. Blanca was always on her shit, and he'd yet to be disappointed in her work ethics and determination to help him keep *Stallion* running. If anything, she was like family. Blanca was Trudy's best friend who'd went off to college in D.C. before returning home after getting her marketing degree. Her profession came in handy once his business was launched and he honestly didn't know how he'd make it without her.

Fifteen minutes later after smoking his 'Woods down to the nitty-gritty, he exited the vehicle with his signature *Stallion* cologne masking his high and a pair of aviator shades shielding his low, red eyes. The quarter length, denim button-down, army green, straight leg, cargo pants, and Balenciaga Triple S sneakers fit his frame perfectly. The braided top knot underlined by his fade let these people know that he'd be fine and fly forever, but that wedding band around his ring finger passed as a warning sign, letting the world know for a little over a year now, that Riley had him locked down with no key to undo the "I do's."

Aside from their staggered quality time these days, the Stallions were happily married.

"Daddyyyyyy!"

Ashanti wiggled free from her mother's lap the moment she saw the rooftop door open and out walked her father. Messiah's long legs allowed him to take bigger steps in her direction, meeting his baby girl halfway before swooping her up in his grasp and kissing both of her cheeks before kissing her lips.

"Wassup, Boop. You miss me?" he asked while calling her by her nickname.

"Yes, I did!" she grinned, wrapping her arms securely around his neck.

Shanti wore a smile that only a daddy could induce, happy that he'd finally made it. His wife, on the other hand, wore the words *bitch with an attitude* across her forehead as she took a bite out of the Monte Cristo sandwich, using her tongue to lap up the juices left behind in the creases of her mouth. Her bright yellow skin was glowing in the sun as he took out the time to admire her features. Those juicy, full lips were still painted in a deep shade of "Fresh Brew" by MAC. The slick bun positioned high on her head accentuated by her swirled baby hairs, hoop nose ring, and no other jewelry made his dick tense up.

Riley was so pissed off at him for being over an hour late to brunch that she refused to acknowledge him, or even make eye contact.

150

With Shanti still in his arms, he bent over and planted a kiss to her cheek, but she wasn't fazed at all.

"Hello to you too then, woman."

Her eyes changed in his direction with an evil scowl as he took a seat across from her. She then took a sip of her water.

"Glad you found the time to show up and squeeze us into your schedule," she spat before popping a prenatal pill.

"Riley, don't start."

"No, *you* don't start."

He reached over and grabbed a few of her fries as Shanti picked up her tablet to finish her movie that was still playing.

"Can we enjoy this date without all the antics, Mrs. Stallion? I apologize, a'ight? The meeting lasted longer than I expected it to."

The meetings always lasted longer than he "expected" them to, but Riley had a headache, and she didn't have the energy to be going back and forth with this nigga.

"How'd it go?" her voice was soft as her mood changed.

There was no point in being nasty when at the end of the day, all it ever boiled down to was that she was missing her husband like crazy.

"Smooth. I like yo' eyeliner like that; enhances yo' eyes and brows."

She smirked at his corny ass complimenting her cat eyes, already aware that he was trying to get back in her good graces.

"You still ain't getting none today."

"Come on, man. Don't be like that. I'm already stressing out enough that Tiri ain't been answering my phone calls."

Riley took a bite of the Provencal Shrimp crepe before responding.

"Babe, she's in college. She's got so much to do and indulge in out there in Trinity. The city is the shit. Her school is the shit. She'll call. Let that girl live her life and take the leash off of her. She has to grow up someday. Ain't shit else out there popped off since the incident, and you know she'll call you if it did."

"Aw, yeah. Like she did when the shooting first happened?" his reply was lathered in sarcasm, causing Riley to roll her eyes.

"Okay, that may be understandable, but still. You see her social media posts. That girl is kicking it. She's making new friends, finding herself, and probably found her a lil' boo and shit too. It was all kind of lil' tenda's up there, so I wouldn't be surprised if she brought somebody home for the holidays."

The look Messiah shot in his wife's direction caused her to hold onto her baby bump and laugh out loud.

"Aye, shut up, Riley."

"Aye, I'm just keeping it real with you. She's beautiful. Who doesn't like chocolate?"

He loved her ability to make him smile. Her cute little wink was messing with both his heads, and after Shanti got dropped off with her great grandmother, Messiah was tagging that shit all night like his name was Chris Breezy.

After placing his order and finally getting a fresh beer to quench his thirst, he reached over the table and grabbed his wife's hand before looking her in the eye.

"What I gotta do to spend a weekend with you, Miss Lady? Alone. Kid and phone free."

"Don't make me any more promises that you can't keep, Mr. Stallion."

"I kept my promise about today, didn't I?" he argued with a smile.

"Nigga, barely. That's alright though. I'll get my side nigga to spend some time with me since my husband has better things to do."

"Quit fucking playing with me, Riley."

"Watch yo' mouth in front of my baby, nigga."

Messiah watched something alright. When she stood up from the table, his mouth salivated at the way her haltered mint green, wide-leg romper hugged her shape. Her nipples were swollen, peering through the fabric like headlights, and with the way her hips switched as she headed for the bathroom without giving him much of a reply, he was torn between feeling some type of way and not being able to pick her ass up in a stall and sit her on his dick since Shanti was present.

Friday came sooner than he expected, and Riley was surprised when her husband sent a car for her after her last personal training appointment that evening. The driver pulled up at the Platinum/Stallion hangar where he was waiting on her, and from there she and Messiah flew out to the west coast. It felt good to get out and enjoy some one on one time with the man who fell out the clear blue sky and took her away from all of her problems.

They did a little shopping, effortlessly blowing a hundred and fifty racks on clothes, bags, and some furniture that Riley simply had to have for her den since she was on this redecorating craze, and of course grabbing everything they could for their baby girls too.

Since they'd arrived in the late evening, shopping was all they could get into for the night before having dinner at Toma Restaurant and Bar. The waterfront eatery was absolutely divine, and nothing was better than enjoying both Italian and Mediterranean food handcrafted into one dynamic cuisine. They shared laughs, jokes, and conversation over squash blossoms, roasted lamb meatballs, mind-blowing entrees that they both were entirely too full to finish after sampling damn near every appetizer on the menu, but they did save a little room for dessert.

Riley sat in her husband's lap sipping on a glass of sparkling wine while he fed her bites of the Warm Chocolate Torte; enjoying the beauty of the waterfront and the crisp ocean breeze from the shoreline. After Messiah finished his cigar, they walked hand in hand back to their vehicle awaiting them and called it a night.

Messiah hated to be mannish. They were back at the hotel now, and with the way Riley's hips were looking in her short and sexy little black dress, he couldn't help it when he followed behind her into the bathroom uninvited. She'd been holding out on him for the longest, and he couldn't take it a second longer. Steam surrounded their hot and sweaty bodies as Messiah penetrated her juicy pussy while she sat propped up on top of the sink. They feasted upon one another's tongues as he continued to dig deeper, prompting Riley to whimper between their every caress. Her husband's dick was so hard she could feel his veins via each stroke with his own panting growing deeper.

Riley threw her head back when he slammed all of himself into her chamber, rotating his hips while gripping on her thighs, sucking on her sore nipples, and holding one hand around her neck. He then repositioned her left leg onto his shoulder before he picked up the pace and started thrusting in and out of her at a speed that had her pussy creaming his dick in a matter of minutes.

Messiah hated to make her feel like he didn't want to be around or that he didn't love her. She was his heart. She was the reason why he'd dived headfirst into self-discipline and showed none of these hoes any attention after the first time he broke her heart. Messiah knew what he had at home would always be too great of a risk to lose for some amateur ass pussy in the first place.

Over were the days when he was running around fucking women who were assessable to any man with a dick and a bankroll. Her love was all he needed. All he wanted. All he cherished, and no matter how many times he'd have to forward his calls to spare a day or two with his shorty, if it kept her happy, then that's what it all boiled down to.

Riley laid between her man's legs after their steamy escapades that led them from the shower to the bedroom, the lounge chair, and the mini bar, now eating on her leftovers since she'd worked up another appetite. Messiah was enjoying a bottle of wine imported from Napa Valley. They sat in a comfortable silence, enjoying each other's company, butterball naked and wrapped up in the sheets with the breeze from the open balcony doors tickling their skin.

"Thanks for being serious about cutting your phone off."

Messiah looked down at his wife, who leaned her head back so she could look up into his eyes. He leaned over and kissed her lips before finishing his glass.

"I know it's been hectic since the launch of *Stallion*, ma. I didn't expect for things to take off like this."

"Babe, I'm not upset with you for being successful, and if it looks that way, then I apologize because that's surely not where I'm coming from. You know I am so proud of you. *And* your franchise is Black-owned? That's the type of positivity that the world needs to see. All I'm saying is, you have to prioritize your time. If it's not about *Stallion,* then it's about business with the Cartel and me and Shanti are suffering from the ramifications of that. We wanna see you just as much as everyone else does too."

Messiah reached down and gently rubbed her belly, eager to meet their youngest princess of the bunch.

"I know, ma, and I'mma do better. But I've been using that shit as an excuse though."

"As an excuse for what?"

Silence consumed them before he grabbed the wine bottle and took a long gulp.

"For Tiri being away."

Riley smiled. It was adorable how much he missed his baby sister. Not to mention how obvious it was that he'd been suffering from a terrible case of separation anxiety — coining the reason for him being busier than usual.

"Siah, hear me out when I say this, babe…You have to let go and let God. You honestly thought that you'd be able to keep her up under your thumb forever?"

"Nah, but after the shooting, I honestly thought she would've been and had me come get her. I didn't expect her to last this long. See, you gotta realize something, Riley. She almost died at the hands of me. Bad enough my Trudy took a bullet and got buried in the process to save her life too. That shit replays in my head on repeat every, fucking, day. Even after it being a few years later. Tiri ain't like other teenage girls these days. She's been blind to so much shit for so long, and I feel like I haven't done my job as her brother to prepare her for the real world. That shit weighing down heavy on my heart, and half the time I be ready to lose my cool, so I stay busy to keep my mind off not going out there and spazzing the fuck out. Don't blame me for loving and wanting the best for my lil' sister."

"No one blames you for that, babe." Riley took his left hand in hers, then kissed it. "Believe it or not, your sister is a lot stronger than you think she is. She's not dumb and she knows how to use good judgment. You think negative and that's what will happen. I agree with you on her sometimes underestimating her family and what she comes from. I know these niggas out here are grimy and will do anything for a come up like going after the princess to get to the king. It's scary. She hasn't seen the world like we have, but you can't hide it from her either…"

Messiah talked with his wife for hours, jumping from one conversation to another. It was a quarter past one when she'd finally fallen asleep, leaving him and his thoughts to run amuck with no barrier to stop them. He was out on the balcony rolling up another 'Woods when an email came through on his phone. He'd been waiting on his squad to present him with some info since Tiri refused to communicate with him. Invading her privacy was never the angle, but his heart wouldn't settle until he knew for certain that she was safe.

"Aye, man. I know y'all niggas lying."

Messiah hopped up dialing Seth's number, disregarding the fact that it was after 3 A.M. in St. Louis.

"Wassup, fam."

To his surprise, his brother was wide awake. He could hear Asim's little voice in the background, meaning that Seth was up on daddy duties.

"What you know about a nigga named Steelo from Trinity?"

"Steelo, Steelo..." the name sounded familiar to Seth until it finally rang a bell. "He work for that nigga Monstrosity. He's an assassin; used to hit licks for that nigga Woo Shields a couple years back."

"Woo Shields? The loan shark from Vegas?"

"Yeah, him. What's the word? We got static?"

"I got some pictures from an investigator of Tiri with this nigga all hugged up and shit. Said that's all the info he had was a few pics and a name since niggas don't pillow talk on nobody from his mob. I couldn't even find out this nigga's place of birth, shit about his background, or none of that. But now that you say Monstrosity, I'm already fucking hip. As soon as I saw this nigga picture, that nigga Marius popped up in my head...

Bro, you mean to tell me that my sister running around with a killa' from the most lucrative crime family in the country? I know that's not what you telling me, bro. Trinity worse than it is here. We low key and discreet with our shit. The Monstrosity move too mufuckin' reckless for me, fam. Never will I knock another nigga's orchestration, but she don't need to be around that shit. Tiri supposed to be marrying a doctor, or a lawyer, or one of these safe ass, corny ass niggas that's gon' keep her out of harm's way. Not put her in the middle of that shit. Bruh, I'm hot!"

"How you gon' want for her something she never been a witness to? All she knows is heavy hittas. If she ain't in no trouble and she happy then why fuck wit' that, bruh? Listen to yo' self right now."

"Fuck all that shit you talking, my nigga. Tiri don't know shit about this nigga Steelo. *You* listen to *me*. I can't even get a full background check on this nigga, but she fucking him? That shit don't sound sketchy to you? Lil' immature and green ass Tiri fucking with a nigga apart of a trade that stops at nothing to hunt and conquer what they want? Like me and you ain't the faces of the states? I'mma say this shit to yo' ass again, dawg. THAT SHIT DON'T SOUND SKETCHY TO YOU?!"

"Fuck on wit' all that yelling shit, bruh. My ears work just fine."

Seth tried to reason with him, but we all know how Messiah is once he's been provoked. The sound of his voice alone and the fact that he was screaming in Seth's ear like he wouldn't swing on his ass for the disrespect if they were face to face, simply let him know that Siah was in a bad headspace. His breathing was irregular, and the way he knew his dawg was pacing the floor out of frustration, was enough to know that there was no taking this situation lightly. So, Seth chunked it up and was ready for whatever.

"You know how we do, bro. Lil' Tiri my baby and you know I don't wanna see her get hurt. So if you think she in trouble then let's go shut that shit down. No questions about it, but we ain't about to roll up in Trinity on some crazy shit and not have a plan. Them niggas own the whole city, so we gotta have all this shit figured out before we pop out."

"I'm already on that. I'm sending a few more soldiers to watch the town and see how shit going on out there so we can work our way around it. We gon' be in and out, but best believe we leaving them niggas a message for tryna finesse me and mine."

"Say no more. Let's do it."

Heart Up For Ransom

"YOU TRUST ME?"

-Steelo

Taug Jaye

Chapter

9

The difference between college and high school was simple: no one was going to force you to attend class. Professors weren't roll calling each period double-checking that you were seated in your assigned seat. They weren't hovering over you, pressuring students to get their work turned in, or encouraging them to be on time, engaged, or attentive. Some professors did, but the majority of them were simply overworked and underpaid, regular human beings working hard for their bi-weekly checks. They didn't give a damn if you showed up or not.

Students took out loans or paid out of pocket for their secondary education, so if they fucked that up, then it was all in their own hands. Entering a zero or an IN for incomplete or an A for absent was much easier than grading *another* discussion board post, pulling apart *another* five-page essay, or docking points for yet *another* student not putting the correct sources as stated on the essay guidelines. Trust and believe that it was no chip off their shoulders at all.

But young Tiri took an oath to remain determined and to complete the goals that she'd set for her freshman year, so she stayed on her grind no matter how often she was forced to shift with the newfound advances of her present life. Luckily for her, all of her classes this semester had a complimentary online access. Her professors recorded their lectures live, giving their international students the opportunity to catch them at their earliest convenience. The only time she saw campus was when she returned for more clothes and any other belongings pertaining to schoolwork.

Outside of her nightly chit-chats and gossip sessions via FaceTime with her girl Ceas, she and Steelo had spent the last thirty days basking in the tranquility of being intertwined within each other's presence. Yes, work kept her man busy, but when he returned home, and she either had the evening or the next few days with him all to herself, it was always worth it.

Every. Single. Time.

Sweet Tiri was rotting Steelo's teeth from the large quantities of chocolate he'd consumed from day one to day thirty. Every time she turned around, her eyes were forcefully being peeled apart, suddenly awakened from her sleep the moment she felt his tongue licking on her pearl. Her cream was like daily nourishment that he couldn't fill up on from one helping, so her legs remained divided as her daily number of orgasms did nothing but multiply once he was done adding, squaring, and subtracting in the correct sequence that forced Tiri to call out his name.

Steelo touched young Tiri in ways that made her want to run and hide away from the world because she was too embarrassed to put into words the yield that emerged from even the slightest touch of his. She wanted to call home and ask her sister-in-law was it supposed to feel this way while engaging with a man and so soon. The butterflies. The constant stampede that overpowered her resting heartbeat. The daily palpitation of her love button even at the thought of him. The way she stared at him when he laid beside her sleeping at night. The way he smiled and pulled her into his arms every day that she marked off the calendar as if it were his first encounter with such a beautiful soul.

Tiri could go on for miles describing the way Steelo made her feel, but the last thing she wanted to do was be foolish over a relationship that they were only two full months into. Hell, it seemed like it was just yesterday when the barrel of his Eagle was being shoved down her damn throat for Christ's sake.

Torn between her heart and her racing mind, Tiri sat along the edge of the bathtub and lathered the thick Aveeno body lotion onto her skin. The rain had calmed, and the cloudy skies were clearing up, but her atmosphere remained tented considering the matte black décor that covered each wall, surface, and piece of furniture in Steelo's home. Mr. P had taste, that was one thing she couldn't deny. Once the sun had set, the mansion almost lit up due to the stainless-steel appliances, modern stairwells and banisters, and the motion lights that illuminated the premises to prevent the use of too much electricity.

It was a beautiful and therapeutic sight to see.

After sliding on a pair of Nike running shorts that were soon hidden by the black t-shirt of her boo's that she paired with them, Tiri stood in the mirror and observed herself. Her skin was radiant. Her smile was genuine; she couldn't remember the last time she hadn't had to force on an act of happiness since the day she lost her virginity to a real one. Her eyes peered over her long acrylic nails, the long violet bundles falling down her back, the long eyelashes, her long legs. And, after a tough deliberation...she honestly admired what she saw in return. A lot of times she couldn't stand the thought of her own reflection knowing she'd been battling with who Tiri Nyree Stallion was for the majority of her life.

She'd been studying nonstop for the upcoming week of midterms, questioning if being Dr. Stallion was really her dream, or the one that her parents and older brother had painted for her. The more she witnessed Steelo's confidence and cocky demeanor; the way he walked tall with not an ounce of shame in his soul for being the man he was, it made her not only question did she have that much credence within herself, but did she truly *know who she was*? Even at this very moment, succeeding the acceptance stamp that she'd placed over the checklist of her appearance. The thought was taunting her brain, so Tiri fetched a notebook and a purple ink pen before flipping through the pages until she found a blank sheet to write on.

She wrote out her full name then drew five different lines where she would soon describe five different artifacts that coined her essence. Off top, she wrote out the word *beautiful,* and it made her smile greatly. Beauty wasn't subjected to her appearance. No, it also referred to her spirits, her soul, her attitude, her passion for life, and the mentality of hers that she knew was still a work in progress, but because she was so ready, willing, and open to grow, she admired the beauty of her faith and tenacity to become a stronger and wiser young woman. To her, that was the epitome of beauty.

Spiritual was her second artifact because where would she be in this world of sin without God's grace? *Family Orientated* was the third artifact, *Purity/Innocence* was the fourth since she knew she'd always be a *Nickelodeon/Disney & Pixar* kid for life, no matter how old she got, but she struggled when it came to the last slot. Should she fill it in with an adjective that further described her character? Or, how about what brought her happiness? What was she passionate about? What did she absolutely love and couldn't steer away from no matter how hard she tried to settle upon a profession that would bear fruits of her labor and not make her look like the Stallion who couldn't contribute to their family fortune?

The irritation that clouded her inability to fill in that last fucking slot sent Tiri over the edge. If nothing made her passionate, then why the hell was Messiah blowing hundreds and thousands of dollars for her to even be there? Why did she even sign up for her Biology major in the first place? Because mommy had said so? No disrespect to her mother, God rest her soul, but did Tiri really even want this college experience? The more she contemplated over that stupid ass slot, the angrier she grew. It was childish to allow something so trivial to choke her up, but was it really? This was her life that she couldn't paint a clear picture of, and by now Tiri was sure that a redness had emerged across her face was the aftermath from her frustration.

Grabbing her gallon-sized freezer bag of premium marijuana, she made her way down to the kitchen and decided to cook her problems away. Roughly two hours later, a shock ran up her pussy when she took a bite out of the infused mac and cheese, oven-fried chicken thighs smothered in a garlic butter sauce, and sautéed kale and collard greens with a side of homemade yeast rolls. Edibles were another product that kept Ceas blowing her up on the weekends. Her Lucky Charm bars, caramel brownies, vanilla Oreo bars, and cheesecake bites kept the college students in a craze, and half the time, she wished she never would've blessed them with those gems. But this meal? This shit right here would run for a dub a plate if she added it to her services.

"Ceas."

"Yes, honey."

"Bitch, why I just made some marijuana-infused mac and cheese, oven-fried chicken thighs, and kale and collards with an infused garlic butter sauce."

"Bitch, my panties just got wet. Run that shit back?!"

The duo broke out in laughter before Tiri rook another bite.

"Ceas, when I say this shit is fire as fuck? I'mma bring you some tonight when I get back."

"Oh, shit! You're blessing me with your physical presence after a month?! You know I'm still pissed at you, right?"

"I know! I know! I'm so sorry! One extra day with him turned into a whole thirty days of-."

"Dick sucking and straight fucking?"

"Ceas, you are a real *freak nasty ho*," Tiri joked.

"*That'll grant all his wishes!*"

"Okaaaay!" Their laughter filled the atmosphere of the phone again after quoting Meek Mill. "Shit, and you can call me Superhead now. This nigga got me sucking nut straight from the sac. No acid reflux once he lets off. No crying. Licking up every single drop then sitting on top of that mu'fucka and sliding down from the tip to the base in slow strides. Making that nigga tell me that his dick is all mine."

"Bitch, you need to write that shit down! That was dope as fuck! You got you the start of some fire shit that you can spit at Kovu's next poetry slam."

Tiri shared the same sentiments, quickly reaching for a paper towel and the ink pen that was sitting on the counter near her. She scribbled the words down as best as she could from her memory before she and Ceas jumped back into conversation.

"Can I ask you something, Ceas?"

"Ask me anything. What's on your mind, babe?"

Tiri twirled the end of a strip of her hair around her index finger to buy some time.

"Did you always know that you wanted to be a scientist and work for NASA? Is that your dream or someone else's?"

"Girl, hell yes. This is my dream. At first, I was afraid to admit that I wanted to be a scientist to my parents and I almost went through with majoring in accounting, but this is all my decision to be here in Trinity. My daddy honestly wanted me to help run our family *business*. You know I'm good at numbers and shit, so he was convinced that I'd be handling the finances. In return he was gonna keep me paid with a six-figure salary, but I didn't want to do that shit. It's just not my speed. I didn't/don't mind stepping in whenever he thinks the numbers are off, but that's not what's in my heart.

"I like what I like, and I'm not afraid to say that I'm a Black woman who loves biology and physics anymore. I'mma be famous for a new line of spacecraft. Just watch, but it's so many haters in this world though, Tiri. People gon' hate, they won't understand your plan, and even if the job doesn't get you stupid rich, get paid to do what you love, then capitalize that shit and grow to where you *are* seeing six-figures if that's what you really want. You'll be miserable tryna live out someone else's dreams and not your own, and I'm glad my mother helped my daddy realize that before they sent me out here...did that answer your question?"

Tiri ran her fingers through her hair.

"It did."

"So what's wrong then? Speak up, baby. I'm listening. Are you second-guessing your major?"

"I'm second-guessing this whole college experience. Before my momma was killed, she'd always walk around bragging how her daughter was going to surpass her RN status and be the doctor that the Stallion family needed." Tiri managed to smile. "Girl, she'd be so damn excited. Every day she had me learning and catching onto the complexities of vocabulary and the background information in the medical field. Bitch, she was teaching me about meds and pharmacology when I was fourteen. I used to dream about that white coat because I knew she'd be honored. So, when the accident happened...I promised God that I'd get that degree to make my parents proud of me in their absence. It wasn't until like two-three hours ago that I realized...hell, I'mma keep it real. I honestly don't know what I wanna be or do. I'm just now finding myself and loving the skin I'm in."

Tiri didn't talk about her parents often, so when she did, Caesar knew off top that it all was from the heart.

"Ri-Ri, listen to me." They looked one another in the eye. "Your parents will be proud of you even in you decided to sell cardboard boxes for a living. It's not about the money. It's not about trying to be the best or having that white coat just to say you got it. Your mother may have wanted that for you, but you've gotta focus on *your* needs and wants. Don't hold the burden of your parents' death on your heart like that. I guarantee you that they would rather witness your happiness than you battling this indecisiveness and not enjoying yourself. Don't waste your time nor money trying to keep a dream alive that's not your own."

Tiri fought back tears while fanning herself. She was grateful that she had someone in her corner who not only listened but understood her troubles.

"Thanks, Ceas. When I say...I really needed that? I'm sorry for crying, but it's just been a struggle for so long, and I'm tired of tryna fill that void with false hope and happiness. I'm too young to be stressing like this."

"Amen, girl, and be glad that you had the heart to address and recognize this *now*. My mother is fifty, and she's just now living out her dreams to sing at hotels. No, the gigs don't pay on the level of gwap that my daddy makes, but Jazz Shields be out on that stage shutting shit down in her cute little outfits and best believe that Woo is front row at her every performance cheering his wife on. I honestly think had I not voiced my beliefs about going to school for what I wanted to do, that she never would've stood up to my father about her own dreams. So, I'm proud of you, friend, for staying true to yourself and realizing that there's more to Tiri than what the eye sees."

"OMG, Ceas, you know I'm a big ass baby," Tiri whined as she wiped away her tears.

"Girl, get those tears out, then you look yourself in the mirror and remind yourself that it's going to be okay, and you step on these bitch's necks with whatever you decide that your game plan will be. It's not a sprint, baby."

"It's a marathon. Words from one of the greatest...God what a relief that was. Thank you so much, best friend."

"You're welcome."

Caesar got her girl caught up on the latest campus gossip while Tiri cleaned the kitchen. By the time she was wiping the counters down and Ceas ended their call to get in a little more studying before she arrived at the dorms, Steelo was walking through the door wearing his signature three-piece Tom Ford suit after chopping things up with Marius. It's been a month since Mr. O'Sullivan was murdered and they'd yet to hear a response from the Irish Mob. While work continued and they remained focused on their monthly successions, Marius and Steelo were also prepared and ready for a war to erupt.

But *when*...when?

"Hey, babe."

"Wassup, mama." Tiri stood on her tippy toes and kissed Steelo's lips. "Smell good up in here. What you throw down on this time?"

"Some marijuana-infused soul food."

"Set that shit out."

Twenty minutes later, Steelo was exiting the shower. His silky, curly hair hung over the front of his face while he exfoliated his beard, brows, and facial skin with the homemade coconut oil and shea butter sugar rub that Tiri had him hooked on. It left his face clear, glowing, and healthier than the Olay he used prior to her arrival. With a towel around his waist and the beads of water still cascaded down his rippling chest and V-shaped back, he exited the bathroom just as Tiri entered the room with his hot plate, a new bottle of Virginia Whiskey, a glass of ice, utensils, and napkins handy. Her mother worshipped the ground her father used to walk on, so caring for a man came like second nature to her.

The first week they spent together, Steelo was convinced that Tiri was busting ass to prove herself...until he realized that's just the way she was raised, and it honestly touched his heart. Because proving herself wasn't necessary at this point. She was already his heart. She didn't have to audition for him on a daily to secure her spot in his life. He knew what blessings the Lord had given him on a single strand of mercy, knowing he didn't deserve this honest and lawful of a woman. Steelo knew he was a bad seed. He knew that him and Tiri crossed paths on a dangerous road, but not once had she judged him. Not once had she attempted to change, demean, or shame him for being a broken man. And for that, he'd always cherish and try his best to treat her like the diamond she was.

She continued to express her femininity and loved on him, even when the adoration became too much for a man who grew up in the streets. A man who'd always had to *prove himself* and show these niggas that the complexion of his skin didn't make him any less of a Black man *who too* was played by the system and a result of the broken Black home.

Tiri offered him unconditional support, love, and affection without him having to bleed for that shit. Not that he wasn't a man who wasn't built to bleed for the goals and aspirations that he'd made for himself, or for her heart, but love shouldn't have to require so many challenges before you could possess and enjoy it.

Steelo grew up with no mother. A mother wasn't around to hug him. To hold him. To nurture him. He retained faint memories of a father whose name he couldn't recollect no matter how hard he tried. He was the only kid at school who didn't have a mother to dance with at those annual parental events like all of the other children did.

He didn't have a grandmother who took him in and restored his faith in hopes that he'd become the man that he was today. His foster parents hated him; since the moment he arrived at the age of five, and that affliction had followed him after all of these years into his adult life. He busted knuckles every day to show people that he wasn't the one to be fucked with. Steelo harbored anger. He harbored pain.

Hate. Vengeance. Animosity.

So when he became a hitta, the title eluded him of that excretion. He hated to admit that his assassinations temporarily patched up wounds that he hadn't allowed to heal just yet. There was no doubt that Steelo retained an excellent degree of self-control. He didn't kill people for the hell of it like a sociopath. He simply did a job that most people couldn't handle and found a sense of peace in that. It was absurd. Sick even, but after leading a life filled with nothing but resentment, what else could he become if that's all he'd ever known?

It was a gamble trying to love a man like Steelo, but Tiri saw past his façade. And there was so much beauty in him being a witness to such a studious woman. She came with a peace offering that he was willing to make as long as he could have her in exchange for shedding some of his toxic walls. It frightened him to a degree, letting Tiri inside. Her heart was fragile, and he was every known opposite that could lead to her destruction; making him too flawed to properly handle her with care.

She knew love and happiness.

He was a product of survival.

In one light, they didn't mix, but her aura held a hypnotizing allure that made Steelo want to bask in his emotions. If it spoke her language, then that was a move he was willing to make. Better to shoot in the dark than to not take a chance at all. She was certainly worth the sacrifice if he could just get his head out of his ass and unreservedly allow her to hold his heart.

"Damn, girl." Steelo took another bite of his food before saying, "You put yo' foot in this shit. Them flavors blended just right too. You know what you doing with that edible shit."

Tiri laughed as she carefully rolled them up a Backwoods. Their faded game was about to be on point. She wanted some of that dick print that was sitting nice in his bath towel. Like, now!

"It did turn out good, didn't it?"

"Yeah, you did that, mama. How was your day?"

Tiri admired the way he looked seated in the chaise lounge chair enjoying his meal: one leg up on the furniture, one foot planted on the floor, and his plate in hand with his drink nearby. Even with the simplest tasks, Steelo held class. And his swagger was so infectious that you marveled at his feet in fascination.

Damn, she *loved* this man.

"It was okay. How was yours?"

"What's on yo' mind?"

It was above her how in tune they were with one another. Tiri felt like she was in too deep, yet past the point of no return to recede.

My, the exhilaration that comes with loving a thug...

"Just been having a lot on my mind."

"About?"

She put the blunt down then looked him in the eye.

"Did you make up your mind about coming with me to St. Louis for the holiday?"

"My mind was already made up the first time you asked me, Tiri. And the answer is still NO; I'm not going."

Come this Thanksgiving holiday, it would be three months that they'd been an item. Tiri knew it would be premature to invite Steelo to meet her family, but she felt like it was needed. Messiah was all she had blood wise in this world with her immediate family, and she didn't want him to worry. She wanted him to know that she was safe and that the man she'd chosen was worthy. He'd been so overprotective since Trudy's death that it surprised her when he didn't put up a fight about her going off to Trinity versus attending a local college.

His grip was so tight; suffocating and draining that Tiri had to get away. It wasn't a matter of her being immature or clingy to her brother. It was a matter of respect, assurance, and compromise. Tiri grew up a lot faster than even she anticipated on doing so, but Messiah had to respect and accept that. She too suffered from malnutrition of love that her sibling couldn't offer. He'd found that angel in Riley, and she'd discovered the same in the depths of Steelo.

It was bad enough that she'd been ignoring her brother's calls. Not necessarily ignoring them but failing to reach out to him in return. Tiri had a new life now. It's not that she wouldn't miss or forget about home, but her priorities have shifted. Was it wrong of her to grow into her womanhood while also remaining family orientated? Tiri wanted to retain her brother's love and blessings just as much as she wanted the two most important men in her life to be on the same page.

One dinner could settle her brother's anxiety and simultaneously show Steelo that family meant everything to her. She knew that family was a sensitive subject, yet foreign aspect to him, but she wouldn't let go of her beliefs to enable him. Steelo was a grown ass man, and he had to accept her, flaws and all, just as she did him. That was imperative.

"No is not a complete answer, Steelo. Why not?"

"No means no, so there is no explanation. Why keep questioning me about it?"

"Look, I know how fragile family is for you, Steelo. I'm not ignoring or saying fuck that at all. You have to understand that there are people out there who will shut the city of Trinity down on my behalf. They'll go to any extent for my safety, so I want to ensure them that I'm safe with the man I have. It's a respect thing, baby. I value the relationship that I have with my brother, and I don't want to lose that. So it would mean everything to me if you came to Thanksgiving dinner with us this year."

"No."

Tiri felt like her face had hit the floor. Her entire spiel clearly went into one ear and out the other, and Steelo didn't give a damn at all.

"Can you take me back to the dorm, please? I've got a busy schedule this week."

She hopped up off the bed and started gathering her belongings. This little getaway was officially over, and she had midterms to focus on. Not this asshole.

"I got you. Let me finish my food and we can bounce."

Tiri screamed.

He was so nonchalant and insolent; it was starting to drive her crazy.

She waited fifteen minutes down in the foyer with her Chanel duffle bags at her side until Steelo came down, dressed and ready with his gun in hand. He politely grabbed her bags as she rudely exited the front door without holding it open for him. Steelo started to say something to her little contemptuous ass, but instead, he decided to hit her where it hurts with silence and tossed her shit in the trunk of the Bugatti before climbing inside and pulling off.

The ride back to her dorm was quiet. Nothing but the sound of the engine roaring sat between them as Tiri gazed out of the window admiring the beautiful scenery until she grew tired of holding her eyes open. She just wanted to get away from him and the pessimistic energy that he was reluctantly harboring.

From time to time, Steelo would look over his shoulder and glance at her sitting there with her eyes closed. He *wanted* to thoroughly explain himself, but he couldn't. There were still shrouds of his past that Steelo wasn't ready to face. He cared for Tiri, honestly, but he didn't retain the strength to be too vulnerable with her just yet for the sake of saving himself.

End of discussion.

"Tiri."

But what he would do was smooth things over with her before she left. Steelo radically went against the grain and decided to be the one to give in first. Even in silence, his little chocolate drop could put up one hell of a fight better than he did, and he didn't want her to be upset with him.

"Yes, *Steelo*."

Her irritation caused him to chuckle.

"You a brat, mama. I swear."

She bit her bottom to keep from smiling or reacting to him rubbing on her thigh, and faster than she realized it, Tiri turned in her seat to look at him. Maybe if she laid it on him real nice and easy this time around with wide, sad eyes, then he'd change his mind. Tiri couldn't believe she was practically begging this man to be mature about all of this, but the last thing she needed was Messiah losing his got damn marbles, so here goes nothing.

"Steelo, I—"

KSHH!!!

171

The sound of the back window shattering caused Tiri to scream and duck when bullets started rippling in the air. Steelo floored the gas and took off like a bat out of hell. Three Lamborghinis were letting off shells at them from what he could see in his rearview mirror. And for it to be a Sunday, traffic throughout town was surely heavy. He switched in and out of lanes, dodging cars and bullets, cutting corners, and manipulated his wheel wildly like he was drifting to keep these niggas off his ass.

"STATIC ON OCEANVIEW! GOING NORTH!" he shouted into his Apple Watch as he turned the car so sharp, they were only riding on two tires.

Tiri looked on in terror, dying a little inside each time it seemed as if they were about to crash before he maneuvered the car just at the last minute.

"Reach in the back compartment for me, Tiri! FUCK!"

More bullets sprayed up the driver's side of his car as he bucked right and merged into the wrong side of traffic. Tiri was frazzled. She hadn't realized what her hands were doing until she pulled the chamber back after loading the clip on the AK-47 in seconds. Steelo was staggered.

"Put that shit to work, ma! Don't hold out on me now!"

Her adrenaline was pumping so quickly, she didn't hesitate to let the window down. Her body jerked each time she pulled the trigger, but when the tires burst on the Lambo that was the closest in range, she smiled inside and kept shooting not giving a fuck about who or what got in her way.

When Steelo noticed the chopper above him through the sunroof, painted in white stripes to signal that his team was present, relief took his anger down a notch. The Lambo's started swerving from the bullets spewing above them while Steelo tried thinking of a plan. When it finally clicked in his head, he grabbed the steering wheel with both hands and looked over at Tiri who was reloading her clip.

"YOU TRUST ME?"

Tiri didn't hesitate when she nodded her head up and down. But before she knew it, her body instantly flew against the passenger's door when Steelo turned the wheel completely to the right once again. The car flew over the ramp and spun in midair until they hit the pavement and he entered the Trinity Tunnel on the lower level of the street. Switching gears, Steelo took off with the two vehicles still behind him.

"Take yo' seatbelt off, Tiri!"

"Nigga, are you nuts?!"

"DO IT!"

He grabbed the gun from her hands after doing what he'd instructed her to do as well. Tiri's eyes widened, now realizing why he told her to remove her seatbelt. They were heading straight for the Trinity River.

"MEET US ON 15TH AND TANNER! WE GON' BE ON FOOT!" Steelo yelled into his watch as the car slowed down. "TIRI, JUMP!"

Everything shifted to slow motion when she swung the door open and tucked her head while jumping out of the flying car. Her body rolled for what seemed like ages until she finally hit a trashcan that caused her to stop moving.

Seconds later, Steelo's car rolled over the curb and rushed along the cobblestone dock until it plummeted into the water. The drivers behind him fell to the same destruction being too slow to exit their vehicles once they realized their targets had jumped from the vehicle.

Tiri's body ached with pain as she groaned out loud from the impact. Sirens were obnoxiously ringing in the air around her, and her eyes were blurred until she recognized Steelo's image standing over her. With blood trickling down the side of his face, he quickly pulled her up to her feet, and they took off. When her vision fully cleared, Tiri picked up the pace and caught up to him. They were dodging the patrons in the street running and screaming, not to mention the bullets whizzing behind them.

She had no clue where they were going, but she refused to stop running. Steelo was hopping over cars, letting off his Eagles, climbing trashcans, and escape ladders, and she followed suit. A good four men were on foot behind them, and they were still three blocks away from their destination.

"NOOOO! STEELOOOO!"

Someone grabbed Tiri by the foot when she tried her best to climb the next dumpster and onto the escape route where he planned on taking the rooftops the rest of their way to safety. Steelo swiftly slid down the ladder with one hand along the rail while airing out his clip with the other, killing two men on impact. A masked shooter held his hand around Tiri's mouth as he tried to backpedal out of the alley with a barrel up to her head. That shit transformed him into an animal. Steelo removed the shiv from his combat boot and tossed it with precision. It bypassed Tiri's face and hit his target in the eye, causing him to let her go and collapse on the ground.

Tiri's eyes grew wide when she saw the last man running up on Steelo from behind. She was quick when she reached for the gun on the ground and fired shots until his body hit the pavement, stammering her man once again from her actions.

Steelo made a mental note of the Irish features on one of the shooter's faces after he removed the mask, then grabbed Tiri by the hand and they climbed the ladder once again.

"WHAT'S YO' ETA?!" Steelo heard coming from his watch.

To his surprise, it was Marius.

"Coming around the corner now!"

The backdoors on the Mercedes Sprinter swung open just in time for Steelo to grab Tiri by the waist and help her into the truck before hopping inside himself and they all got the hell out of dodge. The Irish Mob had finally responded, and it was clear that they wanted blood.

𝕳𝖀𝕱𝕽

Kovu was filled with anxiety as the limousine casually cruised throughout the streets of Trinity on the way to her destination. The palms of her hands were sweating so excessively that she had to reach inside of the kids' diaper bag to clean them with a baby wipe, then air them out as she bit her bottom lip in angst. Her stomach was twisting and turning in knots like a doughy Aunt Annie's pretzel that was being prepared for the oven. She wished the kids were awake driving her crazy. Her little bouncy man Jayce jumping all around the place, and her having to yell at Aubrey's little mean self for being too rough with her baby brother as always.

Kovu was sold on the fact that she was going through a stage of her light-skinned syndrome; a trait she'd surely gotten from her viscous and vulgar ass father because her and Jayce were as cool as a fan on most days. The thought made her smile as she glanced over at her children strapped into their car seats while the motions of the vehicle kept them drifting away in their dreams. She loved her babies. Life with Marius Lionel Usher got better with each day that passed her by, and she couldn't have asked God for anything more but that strength once they finally made it to 8676 Fountain Drive Terrace.

Kovu could feel the air becoming thinner as she unbuckled the kids' seatbelts, knowing that this moment was now or never. By the time she stepped out with Jayce's car seat on her forearm, leaving the baby girl for last, the driver helped her with everything else as he then followed her up the steps and to the front door. KD hesitated, but soon swallowed the lump in her throat as she knocked hard on the locked screen until it finally opened.

She now stood eye to eye with Tammy.

Tears rushed to the surface of both of their eyes. Tammy's heart fluttering from the sight of the grandchildren she'd never met, had the chance to hold, nor had a single picture of to know what they looked like. Surprisingly, her daughter was emotional behind this moment as well. Kovu's been yearning for the love and acceptance of her mother for years now, and she couldn't take their separation a day longer.

The car seat digging into her forearm hurt like hell but the beauty of Tammy wrapping her arms around her neck and holding her close cast away any pain that could've possibly stricken her. Yes, a man's touch was magical, but that love from home? Shit, that love from the woman who brought you into this lifetime just hit different, and Kovu felt like the weight of the world had been lifted from off of her shoulders.

"Oh, Kovu...I'm so sorry..."

We all knew how much of a savage Mrs. Usher was. She'd buss' a clip and kill a bitch in the blink of an eye now; nor did she weep easily, but how could she hold her tears back and refrain from them falling when this is all she'd ever wanted?

"Y'all come on in here and get out of this heat," her mother managed to get out through sniffles.

Kovu handed Tammy over Jayce's car seat as she grabbed Aubrey and their diaper bag from the driver.

"Thank you, Lonzo. I'll give you a call when we're finished here."

"No problem, Mrs. Usher. Enjoy."

Kovu closed the door behind herself and smiled at the sight of her mother holding her grandson. They favored from their toffee colored, rich skin and those big bright eyes. The three of them did.

"How old are they?"

"Jayce will be one in February on the ninth, and Aubrey will be two on June first."

"Dang, you had them back to back! Look at you! They are so beautiful! Aubrey looks just like her father."

Kovu smiled as she rocked her daughter back and forth.

"I know. It's been a crazy...going on three years now...how have you been?"

"Miserable."

Tammy was done putting on a façade. She meant her response with every bone in her body and it instantly made her tears fall once again.

"I've been a—HORRIBLE mother to you, Kovu, and I know that saying I'm sorry can never atone for the shit I've done. It's not that I never loved you nor cared for you, Kovu, I swear I have always loved you. You're my oldest daughter; I'd never just blatantly reject you. There were pains of my past that I never healed from and it was wrong of me to take that out on you. Amber fueled my ways because she'd become the spitting image of me. It's just...the fact that you never took my shit hit me so hard, baby, that it...it made me convince myself that you were the enemy."

"Daddy told me about Auntie Carla."

It was all she could say to try to ignore the bullshit that just left her mother's mouth. Now frustrated, Kovu sat down across from Tammy on the loveseat with Aubrey still in her arms.

"Him killing Carla was an excuse that I used for years. It's all bullshit too...Yes, you did remind me of my sister before all of the drugs made her a slave to euphoric highs, but when I'm the one who's been the problem, there's no point in venturing back to her death. You were always so strong, Kovu, no matter what you faced. You were determined, fearless, and you kept your head up when me as your own mother didn't even have the courage to do so. I was jealous of you and so was your sister. Your sister was obsessed with you, and my dumb ass just turned the other cheek like nothing happened. I'm sorry for putting you out, for the fight with Eric and—"

"Momma." Tammy looked Kovu in the eye after she called her name. "I know and remember all that's happened. It keeps me up on most nights, and I'm tired of venturing back to those toxic ways that I no longer want to taint our future. But just like you...it troubles me still too. Marius and I are getting remarried this upcoming Valentine's Day."

Her mother smiled.

"Congratulations. I thought I heard the driver call you Mrs. Usher, not to mention that big ass saucer on your finger."

"Yeah," Kovu laughed. "Everything he does is over the top. I mentioned that though because...he asked me if I were inviting you to the wedding and when I couldn't give him a clear answer, it did something to me. I've forgiven you for all that's happened, and I want us to have a good relationship, but sometimes, ma, I..." Kovu wiped her face. "Sometimes I still resent you." Gently, she laid Aubrey on the seat where she was previously sitting, covered her with a blanket, then and walked over to the fireplace to gather herself before continuing. "Momma, I know you're sorry, but you ripped me from one end to another for twenty-four almost twenty-five years and that did something to me that I can't keep ignoring."

"Kovu—"

"Ma, you chastised me. You mentally abused me."

"Kovu—"

"And at one point, you fucking destroyed me! For years I couldn't love myself! For years I tried to please both you and Amber, yet y'all hated me!"

"Kovu, I never hated you!" Tammy shouted in return, causing Jayce to stir in his sleep. "I've been mentally sick from the PTSD of my own childhood, Kovu! From never healing from the toxicity and abuse that my own mother bestowed upon me!"

"And you don't think I didn't suffer from the same thing either?! That justified not loving and supporting me?! For dogging me! For never having my back through *anything*! Momma, I came over here to settle things with you, but it's obvious that I haven't healed either! It takes daily strength to walk tall, to love my kids, to love my husband considering the love I never had from you! That shit is hard! The fact that I know my family

177

deserves love, so they don't end up damaged like I did fucking keeps me sane!

That and God's grace! Because I can be just like you and treat everyone the way I've been treated forever to save myself the selfish way, but I don't wanna be like that! But, at the same time, I also have to be honest, get this shit out and let this pain go before it kills me! If it wasn't for God's grace to send my husband and the help of them picking me up off the floor from where you left me then I don't know where the hell I'd be! Look at all of the damage I'm still allowing you to cause in my life! It's fucking sick!"

"KOVU, I'M SORRY!"

Tammy walked over to her daughter and wrapped her arms around her shoulders. She ran her hand down the back of her daughter's hair and repeatedly told her that she loved her. She repeatedly let the words *I'm sorry* roll off of her tongue with tears trickling down her face. Tammy would hurt for eternity knowing that she damn near poisoned her daughter the same way her own mother destroyed her and Carla. No, Tammy didn't resort to crack cocaine like her sister did, but a vile and demonic spirit conquered her soul, and Kovu was the one who suffered from the aftermath.

"Kovu, look at me. Baby, please look at me."

She didn't want to, but KD peeled her eyelids apart and let her pupils settle on her mother's.

"I am so, so sorry, baby and I can't stress that enough. I love you. I just wanna make things right too. I no longer want you to harvest this pain and hate in your heart from my wrongdoings. I'm willing to do whatever it takes. *Whatever*. Whether it's counseling or—"

KSHH!

Pow! Pow! Pow!

Blood splattered amongst Kovu's face when three bullets unexpectedly entered her mother's skull. The bullets continued to blast through the living room at the speed of light, causing her to jump down to the ground and reach for her children. She quickly grabbed Aubrey and sat her on her hip. Tammy had put Jayce back in his car seat before she got up to tend to her daughter so KD grabbed hold of it and crawled along the floor as best as she could until she made it to the stairs and ran to the upper level until she reached her old bedroom.

Her babies crying tore her to shreds as she hid them in the closet. The gunshots were getting clearer, closer, and her eyes glazed with vengeance knowing her children were in danger. She quickly pulled the broken floorboard up and pulled out two dirty .9mm handguns that Collins gave her to hold over three years ago and loaded the clips. A rush filled her blood pumping veins when she closed the closet door behind her and immediately started busting her clips. Both guns relentlessly fired at the armed men running past the door to check out the entire vicinity in search for her until she was spotted, forcing Kovu to duck for cover.

Fuck, I've gotta get out of here so the kids won't get hurt!

A bell rung in her head when she remembered that the guest room was joined by the door across from her bed. The constant thought of her babies forced Kovu to hop up and return shots in the direction of the bedroom door. She took down two more bodies, but another shooter entered the room, forcing her to throw one of the empty guns in her hand, hitting him square in the face. His temporary moment of distraction gave her the advantage to thrust her body weight into his and they went crashing through the holey door that led to the next room.

He knocked Kovu square on her ass with a punch to her nose to get her off of him, causing blood to stain her shirt. Her foot then made one with his face when he tried to climb on top of her and proceed to punch her again. They scrambled around the room, swinging blows, one putting the other into a chokehold until the other managed to get free. He now had his arm wrapped around Kovu's throat with a death grip trying to snap her neck. Her vision was getting blurry as she struggled to reach for the gun that was only meters away.

The children were still crying at the top of their lungs. Still hollering and in harm's way as long as this man lived, and she couldn't have that. Kovu threw her head back as hard as she could and busted his mouth open. The moment he released her, she jumped for the gun and lodged a bullet between his eyes. Her windpipe suffered from the trauma of his arm being around her neck, making it hard for her to breathe while she struggled to stand on her feet. Tears rushed down her face as she swung the closet door open and laid eyes on her unharmed children. She immediately dropped down to her knees and thanked God before scooping them up and rushing out of there.

"Mar-Mar—" she coughed harshly before trying to speak into her Apple watch, but her voice was raspy. "MAR-RI-UUUUUUS!"

The pain shooting from her throat caused her knees to buckle as she headed for the backdoor.

Please let the keys be in the car!

Tammy was good for leaving the key in the ignition since she had a personal garage attached to her back porch. Kovu swung the front door to the Nissan Maxima open and was grateful when she saw them dangling by the steering wheel. She got the kids into the backseat and buckled Aubrey down as best as she could until gunshots started ringing once again. She hid behind the door for a few seconds until she took the risk and climbed into the driver's seat. The wooden door shook uncontrollably from the gunshots while the garage door opened at the speed of molasses.

With seconds to spare, Kovu laid her foot heavy on the gas and backed out before taking off at full speed, finally dodging the rest of the bullets after getting so far up the road. It felt like she drove on for miles before her husband finally answered her calls. Not only was she suffering from an injured throat, but she'd witnessed the murder of her mother before her own eyes *and* almost didn't make it out alive with her kids. She was *pissed* and fucking fed up with her husband's reckless ass life. This shit had to come to an end.

Taug Jaye

"It's okay to love me."

-Tiri

Chapter
10

arius Usher who? The Monstrosity was in full effect at the moment, and there was nothing that a soul around him could do to intercept the rage in control of his actions. Sweat dripped down his steel cut arms, chest, and back as he took a quick break from beating this bitch ass nigga's face to a pulp. His hands were wrapped in a layer of black sparring gauze, and blood was splattered all over his Hermes slacks and complimentary loafers. The Irish Mob member they'd taken captive was screaming at the top of his lungs from The Monstrosity snipping off all ten of his toes prior to his beating. Three of his ribs at the very least were broken, and blood stained his face in forms of trickles and thick, globby blood clots. Marius didn't give a fuck if he wasn't the nigga who'd directly harmed his wife. That shit was unacceptable, and their retaliation wouldn't be taken lightly.

"Cut the fucking music up!" Marius roared after throwing his drink back. He then bobbed his head to the upbeat tempo when Kendrick Lamar's verse on "Mona Lisa" crooned in the air, forcing his heart rate to pump even faster. "Tie his ass down!"

Steelo tightened the chains around this nigga's neck and dragged his body from the wall he was once tied up on, to a wooden chair. Securing his arms behind his back and his ankles to the legs of his seat, Marius soon walked over with a five-gallon tub of water in hand. When Steelo secured a towel around their victim's face and reclined his chair, Marius drowned him with more water than he should have done at once, but his gargling and screams made excellent additives to the music in the background. His body flopped and twitched like a suffocating fish out of water until The Monstrosity finally let up to enjoy his favorite part of the track.

"Ooh, fake smile! Mona Lisa! Mona Lisa! She said, 'Ooh, that emotion!' Mona Lisa! Lisa!"

"Yeah, he get the picture! Mona Lisa! Mona Lisa!"

Marius slapped hands with Steelo when he joined in on the next line to the verse, getting a kick out of this shit right along with his psychotic ass twin brother. The world knew not to piss these two maniacs off, but unfortunately, they were coerced into this behavior. They owned this city. This was their territory. Marius officially staked his claim well over seven years ago, yet niggas wouldn't let him be. Here he was trying to bow down, secure the last of his money, and plan a graceful exit, but you hand out a few turkeys, donate some damn school supplies, and turn into a family man, then niggas assumed they could step in and try him. Marius left bullet holes in niggas' bodies on a good day, played mortician with their corpses to clean his slate, and when he needed to send a message, he delivered those same remains to their loved one's bow tie like a bouquet of red roses before the fireworks exploded.

All he wanted was peace.

Marius would contemplate later over the fact how the city of Trinity was nothing but a trigger to his unbalanced personalities, knowing he'd always feel some type of way about these ruthless streets that scarred him and killed his mother.

But more important shit was on the line right now.

His wife's windpipe was crushed. Someone shot and murdered her mother only meters away with ammunition that would've slaughtered her as well had they been hollow bullets. His kids were in that fucking house! All he could do was watch the security footage he'd installed within her mother's crib years ago in case Tammy ever tried him with the enemy or the law, and it fueled his fury.

What? He had to take all precautions.

The images of KD fighting for her and their kids' lives did nothing but piss him off all over again, forcing him to put the water down and steal this nigga so hard in the jaw, everyone present heard the bone shatter/dislocate since the music was no longer playing.

"Now I'mma ask you one more time, my man. I'm all out of patience," Marius huffed as he wiped his face free of perspiration.

Everyone in the room was so fucking stammered and perplexed that they couldn't help but to watch their boss do his thing. It's been a while since Marius had to get his own hands dirty, but every now and then, even his own team needed a fucking reminder that dishonor was never an option. They'd hate to be the one in the hot seat, and their terrified orbs watching on in fear made that shit obvious.

"You fucked my nigga," Marius continued while taking another drink. "Trust me on this one. Even once they find out that it was you who snitched, you'll be dead before they can even retaliate." He shrugged his shoulders in nonchalance yet got nothing but crickets from out of this nigga.

"Damn, loyal niggas still exist." Steelo shook his head while sizing the halfway conscious man up with a machete at his neck.

Low mumbles began to emerge from the Irish member's lips, causing Marius to hold his hand up to his right ear and bend down at his mouth.

"What's that?!" He was taking too long to respond, eternally aspirating on his own blood due to the hemorrhaging in his stomach. So The Monstrosity uppercut his ass, lodging his bottom row of teeth into his top lip. "Fuck," he uttered. In one swift motion, he pulled his jaw down, knowing this nigga was suffering from excruciating pain with the way his mandible dangled.

The next few mumbles that attempted to form into words only came out as trembling, so after his signal, Steelo removed the nigga's head in one swing for the care package as Marius called this little meeting adjourned.

"Send more teams out. Double up on the doubled security we already had. This ain't the last we heard of these niggas and I'm tryna be ready for whatever. I need a location on Geni a-muthafucking-sap. Should've took that nigga out the day of the picnic with his pappy. That was my fuck up...Pull Tiri and Woo Shield's daughter from out of Trinity University too until we got this shit taken care of. I don't even want emails sent between them and that fucking campus. And anything other than her books on Amazon, get my fucking wife and connections to her family removed from the got-damn internet!

NOW! Nobody runs outside of the county's perimeter unless it's through me, and I need to know all traffic coming in here. Get my men on the polls in less than an hour. Get Mr. Cartwright on the line and give me all you can find out about the O'Sullivan's and legislation from the past six months. I need release records on Geni and anyone else in close relations from ADX. These niggas wanna fuck with me, we gon' serve it to 'em hot and ready. Did Válo make it back in town yet?"

Marius looked Steelo in the eye after barking orders at his tech team who were on a mission to fulfill his front to back, long list of requests.

"He should be here now."

"Handle yo' shit and get in touch with our team in St. Louis. I need eyes on the Platinum Cartel. I don't have time for Tiri's sentimental ass brother. I'm on a killing streak right now, and if them niggas knew what was good for 'em, they'd stay the fuck away from my city. She safe."

Steelo nodded his head in agreement as they went their separate ways.

𝕳𝖀𝕱𝕽

Válo Santiago had an imperative and articulate job description underneath Marius and Steelo: he was the man who kept their weapons, machinery, blades, and war ammo restocked in bi-weekly rotation. Válo traveled frequently to St. Louis, the city of Chamberlain, and even to New York City when he couldn't reach his connect, Tattoo, directly, to meet up, do the exchange, and smuggle it across country.

Steelo met Válo through their foster home when he was fifteen, a year before he started running the streets as a hitman. Válo was two years younger than him, so he was thirteen at the time, but he'd always been solid when they were trying to survive in that roach and mice-infested community. When Marius recruited Steelo, and he started working his way up the chain of command, he reached out to his dawg and helped Válo get on to some real paper so he could elevate and live a better life.

Back in 2016 when Quan, Dino, and the rest of their old crew turned on Marius, Steelo honestly felt some type of way thinking his potna was on some backdoor bullshit too. It turns out Dino had set Válo up.

Amber went to the police about a man smuggling illegal firearms into the city with a connection to The Monstrosity, to increase her claim at the reward money offered for his arrest, and Válo was busted the minute he came back in town. 5-0 were waiting on his ass at the polls.

Things were hectic when Marius was detained, but after KD did her Bonnie & Clyde shit, their operation was back on schedule and running smoothly as if the setback had never taken place. Every month Marius had Steelo run checks on convicts who were due to release from nearby jails and prisons to use as pawns, so when he came across Válo's profile, he took a plane out to Colorado and got him out of ADX Prison with no issues; that's is, after paying a personal visit to the judge who sentenced him. With the right amount of money and a dose of brutal force implemented upon a few other legal parties, Válo's charges were dropped, his background was cleared, and his boy was back rocking with them solid, forever indebted to their gratitude.

They treated Válo vile in prison. Trinity PD flew out there themselves and kicked his ass for hours on in. They tried to get Válo to fold on The Monstrosity and coerce him into being their lead to take Marius down after their unsuccessful attempt at a trial. Busted mouth, swollen black eyes, and all, them white crackers didn't get a peep out of him. Válo knew his chances of being released were slim to none, due to the charges they filed underneath his belt, but running his mouth like a lil' hoe and disrespecting the same people who fed him was out of the fucking question. He didn't rock like that. Therefore, he kept his faith up, never stopped praying, took those beatings to solidify his own code of ethics, and he'll be damned; a month later he was being released and thanking the Most High for His grace.

Since then, the trio had been moving like a plague throughout the city of Trinity, slowly migrating to Chamberlain, and even had their hands around a few business owner's necks in Vegas to expand their territory. Money would always be the main motive, and Válo wasn't just eating good with his niggas; he was feasting with enough leftovers that could last him beyond a lifetime. Marius ran his organization with such finesse and dexterity that he soaked that shit up like a sponge and helped them tie up the loose ends that fit his field of knowledge. You couldn't name a better trio in this crime family shit even if you tried to.

Válo was unloading his last crate from their trucks when Steelo entered the room. The corridor was filled from wall-to-wall and to the ceiling with new merchandise.

Giving his potna the once over as they slapped hands, Steelo now understood the element behind Marius appointing him to be Kovu's personal bodyguard two years ago. She was wanted being on his arm as Tiri was now, and he needed someone that he could trust to watch after her in his absence. Válo wasn't only good with army guns, but next to himself and Marius, he was the next best assassin on their team. His loyalty was undeniable, and there was no one other than him fit for the role.

"Wassup wit' it, bro?" Válo questioned while pulling the chamber back on his strap.

"Gotta new assignment for you. East gon' take yo' spot with smuggling. I need you on 24/7 watch for Tiri."

"Say no more."

Válo reminded Steelo a lot of himself. He was flexible and always ready for whatever. Válo knew that he wouldn't have been reassigned if it wasn't crucial, and hearing that his dawg needed him to guard his girl, had said enough all in itself.

"She can have a lil' smart ass mouth too, so beware."

Válo chuckled.

"Women, dawg."

"Swear to God, bro. She down in the green room."

"I'm right behind you."

𝔥𝔘𝔍ℜ

Down the hall, Tiri sat along the black valor couch cradled into a fetal position. Her heart rate had finally settled down well over two hours later after their surprise high-speed chase. It took a lot out of her to obtain such a mass level of strength to remain solid and not fold, aware that those very actions would do nothing but cause her man to stress even worse than what he was already doing. Everyone on this earth usually knows what they're getting into the moment they approach that fork in the road, but one doesn't *know, know* until that first major occurrence takes place and you're left calling out in Jesus' name to protect you from those demons that will stop at nothing to suck you in without the proper mentality while on this journey.

And that was Tiri's poor little heart in a nutshell.

She unraveled her legs when the door to the conference room she was sitting in opened and in walked Steelo and company. Confused as to what was taking place, Tiri stood to her feet and ran her fingers through her hair before crossing her arms over her chest.

"Tiri, this is Válo. Válo, Tiri. Anywhere you go, he goes, so don't try to pull no funny shit either. With all that's gone down, it's too much of a risk for you to be anywhere alone."

"Steelo, I'm not a child. If I wanted to be on a leash, then I could've stayed in St. Louis for this shit," she snapped.

"It's not about me perceiving you as being a child!" His voice changed pitch with the bass in his tone growing deeper. "Did you forget what the hell just happened a few hours ago or did you think that shit was a dream? I'm a target which makes you a target. Now I said what I said and that's final. He gon' take you to get all yo' shit from off campus and bring you back to the house. I've already gotten in touch wit' ya homegirl's father, so she'll be somewhere safe, too. No more school until this shit is over."

"Steelo, I have midterms this week. I understand what you're saying as far as my safety, but you also have to remember that me and Ceas both have prior engagements *and* that all test have to be taken in person if we're not registered as online students."

Steelo's jaw clenched. A part of him wanted to take control of the situation, shove her ass in the backseat of a car, and keep her locked up in the house. But he inhaled deeply and realized that she did have a lot to lose in the midst of all this shit too. So he turned to Válo.

"Get a team together. Two: one for her and another for Ms. Shields. Neither of them are to be on that campus alone or without a squad for the rest of the week. I need a copy of her schedule emailed to me, so I know what's going on if and when I'm away. Something happens to her, and that's yo' ass, you feel me?"

"I got you."

While Válo went to get transportation and a squad together, Steelo inhaled deeply as he put his gun down. He then grabbed Tiri by her trembling hands and pulled her into his arms. His shorty was present when him and Marius made an example out of their house guest until she was taken away and addressed to wait on him while they got everything else wrapped up. Her quivering reduced at the comfort of being in his arms despite his maniac persona that nearly scared her half to death twenty minutes ago.

For the life of her, she couldn't figure out why this shit still came on as a surprise; like it was something new. Tiri knew the game well enough, and she now understood that it took a certain mentality for a man to hold down his position; and, how that same rank sometimes forced him to do shit that wasn't in his amiable character. It came along with the territory of dating a thug nigga, but for Steelo, she was more than willing to get over her insecurities as far as not accepting her association with a crime family and getting with the damn picture. She *was* getting too grown for her childish antics.

"I'm not tryna take my anger out on you, Tiri, and most importantly, I don't you want you to fear me...I just wouldn't know what to do if something happened to you."

Steelo's tone was soft as he ran his robust hands up and down her back while holding her close. Tiri looked up into his eyes and felt her knees go weak when he kissed her lips.

"I know...I'm sorry for tripping. I know I have to get myself together when it comes to all of this."

"Don't be sorry, shorty. Just listen to me first and try to understand what I'm saying. We can communicate all day long, but if you not comprehending the knowledge that I'm dropping on you, then we'll never be on the same page. Everything I'm doing is to protect you. You see what just happened to KD's ole' lady. We gotta weigh every option that's at our disposal right now and tightening up on our security is the main one...I am proud of you though, shorty. Your silly and dingy ass comes off so fucking clueless sometimes that I don't be knowing what to think, but you handled that shit and held it down.

You got heart, mama, more than you're aware of, and you need to stop second-guessing yourself. From this day forward. Don't let what you've done or hid from in yo' past draw you away from basking in your future, a'ight? We'll talk more later. I've got a couple of other things to handle, so you focus on getting in safe. Válo good peoples. If I didn't trust him, then I wouldn't have appointed him with the responsibility of your life when it's not directly in my hands. Alright?"

Tiri nodded her head up and down with the side of her face buried in his chest. The sound of his heartbeat was soothing.

Therapeutic.

Hypnotic.

Had Tiri not felt safe with him, she would've left Trinity her first day there, truth be told. He had one too many opportunities to slap her face on an obituary and kill her family, knowing the only thing Messiah would want in return for harming her would be blood and bones. It was quite obvious that Steelo couldn't admit to those three little words that held the weight of the world in a single phrase; not just yet, but Tiri knew there was a place in his heart with her name on it. *That* she was one hundred percent sure of.

"Don't think I'm crazy for saying this Steelo," Tiri looked up into his eyes as she gently held him by the sides of the face. She ran her manicured thumbs along his bushy though naturally arched eyes brows, searching for any signs of a red flag before pouring her heart out to him. "It's okay to love me, babe…I promise I won't hurt you."

She kissed his lips and turned away just as Válo appeared in the doorway. He was now ready to escort her out and take her back to their home after all of her business was handled.

𝔥𝔘𝔉𝔕

It was late when Marius made it home last night. 2 A.M. to be exact. Reba Koi was sitting at the breakfast bar sipping on a cup of hot tea with Jayce in her right arm, hungrily feasting on his bottle. His big man was spoiled as shit thanks to him and Kovu. The sight made him smile as he removed his suit jacket. He gently rubbed Jayce's head and kissed his cheek before wrapping an arm around Reba Koi.

"You doing alright, love?"

"Yes, dear. I'm fine. You go on upstairs. I've got 'em."

Translation for, *get your ass upstairs and tend to your wife because she is not a happy camper right now.* Marius nodded his head in agreement after thanking her for all she does for their family then proceeded up to the master bedroom. A dim light illuminated the atmosphere when he entered. The television was on silent with Aubrey's favorite movie, *Shrek* of all things, playing on repeat. His little angel was lying next to her mother with her arms behind her head like she was the one who had the long day, getting a kick out of him.

His eyes changed to his wife. The sound of her fingers thumping amongst the keyboard of her MacBook filled the air in a swift though powerfully subtle melody as her prescription glass rested on the tip of her nose. Donning one of his undershirts, wild curly hair due to the removal of her top knot styled with her natural tresses this time around, and a scowl on her face, he could sense her energy.

After a much-needed shower, Marius entered the room with nothing on but a pair of track shorts. His skin was a few shades darker with a bronze tent from all of the golfing he'd been doing lately, and on most nights, his wife would be jumping his damn bones, letting him ram her pussy from the back while she bent over and touched her toes after his exit from the shower. He was her least favorite person at the moment though.

Thank God the damage to her windpipe wasn't too critical, but there was enough trauma implemented on her trachea to put her in a great amount of pain. The Percocet had her high as hell since they were above the normal dosage a doctor would prescribe, irritating her to the max. Every other word she typed was misspelled, and her deadline to turn in her next book was two days ago.

Kovu was drowning in frustration.

Marius took a sip of her Sauvignon sitting on the nightstand before climbing in bed and laying down next to her. He rolled his favorite pillow up and placed it comfortably underneath his neck while he watched the love of his life do her thing. He knew she wasn't going to acknowledge him, nor did she want to discuss it. So he gripped her thigh with his free hand and told her he loved her, caressing her silky skin with the hope that even such a minor attempt to soothe her uneasiness would turn her anxiety down a notch.

Sleep overpowered him within minutes. Kovu was relieved when his snoring filled the air because the only conversation willing to exit from out of her lips was foul language, and she would've gutted his ass from one end to another.

Before she knew it, dawn was present, and she'd finally hit send to submit her next 120k-plus, manuscript to her editor. Aubrey shifted in her sleep when Kovu picked her up and took her to the pot. She tinkled with her little eyes closed, her head nodding off every so often, which forced KD to smile. For some reason, sleep was the last thing on her mind, so after clearing the bed and tucking Aubrey in next to her father, Kovu went down to the kitchen. Jayce and Reba Koi were long gone and back to sleep by now, so she fixed herself some tea, then stepped out on their wrap porch-deck, being greeted by the beautiful horizon.

Tears stained her precious face without warning, causing Kovu to painfully sob with images of her mother's body collapsing right in front of her, flashing right before her eyes. Mixed with her onset throat pain, KD couldn't keep it together. She'd lost so much at the hands of her husband since day one that it clouded her spirit. All she could think about was planning a funeral and having to answer so many questions for her family back in St. Louis. This wouldn't be nearly as easy as it was with burying Amber.

Kovu's rebuttal was clear.

Things were different when it was just her and Marius living this lifestyle. No, it didn't last long before the kids came into the picture, but Aubrey and Jayce's safety was now their main priority. The tables have turned, and with the way them niggas rolled up on her at Tammy's house, there was no telling what they'd do to get to Marius.

Marius couldn't one hundred percent promise their safety no matter how tall he walked in these streets. He couldn't promise that the Irish Mob or any other cartel wouldn't jump for the opportunity to stake his claim once again after this shit was all said and done.

Kovu knew he placed the blame of the city's peak in violence and brutality on himself since he'd been the one leading the show as an aftermath of his vengeance for decades. He created this shit, so of course he felt some type of way now that he was married and had kids. The bottom line was, Trinity was too dangerous. This city wasn't promising to any of their futures. Marius claimed he wanted to buy out. Marius swore that things would change, and he'd get it all under control, but every time Kovu turned around, it was just one more hit, just one last round, just one last quarterly weigh-in.

The cycle seemed like it would never slow up to present the right time for his departure, and if Marius wouldn't put his foot down then she had to. Kovu had no other choice but to protect her young. If that meant leaving her husband in Trinity and letting him rot at the hands of his own obsession, then that was a plan she needed to put in motion. She refused to lose anyone else she loved to the wrath that hovered over this municipality. Kovu promised to love Marius until death did them part, but when it came down to choosing between her children or him?

She'd pick them first.

Every...single...time...

HUFR

Tiri could barely focus. Her study guide looked nothing like this Biology midterm staring her in the face with mostly blank and incomplete pages, and baby girl was on edge. She knew this shit inside and out. She could recite the process in reverse and with her eyes closed about how blood flowed through the heart step by step, but right now, her mind was drawing a blank. Her anxiety caused her to run her fingers through her hair after dropping her ink pen among the desk in defeat. Was it the intensity of this midterm being one-third of her overall grade in the class? Or, was it the fact that she was being forced to walk around campus with eight big ass niggas dressed in all black surrounding her like she was the president's daughter, that had her so damn worked up?

Peering out at the professor's desk who was nose deep into *Dante's Inferno*, her eyes landed on Válo, who was seated in the corner of the room by the entrance. He could be sweet when he wanted to be. No, he didn't talk much, but he always made sure that she was comfortable and never let her get out of his sight whenever they were in public, simply following Steelo's instructions down to a "T."

Válo could sense her angst as she looked up at him, so when he crossed his arms over his chest with loose hands, telling her to relax in sign language, Tiri inhaled deeply with a head nod. But she tapped on her heart, signaling to him that she was tripping up on the one question she knew she'd have in the bag. All it took was for him to sign the letters *SVC*, acronyms for *superior vena cava,* and a light bulb instantly clicked in her head.

For the last three days, he'd been listening to her stress out about this Bio exam, so he took the initiative to help her study, finding an odd interest in the shit when Válo's always hated school. Sometimes it tripped him up when he decided to drop out of high school during the last semester, but he'd never been comfortable with average or settling when the world obviously had more to offer than a fucking GED and debt.

Tiri managed to finish her last essay question in the nick of time before her professor came around and collected her test. She was the first person out the door, thanking God that this shit was over, and now her school week was completed. She looked forward to her four-day weekend doing nothing but getting high and sucking her man's dick if he'd ever brought his ass home. So, for now, she planned to make sure her vibrator was fully charged, and to schedule a few outings with Ceas and catch up on girl talk.

"Man, I swear you are a lifesaver. How in the fuck did I fumble on the *one* question that I just knew I was ready for is beyond me," she expressed as one of their mobsters held the outside door ajar for her and Válo to exit the building.

"'Cuz you be working yo' self up. Bet if you smoked that blunt like I told you to, you would've been straight."

"Smoking and concentrating on schoolwork just does not mix for me. I would've been in there stuck for real with a blank test and had my damn name spelled wrong. I'm hungry."

"We headed to meet Steelo for lunch now. He wanted to see you before they left town."

That surely cheered her up. Steelo and Marius were running around like crazy these last few days securing the city, and she'd hardly seen her boo's bright smile. It would be appeasing to have a few drinks and get her pussy ate in the back of the 'Lack before she rode his dick into oblivion; thankful to be left with that sacred little fuck for the road until he returned. Tiri was suffering from withdrawals and needed that fix ASAFP!

Ceas still had two other midterms to go that day since it was only 11:30 in the morning, so Tiri had a four hour window to kill time before they were scheduled to go get facials and relax after such an agonizing week with their education.

"Tell me something about you, Válo. Something you think I should know."

Válo reverted his attention from looking out the window as they rode down the highway. He was such an introvert that it made Tiri nervous.

Válo didn't know what she wanted him to say. Socializing wasn't much of his thing unless it was about getting money, so she basically caught him with his pants down asking that question.

"What you mean?"

"I mean...do you have kids? Are you from here or somewhere else? The most I could get you to talk was when you helped me study. It's weird sitting in silence, and it's obvious that we'll be spending a lot of time together, so I'd like to know a little bit about the man guarding my life."

Válo chuckled. She was so prim and proper that it would surprise you to hear her get hip if you didn't know her.

"That's because you have high anxiety, Ri."

Tiri couldn't argue against that; she was always anxious. It's why she smoked.

"You and Steelo both get on my nerves with that. Y'all answer what y'all wanna answer like I'm the Feds or some shit," she pouted.

"No, I don't have kids. I was in the foster system for as long as I can remember, and even after I dug up information on my family, I decided to stay in my own lane. That scratch yo' itch?"

Tiri rolled her eyes. It was clear that he didn't want to talk. Grabbing her air pods, she searched her phone for her Yung Bleu playlist and let her favorite singing ass, rapping ass nigga put her in a better mood.

Twenty minutes later, they were pulling up at this vegan spot called *Crossroads Kitchen* that Steelo had her hooked on. To Tiri's surprise, her man-candy was waiting at the entrance, standing behind the translucent doorway chopping it up with the owner as she exited the car, not waiting for the driver or Válo to let her out. She nearly ran to him until she was abruptly grabbed by the elbow and now standing face to face with a vehement big brother of hers who she thought was minding his own fucking business in St. Louis. His presence came at her so far from left field, she nearly pissed on herself.

"Messiah, what are you doing! Let me go! That's my fucking elbow! Messiah!"

WHOMP!

Válo jumped out of the car war ready and threw a jab at Messiah's mouth that instantly made his top lip bleed. Tiri screamed at the top of her lungs when a goon from her brother's mob held her secure and pulled her away from the scene as Válo and Siah started throwing hands in front of the building.

Steelo barged through the doors quick letting off his clip, knocking niggas off their feet that were retaliating against the small crew that accompanied Válo. He fought his way through the crowd trying to get to Tiri, using his hands and the butt of his gun to knock niggas out. He never saw Messiah pull up on her that quick, nor did he know who these niggas were, but with all they were battling right now, the outbreak had him in assassin mode, and there was no letting up until these niggas were decorating the curb in blood and dead corpses.

Niggas were dropping like flies with the way Steelo was on some *Riddick* shit now, using his blade to skillfully fight them off. That is, until one man rolled up on him in particular and hit him with a combination that caused him to drop his weapon.

Seth was hot.

If him and Messiah could easily roll up on his ass in broad daylight, then how in the fuck was Tiri as safe as she "claimed" to be with her once in a blue moon text messages. No, he didn't weigh the option of Messiah having a tracking device stored in one of his sister's crowns when she had some dental work done just a month before she graduated high school. He didn't bother to weigh the fact that her phone was tapped too, so locating her came to their advantage once they made it on shore via a speedboat since Marius had the city locked the hell down. Tiri must've forgotten that her peoples had this shit in the bag just as much as a fucking Monstrosity thought he did too.

Steelo recognized Seth instantly, but that didn't prevent him from beating this nigga's ass while they continued to scuffle. Each blow that each man threw was applied with more force, immense power, brewing vengeance, and not one ounce of mercy. No one was contemplating over Tiri in the midst of them trying to kill each other. Oh heavens no, that shit went out the window when an animal had a thirst for blood.

Tiri couldn't believe her eyes. Seth and Messiah both had lost their got damn minds, gunshots were ringing, pedestrians were running and screaming for their lives; the sight looked like a war front. She kicked and screamed her damn self with relentless effort trying to break away from this man's grasp, but it was no use. Her eyes kept reverting from Válo's blows upon her brother, her brother's nasty uppercut hitting nothing but Válo's chin. Then, Steelo and Seth scrambling until they broke through the shattered restaurant window and took a hard tumble into a bistro table inside of the building.

Her breathing was constricted from the shock. Her eyes were getting blurry, and her voice felt nonexistent as she screamed all of their names until a darkness swept over her and she blacked out in seconds.

Heart Up For Ransom

Taug Jaye

"My temper; I'm working on that."

-Messiah

Heart Up For Ransom

Chapter
11

There was a trace of unfamiliarity that lingered over Tiri while being back in St. Louis, even if her eyes had only been open for all of two minutes after she finally woke up from her nasty panic attack. No word in the English dictionary could describe what she was feeling right now. She was disgusted with Messiah. The mere thought of seeing him caused a vein to pop out of her forehead; she was so upset. Three henchmen were posted up outside of the backdoor *and* at every other exit around the house as she paced the kitchen floor back and forth, seething. The fact that Messiah was keeping her "detained" enraged her to the max, and she couldn't wait for his ass to show up.

It should've been a pleasure seeing her sister-in-law, Nas, Seth, and her brother arrive after a drawn-out thirty-minute wait that tugged on her anxiety. They were her family; the very people she'd go to any drastic measure to keep by her side. The only family she could ever fathom being born into, but happiness and elation wasn't an option on the menu tonight.

The look etched across Tiri's face alone had shown it.

Her nostrils were flared, fingers curled into two tiny fists that were ready to clean both Seth's and her brother's shit if she had the willpower to do so; her cocoa brown skin was glazed in a shade of red and rage that went out as a sentimental signal to Riley and Nasir, but the men weren't buying it.

"WHAT THE FUCK IS WRONG WITH YOU!" Tiri finally screamed with not an ounce of patience left in her.

Messiah had the nerve to step in her face like this shit wasn't his damn fault, and he was guilt-free.

"Who the fuck is you talking to, Tiri?"

"NIGGA, I'M TALKING TO YOU! YOU'RE THE ONE WHO LOST YOUR SHIT ALL OVER A FEW PUNK ASS, MISSED PHONE CALLS!"

"A FEW?! YOU REALLY WANNA DO THIS SHIT WITH ME RIGHT NOW, TIRI?!"

Messiah's mouth was swollen, one eye was black, and two hours later, this nigga still had the audacity not to clean the blood from off his face because he wanted someone to feel sorry for him and join his side. Seth had a knot the size of a golf ball above his right eye and his pathetic ass was just as banged and bruised up too. This shit was stupid and Tiri was disappointed in both of them.

Messiah took a step closer and invaded Tiri's personal space to stare her in the eye with a glare so hostile that she should've been afraid, but she didn't back down. The days were over when he thought that he could puff his chest out and back her into a corner. He was on edge, she could very much see that, but he brought this shit upon himself.

"This nigga got you disrespecting me, Tiri? He got you turning yo' back on me and thinking you some big bad ass woman now because you laid on yo' back and gave the first smiling ass nigga in yo' face some pussy! You out here fucking a random ass nigga, so now you think you know everything? Huh?! Don't you ever in yo' mu'fucking life say no shit to me like that again! You hear me, *little girl?!*"

"Messiah!"

He ignored his wife's shriek but was stammered when Tiri slapped him clean across the face. The sound echoed throughout the vicinity, causing a vexatious silence to fill the room.

"Whatever I'm doing and whoever I'm doing it with is none of your fucking business, and that does not give you the gall to *disrespect me!* Your pathetic ass has been waiting to say that shit to me! Haven't you! Why do you think I don't wanna pick up the phone every twenty-nine thousand times that you've called! You're a fucking joke, Messiah! All of a sudden you care?! All of a sudden you wanna win big brother of the year award when for how many damn years did I hardly see your face unless it was a holiday before momma and daddy died?! You Casper ass nigga, I see you must've gotten amnesia so let me remind you! You think I didn't feel that shit? You think I swept it underneath the rug because I'm just immature ass Tiri and I'm so got damn easy to manipulate?! Nigga, I ain't forgot, and I'm a whole different breed now!

Trudy had to fucking beg you to start spending some time with me *years* after momma and daddy passed because you was still out here on some ho shit. And now you tryna atone for that like it wasn't you who I was calling back to fucking back just to hear your voice once upon a time! Hoping and fucking praying you wouldn't stand me up for another birthday! For another dance recital! I'll give you a hand clap, you cleaned it up when I turned seventeen, *thanks to Trudy*, but don't never try to come for me, Messiah, all because you think I'm fucking a nigga that wants your spot!

You must really think 'highly' of me to even let that pathetic ass thought cross your mind like I'm just so fucking dumb! Steelo could give a fuck about you and what you do and this dumb ass Platinum Cartel! You wanna get on someone then get on yourself about the lack of preparation for this world that you *didn't* give me, forcing another man to map that shit out so I can stay on my toes! Had it not been for them niggas raiding our house a few years back, you'd still have a binky in my got damn mouth! But I let you do that shit, so you're not one hundred percent the blame *big fucking brother*! And *you*!"

Tiri reverted her attention to Seth. Oh, she was lighting fires up under both of their asses.

"Uncle fucking Seth! You, two, foggy-brained ass muthafuckas get blue balls letting him work you up over a sad ass accusation but got the quote-unquote dexterity to run a fucking drug ring! Where was either one of y'all's brains at when y'all thought of this miraculous ass plan! You just let him coerce you into this bullshit, out there on some nut shit starting fistfights like y'all fucking five damn years old! Yet, *I'm* the problem?!"

"Tiri—"

She silenced her brother with another smack to his face for interrupting her. She wasn't finished!

"And that's for grabbing me like you lost your fucking mind! I'm in college! I'm living my life! Sorry I didn't call more to pacify ya' insecurities, my nigga, but I'm not a baby anymore, and I've told you that! Happened fast, I know it did, yet you the same nigga that tripped into faithfulness after three months of dating, so look at you pointing the finger! Judge ya granny, not me! Man, I can't believe y'all!"

Tiri was so pissed off she couldn't even cry about it. Homegirl was fuming. She stormed off, stomping invisible traces of her footprints into the floor as she proceeded up to her room. Fuck them. Fuck all them.

She'd tried calling Steelo a few times prior to her brother and company walking in with the intent to gang up on her before she blew a couple of caps back, but as she called him now, all the phone did was ring. Her heart couldn't take this. Messiah didn't understand how his actions would make her look in Steelo's eyes, and it infuriated her even more.

Steelo, baby, please answer the phone. I need to talk to you.

He read her message instantly, but those three dots never transformed into a reply.

Not even an hour or so later.

She could whoop Messiah's ass herself if she had the physical strength to actually hurt him.

A bubble bath usually did the trick for her anxiety, but all Tiri did was sweat her hair out and get a migraine from the heat mixed along with her unwavering tension.

Three rolled Backwoods later, she was exiting her bathroom, greeted to the sight of Riley sitting on the edge of her bed.

Tiri remained mute. She put her ashtray on the nearest surface and retreated to her walk-in closet where she lotioned up and changed into an old t-shirt and a pair of spankies. After brushing her hair into a top knot, she finally climbed in bed and fired up blunt number one. Riley let her burn about three-fourths of her green with hopes that it would calm her down before she tried to express her thoughts.

"Messiah was wrong," Tiri blurted, stopping Riley from beginning. "He always thinks the world is just supposed to stop and shift around for his ego like he's the only human being present in it. You cause all of that fucking mayhem over me not responding to some phone calls? That shit is sick, and I know he don't give not two fucks about it either because he's cocky like that."

Riley remained silent. She sat there rubbing her baby bump, giving Tiri the floor to get her argument out of the way until she felt like it was safe to speak.

"Tiri—"

"You married an idiot."

"Are you gonna let me talk, or get carried away with your emotions just like he does?"

Riley's smile caused Tiri to inhale deeply before she put the end of her blunt out. That woman held a level of patience that she wished could rub off on her from contact. It was the only way that she and Messiah's relationship could possibly run a smooth course. Him and Tiri both had that Stallion angst honest, and she knew that nigga got off the chain with her too.

"I'm listening," young Tiri pouted.

"Ri, I didn't come in here to scold you. Keeping it a hunnid, I'm actually thanking you. Yeah, you hit some low blows back there, but your brother really needed to hear that. Yeah, he's told me how he was gone a lot when you were younger, but I didn't know it was to such a degree. Granted, y'all's age difference is a lot to consider, but it's obvious that this tension brewing between y'all has been harbored for way longer than it should've been. His grip on you *has* been tight since things happened with the Kamikazes, but if you honestly think that your brother doesn't care about you, then you really don't know him."

"I know he caaaaaares," she huffed. "Do you know how many people were shot and killed Riley?"

"Yes, I do. His approach may have been wrong—"

"Wrong?!" she interrupted. "Try over the freakin' top! I mean, even if he would've just approached me out there on some chill shit and had a sit down with us like a normal, stable human being would've done, then this wouldn't have happened. He grabbed me and caused me to make a scene like that because he was about to rip my fucking arm off. Riley, his fingerprints are around my damn elbow. How do you think I felt? My nigga runs a crime orchestration. The heat is so fucking hot for him right now in Trinity that Messiah's immature approach did nothing but trigger everything.

Válo stole off on him for grabbing me, then a myriad of Platinum goons just start crowding around like a scrimmage, I'm being pulled away, and the only thing on Steelo's mind is to protect Tiri. Like, come on now, I'm not slow. I know my nigga just as much as I know my brother and had Messiah been an adult about it then I'd be laying up in Trinity cuddling. These fucking midterms damn near kilt me and being cooped up in St. Louis isn't how I necessarily planned on spending my weekend."

Riley laughed which she knew probably pissed her little sister off, but she couldn't help how cute she was talking about and defending her boo. She'd called it a few weeks ago that Tiri was out there boo'd up, but not with a goon like this famous Steelo she'd heard so much about. That was impressive.

"This Steelo got your heart, Ri-Ri. I see it," she grinned.

Tiri tried her best to stifle her smile. This wasn't about her relationship status. This was about Messiah acting like a childish idiot.

"And it's okay," she continued. "I am not judging you. Is this your first real relationship?" Riley probed for more.

Tiri gave in. She was out of steam.

"Yeah."

"And how did y'all meet? It's obvious not on campus."

"Well...we—*did*...kind of, sort of."

She hesitated about telling Riley the truth because she didn't want her running back to Messiah about it. He'd really lose his shit.

"Spill the beans, Ri. It's just you and me. Dinner is already in the oven, so we have nothing but time."

"Yeah, but Messiah is also your husband, and that takes precedence over us. I tell Steelo everything, so I know you're going to go back and tell him."

"Don't throw me shade like that. If you don't want me to tell him, then that's all you have to say," Riley countered as she laid across the bed. A bag of peanut M&M's was at her side as always.

Tiri realized that her comment wasn't the nicest, so she apologized, took a deep breath, then told Riley everything about the shooting up until the day she ran into him at the pizzeria.

"And we've been dating since. Well, he pulled up on me like a week later after ripping my heart into fucking shreds and then we started dating."

Riley wore a smile like the Grinch. This shit was juicy, and she sees why Tiri hasn't been answering the phone. Not only was she big boy toy occupied, but from another perspective, she was scared. Baby sis had grown a solid pair of nuts overnight, that was a given, but she couldn't part ways with her timorous spirit. It's who she was.

"That explains a lot, like, it explains everything, Ri-Ri. Real shit."

They each laughed coolly.

"I know I can call more. I know that, and I also know that I should respond to Messiah to keep him from worrying, but he's hounding me. I don't like that."

"It's a fine line between him being irky, him loving and wanting the best for you, and making up for lost time, Tiri."

That last part of her statement hit Tiri like a ton of bricks.

"Contrary to what either of y'all may think right now, you both hurt each other's feelings today with every intention on doing so. Y'all are siblings; y'all know how to push each other's buttons but using it as ammunition against each other versus coming together to solve the problem, is just as bad. Messiah has kids now, so his emotions are easier to trigger these days, and what you said to him, Tiri, triggered a lot."

"Was I wrong?"

Riley shook her head.

"It's not what you say, it's how you say it."

"Well, he shouldn't have low key called me a ho. I didn't appreciate that shit."

"That *was* out of pocket. Very out of pocket, and I know he regrets it, but he still shouldn't have said it. He got his ass chewed out for that too, but what I want you to do is relax. Give it some time then try to talk it over before you head back. Don't leave here without handling things with your brother. I know you're growing up and living your life, but he's still your brother, and y'all need to lay down some ground rules. I don't like seeing y'all at each other's throats like this. Y'all are so much better than how you're acting, so do me this one solid and promise me that y'all will talk, okay?"

Tiri loved Riley. She had the ability to calm her down and help her understand situations from face value versus her own interpretation. Especially when it came to her egg head ass big brother, and she wholeheartedly thanked God for her presence within the Stallion family. They surely needed her.

"Okay. I will."

"Alright. You go ahead and chill out. It's been a long, crazy day, and dinner will be ready in a few hours."

"Alright. Thanks, Ry. I really appreciate it."

They exchanged smiles.

"Anytime, baby love. That's what I'm here for. Let me know if you need me."

"Okay."

HUFR

"Omg, Ri-Ri. Your brother is crazy as shit! I still can't believe he would come all the way out here and do something like that. With his fine ass. I know he's married; I'm just stating facts."

"Man, Ceas, fuck his ugly ass," Tiri laughed into the camera while fleeking out her baby hairs. It was Friday night, she was bored, and a drink was calling her name. Heading out to Seth's club, *Shottas*, was the ultimate plan to take her mind off Steelo ignoring her. "Should I change?"

The temperature drop in St. Louis compared to Trinity was the cause of her rocking a black and fitted, quarter sleeve, Adidas track dress along with knee-high Christian Louboutin Bianca boots. She was simply dressed but hoped it wasn't too Plain Jane for her outing.

"No, girl, you look great. Get you a popping ass clutch and you're in there. Do something blingy."

Her silver Valentino Garavani, metallic rock stud spiked crossbody clutch instantly came to mind. If her memory served her correctly, it still had a tag on it.

"That's why I fucks with you, Ceas. How's Trinity?"

"You know I got you, boo, but it's Trinity. Same 'ole, same ole.' I'm stuck in this fucking house all weekend due to this mob shit too. I had to beg my daddy to let Glenn come over; with escorts of course. I'm fucking bored and horny. He should be here any minute now with wings and margaritas."

"All flats and blue cheese."

"Yuck! You know I'm a ranch head. Blue cheese is so disgusting."

"No, ranch is," Tiri countered, scrunching her beautiful face. "Get enough dick for the both of us, best friend. I'm spotting a little bit and have cramps out the ass; I'm so pissed. I got this damn Nexplanon to avoid menstrals, yet this periodic spotting gets so annoying sometimes."

"It's better than getting pregnant or forgetting to take a damn pill."

"Yeah, you're right."

"Steelo still being a dick head?"

Tiri rolled her eyes just as she checked their thread. All of her texts were getting left on read and it was starting to get to her. She cleared her misty eyes with a dab of tissue, careful not to mess up her makeup, then appeared back on camera.

Ceas was so cute to Tiri. Her curly hair was twisted in Bantu knots, and she had that same innocent aura as Tia Mowry did too. She was just a little hood and wore gold bamboos.

"You are so fine, friend. Straight ten. Let me get yo' number," Tiri teased.

"Thanks, boo. You can have whatever you like."

"Okuuurt! And ugh, you know he is. Getting on my last fucking nerves. Niggas are so damn sentimental. All I'm trying to do is explain my side of the story."

"He'll come around. He's going through a lot. That man loves you."

"He doesn't."

"Bye, Tiri. You know Steelo loves you. If he didn't, he wouldn't be doing half this shit or dealing with a woman who's so much younger than him—*I'm in the bedroom, babe!*"

Tiri was hoping Ceas said something on the lines of that. She was hoping Steelo loved her because she foolishly loved him in ways that should've been too premature for her to attest to. But when you shared the intimacy, trust, and adoration they'd built in record timing, it was hard not to.

Tiri told her girl goodbye and wished her a good night before loading her clutch and heading out. She and Riley were meeting Nasir at the club, and she'd already pre-gamed with an edible and a few shots of Patron.

She'd heard stories about Seth's luxurious establishment, but rumors didn't do the experience any justice. Half-naked bottle girls were walking around in six-inch heels flaunting their bodies, marijuana smoke filled the air, and the music was popping. That Lil' Baby and Gunna was blaring in the atmosphere as Tiri sipped on her lemonade and D'USSÉ in no rush to finish, throwing her made by Nuri P hips from right to left alongside the beautiful Nasir.

Riley was holding down their valor booth munching on a snow cone made personally by the bartender manning the mini bar on the VIP level. Tiri knew Steelo had her Snapchat tapped and would be watching, so she was sure to flick it up, getting all of her right angles. The shot Nasir got of her with that juicy booty in the camera as she posed from behind was the highlight of her night. After saving it to her camera roll, she decided to give her feet a rest and join the ladies at the booth.

It felt weird, and a tad bit out of place smoking and drinking with her old teacher when they first started hanging out, but now they all were besties. Riley and Nas were her family now, and even though ten years stood between them as well, they treated her with respect, and that's all she ever wanted. They were the big sisters she never had.

"Shoooooots!" Nasir exclaimed with a gorgeous smile when the bottle girl brought over a tray filled with Don Julio. Her laced, neon blue, bodysuit complemented her skin tone perfectly against the LED lights as she handed out the glasses.

Tiri was going to be on her ass tonight mixing white and dark liquor.

"Here, Ry. I got you some apple juice since you all pregnant and shit."

"Girl, fuck you! And I'mma throw 'em back like they the real thing too, trick!"

Tiri joined the laughter with a lime in hand before their three shot glasses, a piece, disappeared. She was officially faded and traveling on a wavelength that she hated couldn't be enjoyed with her man's dick in her mouth. She was dying to let him shove it down her throat before she went ham with the sloppy toppy. To her dismay, he still hadn't replied, and the liquor prompted her to send that, **Miss you**, text along with a couple of freaky emojis. But she was prepared for him to ignore her as he'd been doing beforehand, forcing her to knock off the rest of her D'USSÉ in frustration.

"Can I ask y'all something!" she screamed over the "Going Bad" mixing in with the last song, keeping the club in full swing.

"Uh-oh! She feeling them shots!"

"Nas!" Tiri shrieked with her cheeks turning red.

"Wassup, baby girl. Ask us anything," Riley insisted.

"I think I love Steelo," she confessed.

"And?"

She laughed at Nas' comment.

"What do you mean by, *and*?"

"*And*, as in, tell us something we don't know!"

Was it that obvious that she loved him? No, it couldn't be. At least she didn't think it was.

"I feel like, so crazy and delusional. I know I'm only eighteen and I have my whole life ahead of me, but I just feel something for him that…" Tiri couldn't explain it.

"Let me ask you something," Nasir proposed before throwing back another shot. "First and foremost, does he treat you like a human being?"

"Absolutely."

"Does he treat you like a woman?"

"Yes, while also schooling me on a few things that I've been oblivious to."

"Like a man should," Riley agreed.

"It's like," Tiri sipped her new drink. "It's like, the world sees him in one light, but when he's with me, it's inhibition free."

"Then enjoy yourself with him, Ri-Ri. Don't stress yourself out about how a relationship is 'supposed' to be done; whatever the fuck that means. Let it run its course. Have fun, be adventurous, and have good sex. Have excellent fucking sex but get you some birth control because shit changes when you have kids. Look at Riley."

"Ho, throw another shot at me, okay? You have *three*. You know these hands work just fine, impregnated or not."

Tiri just loved them. She wished Ceas was there to celebrate right by their side. That shit was going up on their end of the year bucket list for sure.

"But yeah, baby, live your life. If it's meant to progress, then trust me, the time will permit itself. A man that truly loves and wants to be with you will hold it down financially, physically, sexually, and emotionally to keep you happy and in his life. But don't forget to want more out of life than being someone's wife. Michele Obama said it best. You need to cop her book like ASAP; sautéed with nothing but gold and valuable gems.

I also want you to read the *TKF Series* by Nako too. I'm sure you'll be able to relate to Savona almost instantly. Make sure you're putting just as much, and hell, *even more* time into being Tiri too. A real man will support and add to the self-care and love that you shower yourself with. Don't let Seth and Messiah fool you. They worship the grounds we walk on. It's gon' always pay being a boss ass, confident ass bitch and don't you ever forget that shit."

They took another shot to being boss ass bitches before turning up with the Cardi B blaring in the air. That Latina had the ability to release every woman's inner ho with the drop of a single beat.

Tiri was twerking like she was tryna get flewed out until the handsome baby face and hazel eyes of Válo almost made her sober up instantly. She thought she was seeing shit until he laughed at her silly ass resembling Marsai Martin in her famous meme.

"VÁLO?!" she questioned while putting her drink down.

Got damn them niggas did a number on each other! She thought in reference to his busted lip and the blue-black bruise underneath his right eye.

Had he not gotten a fresh line up before flying out, he'd be looking like the homeless rocking designer.

"You bold as fuck! I bet you walked up in this bitch like you owned it too!" Tiri joked as she threw an arm around his neck.

To her surprise, he hugged her back.

She respected Válo. No, he didn't know who Messiah was when the chaos erupted but thinking she was in danger, he was ready to do whatever to keep her out of harm's way, and that made him a solid brethren in her eyes.

"You a'ight?" he asked her in her ear.

"Yeah, I'm good. Did Steelo send you out here?!" she hoped.

"Nah, he in one of his moods right now. After all that went down, I just wanted to make sure you was safe and offer an apology."

Tiri smiled. That was very sweet of him, and it was clear that he valued her life and his potna with the utmost respect. Steelo was right. He was good peoples.

"Well thank you!" She hated to scream, but the music was blasting and there was no other way to communicate without doing so. "I appreciate it! Don't even sweat it; it's all good on this end. You wanna drink or something? We have an open bar! These are my sisters, Riley, my brother's wife, and that's Nas, Seth's wife! Y'all, this is my bodyguard/ a good friend of Steelo's, Válo!"

Válo shook hands with the ladies and soon was gulping down a bottle of D'ÚSSE, turning up with them. He hadn't remembered the last time he stepped foot in a club. Steelo always sent him an invite whenever him, Marius, and Terrell popped out for a lil' minute, but his lame ass always turned it down. Preferring to get high in the crib and fuck up a little *2k* by his lonesome.

Válo enjoyed being alone, but it didn't sit right with him not checking on Tiri. Especially during a time like this. Shit was too hot whether she was in her hometown or not, and Steelo would toe-tag his ass if something happened to her. Even if he was being ignorant, fronting like he didn't care about the shit her brother pulled.

So here he was, half a bottle later, drunk as fuck for the first time in a month, vibing with young Tiri and her peoples while a small Trinity squad stood posted up throughout the building for back up. He took no job lightly. Plus, he felt responsible for how shit played out after taking the first swing.

The club didn't clear out until around a quarter after four and Tiri was nowhere near ready to turn it in like her OG's had done. The night was young, she was younger, and after getting a bit of liquor down Válo's throat, he transformed from a grumpy introvert to matching her energy with ease.

That "No Stylist" was hitting tremendous numbers in the speaker system while they rode in the backseat of their Maybach, each rolling up another 'Woods. Tiri's mind hadn't been this free since she'd arrived in St. Louis, and she thanked God for the relaxation.

Getting weary over Steelo's behavior towards her was clearly out of her hands. If he wanted to place the blame on her for another thing that didn't have her name on it then fuck it. She was too busy contemplating heavily on the words of encouragement she'd received from Nasir, which made her ask Válo this.

"I think I'mma invest in my own strain of smokes. Put some paper into the Cannabis business and launch me a line of edibles and soul food. Maybe like a swanky little coffee shop with nice scenery. Roll up and smoke a blunt while you wait on your food; a nice little chill spot. What you think?"

Válo took a deep pull from the blunt before passing it to her.

"Word? That's dope. Everybody getting high. It's beneficial too for mu'fuckas who need that lil' relief while they on the clock. That's some crazy shit, Ri. Go for it."

"Some straight stupid shit, right?" her smile was bright amongst the clouds of smoke engulfing the air around them. "It's a multi-million dollar franchise. And I love to cook too? That's a good look."

"On me. What you gon' call it?"

"Not sure yet," she handed him the new blunt to fire up, stuffed with some lemon drop and laced with wax to enhance their rotation. "I'm just brainstorming for right now, but I'm definitely putting this shit into motion. The way my shit selling now, I already know this is it; my niche in life. I'll finish out the semester so I won't waste my brother's money, but this college dream is a no for me, dawg. It's just not my steelo."

Válo chuckled from her use of slang and personification, causing Tiri to join too. It was cute how much she loved his potna. She was lucky to have him and vice-versa.

"Where we at?" he questioned when the driver pulled up at an old-fashioned building that could've passed for condemned property if you weren't familiar with the setting.

"Uncle Bill's Diner. The place has mixed reviews, but I love their food; plus, it's way better than settling for IHOP."

Tiri normally hated going in public domains wreaking of gut-wrenching cannabis, but her stomach was growling, and this was her hometown. No rules applied. She was as free as a lamb and overly excited that she and Válo were finally bonding versus acting as if they didn't wanna be around each other, afraid somebody might catch the cooties.

Uncle Bill's 70's interior décor was seriously out of date, but the grub made up for it. Tiri was putting down some fried chicken and waffles, sausage, bacon, and grits while Válo smashed strawberry topped pancakes, scrambled cheese eggs, a T-bone steak, and hash browns. All you could hear from their section was the tips of their forks diving into their food, rattling salt and pepper shakers, and finger licking. Their high cranked their munchie level up above normal altitudes.

"Umm-umm. Who you smiling at? I knew you had to be boo'd up," Tiri teased once she saw his reaction to his phone screen. She was getting all of the tea. "Is she from here?"

Válo was as cool as a fan for the time being. His personal life normally stayed between him and the people associated, but he knew Tiri's pushy ass wouldn't go for a half-ass nor smart ass answer. He was feeling pretty wavy, so he let the ball drop and confided in her.

"Nah, but she in town."

"Ohhhh, okay! You better go get you some pussy and quit playing. Your hard up ass needs to get that dick wet."

Válo coughed on his Sprite at her silly ass, needing a pat or two to his chest to clear his airway.

"You wild than a mu'fucka, man." There was laughter in his statement.

"I'm serious. Somebody needs to be getting some, and since it ain't me, then have at it. What's her name?"

"Salt," he responded with a mouth full of whipped cream and other pancake toppings.

Tiri's eyes bulged.

"Salt? *Salt Santana*? Tattoo's little sister? My bish that runs Chamberlain? Shut up! I love her! She...you know with my peoples. That's you, Válo? Oh, snap! I see you like 'em stacked cause' Salt thick than a mu'fucka. Jesus Himself couldn't bypass that ass."

This girl had laughter leaving his lips in overtime. Young Tiri was good company. Good for anyone's soul that she crossed paths with. Like a butterfly.

"Sum' like that. Shorty be curving me like she ain't checking for a nigga but be wanting the dick. I can't blame her though."

"Then put yo' muthafucking mack down and get on that. Text her back and be like you on the way with some beefcake and breakfast. And I wanna hear all about it in the morning. Y'all niggas know y'all love explaining the recaps from y'all's sexcapades."

Yes, she totally just made that word up.

"I'm not about to do this shit wit' you, Ri. Straight up," he laughed.

"Yes, you are. We dun' solidified our bond now! So cut the shit. What's the deal? Do you really like her, like her, or is this just some fuck? Keep it a hunnid."

Válo didn't know how she was doing it, but Tiri was getting him to sing like a canary, and it actually felt good to let some shit off his chest for once.

"Salenthia ain't like the other chicks I've met in Trinity, truth be told," he referred to Salt by her first name to further express his sentiments. "I admire confidence in a woman. Attitude, sophistication, but then again, one a lil' rough around the edges who gon' drank and smoke wit' me. Sensible, business savvy. Hungry; figuratively and literally. Shorty, she all that. So to answer yo' question, yeah. I fucks wit' ha' until the feelings become mutual, which I know they will."

"You know what, Válo?" Tiri wiped her hands while looking over her empty plates and raped chicken bones, spent. Her belly was tight, and her lungs were in need of a relaxation blunt now. "You a real ass nigga and I fucks wit' it. And she will too. You gon' ahead and do your thing tonight. I'mma be okay. No sweat. This ain't Trinity, so kick your feet up and enjoy this mini vacay while we're here. You deserve it."

Tiri was right. Válo felt an instant relief of stress and pressure when he landed on her streets. Sometimes a retreat was the perfect restoration when you were always so busy cultivating, regulating, and killing niggas. He *needed* to be murdering some premium pussy. Damn right he deserved it and knowing that Salt was hitting his line wanting him to eat her pussy then lay down some Santiago pipelines for the rest of the night, he was only one call and a drop off away from fixing that.

ℌ𝔘𝔉ℜ

Easy was going in on her older brother. Frustrations, negativity, and hostile verbiage always flowed with ease because tearing one down was easier than admitting you were wrong. Especially when you had your mindset on going the fuck in, so you studied everything in your head for thirty minutes before you could reach for the kill like Tiri had done.

Now, making up with Messiah? Whew. That shit was a different ball game. They'd been purposely avoiding each other all weekend, and here it was, Sunday evening, and Tiri was on her way back to Trinity.

Riley was throwing silence at her and Messiah both because neither of them had yet to put their pride aside to hash things out. So she was away at Nas and Seth's crib with Shanti and the kids with no pity for either of them. They both were being childish, and if two could play that game, then three would surely break the camel's back.

Messiah hadn't been home on a Sunday to enjoy the quality time with his family in months, and the day it happened, his wife is on bullshit, and his little sister hated him. Boy, was he lucky! Sunday night football, blueberry hill marijuana, and a cooler filled with a twelve pack of Dos Equis Lager beers summed up his doings. The perfect "dad" description, but he was a lonely dad.

"Nigga straight eating pizza on a Sunday because his wife in her damn feelings."

Messiah shook his head before throwing a piece of crust back inside of the half-empty delivery box. He downed three-fourths of the beer he had in hand then belched loudly as he rubbed his rippling stomach.

He didn't notice it when Tiri walked through the door with a plate of food in hand until she came into view along the side of him. Oh, she still had an attitude too, but she'd be damned if she attempted to leave without having a conversation with him. She handed him over an infused plate with tender cooked duck meat, white sauce four-cheese lobster mac, sautéed zucchini and fresh French-style green beans. Tiri loved her green veggies. They grew up on them.

Messiah raised his brow when she sat across from him in the loveseat that decorated his man cave. He nervously eyed between her and the food before saying, "You tryna poison me?" seconds prior to shoving a fork full of each side into his mouth.

Tiri giggled while flaming up a blunt.

"Says the man with a mouth full."

"I'm hip. Woulda' already been dead. This shit good as fuck. Wait, it got weed in it?" or was he just high, high already? The taste wasn't too potent, but again, her blending skills were excellent.

Tiri nodded her head in agreement as she looked around his sanctum. The family portrait that him, Shanti, Riley, and her took over the summer immediately caught her attention. Next to it was one of them with their parents, a month before they died, and it broke her spirits.

"Siah, I'm sorry." She put her blunt down and used her hands to cover her mouth.

Tiri released a mixture of tears and pain that she'd held onto for years now. It was always easier turning the other cheek and sweeping things away than to settle the past. It'd surely caught up with her, and of all people, she needed her brother to get her through the process.

Yes, *him.*

Messiah put his food down and sat next to his sister. He pulled her into his chest and let her cry her heart out; an act of revelation they hadn't engaged in for a while now.

"Messiah, sometimes I can't take this," her cries were muffled in his chest with her tears staining his shirt.

He knew what she was referring to, and there were times when his own heart couldn't bare the same affliction. Messiah always had to be strong for his sister. If he cracked, then she'd surely crumble like a domino effect. Their hearts were one. When Tiri put up a wall to block out the accident, Messiah did the same and hustled harder. Fucked a limitless amount of bitch's hearts out to feel an escape of the tragedy because in those days there was no Riley. There was no woman who, oddly, didn't have to corner him like a child and force him to communicate. The shit was innate with his baby.

Him and all of his hoes were registered on the same wavelength; nuts and goodbyes, and that was okay with a playa like him. Conversation wasn't some shit he was interested in with a replaceable ass ho anyway. And what should've been a one-night stand with Riley turned into a vibe that he couldn't stand a chance against. Hence the ring, the relationship, the children, and the *I do's.*

Contrary to anyone's beliefs, Messiah was just as torn and destroyed about losing his parents, perhaps, even more than his sister was. For years he'd been ghost as she tauntingly reminded him and it hit different when the day they'd all taken that family portrait and sat at the dinner table as one, was the last day he'd seen, hugged, and kissed his folks until they were looking back at him in caskets.

So he cried too. No longer afraid to display his thoughts and sentiments with the fear of hindering his masculinity. Hell, Messiah needed refuge and peace as well. He was only human. And that same humanity forced him to apologize to his sister. He apologized for the neglect. For his distance. For how hard he was on her. For being selfish, controlling, unruly, and ignorant because he didn't want to lose another Stallion.

It was his truth.

"Ny, you know I would never try to hurt you intentionally. My temper; I'm working on that. Exercising rationality and not jumping to conclusions are two of my biggest flaws. I can admit that now. I apologize for putting my hands on you and disrespecting you. I just want you to understand where I'm coming from."

Tiri rose her face from his chest and wiped her eyes. He hadn't called her *Ny* in years. Until she was a good twelve years of age and started junior high, she was his and her father's Princess Ny but felt embarrassed by it since she was getting older. Tiri knew her brother loved her. With everything in him, so she did understand his dilemma. She just hated that he treated her like she was incompetent.

"It's not that I don't understand you, Messiah. You just started suffocating me, and for that to come out of nowhere when I've gotten, *comfortable*, with you being gone...it sent me mixed signals. I've always wanted you to be around, but you were dictating me. I know what's in this world now, and even though your intentions were good, you've gotta work on the display because that shit pushes me away. Riley's right...we're better than this, and all I want you to do is trust me. I would never put myself in a position to disrespect you. Never. Shit's been so up and down since momma and daddy died, but it's finally good to know that I wasn't feeling that shit alone...why do y'all do that?"

He wiped her face.

"Why do *who* do *what*?"

"Why do men run away from everything? That's not masculinity; that's pussy shit, Siah."

He chuckled.

"Society engineered masculinity into us from a one-sided, insufficient, and dictating perspective, and that's nothing but the truth. It ain't an excuse, but it explains men in a nutshell."

"No wonder why Latif be going so hard on her YouTube channel. Sheesh."

"Aye, Tif a different breed. Prodigy got his hands full with that one, but I do listen to her podcast too, and I started back getting into The Word once I found me a preacher I could connect with. You know I ain't been to church in over...ten years, so that's taking some time, but it's transitioning pretty smoothly. Tif, though, she be dropping some knowledge when she ain't on a bashing spree in every other sentence. And I say that to say this: a lot of times, we be blinded to the dumb shit that we find ourselves wrapped up in, slave to, and living by.

A nigga ain't gon' listen unless you disrespect him. I ain't saying go out there and start disrespecting ya' man and whatnot, but you gotta apply pressure and that's why I folded when you chewed my ass out. You was right; I was wrong. There's not much more to it. Seth did try to redirect me when I went haywire about this whole lil' situation wit' you and this nigga Steelo, so you owe him an apology, but you know my dawg gon' ride. Right or wrong."

"What are y'all, five?"

They shared a laugh, but Tiri could read between the lines. Their bond painted the perfect image of trust, loyalty, and friendship for her. She'd always cherish it.

"Same way that nigga Válo packed off on me cuz' you dating his potna. Same shit, different clique, youngin', and I respect it."

"You know I'm never gonna let you forget that shit, right? You really outdid yourself, nigga."

"I bet that ass answer the phone next time, won't you?"

Tiri laughed as he wrapped his arms around her with a kiss to her forehead.

"I love you, girl. Don't you ever forget that shit."

"I love you too, Messiah. I swear I'm okay. A lawyer or a corny ass nigga that you expected me to be with can't protect me like you always have. *You* remember that too."

His baby sister had grown up. Yes, she had an entire lifetime to go and nothing but experiences to live through, but she had to stretch her wings one day. As long as she remembered to value the trust and bond they'd constructed, then who was he to hold her back? Messiah wanted nothing more than the love and happiness that Tiri wanted for herself, and now that they'd established an understanding, she had his blessings and unwavering support.

Taug Jaye

Heart Up For Ransom

"You tell me I'm confusing, more immature than Marques Houston..."

-Drake

Taug Jaye

Chapter

12

One Month Later

The streets of Trinity had been quiet since the altercation with the Platinum Cartel last month. So Still.

Too damn quiet.

As a result, the Irish Mob had yet to receive retaliation from The Monstrosity, and it came off surprising. Marius was a hothead. He reacted off impulse; not only out of impatience, but because of the fact that there were always two or three other executions planned and placed on the back burner for times like this. He was always prepared. *Almost*, always prepared. He couldn't control when or specifically how the enemy would try him, but his army was always on standby like the National Guard to win a war.

And Geni was well aware of that.

Seven hundred and thirty days in the pen. One hundred and four weeks. Twenty-four months. Two years locked away under the surveillance of ADX Maximum Prison did nothing but give him the time he needed to thoroughly orchestrate the assassination of The Monstrosity, and that time would rise with due diligence.

Conner was never the one for confrontation. He hated to clean up a mess that could avoid being made, and that was where Geni and his father clashed. Most of the O'Sullivan family blamed his hesitation and decrease of vengeance on his health and the essence of him aging. He basically handed over the crime scene and embezzlement to Marius without a fight because their pharmaceutical companies in Ireland were doing excellent on American currency.

Trinity PD let up on his family and quickly reverted their attention to The Monstrosity and his orchestration in a matter of weeks. Conner may have taken an "L" on supremacy in the streets, but there was no need to fret when their reputation heavily proceeded them. His family was raking in money he couldn't configure without a financial advisor, and he hardly lifted a finger to do so. That's what he called smart and residual income.

Clean hands, clean feet, and no heat.

All Marius had to do was allow him to make shop in Trinity since he now held the keys to the streets at the O'Sullivan's leisure. Something on the lines of a peace offering, per se. But greed was a venomous sin. He just had to stick his fangs in the one area that kept the Irish Mob living large, and that's when it became personal.

Conner's army was outnumbered by Marius and his crew by ten to one on a bad day.

So much for brutal force.

It was Geni who realized the only way they'd be successful with his demise was by expanding.

Well, the thing about expansion was this. It came with a number of "perks."

The first was money.

The second was an alliance/established peace treaty during the war.

Third was permanent business avenues with the cartel who then became another mouth to feed and more people to keep quiet. Another syndicate they had to develop a list of checks and balances to keep them retained and to possibly exploit and denounce their throne to a nonexistence.

That shit took time, trusted soldiers, and most importantly, fucking money that Conner wasn't willing to waste. He'd rather find a loophole with legislation then to hand over a dime of his hard-earned money to another nigga.

But with his death, that shit now meant nothing. Geni was willing to pay whatever the fuck he could to commemorate Conner O'Sullivan, even if it led to a drought. The Monstrosity took from him what could never be reclaimed, and that was a father.

His best friend.

Marius took from Geni something he'd never understand nor ever cherished because of his own tragic upbringing. That shit was low. That shit was pathetic, and since dogs only knew how to communicate with rage, Geni was coming at his ass using the same tactics against him. Everyone else in Trinity fumbled when the slightest whiff of The Monstrosity's cologne, shielded by hate, infiltrated the air.

Geni didn't give a fuck about none of that shit. The best messages were sent with silence then sporadic incursion, and rounds one and two had clearly gone out to the Irish Mob. Yeah, it was out of the ordinary with a month's window of time resting between the shoot outs, but Geni wasn't sweating shit. He had the availability to go tit for tat with his ass, and each round would get harder. The longer they went, Geni was dropping a plague that would slowly, yet surely force Marius to wave a white flag.

And once he did...by the time their family was through with his ass, his body would be like confetti. Left in little pieces so intricately decapitated that it would take a rocket scientist to put that shit back together. A closed casket funeral for that muthafucka with a fern inside holding little to no ashes. Geni was sure once it was all said and done that nigga's soul wouldn't even make it into the afterlife.

He had to drink to that shit...

The heat waves propelling from Trinity's ninety-seven degree weather entered the back door of Geni's limousine before his visitor climbed inside and the driver quickly took off, merging into traffic. He poured himself and his guest a glass of Midleton Very Rare Irish Whiskey, chilled with no ice for them to enjoy in their few moments of silence before taking the floor to speak.

"How's it looking in South America?"

His guest took another sip of the potent drink before responding.

"Numbers are good. Could be better. Barely making board since the Platinum Cartel bought out Berkeley, but that won't be an issue for long. Timing's gotta be flawless with all of this shit. We attack both cities on my say so, then we infiltrate each territory once I've got all heads on one plate. It'll be a whammy for them pretty boy ass niggas, Seth and Messiah; which, I'm glad that shit popped off last month. We'll keep the clash between St. Louis and Trinity brewing for as long as possible to keep them distracted. The Monstrosity's way in over his head right now.

Never seen him so fucking silly. Slowly yet surely, we'll have that nigga right where we need him then it's one last kiss goodbye, nah-mean?"

Geni caught the tablet his visitor tossed over to him and chuckled at the foolery. Marius had soldiers running around the city onto all known Irish sets caught by their surveillance system, but each property had been condemned, burned down, and moved out. Relocation was a must after they off'd Kovu's mother, knowing that would cause some tension in his *oh so happy home.* They had this nigga running in a maze with no outlet near, and it brought Genu joy for the first time since his family laid Conner to rest.

"Let him continue to look. The enemy will come directly to you once you throw out the right bait. You'll have your moment with him. In due time. I've got six teams surrounding the city with flight backup on standby, so trust me, when it happens, it'll be bloody but quick. Patience, my friend...it's all about patience."

Geni's jaw clenched as he handed over the tablet. His desire to conquer The Monstrosity was so heavy it made his mouth salivate, and his dick grow with excitement. But he couldn't do it without a big enough army and that's where his visitor came in at.

"I'm taking it that's my payment."

Geni's eyes shifted to the four yellow briefcases that held fifty million dollars total.

"Yeah."

"Excellent." The vehicle came to a stop once they reached the driveway of the 4 Season's Hotel. "Remember what I said. Hold your got damn horses. The man will crack. Anything done outside of my jurisdiction will have you and your family buried in Ireland next to your father. We'll be in touch."

𝕳𝖀𝕱𝕽

A month's separation away from the girl he swore on his own heart and soul that he *did not* love made more of a difference to Steelo than he thought it would. His beach house felt nothing like a home without her presence. Without her grace. So fucking empty without the pleasure of waking up to her irises glued to him while he slept on the nights when he wasn't out running the streets like an untamed beast. What once came off as uncomfortable, and maybe even quite creepish, was yet another memory that Steelo was savoring because he was being too much of an ass to be a man and speak to Tiri.

Messiah's pop-up put Steelo's mind into solitary confinement. Never had he once questioned himself, his values, his morals, nor his association with humanity. Not like he did when she was snatched away from that limousine and flown away while he stood back and basically watched it happen. This was deeper than her big brother accusing him of exploiting Tiri for his position. Nah, this shit was intravenous. Bottomless. Another fabrication that he couldn't control and Steelo hated being boxed into a situation that he didn't have the ability to overthrow, so he fought his way out of it and decided that his time with Tiri had expired.

She wasn't fit for this lifestyle, and his heart was too clogged; deadly plagued in every vessel and artery needed to tumefy once he allowed her admiration to fill him, so he too could harvest the same love he knew she needed in return from him. His argument may have sounded convincing, but Steelo didn't realize how he was blocking his blessings and going heads up against God with the affliction of his past being the driving force. Steelo didn't understand how to channel his emotions when he'd grown accustomed to being alone for twenty years. He was confusing himself. One minute he picked up the phone to call a truce and the next, his reflection in the mirror haunting him with that blazing stare forced him to toss that damn phone across the room and pace his home to ease the tension.

Up and down.

Steelo's emotions were like a seesaw that he couldn't seem to balance because he was missing that smiling face who should've been sitting across from him to help enjoy the ride.

But he was the roadblock.

He was the reason.

The cause.

The downfall.

Guilty.

Selfish.

Afraid.

Scared.

Too weak.

My God, a man who reigned supreme over the most dangerous city in the country, had the inability to regulate his own heart, and it killed him. What a fucking weakness of all things to have?

The cool jam gliding against his scalp was soothing as Kovu braided the first out of the two plaits that would give his top knot a little more life, since he didn't plan on rocking a fade anytime soon. They sat in silence. Kovu had shit on her mind, and it was clear that Steelo was also deep in thought.

It was a rare Friday night when the entire family was present. Marius was running around with the rug rats; Jayce sprinting across the floor with nothing on but a saggy Cruiser Pamper; Kovu couldn't wait until he was done with that got damn box because she hated the hang time on those damn things. He was sucking on the binky in his mouth that she tried her damndest to wean him off of too, but that was easier said than done. Aubrey hated clothes too, so she donned nothing but panties and two scruffy puff balls with her name necklace on, rough housing with her boys. Reba Koi sat in the corner knitting while watching the show as Chef Koi whipped up dinner.

Their blended family wasn't perfect, but it was theirs, and for the first time in a while, Steelo realized no matter how unfortunate his cards were dealt as a youth, he still wounded up with a family. It was a blessing.

"I'm trippin', ain't I, KD?" he blurted to interrupt the silence.

"You already know you are. There's no need to confirm it." She used the tip of her acrylic nail to separate the starting piece of his second braid. "You're acting immature about it. That girl ain't done nothing but loved you and got into it with her whole family over you, just for yo' ass to do some ignorant shit like this."

Steelo knew KD would always give it to him nice and raw. Her ass didn't sugarcoat shit.

"Gotta face the facts, young blood. Love is stronger than animosity. *I'm* married."

Marius offered his two cents while lying on his back, tossing Aubrey in the air while Jayce climbed over him like a jungle gym.

"Not for much longer, nigga," Kovu uttered while sucking her teeth.

"Aye, I heard that. Don't get fucked up, KD."

"Watch your mouth around them babies, Marius."

"Yes, ma'am."

Steelo chuckled. Reba Koi was the mother neither of them in this room ever had. She was heaven-sent.

"Kids, y'all momma gon' get A, B, C, D, E, F'd up if she think she going somewhere," he reiterated.

"Marius, wasn't nobody even talking to you, so shut up."

"I ain't doing this shit wit' y'all today," Steelo laughed.

"Nuri."

"My bad, love."

"Reba Koi, tell him to apologize to Tiri for being an asshole. A month is unacceptable," KD challenged while twisting his knot tight like a Japanese bun.

"She's right, baby. Pride is a man's weakest link. Have you checked up on her?"

"NOPE! He lucky Válo good peoples and still been rocking with her. See, Marius knows better. It's y'all young niggas who don't know cat shit from apple butter."

"So you just gon' let KD sit here and pop off like that Reba Koi?" Steelo smiled.

"Kovu can do no wrong in my eyes, but *you,* young man, *do* need to get it together. She's young and vibrant. These men out here fight for a woman like her. Luck had nothing to do with her falling into your hands. Don't be a fool and drop the ball. Too late comes much faster than you'd think."

Steelo ran his hands down his face, sighing with defeat. If only it were that easy not to follow the hollow heart of his that's always ran the show for so many years. How do you just all of a sudden counteract with innate actions? He needed to smoke. A sober mind wasn't his best of friends at the moment.

"Y'all ready to eat?

Chef Koi appeared in the doorway with a hand towel draped over his shoulder after slaving over a hot stove for his family. Reba Koi could get pregnant, but she'd never made it to full term. Even after six tries and being on bed rest as the doctor ordered, her every fetus seemed to never make it past the five-month mark.

Chef Koi hated that he couldn't give his wife the one thing they both always wanted, and after a while, they decided that God knew what was best and moved forward with their marriage. When Kovu entered Marius' life, it was a blessing in disguise. Being a new mother was hard on her, and with Tammy being absent, Reba Koi eagerly jumped in to assist with the upbringing of the kiddos.

The Koi's were the babies' Godparents and it not only brought them joy to finally participate in parenthood, but dealing with Marius, when his alter ego was tucked away, Steelo's as well, and petty ass KD, they had an entire tribe to keep up with and wouldn't change this experience for the world.

"Eat-eat, daddy!"

Marius kissed Aubrey's cheek before he sat up.

"Come on, let's go eat-eat, lil' momma. Let's roll, big man."

"I don't need a big plate, Koi. I'm going out so I'll just get enough to put something on my stomach," Kovu expressed with a yawn after standing up.

Marius turned around with his brow raised like Ike Turner.

"You *what*?"

His wife mushed him in the head as she walked past him, ignoring his comment.

Steelo wondered if that's how he looked at Tiri whenever she popped off with some slick shit. He wondered if he got lost in her beauty with her daydreaming eyes as his brother from another mother did when KD came around. Endless wonders piled his frontal lobe each and every time he witnessed the love he'd watched them build over the years. In all honesty, being their 24/7 spectator gave him hope, which is why he couldn't get both feet out the door when it came to his chocolate drop that he missed to the ends of the earth.

"Come on, Ri-Ri. We need to get out of this house. You've been moping around long enough."

Ceas tugged on Tiri's arm, trying to pry her out of bed. Tiri agreed earlier in the day when her, KD, and Ceas all decided to step out tonight, but now that the time was near, the only thing she wanted to do was lay in bed and watch Netflix until she drifted off to sleep.

"Ceas," she protested.

"No!"

Caesar snatched the blanket from off of her and sat Tiri up on the side of the bed.

"Get up, brush ya damn teeth for the first time in forever and put some damn clothes on. Be ready in an hour or else I'mma drag you out the house just like that; food all over that damn baggy ass shirt, matted hair, and all."

"Bitch, my hair is not matted."

"Coulda' fooled me. Now come on."

Tiri laughed as Ceas switched her cute little booty out the room, wearing nothing but a bra and a thong with her makeup half done and her hair in sponge rollers. Had it not been for her pushy demeanor, Tiri would've rotted away in this room for the last month. When she made it back in town, Steelo's ignorant ass wouldn't even let her in the house. Válo had to bring all of her things to the residence where Caesar was still staying at amid the shooting, and that cut her deeper than anything she'd ever felt since losing her folks. He was acting like a bratty ass, emotional bitch; and the more she thought about it, she was starting to realize that he had some unresolved personal issues that she refused to allow him to direct towards her.

No, fuck that.

Tiri climbed out of bed, showered, then threw some sexy shit on. Steelo could be the only attendee at his bogus ass pity party from now on. She was getting sick of his shit. It was time for her to get back into the swing of things, and if that meant blossoming without him, then so be it.

"Sus, y'all ready?"

Tiri was spraying finishing midst to her perfectly beat face when Válo's chirp came through on her Apple Watch. They'd been thick as thieves since their quality time in St. Louis, and she now had another brother she could faithfully call on.

"Yup, we about to come out now."

"A'ight."

"Well hot-damn, Malibu Black Barbie! Go the fuck awwwwwwwf then!"

Tiri stuck her tongue out and yelped an, "eeeeeoooooow!" in her best Cardi B impersonation while twerking in the six-inch, Versace glass slippers. The silver crystal mini dress clung to her shape perfectly. The spaghetti strapped, V-neck, halter cut out bust showcased just enough of her cleavage where Fenty shimmer body butter caressed her skin. A split went high up her left hip, stopping at her waist where three crystal chains connected from the V-shaped front of the dress to the back.

Baby girl was wearing more skin than clothes, but so the fuck what. It was her nineteenth birthday and couldn't anybody tell her shit. Her hair was styled in a messy, loose curly, blunt cut bob parted down the middle with large diamond hoop earrings to add that pop with her voluminous, jet black, and natural tresses. With a coat of clear lip gloss enhancing her pouty lips and a soft purple blended perfectly with glittery silver eyeshadow, Tiri was looking like the baddest bitch in town, and she owned that shit.

The limousine was filled with a dozen Happy Birthday balloons when she and Ceas climbed inside along with Válo, Kovu, Salt, and Terrell's wife Asia, who was finally in town after months spent in Egypt doing further research on the pyramids of Giza. The plan was to stop at a bar and pregame with a couple rounds of shots, but with the way they were passing around Ace and D'USSÉ on the commute, by the time they'd arrived at the strip club, everyone was already lit before the official celebration began.

Club *Ass States* was a multi-million dollar establishment that's been flourishing now for seven years. One of Marius' greatest investments. Mr. Monstrosity was a sucker for ass and ass shaking. Something about those tall heels, fishnets, and long weave drove him wilder than his Heath Ledger, "The Joker," persona did. Before he crossed paths with Kovu, the booty club was his guilty pleasure. But best believe if him and his wife weren't at the crib jamming with their own little private party in their mini Strip club down in the basement, then they were out popping bottles and enjoying the show as a team when they had the night off from the kiddos.

Kovu pitched the idea to celebrate here since it was not only last minute, but for a while, Tiri's sad ass swore up and down that she wasn't doing shit today until they got her straight. Tiri's never been to the strip club before, and she'd always wanted to see some entertainment live versus on social media videos.

Luxury hardly described the transparent, glass interior palace. 24/7, *Ass States* brought the city of Trinity a winter wonderland that their part of the country rarely got the chance to see. The finest bitches from tall and frail chocolate baddies to the thickest and most confident BBW's were in the building. Women danced on the ceilings from ropes, extravagant jungle bars connected each section of the club where they also got their dance on, and a few, ten-foot tall martini glass statues were scattered throughout the club where women danced from the inside with foam bubbles surrounding them.

Tiri was amazed. Her head was so far gone that Kovu had to give her a tour around the building while the gang grabbed a booth upstairs in the VIP section that overlooked the club. A night out is just what the doctor ordered, and Tiri would surely let her hair down. Every track that spun, the chocolate goddess was spitting them lyrics like she wrote the shit herself into Ceas' camera who was recording her every move. Everything about Tiri was flawless tonight from her highlight down to her pedicured, peach painted toes.

Niggas from the lower level were sending endless bottles and messages up to her section like crazy, loving how she stole the center of attention that night. The gangstas desperately wanted a taste of the cocoa, not knowing that the silly shit would come to an immediate halt the moment Mr. Krabby Patty, King Nuri P, himself walked through the door with Marius and Terrell in tow.

It took a little more pep talk from his married potnas to make Steelo realize that women like Tiri only came around in certain seasons and he needed to right his wrongs. That's all it really was to it.

Steelo never had to do much whenever the time called for him to get fly, but for his baby's birthday he decided to ice himself out with three Cuban linked chains, two rose gold and the middle piece silver as they aligned his neck in a tri-level fashion. His left wrist was decked out with three corresponding cuff links and the right with a fly ass Richard Millie wristwatch, designed with a rose gold face.

234

The black, Christian Dior, linen button-down worn partly unbuttoned with no undershirt, and the Dior cargo pants that stopped above his ankles to display his Dolce and Gabbana Sorrento slippers was an excellent and edgy, though clean look for him. His line up and fade was fresh, mustache had gotten thicker as it perfectly outlined his insatiable jaw structure that drove women wild, Dior round-framed shades shielded his eyes, and Tiri could instantly smell his *Sauvage* cologne once she felt his presence in the building.

It could've been all of the weed and liquor in her system, but baby knew when her man was around. His aura was filled with such an eminence that it shook niggas in rooms where his feet had never been in before. She did a quick scan around the building, disappointed that her intoxication was playing with her emotions before she jumped back into turning up. A naked bottle girl soon bought out a large tray with sparkles firing to their section. Her eyes got glossy when she saw the number 19 shaped with vanilla cupcakes and lavender icing that Chef Koi had prepared for the night.

Tiri couldn't believe she was surrounded by so much genuine love when for years she walked around as an outcast because bitches were too damn jealous to attempt to build a friendship with her. She was boohooing like a little baby with all eyes and cameras on her as they sang happy birthday.

That is, until *their* eyes finally met.

Everything around her stopped when he climbed over the last step leading to their section. The insides of Tiri's legs reacted to Steelo's appearance with the snap of a finger; her clit instantly twitching and catching convulsions, begging those full pink lips he'd just habitually licked, to lick and suck her into an orgasmic coma right then and there.

Steelo's heartbeat grew erratic as he made it closer in distance to the most beautiful woman in the room with one of her gifts in hand. His mouth dying to trail kisses up those long and lean legs of hers. From her fingertips to her neckline and jawbone. Then down to her breasts, along her washboard abs and her pussy lips until he made it to the pink pearl that only reacted to his adjure.

Tiri was all his. Every part of her body. Every hair on her head, and he was torn between the world needing to accept that shit, to him not being so afraid of losing her when he knew she'd already been bagged and tagged.

Ceas' man candy, who was also in attendance, held her around the waist as she cheesed into the camera. Excitement filled her watching Steelo grace Tiri's neck with an exquisite million dollar diamond necklace. It was crafted into an upside-down tear shape that ended with a deep purple ruby centerpiece. The surrounding gemstones suspended lavishly with 18k gold branches that housed cushion cut, pear-shaped, oval, and Asscher-cut diamonds, giving the jewel a dainty rose vine effect. Steelo put some muthafucking ice on his baby, giving a damn about the price.

What other or better way was there to say *I'm sorry,* knowing that diamonds were a girl's best friend?

Tiri was speechless. The necklace radiated amongst the ceiling, adding a beautiful effect with the atmosphere. She wrapped her arms around Steelo's neck when he pulled her into his embrace after snapping a picture of her looking like nothing short of royalty. Low-key, he was just happy to have his girl back.

They were a beautiful pair; merging together perfectly, them each bringing to the table what the other lacked and damn it that's what you called a blessing.

Tiri melted in his arms as he held her close; one hand gripping that ass and the other clinging onto her waist. She loved him so much and didn't give a damn who was there to judge what her heart felt for this man. As long as they were on the same accord, then that other bullshit was above her.

Tiri knew that she and her man needed to have a sit down and get a few things off their chest, but there was a time and place for everything. She couldn't see his eyes behind his shades as he sexily chewed on a piece of Double Mint gum, but from the looks of it, he was high as a damn kite, homegirl was both, and the music was live.

By now, everyone in their crowd was boo'd up, doing their own thing in their own personal bubbles outside of passing the three blunts that were in rotation. Tiri was glued to Steelo's lap, mouthing to the Cardi B the DJ kept in rotation until that "Ice on My Baby" by Yung Bleu filled the air. Any one of his melodies could spin, and Tiri was instantly enchanted via the voice of his that's always connected her heart to Steelo's.

That booty-shaking beat dropped as the chorus began and every woman in their section started grinding on their man's wood on cue. Steelo sat back vibing to the beat with a blunt in his mouth watching Tiri work that shit. Good Lord, she looked so fucking good in this got-damn dress that he could hardly control himself from ripping it off of her so he could feast upon her Nutella.

A pole was stationed off to the side of the booth, closer to their end of the couch and Tiri had too much liquor in her system to hold back what she was feeling. She could sense Steelo's eyes locked and loaded on her legs, ass, and hips as she climbed the platform. Hell, KD was straddled in Marius' lap, a zipper away from riding his dick, Válo was tonguing Salt down with his hand up the back of her dress as she sat outstretched across his lap, Ceas' little rachet self was bent over between Glenn's legs touching her toes, and Asia's drunk ass was standing on the couch with her shoes off, dancing between Terrell's legs. Nobody was gonna outdo her on her damn birthday, so she had to dance for her man.

Each and every day Tiri was growing into a high-toned and seductive woman, and that shit kept Steelo's dick solid like it was now. So when she grabbed that pole and swung around it with her hair flying and those ass cheeks clapping in her dress, he was her number one fan. By the time Tiri turned her back to him, dropped it low and started popping that ass while running her fingers through her hair, Steelo was up on his feet with hundred dollar bills fluttering around her as the smoke from his blunt fogged the atmosphere. Tiri kilt that shit. Her body would make a snake envious the way she slithered with grace and threw her hips with her hands caressing her curves.

Steelo was stuck in a trance standing there sipping on his drink watching her move. She flowed to the lyrics with poise; a sexiness that had his dick bulging. Man, shorty was riding that beat like Floetry as she licked her lips, veering into his soul with those big, doe-shaped eyes of hers; her charm was effortless mixed with the way she kept twirling around and showing out until she stepped down and hopped up into his arms.

When Yung Bleu sang, "We gon' fuck all night, she drive me crazy," Tiri felt that shit deep down inside of her soul. She was gonna fuck this man all night because it drove her crazy being away from him for so long...as if their spirits weren't tied.

Young Tiri didn't remember anything else that happened at the club once the track was over. In the blink of an eye, she and Steelo were on a G6 with a destination unknown because she was too busy laying back getting her pussy ate. The liquor set in her system like a ticking time bomb patiently waiting to go off. Steelo had her chocolate legs kicked in the air as he licked on places that she could've sworn he'd never ventured before. His tongue twirled around the inside of her opening while he slurped up her honey before using two of his fingers to bring her pleasure so his mouth could return to her juicy nub. She dripped with bliss. One of her breasts were exposed while Steelo used his free hand to pinch and tug on her budding nipple and it made her body shutter. Mixed with the elation that filled her from him groaning against her flesh, Tiri was spent, and her serum was crashing onto his wanting tongue.

He had her cumming back to back at a rate that made Tiri's body fog with fatigue. She could taste blood from gnawing down so hard on her bottom lip as she watched her man French kiss her kitty cat with his eyes closed. A rush crept up her spine, causing Tiri to buss' once again while screaming his name like it was going out of style.

Steelo missed this pussy. The way it got wet for him. The way it blossomed then coiled around his shaft. He missed the way she'd climb on top of his face, and he'd suck on her clit from behind as she held onto the headboard or the back of the couch. His hand eagerly pumping the hard dick of his until she was dripping with too much desire, yearning for the need of him enter her.

Tiri's nectar was so sweet her name should've been at the top of every diabetic's "Foods to steer away from" list. He was like a beastly animal who couldn't get enough of its prey, so Steelo zoned in and focused solely on her taste. A flavor too fucking delightful to share with the rest of the world or any other man on this earth as long as he was breathing. Marius warned Steelo and looked him in the eye when he advised him not to fall submissive to madness when it came to his love for young Tiri. He didn't understand that shit a few hours ago, but now as he licked on her flesh, letting his tongue do all of the apologizing for him, Steelo realized that he *did* love her.

He was madly in love with Tiri, and that's why his soul was drenched in hesitation. He loved no one. Not a soul. Not the way that he cherished the sweet little angel that wasn't ready to endure the aftermath of all of his pain and suffering. He didn't want to expose her to the side of his heart that kept pushing him away, but Steelo was selfish and wanted her in every way, shape, or form no matter what it took.

No matter how often his emotions fluctuated.

He knew he was unstable.

Steelo knew that it was a struggle trying to maintain a healthy and normal lifestyle that was strife free, but when he looked at Tiri? Like he was doing now after sliding his rigid soldier so deep that she had to inhale and brace herself for the pleasurable pulverizing, she was seconds away from receiving. One look into her eyes and the way that heavenly smile of hers softened up his heart, it gave Steelo the strength and motivation to make those changes he so desperately needed.

"I'm sorry, Tiri..."

Her eyes crossed from the mixture of his sincerity, his heartfelt apology, and the deep panting that was serenading in her ear. The rumors about "I'm sorry dick" were all true got damn it. His stroke game felt deeper, more intense though so heavily magnetic that her pussy reacted without her say so and she was showering the dick of his that continued to work her middle.

"I know it's a lot to ask," he panted in the midst of licking and sucking along her earlobe and neck. "I swear I'll give you the world if you just be patient wit' me, mama, *shit...*"

Steelo's heart was vulnerable in the moment. A portion of it had something to do with the gooey and silky pool of chocolate heroin that his dick eagerly, though sensually, obtruded in and out of. Only with her permission to do so, of course.

He was raw.

Unfiltered.

Defeated.

Chained to the luxury and possibility of having a promising future with this woman. As long as he yielded to the peace treaty needed to grant him with the access to her everlasting love, then that's what he'd do. He wanted a foundation so solid with this woman that his fears and doubts wouldn't easily break it. He needed a miracle. He needed God; someone he hadn't called on for as long as he could remember, and Steelo knew it was absurd of him to neglect God when it had been His grace that kept him alive and well. Even with the lifestyle he led.

"Baby, you've gotta have more faith in me..."

Tiri's words were faint, but they were sound; so sound that it caused Steelo to pause and look down at her as his chains dangled around his neck. Her eyes were firing like two beautiful Hennessy brown stars as she held him by the face with both hands. Tiri's thumbs glided over his bushy eyebrows, her favorite thing to do, as she flashed him a soft grin, knowing he was taken back by her response.

"It may seem, naïve of me or even dubious." She bit her bottom lip, trying her best not to get swept away in how sexy he was hovering over her. The muscles in his ripped arms bulging, that smooth marigold colored skin of his, and the way his lips just sat there, begging for another kiss. "But I'll do anything for you; anything that's in the bracket of my values and morals of course, but what I'm saying is, don't fabricate things between us with thoughts and scenarios that haven't even, and nine times out of ten, *won't* even happen. You're tryna put this fire out between us, baby; just let that shit burn. I'm with you through everything and I've shown you that. I just need your heart to be on the same page."

Tiri was on the nose with her expressions, causing his chest to tighten because the truth was also present in her eyes. It's not the fact that Steelo couldn't put Tiri together; that he'd already done. It was the fact that she was so damn intimidating and threatening. *That* was the shit that pushed his suspension. She was the ultimate challenge that he couldn't physically bring himself to complete, and for that push to do so, he'd always *love* her.

A groan escaped Tiri's lips when Steelo leaned in and deeply kissed her, their tongues colliding in ripples as his thrusts started back up. He'd heard and understood her loud and clear, but until he was one hundred percent ready to be *that open* with her, he'd continue to make sweet love to her body until their plane landed at their destination.

HUFR

Geni hated walking in the shadows of another man. He'd done so all of his life. Geni loved his father with every bone in his body, but he too hesitated in handing over the throne that he so rightfully deserved. He couldn't understand it, but at this point, it wasn't meant to be understood. Tables have turned, bridges were burned, and an alliance was already in effect.

He made the mistake once by treading softly when he was given orders to hold off on The Monstrosity, just for him to end up in prison. He'd be no fool the second time around. Geni might've came up out of fifty M's to secure his spot in the game, but he was sure that once Marius was handled that his new "business partner" would be too.

One thing he learned from studying The Monstrosity was to always let your opponent believe that he was a few steps ahead of you before going in for the kill. Hell, they could've been a great team putting the city of Trinity into a recession if they both weren't two heartless, carnivorous savages, but since Marius wanted a war then he'd gladly be served with a plate of disaster since he was riding around like shit was just so kosher these days.

After his meeting with his visitor, Geni caught a plane out to Ireland to catch up with his family: kiss and make love to his wife, play with his children, and have a few beers with his best friends who were watching over his family in his absence.

Christmas was around the corner, and with the way their war tactics were balancing on a quiet beam, he decided to take advantage of his getaway and get started on the mile-long Christmas list that his girls were eager to see fulfilled once Santa did his nightly drop off. Geni was never really a holiday person himself, but his wife was the most festive person he knew, and just like any other man in this world, he followed suit and forked over the cash once he received the bill.

Geni called Alma to let her know that he'd be home in an hour to see her and the girls for dinner after checking in on the O'Sullivan Pharmaceutical warehouses to make sure that everything with their next delivery was up to par, but she didn't answer. He found it a little strange since she was always glued to the phone, anticipating his next call and wanting to know how things were in America. So her missed call definitely raised a red flag.

Shit, speaking of red flags, he couldn't remember the last time he'd spoken to her in three days since he'd been so busy.

"Straight to the house, eh."

His driver nodded his head in agreement as Geni fixed himself another drink. He prayed that it all was in his head and his uneasiness was taunting him simply because his hands were tied, and his army was waiting like sitting ducks under, yet another man's say so. The bottle of whiskey at his disposal was a swig away from being empty when the driver finally pulled up to his estate.

Dublin was a beautiful city cascaded with ancient cobblestone pavement, pubs on every corner, and the traditional building formation that resembled other cities with the Victorian architecture coining their real estate enchantress.

Geni's Victorian styled mansion gave the St. Mary's Pro-Cathedral a run for its money with its eight pillar, house front design. Along with the enormous and impressive sculptures of Irish promenades all made using the lost wax technique in bronze and hand finished with a precious patina in light green hue, the view was breathtaking. His Ferragamo slippers created a melody against the cobblestone until he climbed the stairs with a bouquet of red roses for his wife, daisies for his princesses, and a bottle of wine to enjoy over one of Alma's exquisite cuisines.

A faint smell hit Geni's nose the moment he opened the front door, causing him to drop the items in his hands and withdraw his .38 Special revolver. The smell grew even more sickening as he crossed over the foyer and headed to the dining room where one, low voltage light was lit. When Geni flipped the switch, tears trickled down his pale cheeks as he fell to his knees and released a scream filled with rage. Hurt, perplexed, and disgusted were only a handful of adjectives to throw out there, hardly describing what this man was feeling.

Chunky, white vomit climbed his throat and spewed from out of his mouth onto the eggshell-colored carpet floor that was soaked in three-day old blood. His wife, daughters, and best friends' bodies were all seated at the table, tied up to their chairs with their heads detached. Each of their heads were lined up across the dinner table on silver platters with apples in their mouths, eyes visibly crossed because their lids were wedged open due to rigor mortis. Blood dripped into the carpet from off the sides of the table and from all of their chairs.

Geni threw up again, this time more brown than white vomit emitting from his lips, a mixture of now whiskey and the steamed veggies and potatoes that were eaten on board his flight, the taste intruding his mouth followed by the horrid bile that didn't add a welcoming fragrance when combined with the decaying bodies. His eyes flushed red when he noticed the words *Round Three* carved into his wife's forehead.

Marius allowed that nigga to believe he had his army on search for people in Trinity that he knew damn well wasn't there. Shit was a scare tactic. While Geni and company were so damn busy laughing and drinking to his quote-unquote "foolery" earlier that day, three nights ago, Marius, Steelo, and Válo personally paid his people's a nice fucking visit. Marius had a family himself but fuck the element of sentiment. Who was sentimental when they ran up on Steelo and Tiri? Who the fuck was sentimental at Tammy's house? Threatening his family was the lowest blow you could possibly make against him, and Mr. Usher got real petty when it was time for him to get his lick back.

Since they were playing *12 Rounds,* level three not only had his name on it, but so did rounds four and five once Geni developed the courage to walk upstairs. He not only realized that he'd been robbed of the deeds to the O'Sullivan pharmacological companies, but his mother's ventilator had been unplugged as well, instead of lying in bed with a decapitated head and a dismantled shriveled body like Marius intended on doing before his heart gave in a bit. The blow of his people seated at the table was enough to show this nigga that shit changed over squalid.

Round number six nigga.

Where the fuck ya' at?

Heart Up For Ransom

Taug Jaye

"I know you've been through more than most of us."

-Jhene Aiko

Heart Up For Ransom

Chapter

13

Four Season's resort, Bali @ Sayan

T he air in Bali was crisp; as if the trees deeply rooted in their sacred grounds gave off a source of oxygen and energy that was too precious for the United States to possess.

6:00 A.M.

Every morning Steelo was up at the crack of dawn despite what time zone he traveled to. When God said rise and be thankful for your daily awakening, the blessing was never taken for granted.

Tiri slept peacefully in their master bed; her moderate sized breasts exposed as she laid on her back, eyes half open, lips pursed, one arm above her head, and the other resting against her mahogany colored skin. It caused Steelo to chuckle as he sat across from her along the modern styled loveseat. His bare feet were propped up amongst the ottoman as the pencil in his left hand shaded in her wild and frizzy hair that his fingers have been intertwined within since they left the states.

He bet she didn't even remember them landing in the wee hours of the night since the time zones were evidently different and she was fucking wasted. *He* remembered cradling her long body in his arms after they arrived at the hotel and checked in. During that first take when she somehow came back to life for a good twelve minutes, like she'd done multiple times throughout her off and on drunken coma, Tiri acted a fool when she dropped down to her knees and sucked his dick like she was auditioning for the #SHEAWINNER cucumber contest. That was one round he'd never forget.

He'd nut twice when she put that sloppy toppy on his ass that go around, and he'd never experienced such greatness.

Both of their clothing from her birthday celebration were scattered around the bedroom, shit was knocked over; her pussy juices stained the end tables, the sheets, the couches, and no matter how many times Steelo had washed his face, he could still smell the remnants from her sexual prowess embedded amongst his top lip.

He underestimated young Tiri. She hung all night until she hopped up out of bed an hour ago once they'd finally fallen asleep and he was holding her hair back while she vomited cupcakes and D'USSÉ into the toilet. She brought her nineteenth birthday in going hard on the paint, and her man surely wouldn't let it stop there.

Steelo was shading in the purple ruby hanging from her neckpiece since its all she wore other than the white bed sheet covering only a portion of her legs, when Tiri groaned and started to stir in her sleep. He didn't understand how she'd always been so comfortable sleeping on her back. The shit gave him nightmares. Tiri squirmed a little more, her left hand reaching over on the other side of the bed hoping to feel his nice and warm body next to hers, but she didn't.

Something didn't feel right. With her memory failing her and not knowing what the hell happened after they left the club except for those sinful licks against her swollen clit and his thick dick further turning her out, Tiri sprang up out of her sleep and frantically looked around until her eyes landed on a chuckling Steelo.

"What's funny?" she groaned with a half-smile while scratching her itchy scalp.

Steelo didn't respond. Instead, he watched her climb out of bed, her breasts slightly bouncing with each step she took, her radiant skin glowing in the sun rays, and those engaging hips swaying from side to side as she entered the bathroom. She took her time handling her hygiene, then made her way back over to him. Tiri made herself comfy at his side, resting her head on his chest as he put his arm around her and kissed her forehead.

"You barely slept," he spoke in a low tone, his hand rubbing on her bottom.

"I feel like I got hit by a car."

Steelo chuckled.

"Mu'fuckas turned the fuck up last night."

"I'm mu'fuckas?" She joined his laughter. "Wait, first things first. Where are we?"

"Bali."

Tiri's eyes magnified. There was no way in hell they went from Trinity to Indonesia in one night.

"Wait, wait, wait. How long were we on the plane? I know I didn't sleep the whole way here, did I?"

"Nah, not the whole way, but you ate this dick for a good fourteen out of sixteen hours though."

She playfully pushed him in his bare chest while sucking on her thumb. It was a sporadic habit. Faint then vivid memories started coming back to Tiri of them rumbling around the G6, sipping champagne, and laying up naked as they were doing now. The insides of her legs were sore yet still tingled from the excitement.

"Missed you, Steelo." Her voice was soft as she grabbed his hand and kissed it before looking at his sketchbook. "Never! Is that me?"

Steelo handed her the pad so she could further observe his work. It wasn't nearly finished, but her long and lean, velvety chocolate frame in 3D amongst the manila paper was an amazing sight to see. Steelo drew whenever he was up for it, which was rare, but he couldn't resist the beauty of her lying in bed.

"I do sleep with my eyes open."

"What, you thought I was lying?"

"Um, yes." Her eyes were glossy. Steelo paid her more attention than she thought so. It was majestic in her opinion. "This is so dope, babe, like really. I love it already."

It reminded her of that famous scene from the *Titanic* when Jack drew his dear Rose. Tiri knew she'd always treasure it.

"Still got a long way to go, but shit, if you like it, then I love it." He sipped his mimosa, concocted with more top-shelf champagne than orange juice before saying, "And I missed you too."

"Did you really?"

"Don't start with them stupid ass questions, Tiri."

"Just answer it," she pouted.

She knew Steelo hated to repeat himself, but Tiri loved it when he reiterated his feelings for her. It was self assuring and fulfilling.

"Yeah, I really missed you, girl. What I'mma lie for?"

"Then why'd you put me out? I swear you're worse than a male Cancer and a Taurus put together sometimes."

Knock-knock!

Steelo was luckily saved by the bell with the knock to their door. He tossed Tiri a sheet then slipped into his boxer/briefs that were lying next to one of the end tables before letting the bellboy in with their fifteen foot table spread. Breakfast was set up with fresh sliced fruit, coconuts filled with Pina colada mimosas, diced smothered potatoes, pancakes, waffles, bacon, sausage, eggs, and fresh salmon fillets. Tiri's stomach growled the moment her nose caught a whiff of the delightful fumes. After using the bathroom once again, she was greeted to a tray with a plate and a drink prepared by her man before he went and fixed his own.

She fueled up on the starches to soak up as much liquor as possible to hopefully ale her headache.

"Come on. Let's go outside."

Tiri took a quick sip of her drink before grabbing her tray and followed behind him. Their view was stunning. An infinity pool surrounded the lounge area of their villa as the tallest and pure, deep green Sayan Valley treetops circled around their skyscraper residence. They ate breakfast in silence, taking in their enthralling private sanctuary while getting faded too. The nature in Bali was gentle. Soothing; calming to each of the senses, the mind, body, and the spirit. Steelo had flown his woman out to paradise, and it eluded a sense of peace that they'd both been missing.

Half an hour went by as they casually enjoyed the scene and the chirping birds while jamming to a few throwback R&B tunes. That is, until Tiri's closet freak was suddenly rebirthed, thanks to the Mary Jane.

She eyed Steelo sitting across from her: legs open, balls out, one arm outstretched along the back of the full sized lounge chair. That thick dick of his hanging down his thigh, even in its flaccid nature. She was getting hot for him. Tiri never in a million years would've imagined the burning rage to sit on and suck a man's dick the way she did when it came to her Steelo. She could feel her nipples hardening and her nub gyrating at the thoughts of letting her tongue circle around the tip of that monster before she French kissed and swallowed it.

Steelo saw her looking. He recognized the intensity in her eyes, so with the blunt hanging out the edge of his lips, he gripped his wood with his free hand and started stroking it for her. Tiri had a sick obsession with the way he beat his meat; the sight would almost make her cum instantly. She lived for his sporadic, explicit videos and hearing her own voice hit an octave once he let that nut go. And like the freak he was, he'd then massage it against his thick, hard wood, and keep stroking because he knew it made her pussy drip.

Steelo looked her in the eye as his hand pumped up and down his ten-inch shaft, his dick elongating with each second he continued while Tiri played in her pussy for him.

She then stood up and climbed onto his lounge chair, sexily crawling over to him with a nice heaping of saliva building up in her mouth until she let her emissions drip all over his flesh. Her heart raced as he increased his speed, now catching a steady rhythm. A little WD-40 always seemed to do the trick, and now a swishing noise filled the air followed by a low, though gut-wrenching, grunt from the pit of his stomach. Tiri wrapped her lips around the head as he stroked the base, making a popping sound each time she released him as if he were her favorite watermelon flavored Blow Pop.

When she removed his hand, Steelo got comfortable as she pulled her hair behind her ears and hungrily looked in his eyes.

"You turned me into your dirty little whore, Steelo. I love it..."

His dick then disappeared down her throat as Tiri bobbed her head with style and grace all over him. Her tongue twirled around his rod like a moderate paced windmill as saliva trickled out the corners of her mouth. Tiri went from having shark teeth to being young gummy on the salami in a matter of tries, and now she'd been giving him some of the best head he's ever had. No cap.

Steelo's teeth were grinding as he watched her saturate his nuts before taking them in her mouth. She started gargling as if she were trying to make her dentist proud. Tiri loved how it felt swirling his sacs around her wet tongue, knowing from the muscles showing in his legs that her man's toes were curling from the pleasure. What felt ten times better was when she inched that monstrous meat down her throat and held him captive; the blood in his shaft rushing so immensely, the hypertension in his dick caused him to pulsate against her esophagus. He'd throw his hips forward, shoving himself so deep that Tiri could've sworn she felt the tip of him tapping against her chest.

She exhaled deeply after releasing that thick dick, glaring at that wood coated with a clear glaze as pre-cum oozed out of his third eye. Tiri licked it all up, using one hand to smear it up and down his length before she continued making love to him with her warm and slippery abode.

Steelo soon stood to his feet as his little slut got up on her knees. He wanted to watch his dick thrust between her "O" shaped lips while she squeezed her breasts and played with her clit. He held onto the back of her neck with both hands, steadily puffing on the blunt that was still burning, fogging up the atmosphere. Tiri opened wide and let him fuck her face, gagging when he reached a certain depth of her throat. Her sticky right hand rolled his balls like two dice to ensure that he scored a lucky number seven when he was ready to shoot off. He was the greatest taste of sin. She could give this man head for the rest of her life if he asked her to.

"Where you want me to nut at, mama..."

Steelo's words got choked up in his throat as Tiri pushed her breasts together and slid his rigid instrument between them after it slipped out of her aperture. His chest rose and fell in slow motion at the sight of his dick working in and out of her slippery tits. He had to take over and pinch her nipples; twirl them between his thumbs and index fingers before picking up his speed at the feeling of him about to explode.

"On my face...in my mouth...on my lips...between my girls...pick a spot, baby. No matter what, I'mma still lick all that shit up..."

"Ahhhhh, shit!"

Steelo swore that girl always knew what to say and just at the precise moment. He skeeted his cream onto her chin, some of it in her mouth, a nice heaping on her lips, and as he pulled out of her bosom, he left another lovely trail of his kids down her chest. She held her mouth open knowing her man had a little more of his essence left and felt her cervix contract as he sexily stroked the remnants onto her tongue.

Bali's beauty was unmatched in Tiri's eyes. After letting her man plunge her pussy and pull her hair from the back during their morning shower, they hit the Indonesian streets and enjoyed the countless festivities that would take their entire six day stay to put a dent in. Tiri admired her man's regression when it came to them. To their relationship.

Nothing was too lame, no experience was omitted, and when they traveled this enormous world as one, Steelo's mind wasn't just open, but he was focused.

Engaging. Existing.

Both of their cameras getting full from enjoying their tours at the Sacred Monkey Forest Sanctuary and the Ancient Hindu Uluwatu Sea Temple with water views that evoked her voice as if Queen Ursula ruled that part of the ocean. Towards sunset, they acted their shoe sizes versus their numerical ages and rode every slide, raft, and slippery attraction at the Waterbom Bali Indonesia Waterpark.

The soles of Tiri's feet burned like a raging fire when they turned in that night. Just to enjoy a five star Balinese dinner at the Four Season's bistro, then make love on their balcony and into the sunrising hours of the morning until they began with an endless day of shopping at the Beachwalk Center.

Tiri felt sorry for their poor driver who made endless trips back and forth carrying her Chanel, souvenir, Alexander McQueen, Fendi, and other designer merchandise bags from the entrance to their truck. She could get anything out of Steelo. If she wasn't grabbing something for Shanti, her baking second niece, Ariel, Seth Junior, and little Asim, then she had him buying her and Ceas matching friendship diamond necklaces or came across yet another pair of shoes that she absolutely had to have.

Not to mention that she'd picked out a shit load of fly outfits for his fine ass to don, too. All with matching loafers, kicks, or slides. He came out of fifty grand easily. Tiri was a product of currency, so baby girl had no issues nor complications with knowing how to spend the true value of a dollar. Seeing her beautiful chocolate face light up in excitement was all that mattered to him. If anything, he had the tendency to shop until he dropped just as bad as she did with fashion being another similarity they had in common.

Their teenage fever was heavy. Hand in hand, arm in arm, they clung to each other's side like Siamese twins. Licking on ice cream cones from the most popular creamery in town and having a ball in the enormous candy shop that took up all of five thousand square feet of rental space alone.

Time progressed quickly, but every moment spent with her man was savored and priceless.

It was night number four, and they'd just made it in from a late dinner and Balinese dancing that they each absolutely enjoyed. The couple beat the rainstorm by minutes as the pouring, tear-shaped drops created a clapping melody against the outdoor patio. Steelo was unzipping her evening gown when her phone rang. It was a group FaceTime from Kovu and Ceas checking in on her since she'd been ghost following their celebration at *Ass States*.

Following a light peck to her exposed, silky back, Steelo excused himself and let Tiri enjoy her moment with her girls. He removed the three-piece Alexander Wang suit and changed into something more lounge worthy. Comfy Gap joggers did just the thing as he grabbed an ashtray and rolled him a blunt.

He hated the rain and the darkness that associated with it. The ugly grey skies that suddenly clouded his once free mind, pushing him into a pool of anxiety and contemplation. Majority of their patio was shielded with a beautiful wooden roof, and despite the weather not being of his liking, he laid in one of the soft and relaxing lounge chairs while Alexa played Drake's *Views* album.

He lost track of how long he'd been sitting outside with grey eyes to match the firmament brewing above him, until his boo exited the sliding doors to join him. Donning one of his t-shirts, no panties, no bra, and a $20,000 solid gold ankle bracelet with tear-shaped diamonds surrounding the roof of her foot, Tiri made her way over to him with her hand covering her mouth to conceal her yawn. She was beat, but not as much as her man mentally was since he was vibing to this particular album. Champagne Papi was encompassed by a dark mentality when he wrote and produced *Views*. All true Drake fans knew that.

Views was another binding force of theirs. It posed as a truce; the wave of a white flag when they were over the notion of not seeing eye to eye, indicating that they were ready to talk. And even though they weren't into it, the fact that "U With Me" was on repeat had let her know that something heavy was on her man's mind.

Neither of them spoke when she took a seat next to him. Mary Jane and the assailing though mind-numbing lyrics were the driving energies at the hour. Tiri could see the aggravation, the frustration; the discomfort and irritation that dominated his vibe, and she didn't like it not one bit. She hated how he still hesitated to be emotionally open with her.

More so sentimental. They were partners in crime. Steelo knew she'd never judge him, his past, or the things he'd done, but that little voice in the back of his head was always coercing him to dive into these bouts of dismay and disdain. He submissively put himself through this nauseating pain that tore her own heart apart from simply being a witness to such treachery.

Tiri knew his actions embarrassed him whenever he clammed up in such nature before her. Since day one she'd always stirred things within him that he'd never felt before, so for her to go from shopping, fucking, sucking, and dealing with a boss to observing his...nightly mental breakdowns, it simply ate away at his masculinity...

At his heart.

At his mind.

"You know what, babe?"

Tiri's voice was soft and welcoming. Steelo took one last toke from the blunt before turning his head towards her and passing it along.

"What?"

She smiled as she wrapped her lips around the cigarillo and inhaled.

"Not even...five months ago, would I ever imagine being here. In this mindset, living this life, becoming this type of woman. It's not that I wasn't ready for the world, even though that was very evident since the day we crossed paths, but..." Her voice trailed as she exhaled. "I was afraid of the world. Ignorant to what was out there because I'd been confined to this little bubble that my parents and my brother kept me trapped in. Messiah did one hell of a job concealing the Platinum Cartel; the guns, the goons, and the drugs away from me. I knew nothing about being the baby sister of one of the biggest drugs lords in three different countries. I was oblivious to hustle, to street code, to dire ambition, and survival because I was brought up on love. I know that's the major difference that still sits between us, so with you seeing the world through a completely different lens than I did means more than I could possibly and efficiently process all in one setting when we first had this conversation."

Tiri climbed in front of him and sat between his legs so she could have his undivided attention. It was so rude to her when he peered in every other direction as they spoke, him being overwrought from the intimacy that eye contact ignited when the tables were turned, and he wasn't the aggressor.

"I know you hate it when I'm repetitive and how aggravating it gets when my actions and questioning can easily come off as an attack...Steelo, you've dropped over two million dollars on me in less than a week. You've risked your life, your position, gone against the grain and your street morality by not killing me on numerous occasions...I know that you love me."

The suffocating fear was written all over his still though contorted face. It made her smile.

"There's no doubt in my mind about it because I know for a fact that, in the same sense, I dangerously love you too. But when you mentally revolt against me, which leads to you physically putting a distance between us, it insults me because *I know* that *you know* that we're a lot more in sync than you want to admit. And yet your stubborn ass still begs to differ. You're out here sitting in the rain listening to draining, though good music I might add, instead of letting that hurt go and confiding in me like you always encourage me to do with you. I know that words will sometimes fail you, baby.

I know that life has previously opened you up to things that make you keep that last foot out the door on me. But it's not fair. We're a team now. A union, and Steelo, I hate to see you like this. The shit enrages me because I know for a fact that you're a good person, and you don't deserve this baggage that you keep shackled at your feet, your racing mind, and your wrists...What I'm ultimately saying is, there comes a time in life when we have to shift and make changes so that we can expand. That was me growing the fuck up, and now, I need that to be you making amends with your past so you can stop bleeding on the people who are trying to love you...especially me...Steelo just talk to me...just let it out...I'm listening with the intent to understand. I want this just as much as you secretly want this for yourself too, so let's hear it."

Tiri could ask this man to slit his own damn throat, and he'd tell her to hand him the knife to do so. Her ways with words spoke a language no other woman on an intimate level had ever done for him, so he felt gyved to her every request; a request that he presently didn't have the energy nor the restraint to conflict with.

"I've been down for so long, Tiri."

Her heart shattered to pieces at the melancholy present in his tone. This wasn't her Steelo. This wasn't the man who loved all over her and protected her from the demons in this catastrophic world. It may have sounded senile, but Steelo's soul harbored monstrous inhibitions that ate away at his livelihood, and he was too precious to be tamed by such a hex. She felt that shit *for* him. It was a hindering numbness she couldn't believe that he continued to stomach.

"Every day I continue to ask myself *why did I save you*, trying to come up with an answer that not only I can understand, but also accept. It might sound cliché, but the shit frightens me what you do to me, ma. What your eyes have always done to me. Your presence; just being around you, shorty. That shit is scary. I feel shit for you that I've never wanted to imagine. Shit that I've never had the urgency to want or desire. Considerate of the fact that I was never shown that same admiration from the people who brought me into this world...I found out that my mother was alive and well about...a couple weeks after me and you started rocking together...imagine how that shit made me feel, Tiri..."

His voice croaked. Steelo wasn't the one for the sentimental splurging, but he couldn't bottle up his anger nor frustrations another second. He knew Tiri wouldn't allow it, so his eyes glazed with pain as he clenched his jaw to stifle the tears that he'd be damned if he shed.

"That shit hurt, ma. Like a nigga drove a knife right into my jugular. I don't feel it in my heart that you knew, but that shit was still hard to accept, and it still hasn't resonated with me mentally with how close to home it hit."

Tiri was confused. She wasn't catching his drift.

"Knew about what? Baby, what are you saying?"

Silence...

"Apparently, I have an older brother and an older sister. Children that she's raised. Children that basked in the opportunity to have her around to love and care about 'em, you know? *That. Shit. Hurt*...Every day until I was bout, seven, I used to pray and beg God that she'd miraculously pop up and come get me after living with how my 'father' and stepmother left my ass in the rain for what, the owner at the orphanage said was a good ten hours, on their doorstep, according to the security camera before they found me out there...That's why I fucking hate the rain...are you pregnant?"

His last question was sporadic, but Tiri shook her head no, knowing there was purpose in him asking.

"I'm on birth control. We're good for the next three years unless I decide to get it removed." Off instinct, she reached for her arm and glided her long acrylic nail over the plastic device that was borderline skin deep. "I would've said something if I was. You know I would've came crying my damn eyes out with the stick asking you to get it out of me."

Her comment lightened the mood, but his face never twisted.

"I was hoping you was taking or was on some kind of contraceptive. I been carelessly nutting up in that good shit just knowing you was gon' hate me when I proposed an abortion. I ain't 'em gon' lie."

She giggled. She wouldn't have had the baby anyway, so his comment didn't offend her at all.

"You can nut up in this pussy all you want to, baby. We got insurance; plus, it's yours."

Steelo lost his breath when those words escaped her lips, forcing him to get up and pace the floor. He was weary. So fucking weary. So fucking out of place and uneasy that he couldn't keep still.

"I wanna believe that shit, Tiri. Wholeheartedly." Steelo shook his head, praying to God he could easily shake his emotions in the same breath. "I've never had *anything...anything* in this world that I could call my own. Nothing but biological parents who gave not one fuck about me, and foster parents who only cared about the funding they received from the state as long as I was breathing...Money don't mean shit to me, Tiri, because no matter how much of it I've accumulated, that shit couldn't and still can't put together the pieces of me that was gon' mend this eternal affliction.

My bond is so solid with Marius because he took me in, and he introduced me to the brotherhood and loyalty that I only knew outside of me and Válo; two lost ass teenagers who were just tryna survive. That shit saved me, ma. It saved us all. I consider them niggas to be my brothers, you know, but at the same time, I don't feel entitled to that if it makes any sense. Yeah, KD, that's my big sus all day because she too struggled with a toxic and nonexistent relationship with her moms, so we could relate on every level when it came to that. But I still don't feel entitled to or one hundred percent secure to her either. I'm tryna make sense of this shit, Tiri, like..."

He was so frustrated. He knew what he wanted to say but couldn't formulate the right expressions to defend himself. It made him feel hopeless.

"I only have that sense of peace and surety wit' *you*, shorty. Like, I don't think you fully understand what you do to me. The lines for everything when it's come to me and my life have always been so fucking blurred that it takes a lot out of me to make sure that our picture is crystal clear. I don't wanna control you, Tiri, not at all, but you...you are *mine*. Not in a possessive way, but at the same time, you the grand prize, ma, and I... I keep questioning that.

I keep doubting that, stupidly engaging in the same antics that I hate because I've never had a single soul in this fucked up ass, cold and brutal world to love and cherish who the fuck Nuri P really is. Not until we crossed paths on the wrong road, and I found you. I'm being one thousand wit' you right now, Tiri. *That. Shit. Makes. Me. In-se-cure.* That shit has the power to mentally shut me down because I'm afraid to lose what's mine. No matter how many times you've reassured that shit to me, Steelo ain't a hundred percent settled with the fact that you won't easily walk away or someone else won't take you away from me.

The fuck I'm throwing hands with that nigga Seth for when I could've easily whacked him and yo' brother with two pulls of a trigger no matter how chaotic that shit was. I'm heavy with the steel, you know that. Niggas don't call me Steelo for nothing. Them niggas would've been six feet deep, and I wouldn't have lost a wink of sleep over it. Yeah, I'm nocturnal, but ain't no nigga's death gon' ever have me tossing and turning at night, and that's a fact. But for *you*, I hesitated...like I always have.

I couldn't do that to you. I couldn't...I try not to intentionally hurt you, ma, but that's another thing that's failed me too. That day when they flew you back to St. Louis, I felt like them niggas ripped my fucking heart out of the socket. Evoked my ability to breathe, to see, to think. The fact that you have so much power over me and my sentiments, shorty, is why I've always pushed you away. I couldn't handle it. It felt like another mu'fucka was choosing over me, and after being down for so long, it makes me second guess everything...

You keep asking me what I'm afraid of? Why did I save you? I'm scared to lose you. To abuse you. To hurt you. I saved you because you

259

triggered pivotal emotions in my heart without saying not a mu'fucking word to me when them niggas was tryna kill you. You ignited shit that I never knew I was looking for until I was handed the challenge to love and protect you. I'm afraid of not being what you need.

Of not being able to properly reciprocate yo' love and energy...because the woman who was supposed to teach me that shit abandoned me... and considering all the hate for her that I've been harboring after all of these years, shorty, I would've been forced to splatter her shit across the table at Thanksgiving dinner. Simply because I would've had to face her after all this time, knowing damn well she ain't gave not *one*, *single*, *fuck* about me... My full name is Nuri Princeton Valentine; which makes Nasir, my older sister, Ali, my older brother, and Catori, my fucking mother. The bitch who destroyed me..."

𝕳𝖀𝕱𝕽

Every time you look at me, all I can see are my failures floating out in midair right where you left me.
You never even gave me a chance.
Instead, you threw me out right on my ass as soon as you could; oh so effortlessly.
Modestly cleansing your hands.
You had me trapped within these four walls for days (years) second-guessing my character.
Wondering if I was ever good enough for your presence, as if I didn't measure up to your standards.
You could never look me in my face to address me with such essence.
I was your greatest embarrassment.
To others, I was a major comparison.
Something you could no longer cherish...

Steelo didn't have many tattoos. A total of two marking his body: the poem above with a chopped and screwed excerpt from Kovu's poetry collection located on the inside of his left upper arm. The shit spoke to his soul since the first time she read it to him around the time they first met. They shared the same sentiments and disdain towards their mothers, and she'd put that pain into words that he could never...

And now, Tiri's name that was officially two weeks old and healed in exquisite, handcrafted calligraphy covering the left half of his left hand on a vertical horizon. It coined tattoo number two.

Her eyes had been glued to it once she was able to unscramble the letters in the fancy script that smoothly graced and merged with his skin.

Tears and Steelo just didn't go in the same sentence, but today that acclamation had come true. They laid in bed, hours after he'd poured his heart out to her on a silver platter; his head resting on her bosom as she ran the tips of her coffin-shaped nails against his bare back.

Tiri was sick.

It infuriated her to know that Ms. Catori had single-handedly corrupted this man. She felt like shit for begging him to come to St. Louis for the holiday, now fully understanding his objection. Catori was so loving. So supportive. She'd move heaven and earth for Nas, Riley, their children, her other granddaughter, Boo, and Ali, so it made no sense why she'd blatantly and selfishly abandon her youngest son. It would've been one thing had Catori been a drunken crackhead, a meth addict, or strung out on some other heavy and mind-altering drug. Something over the top to explain why she'd left him halfway across the country with a deadbeat ass father who did the exact same fucking thing.

Tiri didn't want to believe the sweet woman whom she'd grown to love, and respect was a dirty fraud who washed her hands with him. Her heart ached. It didn't make a lick of sagacity, and she prayed to God that Nasir had no knowledge of this shit either or else she'd get cut the fuck off too. It was wrong of Tiri to blame them, mainly that damn Catori, when the full story hadn't been explained yet. But not once had she gone out to look for him? To check up on him? To see that he was alive and well? She'd never wondered how her son turned out? Sent him a damn birthday card? Had the desire to see what he'd become in a world that's repeatedly chewed him up and spit him back out because he was built too tough to physically destroy or digest?

No wonder why the price and value were set so damn high to release this man's heart out from ransom.

Steelo had war wounds that no dime or addition of hundred dollar bills could ever buy. Fuck being broken; this man's entire infrastructure was in a desperate need of reconstruction if he was ever going to love properly. It's the reason why children were the last thing on his weary mind right now. Thank God that Tiri agreed. She was only nineteen, and there was an entire world out there that she'd hid from for long enough.

Children could wait.

They were going to wait.

Steelo wasn't mentally prepared to properly raise a child, knowing he needed to fix a myriad of complications within himself before trying to knock his sweet little Tiri up. This relationship shit was tough as is. Things between them were progressing with a lack of gravity to pull them back, and he was trying his best to keep up with that.

Steelo swore Tiri wouldn't hear him out. He swore she wouldn't comprehend the information even if he did communicate it with her about his eternal quandaries. But once again, he'd misjudged her and the sovereignty she possessed to deal with a thug nigga such as himself. He could finally believe it when she vowed to love him like she'd never loved someone else. Steadily blessing him with shit he never would've fathomed to ever *need.*

Women were the mold in any and every relationship. Steelo was lost without young Tiri, and here he was going on twenty-six years of living come next March, thinking he had his life mapped out or had a grasp on his future. She came into his world, knowing exactly what to do with him, and he cherished her for that. Steelo didn't expect Tiri to take on the role of evoking his unresolved issues, but she did a damn good job of opening his eyes to envisage the bigger picture and assist him to make the initiative to be a better man. One who'd eventually arise and overcome the aspects of his past that he'd foolishly swept away to deal with on another day. A day that they both knew would've never come hadn't she given him a little push.

She was the definition of *from his rib.* The face of change he'd been hurting for. The love and completion his life had been missing. Since day one, Tiri's always kept it so real with her nigga that, he'd never allow his ego to leave them divided as long as there was a breath left in his lungs to breathe.

That was one promise Steelo was determined to keep.

"Look at you, got me ruining the mood with all of these emotional ass interventions and shit, mama."

Tiri giggled with her eyes closed as he placed those deep, tantalizing kisses to her collar bone. The sensation had her wrapped up in a spell so powerful that she couldn't respond right away.

"Bali's gon' always be here, babe. It's nothing to fly back out here and take another six days or so away from reality. If we can't enjoy this experience on the same accord, then what's the point? Your mental is more important. When you hurt, I hurt. When you're off your square, guess who's gonna help you get back on track? That's what love does, Steelo. It releases our hearts from ransom and being selfless is the key ingredient in order to make things work."

Heart Up For Ransom

"Don't come until you bring the lockbox! Tell her! The lockbox! The fucking lock booooooox!"

-Catori

TaugJaye

Chapter
14

There was a thin line between love and protection when it all boiled down to throwing a family member inside of a psychiatric ward, and Catori was livid. The words, "Ma, you're not stable," and "You tried to kill yourself," simply translated in her mind as,

"Bitch, you're crazy."

"You need to be detained."

"Your psychotic ass is back at it again."

And now, Catori didn't know who to trust.

The hospital gown was hideously draped over her long and lean stature in a wrinkled and baggy nature, stopping right above her knees. Her pixie cut was brushed to the back for an attempted sleek look, but hair appointments and beauty shop privileges weren't an option at the St. Louis Psychiatric Rehabilitation Center.

The hairs on her arms were standing at attention, desperate for an *at ease*; the air was so got damn cold in the building.

She wanted to chuck the hideous ass royal blue non-skid socks on her feet out the window; they disgusted her.

All of her jewels had been confiscated upon her arrival, so she felt empty without the two Tiffany & Company heart lockets around her neck that she wore twenty-four/seven.

Her nails were horrendous, in a desperate need of a manicure and full-set since the staff popped her previous ones off. Utterly leaving her with damaged nail bids.

Catori couldn't even floss her teeth.

It's not like she ate much with the bird food they'd been offering her, but to have such a minor right taken away from her made the woman feel like she was in chains. All she was missing was a pair of shackles.

The color white was associated with holiness according to your typical Google search bar, but to her, it was everything far from godly. She stared at her twin sized bed positioned in the center of the room, the white walls, and the 4x4 window in diameter, barred up to prevent an escape. It only illuminated her quarters with just a pinch of sunlight. Lastly, one little desk that sat over in the corner with the Holy Bible decorating the top of it summed up her "lavish" living quarters.

This shit was hell.

Everyone thought she was truly crazy. Her own children had voted against her instead of siding with their mother and listening to her truths.

But did I give them the option to do so?

Ok, maybe Catori *was* going nuts. She couldn't clearly nor thoroughly explain the words that were jumbled around in her head because they too were out of order, but one thing was certain. Catori Naomi Rutger wasn't *crazy*. She wasn't psychotic, a lunatic, or so far gone in the brain that she needed to be locked away with other individuals who skipped around in circles all day; menacingly chanting repetitive phrases until their medications put them to sleep. She was too alert and orientated to be caged in with the same people who had to be physically detained by four or more staff members just to receive a shot in the ass for their Schizo meds.

Yet, her *family* insisted.

Was she traumatized? Suffering from PTSD of her previous life?

Absolutely.

But deranged?

Absolutely the fuck not!

Catori could admit that she may have gone a bit overboard with the loaded gun that she and Nasir had to struggle over. We're all human. We can only take so much. Face so much. Accept so many got damn disappointments until we all just mentally need a break.

And here is where she stood.

Mentally drained. Mentally defeated. Mentally fed up with the bullshit that she'd been forced to conceal and never reveal for over...twenty-five years now.

Damn, that's a lifetime.

"One little outburst and some discovered prescriptions for a little dose of Pristiq and QID Xanax surely makes everyone view you differently these days." Catori laughed to herself following her comment, because, who else was there to converse with? "Damn, Catori, girl. Look at you."

She stood in front of the surveillance window disguised as a mirror and laughed out loud from the sight of her reflection. She was a mess; looked a mess, felt a mess. And with the twist of a doorknob, that same pile of mess she was currently surrounded by had instantly been mushed into shit. Shorty was down on her luck by a long shot.

"Catori Rutger," the deep voice growled as he closed the door behind him. "Been a long time since I've seen that name in my books. Still got those nice legs on you, I see...that beautiful face...those eyes..."

The security officer slowly cornered her into the wall with a good six feet left between them. He swung his double set of keys around in circles while biting his bottom lip. Washed up and pale she may have been from a month's time "purging" in the devil's den, but true beauty was always retainable. He had to admit, even with twenty-five years of aging tacked onto her since the last time she was there, she was just as beautiful as she was in her twenties.

"Get your fat ass out of here you big, small dick ass bitch! Two and a half decades later and you're still hurting for pussy! Pathetic!"

The guard chuckled as he grabbed his nuts, his penis swollen to its capacity at the thoughts of what he was only minutes away from doing to her.

"Still feisty, huh? Oh, baby, this is going to be a long night, but first, you have a visitor. Ten more minutes and," he licked his tongue out at her and growled once more, highly anticipating hovering over her body until he reached a climax. "It's just you and me until 7 A.M."

"Go eat a cookie or something, bitch. Control yourself until I'm gone, alright? Fuck out my sight."

Catori lost all feeling in her legs when the door opened once again and in walked a living ghost whom she'd assumed was dead after all of these years. Down on her hands and feet, she crawled backwards away from him with tears descending her face. A loud gasp spewed from her lips when she hit her head against the wall from not seeing where she was going.

Her heart was seconds away from exploding. It thumped in powerful, irregular beats, her airway was closing in, and she could feel hot, golden piss running down the insides of her legs, creating a puddle underneath her.

This was all a dream.

It had to be.

It fucking had-to-be!

Everything she managed to escape from for twenty-five long and agonizing years had emerged from a dark and hidden crevice with the snap of a finger, and she was shambled. Pieces of her heart, of her sanity, were lying on the floor in her bodily secretions right along with her. The wetness forcing her to catch convulsions from the low temperature whisking against her skin like the hard, Antarctic air.

"What the fuck are you doing here!"

Her voice roared in a terrifying rage; her trembles oddly filling the room to such a degree that her words echoed against the walls.

"Is that any way to greet your husband, Mrs. Valentine? I've missed you."

He was such a chastising lowlife.

"FUCK YOU, HEZIKIAH! LOOK AT WHAT YOU DID TO ME! LOOK AT WHAT YOU DID TO OUR CHILDREN! TO MY LIFE FOR SO MANY FUCKING YEARS! YOU GOT THE NERVE TO JUST FUCKING POP UP ALL WILLY NILLY LIKE YOU DIDN'T DISAPPEAR OUT OF THIN FUCKING AIR! HOW FUCKING SICK ARE YOU?! AND WHERE THE FUCK IS MY SOOOOOOOOON! YOU SET THIS SHIT UP! I KNOW YOU DID, YOU DIRTY BASTARD! FUCKING ANSWER ME!"

Catori watched him arrogantly pull a cigar from out of his Alexander Wang trench coat and put it up to his lips. The smell of Cuban tobacco filled the air with a welcoming fragrance in comparison to the formaldehyde fluid lingering around. Housekeeping tried their best to hide it from outsiders, but their illegal shrouds were slowly yet surely beginning to surface.

She couldn't believe the audacity of this man to just conveniently pop up when it was obviously good for him; as if he hadn't been missing in action for almost thirty years.

Because of him, she was right back in square damn one. Because of him, her daughter and son had deceived her, and she was on the verge of losing her job, and all of her got damn marbles for sure this time around, with no possibility to reverse the damage.

This filthy piece of shit whom she'd once loved, who she once thought she'd spend the rest of her life with...was the fucking devil himself. And considering the smug look plastered amongst his face, he still could give a damn about her or their children, pushing the hate for him in her heart to simply multiply.

"Jamie-O, where the fuck is my soooooooooon!" she demanded, uncontrollably stomping her feet and banging her fists against the walls.

"That should be the least of your worries, love. He hates us both. More you than me, but that's neither here nor there at this point in life. I just came to collect what was mine and go on about my business."

"He hates me?"

Catori's voice was barely above a whisper. Her heart shattered into a million tiny little pieces of shards that would harm anyone who attempted to put them back together. She could've died right then and there. Not only from the thoughts of him being alive, but from her precious little Nuri Princeton Valentine, whom she'd always loved, hating her. It wasn't her decision to be separated from her baby boy. It was his own father who took him away from her. He'd singlehandedly birthed this psychotic fuck fest that she'd been sucked into since the moment she recovered from after giving birth. It was a nightmare.

"WHERE IS HEEEEEEEE! BITCH, YOU'VE GOT EVERYBODY THINKING I'M CRAZY WHEN I KNOW GOOD AND DAMN WELL—"

"Where's the key to my mother's lockbox, Catori? Quit fucking with me; I've got shit to do. I've been gone for twenty-five years. Do you honestly think I give a fuck about you? You were something to do until my name was cleared in the judicial system and all of my trafficking cases were dropped. If that hasn't been obvious, then there's no one else to blame for the point of madness that you've driven yourself to. I mean, look at you."

The room was spinning. Catori couldn't feel her body, her vision had blurred, and the condescending look in Jamie-O's eyes matched the very words he was spitting to her. He never truly loved her. He manipulated her and used their flashy relationship as an alibi while his soldiers did all of the dirty work. She and their children were nothing to him, and that was one hard pill to swallow.

"Look, woman." He pitifully shook his head at her while rubbing the inside creases of his orbs. "You're sitting on the floor in the middle of a piss puddle with bags underneath your eyes, and you're addicted to prescription medicine. So tell me, what have I been missing out on? Nothing but a psychotic ass old bitch still working retail in her late thirties. At least Nasir had more sense than you and left me with something that won't depreciate in its value. The Platinum Cartel is excellent collateral.

Nuri's got the west coast on lock for me, and once y'all are out the way, my life becomes that much more easier. So clean yourself up, alright? From the looks of it, you'll be here for a while, so get it together. Thanks for burying my mother and handling all of her finances for me a couple of months ago. You were always up to par on shit like that. I'll take all of her assets and be on my merry little way while you live in this hell you've created for yourself. Just give me the location of the key and I'm out of here."

"Fuck you and your dead ass mother and those fucking keys that are buried six feet deep right along with her ass, bitch!"

"Yo', you've got one more time to—"

Hawk-twat!

Jamie-O tried to reach down and put his hands around her neck, but Catori lathered up a huge glob of spit and showed him how she really felt since she was nothing to his ass. They both knew she was lying about the keys, trying to sabotage and reroute him as if Glenna didn't leave everything to her. Catori hated that old bitch, honestly.

Glenna swore she was the one who ran her son off, but Catori was the only person on this planet who bothered to care for *or* look out for her. Hell, if you knew you were going to be promised over four hundred thousand bands once all of her investments, savings, and the monetary value from selling her house was added up, you'd stick your Black ass around too. Not to mention that broad's million dollar life insurance policy?

Nigga, please.

Glenna only had one other son, who's dead now, and with them both believing that Jamie-O was honestly dead too, to atone for being a horrible grandmother to Nasir and Ali, she left them something behind that would mean more to them each than an overdue and forced *I'm sorry.*

Jamie-O exhaled, clearly out of patience as he wiped his face. Time wasn't on his side, so now he had to go trash her apartment like he should've done from the get-go. A part of him had this slight desire to see her after so long. Back in their days, her pussy was good as shit, *and* she wasn't a bad wife. He just didn't love her. Didn't want her. Felt no connection to her whatsoever but did what the fuck he had to do because he knew Catori would hold him down without asking many questions. Hell, if any at all.

She played her role well, and now it was time for him to permanently make that part of his life disappear. The woman he loved was down in Costa Rica waiting on him to return home after conquering all of his territories in the States so they could continue to recklessly spend their drug money and happily fuck into the sunset like rabbits. He was on a tight schedule that he wanted to keep and arguing with Catori's dumb and delusional ass wasn't on the agenda.

"Suit yourself, bitch. Chauncey, have fun."

Catori hopped up to her feet and jumped on Jamie-O's back as he turned to leave. She bit down on his neck, instantly breaking the skin while throwing wild punches at his head and face. She was relentless, lashing out on him with a rage that she couldn't contain until they both pried her from off of his back and she was roughly thrown into the nearest wall like an animal.

Stars were dancing around in her head until she felt the guard grab her by the ankle and pull her underneath him. She fought against him with all of her might until he backhanded her, and she fell back against the floor. Blood stained her gown, her breaths were short, and she felt twenty-one again as Chauncey unzipped his pants and roughly grabbed her by what little hair she did have. The moment he shoved his shrimp sized penis into her mouth, she bit down with so much adrenaline pumping through her veins, that a gust of blood spewed into her mouth.

Chauncey's screams were horrific. Miles of tears streamed down his face as he repeatedly punched her in the head to get her mouth from around him, but to no avail. She clenched harder, digging each of her teeth so further into his penis that with one vigorous yank of her head, she bit that little motherfucker off and spat it out across the room. Just as she pounced on him and started beating the shit out of his face with the baton he'd dropped on the floor, the door was shoved open, and three other guards pulled her away.

She looked like something out of a horror movie, the room being her stage set for filming; there was so much blood on the floor. The energy running through her was endless as she proceeded to fight against them too, giving the guards no other choice but to relocate her to another environment.

"Tranq this bitch now! Then take her crazy ass on down to solitary confinement!"

Catori was slammed into the slippery, cold floor and pinned down; her body twisting and turning like the exorcist, trying to get away. She wasn't going out without a fight as they could clearly see.

"Call my fucking daughter! Noooooooooooow! Naaaaaaaaaas! Nooooooo! Come and get meeeeee! Bring it! Bring the box! Don't come until you bring the lockbox! Tell her! The lockbox! The fucking lockbooooooooooox!"

Catori's screams drifted away when the needle was inserted inside of her arm, and she was heavily sedated. In seconds her ferocity dialed down, her eyes rolled to the back of her skull, her head slumped over, and her body went limp.

The guards were all heavily breathing, stammered, and surprised at her horrific outburst. They hadn't had any excitement like this is weeks.

And now that she was out like a light, two of them were able to roughly grab her by the arms and drag her body down the hall to the isolation chamber, where a stray jacket with her name on it awaited her.

HUFR

After having three children, the lives of a man and a woman, who decided to spend the rest of their days together would never be the same.

Nasir couldn't remember the last time she and Seth shared their bed alone: SJ, Ariel, and Asim free.

She'd been spaced out for the past month or so, ever since Catori was checked in down on Arsenal, and Seth knew this situation was draining his wife. So he got the kids fed, bathed, and put them to sleep a little earlier than usual tonight, since they normally liked to party like mini rock stars into the wee hours of the morning. He simply hoped to buy some alone time with his lady and try his best to ease her mind.

The dreadful and distraught look she'd permanently worn etched across her beautiful face was heartbreaking. He hated to see her so out of place. So out of body. So with her left foot in hand, her pretty toes polished with a hue of pink and a glittery overlay to enhance the color, he eased pressure points that caused her eyes to close while she bit down on her bottom lip.

Seth admired his beautiful wife. She'd also been stressing out over her weight gain since she had Asim, packing on an extra twenty-five pounds that pushed her from a size twelve to a sixteen, but it looked divine on her body structure.

Proportioned to perfectly fit her wider hips, fluffy thighs, rounder ass, and that little pudge that he absolutely loved grabbing on, Nasir fucking Platinum still got his dick hard as a motherfucker! Her beauty hadn't faded, thus, making her even more attractive in his eyes. He adored the time she still took and the effort she continued to put into rocking the hottest wardrobe; still flaunting nothing but skin with a side of clothes and tall heels that coined her signature seduction.

She was perfect.

Even now donning nothing but his white undershirt, those pierced brown nipples bulging through the thin layer of fabric that hardly shielded her perfectly waxed pussy and curvaceous frame. Her long and curly hair was all over her head, a tad bit wild after combing out her tight curls. She had the mane of a lion and damn it he'd be her Simba every fucking day of the week.

Her plump, heart-shaped lips were the most beautiful feature along her gorgeous face outside of her Hennessy brown eyes. They captured him in a love so deep that it was pointless to fight his way out of it. Going on three years now, he'd drifted along the pools of her irises with nothing but content; peace and unwavering tranquility, knowing that God had blessed him with a woman of her supremacy to spend the rest of his life with.

Nasir's eyes opened wide when she felt the tender caress of her husband's lips gracing the top of her foot. Shivers slithered their way up and down her body as Seth continued to trail those sinful kisses along her ink covered calf, then to her trembling thighs. She'd been so worked up that making love to him had also been the last thing to cross her cluttered mind. As he looked up into her raging, fire breathing eyes, his lips now getting closer to her sweet heat, Seth could see from her body language and the dick hardening submission taking over her, that she *needed* him.

You could only do so much conversing, cuddling and coddling with your spouse until it was time to take shit up to a sexual notch. Nasir needed a natural release. She was ready to mount her man's hard, throbbing dick and slam up and down on that vein coated shaft until her pussy created a velvety, milky oasis amongst the outskirts, just so she could suck it off and repeat. She knew her man craved for the prowess of her wet and fat pussy just as much as she was starving for the cock.

Seth hadn't gotten lost in her honey since the morning he bent her over in the closet, so it made her pearl throb with excitement; already aware that her man was about to ram-shack her canal until the ceiling secreted a leak that one round couldn't settle.

Nasir drew in a sharp breath the moment his tongue slid between her pussy lips then swept along her hardened gem. Seth's face was smothered in her love as he swiftly glided amongst each crevice that instantly triggered an orgasm. Oh, she was backed up to the point where the sight of her husband alone had the insides of her legs dripping before their foreplay could even take place.

Seth held her legs spread as open and as foolishly wide as she lovingly had him. His head rotated with each lick of his tongue lapping up her essence until the sound of Nasir's ringing phone interrupted them. It was well after midnight. Riley's pregnancy had her in bed before ten on most days, so he could only imagine who it was, yet most importantly, pray that Nasir would ignore it and let him continue chowing down on her gourmet pussy. He'd just removed his dick from his shorts for crying out loud to begin stroking it until it reached its full, ten-inch length.

But...that was short lived. When Nasir recognized the number from the rehabilitation center as it appeared across her screen, she lunged for it, utterly smashing her husband's face so tight between her thighs that it blurred his vision.

"Hello?" she panicked, praying that nothing bad had happened, but why else would they be calling her at a quarter past twelve?

When Seth's vision finally cleared after sitting beside her, he could automatically sense her uneasiness. The tears trickling down her now pale face triggered his heart rate to increase, their bodily reactions undeniably in cahoots.

As the nurse on duty at the asylum continued to be the biggest bearer of bad news, Nasir's body sunk more and more into both the headboard and the surface of the mattress with her mouth agape and her chest vacillating with rapid motions. After a while, she couldn't take anymore. The phone slid from out her hand as she solemnly sat there, vocally mute and her eyes now gazing out into outer space.

She couldn't hear her husband calling after her, trying his best to get her attention. She couldn't feel him shaking her, trying to snap her from out of the mental hex that presently held control over her every involuntary motion.

Nas was somewhere on another planet.

Trapped in a vortex.

Crash landed on uncharted territory.

Forcing Seth to reach for her phone and have the nurse fill him in since Nasir was compelled by the moment.

It wasn't until thirty minutes later when Falcon arrived to sit with the kids had Nas come down from off her mental high. She couldn't tell left from right and struggled immensely while sliding on clothes and shoes that didn't match a lick. Her head was so far in the clouds that she exited her dressing room bra-free and with the girls, on display in the undershirt she still wore as if she were buying in for a wet t-shirt contest. No hat. No gloves. No scarf. No coat. Hell, she was wearing two different damn shoes: one UGG house slipper and an Air Max 95 on the other foot.

Like her poor mother, she too was a mess.

"Put a bra, a coat, and some matching shoes on, Nasir so we can go. I know you got all kinds of thoughts and emotions and shit running through yo' head right now, but you can't leave the house like that."

Her husband's tone was so demanding, even when he tried not to be. Seth's dominance was still one of his greatest features, so his words pierced her like venom that cut through her daze. A little more focused now, she got herself together before they finally headed out.

Nas didn't know why the lockbox meant so much to her mother. She'd brought it home with her that day after their little episode, something in her gut telling her that it would be important, but it was filled with nothing but old polaroid pictures that she must've flipped through a hundred times looking for a sign to lead to Catori's madness.

"I mean," she released an exasperated breath while wiping the tears from her eyes. The commute was a bit far for them since they lived out in Chesterfield, MO, but with Seth driving like a bat out of hell, they'd reached the city in record timing. "I just don't get it, Seth. Like...what's the deal? There isn't shit but a box of old pictures of me, her, and Ali from the 90's and this damn gun. It's not making sense to me. Why is she acting like this?"

His baby was crushed. Taking his eyes from off of the road for a second, Seth reached over and thumbed away some of her tears.

"You don't notice nothing out of place?" he questioned, now flying down S. Kingshighway Street, running through a slew of red stoplights.

"NO, I DON'T! THEY'RE JUST SOME OLD ASS PICTURES, SETH!"

"Calm down and look again. Feel around in the box and make sure ain't shit taped to the top of it."

Puffing her cheeks out like a bratty little kid who'd just swallowed their tears and a hard cry, Nasir followed his suggestion. She felt around until what felt like a key taped in the top left corner caught her attention; it still didn't solve anything. They were about seven minutes away from their destination now, so with nothing else left to do, she gathered the pictures and decided to flip through them once more.

"I'm sorry, babe."

Nasir's voice was soft as she eyed her mother's wedding photo this time around, not remembering it the first six times since her mind was so boggled. She hadn't seen many photographs of her father. Catori kept the ones she did save hidden throughout her childhood, so to see them on their wedding day along with her and Ali had inevitably struck a bundle of nerves.

Jamie-O was as handsome as her mother said he was: six-feet-four inches in height, mocha-colored skin and piercing hazel eyes that reminded her of the youthful DeVante Swing from Jodeci.

Her mother appeared to be madly in love; the happiest her daughter had ever seen her before, and it burned a loving, deep fire in the pit of Nasir's heart. All she ever wanted for Christmas was for her mother to be happy. Both of her parents looked to be dangerously in love as they gazed deeply into one another's eyes, so what could've possibly torn them apart? Why would her father just abruptly leave his family? That was the ultimate mystery. Well, one of them at least.

Nasir studied the photograph until they arrived at the guarded gate where her mother had been residing. Just as they were buzzed inside, the fact that her mom was pregnant in the photo had finally hit her. Catori was obsessive about her figure. She'd always taken pride in her slim frame up until this very day, so pregnancy was the only possibility behind her round cheeks and protruding belly.

Oh, her cover up was on some Michael Jackson, *Smooth Criminal* shit with the way her dress precisely cascaded down her frame with a flare to sell the camouflage. But if you really looked at her as her daughter was doing now, you could see Catori carrying her youngest child.

The wind had been knocked out of Nas once she realized that one little significant detail. Flipping on the overhead light, she blinked twice just to make sure that her eyes weren't playing any tricks on her before reaching over and patting her husband's arm.

"Seth, she's pregnant!"

Her news came on just as shocking to him as it did to her. Catori didn't have any children other Nas and Ali, so what in the entire fuck! And how could this be?

"What you mean she pregnant? You and yo' brother her only kids, ma."

"*Well*...apparently we aren't..."

𝕳𝖀𝕱𝕽

Yellow tape meant cops. Yellow tape meant dead bodies, but most importantly; it meant fucking nosy ass, White supremacists, bitch made ass niggas, aka, the St. Louis legislation, had just got one more reason to keep their eyes and ears open for the Platinum Cartel. Cops meant killing paid witnesses. Cops meant yet another drug trafficking and gang violence story that was floating around every news station in the Lou, and Seth was at his wit's end with this shit.

He knew it was risky going anywhere within a ten-mile radius of any crime scene in this city, especially a crime scene where all fingers would eventually be pointed back to his involvement. But with the way he was already feeling, considering this fucked-up ass situation with his mother-in-law, the animal within him had not only been awakened, but his fury was being fed as well. He had to see this shit with his own eyes; up close and personal. Wanted to be near the dead soldiers of his who were outlined in white chalk.

A five hundred thousand dollar drop was scheduled to be made tonight, yet here he was with his hands tucked away inside of his black, Nike track jacket, staring at one of his frontline soldiers. Pitifully lying in the alley right at the intersection of Natural Bridge & Fair with his brains blown out all over the pavement. And his partner, Rich, hanging from a noose attached to a light pole; eyes bulging, one of them bitches barely hanging on by the optic nerve as it hung down his face like some shit off a horror movie. He was pants less; naked from the waist down with his penis detached, and acid burns eating away at the flesh along his exposed thighs to match the scourging on his face and the chemical burns on his partner.

With the hood hanging low over his eyes and his hair tucked down his back, to avoid exposing his identity, the velvet dark sky that swept over the northside kept Seth camouflaged as he continued to shake his head in disgust. His jaw clenched in frustration. This wasn't an ordinary homicide, nor some random ass hit. With Gunna and Rich both dead and being 500k in the hole, it was clear to any and every nigga associated with the game that this shit was a well thought out execution.

Seth kept his distance, being sure to remain hidden in the shadows of the night from across the street as he began to blow into the chrome whistle. He'd seen enough of this shit. The four Canines roaming the unit eagerly shifted their attention from the crime scene, now hypnotized and aroused by the ultrasonic sound that was piercing their ears. Seth was terrorizing each animal, blowing into the cylinder with horse-powered lungs to enhance the intensity that viciously penetrated their eardrums. Howling filled the air causing heart racing and grim barks to echo in the atmosphere.

Officers began drawing their weapons and heading out in search teams, hurriedly going after each dog that were racing away from the crime scene. On cue, a dark shadow emerged from behind a dumpster, knowing she only had a good thirty to forty-five seconds to snap as many low-light photographs as possible. Shorty was so smooth at her shit that she managed to come across a piece of evidence that hadn't been numbered or tagged by the crime scene investigators.

Seth casually walked further down the block, blowing into the whistle, now in a different direction to keep the dogs going wild once they began to head back in route to the murder, giving his girl a little more time to gather her findings until she left just as quickly as she'd came.

Twenty minutes later, he was knocking against a barred and visually condemned backdoor four blocks over on Lee Street. He dapped up the six-foot-seven, three hundred pound guard manning the entrance before descending the stairs that led to a vacant basement. A few minutes passed by with him sending his wife a quick text message, checking in on her and Catori, until he lifted the heavy cemented trap door and descended another flight of steps into the cellar.

Messiah was hot. I mean, you could see veins bulging through the skin on his forehead he was so T'd.

Prodigy was by his side, nursing a bottle of water like it was Hennessy while their girl, Portia, a skilled crime scene investigator that had been working with them for years, sat before a computer screen doing her thing. She was trying to find a matching print from off of the 40 Smith & Wesson brass shell case she discovered while taking pictures.

"White stripes," Messiah spat as he dropped the printed photographs on the ottoman that Seth stood next to.

Most assassins left their mark on a victim after a killing. Some left symbols, others mutilated in a specific format to coin their fatalities, but it was strange to see the white spray-painted vertical lines on the bottoms of Gunna's Timberland boots and along the back of Rich's bloodied black shirt. Shit was odd. Shit didn't make not a lick of damn sense. Everyone knew what and who two white stripes signified when you were familiar to this gang shit, but when it came to an execution, this shit right here wasn't his style.

"Nah, fam." Seth put the pictures down while removing his hood. "This ain't The Monstrosity's mark. His symbol that his team is on scene? Yeah, but not for an execution. And you know that. Whoever did this shit tryna shake sum' up, hoping we fell for it like yo' pressed ass just did. This a ploy."

"I tried to tell this hot-headed ass nigga that shit, but you know how he get," Prodigy co-signed after removing the bottle from his lips. He had cotton mouth like something terrible at the hour.

"Man, fuck y'all."

"Nigga, fuck you. Use yo' mu'fucking head for a change. We supply Trinity. The fuck them niggas want smoke wit' us for? Marius tax they ass, he don't orchestrate that shit. This ain't even logical, and real shit, you can take yo' sentimental ass back home if you about to be on some ole' ho shit. We got more important stuff to be tripping off of," Seth countered.

It was obvious that Messiah still felt some type of way about Steelo rerouting his innocent little sister's head, so being the overprotective big brother he was, he'd run with any little thing to prove himself right like the enemy had plotted. Thank God Seth wasn't listening to his shit this time around. They didn't need any more setbacks. Their little pop up in Trinity was already being used against them, so now they had to be mindful of what they responded to and how they did it.

The Lord was still working on Messiah. He simply didn't want anything to happen to his sister, but he'd get it together one of these days.

"These niggas would've been headless, fam. You know how he get down," Seth continued.

"Shit, fuck that. What bodies? Nigga would've 6F'd these niggas and shipped they heads with a cherry bomb shoved in they damn mouths to one of our traps *after* robbing us if that was the type of shit he was on. And even if so, that still wouldn't add up. Pushing weight ain't his MO."

Messiah hated to admit it, but his brothers were keeping it a buck fifty, spitting nothing but facts, but that still didn't stop him from asking this.

"So who else got beef with that nigga that could possibly be linked to us? Make it make sense."

"Does the name Hezekiah Clemet Valentine ring a bell?"

Seth damn near snapped his neck when he heard his wife's maiden name leave from out of Portia's mouth.

"Say what?" he questioned as he now stood behind her chair, eyeing the computer monitor.

"That's whose print was found on the shell case. Street name is Jamie-O, but after paying off some officials, getting his name cleared in the Witness Protection Program by paying an inside source, then relocating to South America, down there, they know him as Erasmos Gonzalez. The Costa Rico drug lord."

Another one of Portia's handy skills was cyber hacking. Some cases could give her a run for her fucking money when the security system was nice and tight, but for the most part, she could almost break into any system for information.

"You gotta be shitting me." Messiah wiped his face before looking over at his boy, Seth.

Him and Prodigy both could see the vengeance brewing within his glowing eyes before he began reading over Jamie-O's files. For damn near twenty-eight years of his wife's life, she wondered where her father was; emotionally torn and unsure if he were truly dead. She never had the courage to give Seth the okay to look up the information for her, realizing that his bitch ass didn't want to be found, so why go digging around in the devil's backyard? But hey, maybe doing so would've prepared them for this moment.

"Shit still don't make sense though. The fuck that nigga got to do with us, and why he tryna make static with the PC and the west coast?"

A lightbulb went off in Portia's head following the resonation of Prodigy's comment. And nah, he wasn't back in the game, but for his brothers, Noel would always ride.

"Remember you had me do a little more searching in Trinity, Siah?" she questioned with her fingers thumping against the keyboard.

"Why? You got some background information on that nigga now?" he inquired.

That was the main reason why he couldn't fully trust Tiri's and Steelo's union. The nigga was a walking ghost.

"Nah. Steelo got his shit on lock and key. According to Trinity, he's not even a resident, but check this out though." They each stood around her until she pulled up an image on the computer. "That nigga Conner O'Sullivan who used to run the Irish Mob was wacked back in September. He owns the two biggest international opioid connections with the United States out in Ireland. This is his son, Geni O'Sullivan, shaking hands with our killer, Mr. Jamie-O."

"So The Monstrosity beefing with the Irish Mob?"

"Uh-huh," she answered Seth's question. "And according to this picture, these niggas must've formed some kind of alliance. You see the briefcases in this picture right here? Gotta be a monetary payment. I'm just a CSI but if you ask me, these niggas tryna kill two birds with one stone and use y'all as puppets to wipe each other out."

"How the fuck does that even involve us though, P? This nigga just randomly start making hits on us? Somebody in the crew know something. This shit sound sketchy as fuck. You gotta give me more than this. It's gotta more to the story."

Messiah was tired of all these damn games and reading between the lines. The neurons in his head were firing too intense to comprehend right now. He needed this shit spelled out.

"It's obvious that nigga want our spot, bro. He used to move weight back in the day. Check this, we bought out Berkley from BTG in 2016. Berkley had ownership over Cuba too, so he ain't really making no money right now because his connects making shop with our product in both locations instead of from Costa Rica," Seth explained, making sure he understood this shit himself. It was the only logic he could come up with.

"I understand all that. That's obvious. Shit still don't explain why that nigga coming at us using The Monstrosity as bait. Somebody from that nigga's clique got something on us, or something to do with us that involves this nigga Jamie-O. Know what I mean?"

This was the Messiah who Seth got money with. This wise guy right here; not that emotional ass nigga who almost got hung up when they used the white stripes as a gimmick to bait their trap.

Seth could've sworn he turned his ringer off, but when the chime cut the suffocating air in the room, he pulled it from out of his pocket and read over the text message in disbelief before his phone chimed again with picture mail.

"Never," he scoffed with squinted eyes, reading over the message a few times before he looked up and peered at his dawgs.

"What's the word?"

Prodigy crossed his arms over his chest, following his statement. What the fuck else could've possibly gone wrong?

"Nasir got a lil' brother that's three years younger than her...and he dating yo' lil' sister, fam." Seth showed them the picture on his phone; a very rare photograph of Catori in the hospital holding onto a baby boy with both Nasir and Ali sitting in bed with her, and another of the baby's birth certificate. "Nuri Princeton Valentine, better known as, Steelo. He that nigga's Jamie-O's son, too."

Taug Jaye

"Be better, do better. But most importantly? Don't be like me. The chains are harder to break at thirty-three."

-Marius

Heart Up For Ransom

Chapter

15

Closure is an act or process of closing something. A sense of resolution or conclusion at the end of an artistic work. A feeling that an emotional or traumatic experience has been resolved.

It took a lot to rattle Steelo.

To kill his vibe.

To get inside of his mind and cause him to double back.

A man like him had almost mastered his peace down to a "T." But Tiri knew what triggered him. She held the cheat codes in the palms of her hands that would expeditiously revert him from zero to one hundred, and the killer in him right now wanted her fucking head. They'd only been back home from Bali for all of a week, and just that quick, she'd already succeeded at pissing him off with running her damn mouth and asking a bunch of dumb ass questions that had him ready to catch a damn case.

His temple was so disturbed, you could see the vibrations from his anxiety quivering amongst his flesh. Hell, even his goosebumps had goosebumps. His stomach was churning, mouth was dry, eyes were crossing, bowels were trying to move without his permission. A sickness had yoked Steelo up in a chokehold that he physically couldn't fight his way out of, and any minute now, he was bound to regurgitate everything he'd eaten in the last twenty-four hours.

Steelo hated what she did to him. The stupidity and weakness wrapped up in his love for young Tiri would surely be his fucking demise. Just that quick she had all odds stacked against him, and his head wanted to explode. The pressure was too heavy. The walls of his home were slowly closing in, and no matter how much he tugged on his collar, perspiration began to dampen his clothing until he snatched up his car keys and headed out the front door.

At first, he was convinced that the fresh air would do him some justice, but it did nothing but drive him deeper into a sulking rage of paranoia. And if something didn't intercept him quick, there was no telling what he'd do if his anxiety had succeeded at pushing him to the edge.

He felt a little better; a minor release of his agitation had diminished when he pulled his Bugatti up beside his brother's Batman-inspired Lamborghini and shut off the engine. He damn near rubbed his hands raw wiping the sweat free from his moist palms. Steelo gazed out into space for a good thirty minutes proceeding his arrival until Marius came outside to check up on him.

The sight before Steelo was too got damn hilarious not to laugh.

His potna stood there shirtless with Jayce asleep inside of the baby hoist that was strapped around his muscular frame. He had this daddy shit down pact. Aubrey was walking like a pro in a pair of her mother's heels with nothing on but a t-shirt, panties, and sixty layers of lip gloss painted on her miniature heart shaped lips. Marius certainly had his hands full with his little diva already.

He was an iconic and untouchable assassin; one of the fucking best to ever do this shit in history, but he was an impeccable father, and Steelo had always respected that about his dawg. The growth was rewarding to witness.

"Yo' ass been out here crying in this damn car for almost an hour," Marius chuckled as he approached the vehicle. Best believe that Aubrey was in tow with her heels click-clacking amongst the gravel, racing for her Ste-Ste, too.

"My moms want me to come see her."

Steelo wasn't sure how the words were able to fly out his mouth with little to no effort, but they did. In one bop. Almost with force, and just hearing those words escape from him caused his stomach to twist into the tightest knot, yet.

Marius scratched his wavy head perplexed, not knowing how to take on his boy's confession. Steelo didn't discuss his past. Not about his parents. Not about his problems. It was one thing when he admitted to the obvious love he'd developed for young Tiri, but the declaration of mentioning the censored evocations from his childhood was a totally different ball game.

"She's alive?" was the only thing Marius could come up with right off rip. Shit threw him through a loophole for sure.

"Yeah, that bitch alive."

"Ooooh. Emotions."

Steelo cut his eyes so hard in Marius' direction, the notion could've slit his damn throat. He was really feeling a way and wasn't in the mood to be chastised for doing so.

"You know I'm fucking wit' you, man. Light skinned niggas stay in they damn feelings. Let's finish this inside. Bri-Bri, come on—aye, put that mulch down."

He was wondering why she was so damn quiet.

"But daddy!"

"Get yo' lil' butt in here, girl. Hands smell like shit now. Come on."

Steelo gathered up the Louboutin pumps that fell from little Aubrey's feet after her father picked her up and followed them inside.

It was nothing for Marius to get Jayce settled since he was cast away in a deep slumber, but his daughter? It was hell getting her hands washed/drawn away from the sink because she didn't want to quit playing in the water. Her little fake cries filled the atmosphere until Marius got her settled with a small bowl of "Trawberr" what she called strawberries, and put on *The Secret Life of Pets* to hold her attention while him and Steelo chopped it up.

Their women, Ceas, The Koi's, Válo, and a small squad were all out in LA testing a few different strands of marijuana for Tiri to choose from for her café that afternoon. Once Tiri revealed her goals and aspirations to her man, Steelo didn't hesitate to get her licensed to manufacture and distribute Mary Jane. That way, she could legally move forward with her dreams. So here they were with the kiddos, sharing a bottle of Whiskey, and moments away from engaging in deep conversation.

"How'd you find her?"

Steelo released an exasperated breath as he held onto his empty glass. The ice cold bottom of it sat along his exposed knee due to the rips in his distressed denim capris pants, sending a slight chill up his spine.

Or, was he just nervous?

He honestly didn't know where to begin, but he also knew since the cat was out of the bag, that he no longer had the right to remain silent. His days of pleading the fifth were pretty much overthrown.

"Doing a lil' background check on Tiri some odd months back. You knew?"

Marius shook his head no, and that was the honest to God truth.

"You a grown ass man, Steelo. I trust your judgment. Did I start to do a search of my own on Tiri? Damn right, but I left that for you to handle. I knew all I needed to know about them niggas Seth and Messiah and their involvement with the cocaine trade, and that's all it is to it. BTG signed them off as well trusted niggas, so I took my potnas' word. Sometimes you just gotta step out on faith, man."

"Seth's wife is my 'sister.'"

Marius choked on his drink when it started to travel down the wrong hole. He had to be hearing shit. How in the hell didn't he peep that?

"Come again?"

"Now you see why its got me feeling some type of way."

"Seth wasn't married when they bought Berkley from BTG. That I remember."

Steelo cracked his neck, trying his best to unwind, but that was all easier said than done.

"Shit's blowing me, man."

"You gon' go?"

"The fuck I know?"

He could front all he wanted to, but Marius could read his boy; very well. Steelo couldn't hide the eternal battle he was fighting, and what came out of Marius' mouth next startled the both of them.

"Go."

"Go?"

"Exactly what I said, youngin'. GO." Mr. Usher downed the rest of his drink then chuckled at his little crybaby, laid back, quiet as a mouse now just a chilling. She'd be nodding off soon. There was no need to bet his last dollar on it. He knew his seeds like the back of his hand. "If I had the chance to speak to Lena; even if it was only for five minutes, man...I'd do it." He poured them each another round. "I got caught up in fucking this city to atone for her death. To feel closer to her. To show her that her son didn't take it lightly when he stepped to the very outlet that destroyed her.

Real shit, I felt a lil' resentment towards her in doing so because she was the reason for all my hatred. But when the shit was all said and done, all I ever wanted was for her to love me, man.

You don't wanna be in your thirties still mentally and emotionally sick from not letting that shit go. Shit's not healthy. Shit's for damn sure not worth it, either. You've spent your entire life wondering where she was. Why not go and hear her side of the story? It's obvious that it's eating you up, man. So fix that. Be better, do better. Take the time to hear her out. If it's bullshit, walk away. But if it's not?" Marius looked his little brother in the eye. "Then it's up to you to decide if you wanna proceed to make amends or keep living how you been living. It's a reason why you haven't done a DNA search. It's a reason why you haven't gone the extra mile to find her or ya sperm donor until now."

"Could really give a fuck about Hezekiah, bruh. Straight up. Nigga gave me away when I was five years old. How can I ever respect a man like that? His ass done disappeared off the face of the earth, though. Ain't no trace of him around. Info show he's my father, but I couldn't get nothing further on him...I remember his ass though, now...the night him and that crackhead ass bitch he was fucking with left me on the orphanage's front porch in the rain...in the middle of the night...it's some shit you'll never forget. It's like you try to convince yourself that you did, but mentally, you can't run away from the truth."

"Not at all, man. And it's a'ight to admit that you still afraid. I ain't gon' judge you. It took me and KD getting into it about a damn dog a couple years back for me to realize that, what I've been holding on to was hurting me more than it was to accept it and finally find peace within myself. And speaking of dogs."

It wasn't long until Marius came back from the side door with Dottie and Rayman racing for the living room right behind him. Aubrey jumped up in excitement when they came charging in her direction. She too knew that they couldn't sit up on the couches, so she brought her bowl of fruit down on the floor with her and snuggled up in the middle of her babies who would always be there to protect her and her little brother. The Ushers were slowly yet surely growing into a well-rounded family. The only thing missing was the white picket fence.

"You need closure, youngin'. Ain't nothing wrong with that." Marius took a seat after peaking in on Jayce sleeping in his play pin. "It's your call though, but you and I both know you really want to. Strangely and in ways you'll never be able to understand, you harbor more love for her than hatred. Take it from a man who always told his mother that he loved her despite the shit she put him through. A mother's love hits different, and lil' bro, if you got the opportunity to jump on it and make sense of it all, then I'd do it without hesitating if I were you. And nah, that shit ain't gon' be easy, but at the end of the day, it's gon' be worth it. Release yo' self from this mental slavery, man. You and young Tiri crossed roads for a reason."

Steelo could see the darkness overpower the whites of Marius' eyes once he changed his attention to his phone. Those were the eyes of death; blood and assassination, and that quick Steelo's demeanor changed to match his brother's.

"What's the word?"

Marius had blocked everything around him out for the time being. The email he continued to read through held his undivided attention until an imaginary light switch was flipped, and The Monstrosity went back into hiding.

"Aye, man. What the fuck is up? We got static?"

Marius shook his head as he coolly sipped his drink, now unbothered.

"Nothing that concerns you. Go see ya moms, a'ight? That should be your main focus. I'mma hold shit down here while you out."

"Mar—"

"Do what I said." The bass in his tone was assertive, proving to Steelo that brotherhood was something every man in this world needed to make it through life. Marius truly did have his back through whatever. And he was grateful. "Remember what I said, a'ight? Do better, be better. But most importantly? Don't be like me. The chains are harder to break at thirty-three."

𝕳𝖀𝕱𝕽

"So, which two strands did you narrow it down to, Tiri?"

Kovu damn near coughed up a lung while puffing on the Backwoods they were passing back and forth. She and Tiri had been getting high all day considering their visit to LA while they were doing the marijuana testing. They should've had dry mouths at the rate they were going, but after having lunch and getting fucked up off of mimosas, it was only right to spark another flame to keep this party going.

"It's between these two: this one reminds me of that Blueberry Hill and this one gives me Lemon Drop vibes. What do you think?"

"I personally fuck with the Blueberry better, but maybe you should make two different plates using one of each and we'll go from there."

"Yeah, that's what I was thinking, too," Tiri agreed as she closed the Ziplock freezer bag. "Damn, we made it to St. Louis already?"

Lo and behold, their jet was landing at her people's hangar as if they hadn't just boarded this bad boy roughly an hour ago.

Uneasiness had begun to plague her body as she unlocked her phone and realized that Steelo still hadn't responded to her text message. Tiri felt stuck between a rock and a hard place once Nasir hit her up and voiced how she and Catori would love to see him if he was up for it. She didn't appreciate Steelo cussing her clean the fuck out when she relayed the message as if she were the master behind this entire orchestration. But she also knew that their family union wasn't only overdue, but it was imperative to occur. After hearing about Catori's breakdown and learning the truth, Tiri couldn't allow Steelo's hatred and unstable emotions to be symbolized as the divider between them any longer. Whether he liked it or not, his mother deserved an explanation and so did he.

"Do you think he'll come?"

Kovu could see the plea in Tiri's dark brown eyes as she turned and faced her. She cared so much about her brother from another mother, and KD admired that. It was unbelievable the way she entered his life and honestly gave him purpose. Light skinned niggas were drama queens, a hard code to crack, and the perfect recipe to end up on *Snapped*.

And that man was suffering from twenty years of affliction? KD had to give her girl a hand clap. Whatever Tiri was doing, which she knew was loving him unconditionally, she hoped it never stopped. I mean, who else was better for ya boy? Let's go ahead and keep things one hundred.

"He will. Just watch. Steelo stubborn as fuck. He probably back at home crying to Marius right now looking for insight. His ole' emotional ass ain't fooling nobody."

Tiri couldn't help but laugh at the way KD's St. Louis lingo paired with that Trinity twang rolled from off her tongue to induce both the humor and realness within her comment. She was beautiful seated across from her in a red, Shane Justin racer suit and over the knee, fuzzy knitted socks, courtesy of Reba Koi. The glow in her toffee colored skin was radiant, illuminating the area around them with nothing but good vibes.

"Those two are such a toxic combination, girl. It's like when physical abuse links up with emotional abuse."

"Biiiiiiiitch, I swear to God!!! Nut shit ass White boys!" KD blurted while falling back in laughter.

"Thanks for coming with me though, girl. You didn't have to."

"Ain't no need to thank me, baby. What are girls for? You solid, Tiri. I keep telling you, after almost being in Trinity for ten years, I still ain't met a bitch any realer than you, Asia, and Ceas. I got yo' back like fo' flats, *Tootsie Pop*. You know that. Plus, I know how much this really means to Steelo. We used to sit up and talk about that hurt from our mothers all the time before he completely blocked those thoughts and sentiments out. And Steelo don't open up for shit. I'm glad you got him to let his guards down so he could confide in you. He not only needs this shit to happen, but he also needs his girl and his sister to be there ten toes down behind him. This ain't gon' be easy by a long shot, but if I know him like I swear I do, then he'll be here. Trust me."

𝕳𝖀𝕱𝕽

Falcon's voice echoed at a light pitch as she hummed a Hawaiian lullaby that Meme Aruba had taught her years and years ago, right before she gave birth to Seth. Her head was resting gently on top of her best friend's. She held Catori in a loving clutch and slightly rocked her back and forth while rubbing the back of her hair. Falcon could feel her pain.

They almost shared the same numbness that's held her girl captive during these last seven days post her leaving the psych ward AMA.

And as much as Catori wanted to cry and weep, her glazy irises wouldn't allow it. The woman was mentally and physically drained as is. So she laid there staring off into space with her head in Falcon's lap and watched as the little white flurries scurried past the windowpane, swept away in the current of the icy winter winds. She hadn't left the room of hers inside of her daughter's home for the past week either. The only reason she allowed Nasir to pull her out of bed and scrub her down in the bathtub while Falcon changed her sheets was because she was hopeful and desperate that her son would arrive. So when Tiri and Kovu walked through the door, their presence kicked her anxiety into high gear, knowing that the moment she'd waited on for the last half of her complicated life was finally near.

Other than Falcon's soothing voice, Catori's sanctum was pin-drop quiet. The blazing fire from the built in, brick fireplace even roared at a low tone, thus, keeping the ladies comfortable and toasty in her thousand square-foot, roomy abode. Nasir was laid across the front of her mother and Falcon, up on her side while holding Catori's left hand inside of her own. Riley sat in a loveseat only a few feet away from the bed while Tiri and Kovu both laid snuggled up on the oversized, round, and rotating ottoman on the opposite side of the bed too. No one would dare bring up a conversation. Talking and sharing anything on their minds wasn't necessary in the moment. Just the love and surety of them all being a family and having each other's backs through whatever, was just as rewarding until there was finally a light knock at the door.

All of their hearts paused on the same electrical beat succeeding the disturbance. They each turned towards the entrance, Catori now sitting up straight, all six of her senses alert, shoulders back, head held high, and her heart galloping at a speed so heavily that she could hear the palpitations deeply embedded within her tympanic membrane. This was the moment that it all had boiled down to, and with everything in her, she prayed that the Lord would order their steps as everything soon began to unfold.

Steelo stood on the other side of the door regretting hopping on that jet, let alone being in *Nasir's* house as is.

Why was he there?

What was the point?

Was this moment of truth, this moment of faith, this moment of closure going to be worth it?

He was terrified.

Why the fuck did I let that nigga talk me into this shit?

Steelo exhaled a hard and perturbed breath as he stood there with his left arm above his head since he'd never removed his hand after knocking. The right hand clung to the doorknob as he pressed his forehead against the mahogany, seven-foot door shielding him from his worst nightmare, yet greatest dream come true. His ears were ringing, damn near bleeding from the suspense. Stomach flipping in summersaults, legs growing weaker, orbs desperate to shed a few tears; heart one tick away from bursting through his chest and erupting at his feet like a dormant volcano.

He wanted to turn around right in that moment and act as if this day had never come, but instead, he foolishly found himself twisting the doorknob, eternally counting to three before stepping foot inside.

The silence was suffocating after he slowly removed the chinchilla fur hood from hanging low over his still frosted face that was due to the harsh weather.

Catori held her hand over her mouth to stifle her cries once he revealed himself to the room. Tears soared down her cheeks like blazing comets while her throat begun to constrict with a vice grip.

Her son stood tall.

Handsome.

Was filled with a cockiness that spoke volumes despite how much this moment was feasting upon his insides.

His lining was perfect.

Facial hair and beard trimmed to precision.

His jaw structure was fucking beautiful; beyond anything any woman on this earth had ever seen before in all of her life.

The COLE trench coat, corresponding black cashmere sweater, jeans, and calf length revolutionary boots fashionably draped over his frame, hugging all of the right areas to give him a clean yet swagged out appearance.

He was everything she could've ever dreamed of him becoming.

Slowly, Catori crawled out of bed and stood in the middle of the room with a good ten feet keeping them at a distance.

Sadly, there was vengeance in his eyes.

Affliction.

Sorrow.

Yet, and still, there were also faint traces of...*hope.*

The tears flowed in overtime down Catori's face as she reached back with the hand of hers that wasn't around her mouth and nervously scratched her back. Her mind kept telling her one thing, desperately trying to encourage her feet to tread closer to her youngest child, but the communication from her brain to her physical motions were nonexistent. Instead, she doubled over in pain, sobbing from the pits of her aching soul, so wound up in mounds of disbelief that this shit was no longer an illusion.

He was beautiful.

As beautiful and fucking gorgeous as a man could possibly be, and that onset of pain fueled from deception, neglect, and failure, on her end as his mother, had attached her like a plague from the medieval times. One with no known cure to possibly rid her of the trauma she'd caused him.

Nasir nervously ran her fingers through her silk press as she sat up in bed, horribly shaking with red eyes and a tear-stained face that matched her mother's. She and Ali had a baby brother...a baby brother who was deprived of the childhood that they lovingly got the chance to spend together, making endless memories that they'd always cherish. Ali wasn't flying in until tomorrow morning due to the surprising weather advisory down south, so she was here on her own/without him, to face the music that she too couldn't handle.

When Catori felt her sobs reducing, she inhaled deeply before standing up straight and forced herself to make eye contact with her baby boy.

Steelo's anxiety plummeted as she began to take small, baby steps in his direction. Each time she stepped closer, the motion of her bare pedicured feet hitting the carpeted floor felt like the plunge of an Asian bass drum against his chest. It made him feel as if he were sinking into the floorboards; deeper into a deadly quicksand of some sort that was seconds away from swallowing him whole. Her steps kept igniting in his eardrums like bombs exploding on a war front in Iraq, causing him to tremble without his direct control.

Off rip, he gripped the handle on his Desert Eagle, tempted to withdraw it from his coat pocket and lodge the full extended clip into his mother's dome; and sadly, with no questions asked nor any second thoughts due to his sudden emission of rage. It took everything in him to retain his composure and not act off impulse, but when Catori started closing in on him, now only three feet away in distance, Steelo suddenly found himself...taking a step...backwards...

His actions felt like a slit to her throat, forcing her to howl out in pain.

"Nuri..."

Steelo took another step away from her. Away from *his mother*. Anger rushed through his veins like angry bees after a predator. This bitch never loved him. This shit was all a scheme. A scam. A trap to catch the oh so famous, big and bad, ruthless reputation having, Nuri "Steelo" Valentine slipping, and he had to admit that they'd succeeded at manipulating his mental.

Shit, he was there, wasn't he?

Touché!

Nonetheless, he was a fool to believe that this moment would mend all of his pain. Perhaps, to permanently patch all of his lesions? Pose as the coronary by-pass that would allow his broken heart to continue to beat firmly against his sternum instead of bleeding out?

No.

He was wrong.

This was wrong.

He shouldn't have come.

By this time, he'd taken so many steps in the opposite direction that his back was now stationed against the door that he should've never entered. Emotions weren't his cup of tea, of course, we all know this, but he couldn't hide the tears that welled up in the brims of his eyes as he gave his "mother" a quick once over. She was beautiful. He couldn't deny that...but...he simply didn't belong here. They were better off apart no matter how much she stood there and tried to attest that their separation was never a part of the plan.

It happened...

It lasted…
And most importantly…it destroyed him…
The shit conquered him in ways that he hated to plead guilty to in court, and right now…those negatives greatly outweighed the present.

He simply wasn't ready.

"I…" his chest felt restricted of all air. Like an anaconda had him secure in a deadly grip that none of his killa skills could ring him free from, and on everything he loved, he thought he'd collapse in the middle of the floor because the pressure was too got damn heavy for him to bear.

"Nuri…please, just—"

"Nah…this ain't that."

Catori crumbled when the bedroom door slammed shut behind him. Once again, she was being blamed for an instance in her life that she had absolutely no control over. Her knees hit the ground as an instant reflex while she attempted to rip out her hair and cry her eyes out. She loved her son so much, and he didn't even know the half of what their separation had done to her. What mother could handle such a low blow?

As Nasir hopped up and ran to her mother's side, Tiri kicked the covers from off of her legs and ran after Steelo's emotional ass. She wasn't sure if she should be upset or comforting about his actions, but one thing she wouldn't do was allow him to walk away and fly back out to Trinity. That shit was not about to go down.

"Steelo, I know you hear me calling after you! Got me running and yelling in this damn house. Steelo!"

But he continued to ignore her. The quicker he got inside of the limousine, the quicker he could make it to the airport and get the fuck from out of there. He was so good on this shit; he was good on *all* of this shit. Nothing anyone could say or do would possibly change his mind. Just seeing Catori for the first time in his life had ripped his manhood to shreds, and he couldn't handle it. It was easier to leave things alone and accept the fact that his "family" were doing just fine without him than to crumble at that woman's feet.

He'd be damned.

Steelo was so deep in his thoughts that it startled him when the door to the limousine that he'd just opened, was slammed shut, and a vehement Tiri was only meters behind him once he turned around.

"Tiri—"

"What the hell was that? You came all the way out here just to slam a got damn door in her face?" she spat.

"*Tiri.*"

Steelo was trying his best to remain calm. His eyes were seconds away from flushing into a killa state of mind, and off vibe, she knew better than to provoke him. But she called his bluff.

"Grow up, Steelo. I don't give a damn about you getting mad. We've already had this conversation. We've made it through the confessions. Just sit there and listen to her. Acting this way isn't gonna make it any better."

"You think this shit is easy, Tiri?! You of all people know what the fuck I've been through, yet you still tryna force this shit!"

"Did I say it was going to be easy, Steelo?! What in your life has ever been easy?! Do you wanna be this fucking damaged forever?! You and I both know that *getting over this* won't just happen because you *still* can't let it go! If you're afraid, then that's one thing, but don't stand here and try to insult me like you haven't been waiting on this to happen for fucking ever! If your mother was on bullshit, you would've been and called it the moment you felt the vibe in that room! So give me another excuse! Give me a legitimate reason as to why *this ain't that*, Steelo, and you'll never hear my mouth about it again!"

The adrenaline was pumping so fiercely throughout her blood that Tiri didn't realize how cold the twenty-three degree weather against her bare skin was since all she wore was a Champion t-shirt, matching leggings, and a pair of corresponding flip flops with no socks. A mountain of snowflakes were piling on top of her head as she stood firm with not a weak bone in her body. Steelo knew Tiri wouldn't coddle him about this situation. How would he look as her man? As the man who was placed in her life by the grace of God to guide and protect her, to selfishly turn his back on this shit after the way he folded in Bali? No, Tiri didn't set this ordeal up. She'd gotten intertwined in the middle of this shit just as he had too, once Catori took the initiative to finally go after him. They both were stuck between a rock and a hard place...but the best thing about it though? About them? It was simple. Together, these two could conquer anything, and that's why he loved her.

"I'm waiting," his little chocolate drop challenged with her arms crossed over her breasts and her perfectly filled in/thick eyebrow raised, waiting on his bullshit.

Defeated, Steelo sighed with his brows all wrinkled too as he removed his coat and wrapped it around her. The last thing she needed was to get sick. And even though it was against his better judgment, he pulled his feisty and technically right girl into his arms while placing a kiss to her forehead. Lil' smart mouth ass was always right. What in the hell was he going to do with her?

"It's not that I don't appreciate you for holding it down and having my best interest through all of this, shorty."

"Baby—"

"Just...give me a minute, a'ight? This is a lot to process all at once, and I know you feel me on that."

Tiri exhaled while looking up into his eyes, her lips forming into a slight smile. She hated how she got so weak for his sexy ass.

It was so silly.

"I just love you so much, Steelo. You know I wouldn't push you to do anything that would end up harming you. I want you to heal from this."

"I know, mama...Trust me, I know." He lovingly kissed her lips, sending a rush up her spine. "And I love you too. You hear me?" He held her body close while gazing deeply into her blazing brown eyes. It was crazy how much the Lord loved such an imperfect version of him that He sent this angel in his arms to love him in human form. It was the best blessing he'd ever received. "I love you, girl, and I'm not afraid to say that shit anymore."

Tiri's legs felt weak as she melted inside his embrace. She didn't expect him to reply. She never wanted to force Steelo into "convincing" himself that he loved her, especially when she knew that notion would leave him unsure of doing so. She wanted him to be honest and truly know it in the depths of his soul what it felt like to bask in the sacred purity of love once you'd allowed a stranger inside of your heart. And with the tone of his voice, the fear present in his eyes from revealing something so sacred and fragile from such a brute and broken man; she could tell by the way he held her and kissed her juicy lips that Steelo truly meant every last word when he admitted to loving her.

Anything that isn't growing is dead, so it was good to know that the Lord was watering the flowers in their garden for a glorious harvest.

"Just give me the night to myself, a'ight? I need a minute..."

Tiri nodded her head in agreement as she firmly wrapped her arms around his neck. She could give him that and pray that his family understood.

"I'll give you until Ali shows up here in the morning, babe."

He chuckled.

"You still giving me ultimatums? Even after all that?"

"Yup, because if I don't, then you won't take me or this situation seriously." Pulling back, she cupped his face in her hands before gently kissing his lips one last time. "Let's fix this, okay? Together."

"That's the only way I see fit, shorty."

HUFR

One of the most beautiful things about life in Trinity was the sunshine and its welcoming eighty degree weather during the peak of winter. College girls walked around in their skimpy clothing. Freshly waxed convertibles glided amongst the streets and the freeways with their tops back, music blaring, and nine times out of ten, the baddie in the passenger's seat had a good four to five bundles of Kendra's Boutique blowing into the wind while she recorded the moment on the Snap too.

Unfortunate for Mr. Miguel Samuels, the mayor of Trinity city, he missed the opportunity to enjoy that sunshine since he didn't leave his office until nine o'clock that night. He was more fearful than pumped or exhausted after working fifteen hours today with a lawyer on a case that they were sure to win. Every time the city went after The Monstrosity, it not only cost them millions, but each person in legislation who tried him wounded up dead or missing. Even though he was one hundred percent confident this time around that once they brought him in and got him convicted, death row would be his new home until his untimely death had arrived. Things weren't looking too good for Mr. Usher from their perspective, but the shit still had them as nervous as a first night stripper.

Taug Jaye

Considering Marius' reputation and his ability to slither his way out of situations that no other human being on this earth, well, to the mayor's knowledge of course, could ever do, that conception alone had him sweating bullets on his twenty minute commute home.

But he felt safe once he entered his three story sanctum, away from the world and all of its strife that he didn't allow to enter his front door. It was out of the ordinary to come home and not be greeted by his beautiful wife and children with dinner already on the table, but weighing the present circumstances while planning to execute Mr. Marius Lionel Usher, to take all measures and precautions, he sent them away on a trip to the Dominican Republic for a week as an early Christmas gift.

Loosening his tie, Mr. Samuels shot his mistress a quick text message, informing him that he was home and how it was okay for him to be in route. His feet were killing him. He needed a massage and his dick sucked like yesterday. The Absolute vodka burned as it rushed down his chest after fixing himself a chilled glass and lighting a cigar to help him unwind. He hummed along to a catchy tune that hadn't left his head since his ride home from off the radio as he proceeded up the stairs to the master bedroom.

The chill that swept over him as he flipped the lights on had startled him; well, the lights that he *expected* to flip on. The French styled windows over on the right side of the room roughly flapped back and forth as a brisk and harsh wind blew against his home. Rain began to pour like a raging typhoon, sending a double chill up Miguel's spine as he put his glass down. He took slow steps towards the window with his heartbeat increasing. A lump the size of a man's enlarged prostate got stuck in his throat as he looked over each of his shoulders in fear.

Just as he was about to reach out and close the windows shut, Mr. Miguel was grabbed by the back of his neck and thrown over the ledge, screaming at the top of his lungs as he fell down three stories of height. By the grace of God, his body was stopped just seconds before he would've hit the ground and faced a number of possible injuries. The blood in his body rushed to his head as he felt a harness on the back of his pants quickly pulling him back up towards the window. He could feel hot yellow piss trickling down his legs and chest, disgustingly seeping through his white button-down and onto his pale white face out of fear. A pair of hands grabbed him by the ankles while another set wrapped thick, grey duct tape around them.

Miguel screamed out loud when his body was roughly pulled back inside from out of the rain, and he hit his head along the hard wooden floor that he was dropped on.

The Monstrosity stood towering over him with a menacing glare present in his black eyes. He watched as one of the henchmen used a box cutter to remove his shirt before taping his arms behind his back while holding a black cast iron rod in hand.

Miguel's heart rate was so high that his blood pressure shot up to stroke level. His eyes were getting blurry, causing a formation of yellow and red colors to ricochet in view of his vision as Marius stuck the rod inside of the fire that was now present in his fireplace.

"P-p-please!!! I d-d-don't want any trouble! Ahhhhh!"

Miguel cried out in agony when the two beastly built henchmen started implementing harsh kicks and punches to his rather thin and frail body. Each blow felt like a limb in his body had been broken. Their fists were like iron; hot and heavy. The Timberland boots kicking along his back had surely given him a slipped disc or two. The last kick to the back of his balls caused him to throw up the previous drink he'd taken only minutes ago.

Why was God punishing him? Why was it such a horrible deed trying to get the city's most notorious criminal from off of the streets and behind bars? It wasn't him breaking the law. Him killing innocent people. Marius Usher was the demonic seed plaguing their town and running folks out of business with his illegal tax evasions and other physical and unlawful crime, so why was he suffering from the consequences of being an abiding citizen?

"That's enough."

With sweat dripping from their foreheads, his henchmen followed their boss' request and stood with their muscular chests heaving up and down from the excursion.

Mr. Samuels laid there stiff as a board, hoping if he appeared to be unconscious that The Monstrosity would just leave him be, but he'd been a witness to how this man operated for almost a decade now. He should've known better than that. His eyes flew open as screams erupted through his lips like a mad man when the piping hot branding rod was pressed against his ribcage. He cried like a baby. Howled like a dog at the moon. The heat ate away at his tender flesh with a raging intensity that made him lose all feeling from the waist down.

When The Monstrosity felt that he'd had enough, he pulled the hot iron away with a minacious glare in his eyes. To him, it looked as if a fist sized "W" were branded against Mr. Samuels' side, but every day for the rest of his life, if he lived, when Miguel looked down at it, from his perspective, he'd see an "M" and know who and what it referred to.

The wires in Marius' head were a bit crossed in this moment. More screws and bolts were loose in that got damn noggin of his than usual, and performing as the darker side of himself gave him an unfamiliar fit of rage this time around.

Mercy was absent from his soul as he now stood at his feet watching Mr. Samuels squirm and holler for his life, buried in pain. Yet again, somebody was tryna' play him. Just when he figured he had his retirement down to a "T," it was monkey ass niggas like the mayor who liked to add another round to this shit. This is how he got entrapped within that cyclical, revolving door. A part of him couldn't resist the bait. Could resist the challenge, but he also knew that all good things had to come to an end at some point. The only reason why The Monstrosity wasn't chopping this colonizing, White piece of shit up and feeding it to his "mistress" was because he had a little proposition for the sum' bitch that would be satisfying for the both of them. So he better had gotten it together and quick. They had business to take care of.

"Cut this shit the fuck out, alright. You're a grown ass man lying here begging another man for your life instead of dying on your feet. You've done enough to show how pathetic you people really are, but, check it. First, I have to admit that I do feel some type of way about how y'all plotted to take me out. I mean, that's cool and all. Fair game with the way someone from the Irish Mob was able to leak you information about my involvement with Elixir. It's a shame really. The same nigga's neck I saved a few years back still had the audacity to shit on me because he felt the need to be threatened by some potato worshipping ass crackers. He'll spend the rest of his life in hell thinking about his mistake, if you can catch my drift...So, Mr. Samuels..."

Arrogantly, The Monstrosity removed the fresh Cuban cigar from out of his breast pocket and lit the end until thick, white clouds of smoke filled the perimeter around him.

"Since you niggas are so comfortable gambling wit' ya life, then let's bargain. Roughly one day from now. City Hall. 1:00 PM, and not a minute later. You're gonna get the District Attorney, your Chief of Police, his Commissioner on my case, and the cities' Judge to show up. Listen to me closely, Mr. Samuels. Listen to me good. It's obvious with the way you all planned to surround my house tomorrow afternoon and take me into custody, that, you simply want me off your streets. I'm a *Menace to Society*. Alright, I get that.

So for the surety of my freedom and for the hunt to end, I'll give you exactly what you want and disappear. You niggas don't seem to take me seriously when I try to do shit on paper, so now I have to take things into drastic measures, meet with you all as a public, though private party, and then threaten not to have my men slaughter any of your families. I mean, I guess the Dominican Republic was a smart and rather cheap ass move, but just like you quote-unquote 'got eyes on me,' I got eyes on you, my good man."

"Don't you touch my fucking family, you filthy bastard!"

Mr. Samuels' words were so harsh on the way out, drool seeped down the sides of his mouth like an infested dog with rabies.

"Then call the fucking meeting."

"I need to know that this isn't some bullshit! Ahhhhh!"

The Monstrosity chuckled as one of his goons kicked the mayor in the middle of his bare back, encrypting a permanent boot print along his spine.

"And I need to know that we have a deal."

A sizzling noise filled the air along with deep wailing as Marius dug the piping hot iron into his side a second time, burning through his already raw tissues and exposed white flesh. He pressed the rod in further, and with more pressure, the hot metal continued to cook through his abdomen, slowly penetrating down to the bone.

"Yes! Yes! Yes! W-w-we h-h-have a deeeeeeeeal!!!"

Marius tossed the weapon onto the floor and turned his top lip up, modestly using his tongue to rake his teeth as he studied the submission in his opponent's tone and body language. That shit would always get a thrill out of him.

"Good choice, my man. Now let's get you up and ready to place a few phone calls. We're running out of time."

Heart Up For Ransom

"Lookin' back at my life made my heart race
Dance with the devil and test all faith
I was thinkin' chest moves, but it was God Grace
Crooked as whoever, 'til we all straight..."

-Nipsey Hussle

Chapter
16

Do you honestly think that Steelo had a wink of sleep last night? He tossed and turned for hours, his cognizance running on nothing but mind-numbing fear and adrenaline.

And that was one hell of a combination.

Mr. Valentine tried his best to remain calm yet found himself consumed by these heavy fits of rage that coerced him to drown his liver with a fifth of Black Whiskey. And even once the bottle was empty, to his dismay, not only was he still pissed off, but now he'd foolishly transformed into a pissy ass drunk who was easily triggered with little to no effort. Something as minor as him hearing the wind blowing against the windowpane would irritate him to the core, and the desolation made Steelo feel as if he had nowhere to turn.

He must've paced the hotel room a hundred dozen times over until the knock at his door forced him to approach it with two fully loaded burners; impatiently ready to make something shake from the mere sight of anything in motion. He wanted to kill someone, something; hell, any damn thing at this point to rid him of the anguish. Nevertheless, he was hit with nothing but mounds of deception when that short-lived boast of desire was eliminated upon his opening of the door.

He didn't know why Tiri was so got damn hardheaded. So got damn adamant to disobey a single request, which was to leave him be for the night while he tried to figure this shit out on his own whim. For the life of him he just couldn't seem to understand why she never listened to her man, as if his words held not an ounce of weight when it came to her. Maybe it was because she knew she was his weakness...She wanted to get sick from leaving out the house in the wee hours of the morning with miles of snow steadily coating the pavements of those dangerous St. Louis streets. But not even that had stopped her.

He honestly didn't know how she did it...how she just...knew when he was in need. Knew when he was hurting. Knew when to wrap her arms around him and talk him down from off the ledge...once, a-fucking-gain... especially when it wasn't her responsibility in the first place to heal yet another damaged Black man... not when he was the known perpetrator who'd driven himself into a boundless trench of melancholic absurdity. He wouldn't dare hand that burden over to her when it was time for him to put his pride aside and seek his own refuge.

But her effort to always push him to stand tall made Nuri a slave to her every command. She showered him with a sense of loyalty that could never be bought, and for that, he'd forever be indebted to their love.

Neither of them could verbally use words to describe the way Steelo made love to her that night. The powerful yet gentle way he touched and handled her body like the delicate gem she truly was.

One moment his tongue was so far down her throat that young Tiri swore she could instantaneously feel the tip of it stroking against her tender nub. Then the next, he was holding her legs on his shoulders, tightly gripping her thighs, pounding away with such intensity that each thrust sent an instant shock of electricity thrashing up her warm and silky middle.

He fucked her with years of pain that ironically converted into nothing but pleasurable palpitations; such tantalizing tremors that he had Tiri's pussy squirting around his throbbing cock that was buried deeply into the roots of her loam. He'd pinch her nipples, and round after round, continue to shove his raw rod with such desire into the pits of her essence, greedily enveloping himself into her quivering wetness because he couldn't seem to get enough; impeccably rotating his hips, making sure that pussy knew what he felt like from each and every angle that he had in him to give it.

Steelo took out all of his mental frustrations between her thighs. Thankful for the momentary escape. Thankful for the sexual release that kept his alter ego from rising to surface and stupidly adding another murder to his name. It was sick how he was suddenly stuck in the motions and couldn't seem to get a grasp on his sentiments for the time being. The ambivalence had him torn between infuriation and forgiveness. Love and hate. Vengeance and grace; no, more so mercy and rage. He'd never wanted to hate an individual as much as his mind kept trying to make him perceive Catori as the enemy, but when he released his seeds inside of Tiri for the last time that night, Steelo felt the chains unbinding from around his wrists.

The rope was cut from his neck.

The ransom was paid.

It were as if an epiphany had swept over him, simultaneously forcing him to tap out sexually and mentally. In a matter of strokes there was no longer this repressive constraint weighing him down. There was no further need for him to reload his machinery with ammunition, nor to make any preparations for the ongoing war he'd been fighting for years. There was no need to continue.

He was done...

Steelo could've sworn that he'd closed his eyes only minutes ago just as the ringing of Tiri's phone woke them up around 10 o'clock that morning. "His brother" had arrived in town thanks to Seth sending out a jet since the Atlanta airlines were still delayed.

Nuri couldn't describe the way he felt once he pulled up in front of Nasir's house an hour later after they made one last round of sweet love, then showered before leaving the hotel. His stomach was nothing nice in this moment, twisting and turning in such a degree that it caused his chest to rise and fall with pain. It wasn't until he felt Tiri reach over the console and grab a hold of his hand, had he looked her in the eye after staring off into space for quite some time. She greeted him with a soft and timid smile to try and lighten up the mood.

"Babe, you can do this. God is with you. He's always been with you despite your previous sorrow. You have to believe that everything happens for a reason. Even when you don't understand it."

Steelo exhaled the last of his discomforting angst once she leaned over and kissed his lips. He was so got damn tired of fighting that he threw in the towel and finally exited the vehicle.

Minutes later, Seth, *his sister, and his brother* greeted them at the door before letting them inside. The silence engulfing the foyer as they all stood around staring at one another, as if they were telepathically asking, *What's next,* was eventually cut by Tiri as she cleared her throat.

Somebody had to be the voice of reason and decide what the next move would be.

"Umm, we'll give y'all your privacy and let you all talk before Catori comes down. Come on, Uncle Seth. Are y'all cooking? It smells good. Is Momma Platinum still here?"

As the duo disappeared down the hall that led to the kitchen, Steelo removed his coat before Nasir walked up to him and smiled.

"I'll take that for you if you want me to. I'm Nas, well, Nasir. Your big sister. I'm sure you already know that, but I still feel the need to introduce myself. I know yesterday went a little left with how overwhelming this all is, but I'm happy to meet you...Can I have a hug?"

Steelo knew right then and there that this shit wasn't about to be the least bit easy. Nasir's heart was pure. He could decipher that from her voice, her energy, and the odd connection between them as they embraced before she took his coat.

"And this is Ali, our older brother. If I'm not mistaking, I think Ma said that we're all three years apart. Something like that?"

"Wassup wit' it, man," Ali greeted with a hand slap. "Yeah, you are our lil' brother. You look just like us. Welcome home. Can't imagine the shit you been through, but I'm glad we about to get this all cleared up. This make a lot of sense, don't it, Nas? With the way moms been acting after all of these years. I never expected it to be as big as this, but shit, it's all on God's timing. Not ours."

Steelo agreed with his *brother's* words of encouragement one hundred percent. He wasn't the perfect follower of Christ, and he also knew that he could have a stronger relationship with God, but one thing he did believe was that Jesus is Lord and in the power of the Holy Spirit. It's what kept him going after all of the trials and tribulations that were so close to breaking him, but even on those dark days when it seemed as if he had nowhere else to turn, one thing he always did was hold onto his faith.

As Nasir went to do away with his coat, Ali went to grab their mother from her room once they showed him to the sanctum where they all would be having their family discussion. Steelo stood inside of their open-floored conference room alone with one of his hands in his pocket as the sun shined through the ceiling-high window. A sense of peace was trying to mend his clouded mind as he watched a red fox scurry across the backyard, leaving its deep footprints inside of the six-inch high, white snow covering the grass. He sipped the same glass of 1942 that he was offered when he'd first arrived, slowly, to help with the aftermath of his slight hangover and nerves. It was quite odd how another round was the magic antidote to suppress your nausea from the overkill of the same poison.

The thought tripped him up for a few minutes before he heard the door to the den open, but Steelo didn't bother to turn around. Watching Nasir and Ali's reflections in the window was all he could cowardly do until Catori arrived in tow and shut the door behind her. Then, he turned around. It was then when he put the glass down and searched her face with blazing eyes. She was sick. He could see it. He could feel it. Sick for reasons he was only moments away from learning. Sick from the depression, the separation, the heart break…

Steelo could *feel* that shit.

So when Catori's swollen eyes landed on her son, the tears raced to surface like a chain reaction. She held an old photo album in her arms, the leather hardcover a bit damaged from the house fire of '97, but the untouched remains stowed away along the inside were all that really mattered. She placed the rather heavy booklet on the table before she headed over to her youngest boy. Praying to God that today he had the strength. Praying to God that he'd discovered the ability to hear her out first before passing judgment on her complicated shrouds and dilemmas from the 90's. Some that Nasir and Nali aka Ali weren't even aware of.

Their heartbeats were in sync as Catori began to close in on him. It was as if each *lub-dub* from the powerful contracting of their weary hearts were bouncing against the walls like sound effects from a thriller film at your local movie theater.

Six steps away…five steps away…four…

Steelo found his breaths growing deeper, quickly transitioning into a fearful pant as she had made it over to him, now at an arm's length.

Three steps away…two steps away…one…

Catori crumbled and fell into his arms the moment he pulled her into his embrace.

Steelo was…officially tired of fighting y'all.

He wrapped his arms around his mother's back and cried on her shoulder as she soaked his shirt with her own tears. Catori clutched her baby tight. A gust of completion, tranquility, and relief wrapped them up in a whimsical vortex, joining their lost and broken souls as one. Emerged a splash of color back into the nightmares that have been nothing but grey and white for as long as either of them could remember. Those same emotions and sentiments from the moment she walked in the door just seconds ago came rushing at Steelo as he held her tighter and cried in her arms like the night be broke down and willfully disintegrated in front of Tiri.

This is why he couldn't kill that girl. This is why he saved her. This is the reason why Marius went back on his word about that very day, her first day on campus, and told him and KD to take care of some last minute business for him while he was away instead of pushing it off. Not only was Tiri the girl of Steelo's dreams, but God allowed everything in their lives to fall apart so that this moment could come together. That was the ultimate answer to the riddle.

"Nuri...I." Catori inhaled deeply, feeling the convulsions taking over before she could begin. "I'm so, so sorry, baby. I...I didn't know what happened to you. One moment I was holding you in my arms, and when I woke up that next day, I...I'm in a psych ward heavily sedated, hooked up to all kinds of IV's fresh out of surgery. Something in my heart kept telling me; my intuition kept forcing me to ask about you, son. To question the whereabouts of a child that so many people tried to convince me that I didn't have no matter how well I hid that pregnancy. They all told me I was crazy. They all tried to make me believe that it was all in my head, but deep down inside, I knew it was true."

It was abrupt when Catori pulled back and looked him in the eye, making sure that he'd *heard* her when she said what was next.

"Nuri, I never would've left you. I never would've neglected you. I never in my life would've cast you away and left you out there all the way across the country, and in a city that I knew nothing about. I know that you think I didn't fight for you. I know that you've hated me and that you have twenty-five years of resentment built up against me because of this. Baby, I'm not that kind of woman, that kind of mother. I'm not the monster that your father made me out to be, and I pray to God with everything left in me that you find it in your heart to forgive me. Being separated from you was never a part of my plans, and I'll do whatever it takes to prove to you that I've always loved you. That I've always cared for you and prayed for your safety. I don't know what it was that I could've possibly done to you all's father to make him leave and destroy this family the way he did. He was so fucking sick in the head that, against my better judgment, he even forced me to name Ali after someone else because he was convinced that I had stepped out on him. And even once the DNA test came back proving that you were his son, it still made no difference and your name was never changed."

A confused look was etched across Ali's and Nasir's faces once their mother peered in their direction.

"I'm sorry. I haven't been completely honest with any of you. Momma fucked up. She let y'all down. It's deception at it's fucking worse, and I pray that one day we can put all of this in the past and just move on."

Catori had been afraid throughout her entire life that her children would never look at her the same once she sat down and kept it real about their father, so as a defense mechanism, she always brushed the fact off and let their minds wonder to keep herself at peace.

Those days were over.

Every one of them in this room needed her to iron out a plethora of details that would heal them all, and now that Nuri was not only around, but alive, she had no choice but to face the fears that she no longer wanted to haunt her. It had to be done.

"Come on. Let's have a seat."

Steelo's voice was lathered with care and concern as he directed his mother to the couch following her introduction. She was jittery and a little unstable on her feet, and from the looks of things, this was getting ready to be a long morning. They all needed to get comfortable to prepare for what was soon to come. So he sat down on one side of her, Ali sat on the other, and Nasir took a seat on the floor, resting her head on their mother's lap with tears trickling down her own face too. The moment was overbearing.

"Curtis Chambers is not your father, Ali. He's your uncle; Hezekiah's, aka Jamie-O's, older brother. Jamie-O was so convinced that I'd slept with him because of the bond we had that, I allowed him to humiliate me in front of everyone when I printed Chambers out on that birth certificate. I was young, I was dumb, I was in love, I—I really had no other choice, honestly. I blame it on myself all the time for not being rational about the situation with y'all's father, but at fifteen and sixteen years old, what else could I possibly do on my own? Now, as I had gotten older, *yes*, I was the only one who should've been held accountable for continuing to sacrifice my sanity, my dignity, and my reputation as a woman just to say that I had him. For stupidly sticking around. A part of me was afraid to leave after so long because Jamie-O was all I'd known for *years*. He showed me things in this world that I didn't know existed at the age of fifteen, and you can only imagine what that shift for me was like back then. But one thing I'm not going to do is sit here and act like I didn't know that man was using me. That I will not do.

Did he have love for me and the bind that I helped him get out of? Yes, but majority of that shit was all in my teenaged head, and that's a loss that I've had to accept. I always wondered why he kept threatening to leave me by the time Ali was five and Nas was three. It made no sense to me until he told me straight the fuck up to my face last week how I was nothing but a safety net for him until he could live the life he truly wanted. At the end of the day, he was using me to steer clear of the laws who were trying to put him in prison until he beat his cases and his name was cleared. He never even wanted kids. I was on birth control the entire time we were together, it was one of his stipulations as far as our arranged marriage **went**, but I still ended up pregnant. It was a *real* shock when I got pregnant with you, Nuri, because seeing as though the pill wasn't as effective for me like it was for other women, as a result, I was switched to the patch by my gynecologist and per Jamie-O's request to ensure we didn't have any further slip ups, but God had other plans.

Jamie-O put on a nice front for the cameras as if we were happily married, but, baby, if the walls in our home could talk? That nigga was miserable, and I'd known for a fact that he'd cheated on me for majority of our relationship. But what did momma do? Let that man cheat in peace because he was my everything, and he'd succeeded at mind fucking me to where all I could see was him. It's like, knowing that he was truly unhappy pushed me to oddly love him even harder. It pushed me to want to please him and gain his acceptance so much that I was willing to do anything for him. I was blinded by the façade we were putting on for the people around us. I *can* admit though, at one point and time, around when we first met, that, he *did* love me. It was almost too good to be true, really. It all happened so fast. He was on the run, he was this fine ass, mixed,

Black and Asian dope boy that no woman in town could resist. But no matter how chaotic those days were for either of us, I could tell from the first time when he laid eyes on me that he felt something beyond our arrangement. For a short while...I was living a fucking dream until it all came tumbling down much faster than I could savor the memories, and that's why I was so nervous when Nas had first told me about her dating Seth.

I just knew what it looked and felt like to have the wool be pulled over your eyes in the snap of a finger, but I thank God that my son-in-law was—*is* nothing like that bastard. I know y'all keep looking at me crazy in regard to the arranged marriage part, but it's true. Hezekiah was an illegal immigrant at the time, and he was not only facing deportation from here, but he was also facing the death penalty where he was wanted in the Philippines for capital murder. He left Asia in sight for refuge and ended up in St. Louis after Curtis sent for him to help him escape his charges. He's been changing his identity for years, way before he even met me. By the way, Jamie-O is fifteen years older than I am, so put that shit in a pipe and smoke it. But yeah, even with all of the identity changes he was doing, he'd finally gotten caught up out here when he was busted for drug trafficking. The idea about the marriage came around from the 'great wits' of Curtis. He was dating my sister, y'all's aunt, Catrina, Riley's mother, at the time, and that's how I ended up crossing paths with Jamie-O. Curtis would do anything to keep his baby brother out of trouble, so he pitched the idea to my mother that he'd pay her twenty grand to marry me off to keep Jamie-O from getting deported.

In Missouri, its legal for parents to consent at such a young age, so boom. Never knew a thing about this nigga, had never seen him a day in my life; hell, I didn't even know that Curtis had a brother, but I'll be damned if Valentine was slapped on the back of my name quicker than my mother could get me to understand what was going on. With the right amount of money, they had the marriage back dated to show proof that we'd been together for a while to help stop him from being extradited. Back in those days, it was nothing to pull that shit off. Immigration laws weren't as strict as they are now. So... they were able to avoid him getting sent back out to Asia, but now he's in the limelight for drug dealing and it's like the madness would never end. My momma had married me off, my 'estranged husband' was out on bail with a trial that kept getting pushed back because cash rules everything in this damn world. Still moving weight like the shit was nothing because he was laying low with his operations, breaking all kinds of fucking laws, and just little ole' dumb me was stuck in the middle doing whatever the fuck my man told me to do because I didn't have a voice.

I guess what also hurt me the most and made me feel like I had nowhere to run is because of what my mother did to me. I lived lavish with y'all's father, so to know that she only pocketed twenty thousand punk ass dollars to marry me off was just pathetic and grimy. It made me feel like she didn't really care or give a damn about me, so I was convinced that Jamie-O was all I had. She didn't give a fuck what anyone in our family had thought of her, she didn't feel bad for doing so, and that shit broke me. Jamie-O might not be shit but one thing he did that your grandmother didn't was take care of me."

"I mean..." Nasir wiped her face and cleared her throat so she could clearly speak. She didn't mean to interrupt her mother, but baby girl had an important ass question that couldn't wait. "But why take Nuri away from you though? Despite all of that. Not saying it doesn't matter because it does. It explains your behavior and every single move you've always made since Ali and I were old enough to realize that something was out of place, but why put you and y'all's son through all of that? And deliberately? I don't understand. It's just not making sense to me."

Catori took a deep breath so she could continue to settle her daughter's weariness. It brought tears to her eyes just knowing that Nas and Ali were so accepting of their brother after all that's happened.

"Once his name got cleared, it was like fuck the life he never asked for. We both were literally forced into it...He was a manipulator. He still had resentment towards Ali no matter what the DNA test had proven. He never wanted a daughter; it was frowned upon in the Asian culture, and that left your little brother. Nuri was his opportunity at beginning a clean slate; something he was proud of since the three of us obviously didn't make 'the cut.' Jamie-O was selfish and wanted to move on as if none of the past had ever happened. The nigga turned around and paid y'all's grandma another fifty thousand dollars in exchange for him taking Nuri and making her put me in the psych ward to attempt to make me forget about being pregnant. It's the main reason why he made me hide the pregnancy in the first damn place, and I'm just now putting all of the pieces together. He'd always planned it. Nas, baby, you and Ali were so young that y'all don't remember me being away down on Arsenal for a year; strung out on all kinds of shit. I just couldn't believe that man really used my pregnancy against me to make my charts look good since he'd illegally put me there, saying it was the postpartum depression that led me there if anyone got suspicious about it. That shit made me delusional. I'm surprised anxiety medicine, and Seroquel is all I've been on to keep me sane when those faint memories would haunt me for years and years until I just couldn't take it anymore."

"So that's why you and grandma don't fuck with each other? She fucked you over, *twice*, for some damn money? Money that she ain't got shit to show for?"

Ali was hot. Nasir had always been the forgiving one out of the two of them growing up, but if he didn't fuck with it or you, then there was no need to fake, front, or stunt. It wasn't in his character.

"Yes, son. Yes..." Two tears slid down Catori's face. It surprised her when Steelo reached up and thumbed them away, forcing her bottom lip to quiver. "I wish I would've had the strength to tell y'all sooner; before it ever got to this point. Nuri, no matter how many private investigators I hired, your father made it certain that I couldn't find you. You technically didn't exist because he made it look that way. The foster home you were at? He paid them off. Your sister's husband was able to do some good digging once some things with the Platinum cartel popped up. He'll be able to explain all of that a lot better than I can...but, Hezekiah was sick. He gave you away because he eventually grew tired of seeing so much of me and the life he didn't want to remember through you, and you didn't deserve that. All I ever did was foolishly love him, despite how inhumane and crazy it was. Despite how fucking farfetched and unreal it may have been. I coasted my way through a lot of my life posing as a porcelain doll, listening to whoever and doing whatever it is that they demanded of me, just to have all of those same people turn their backs on me once my services were no longer needed.

All I've ever had unconditionally in this world was the love from my children, and I owe y'all my life and what little sanity I had left for that salvation. So...when y'all put me in that psych ward five weeks ago...that tore me to fucking shreds. I knew y'all weren't aware of the circumstances and I know that y'all had to take precautions after that stunt I pulled with the gun, but that fucking asylum is where it all began. I had so many abortions in there during the year I stayed, that the facility did pay for to keep state off their backs and Jamie-O's secret safe. The guard who looked after my cell raped me from the day I got in there to the time I was released and that really took a toll on my mental. Catrina got me from out of there, but it still took me a good six months to another year before I could even come down from off of the addiction to all of the meds and could cuss her ass out then thank her before I ended up killing myself. I knew she knew about what our mother did to me, but I was so weak and overwhelmed that I just let it go. Focusing on the fact that she had the decency to be a part of the solution and not the problem at that point. It saved our relationship in all honesty...

I know this is a lot to take in and process all at once, but y'all just don't know what a relief it is to get this weight from off of my shoulders...I love y'all so much. Y'all are my babies. My children. My fruit. I bore y'all. I will fight for y'all. Steal. Kill. Do whatever it takes for y'all's safety, so Nuri, when I couldn't find you...that shit destroyed me. I will apologize for all of the things you went through for your entire life until the day I leave this earth. I am truly sorry. Ali, my Nali, no matter how much you hate your government name." A genuine smile covered their mother's face as she looked into the eyes of her oldest boy. "I'm sorry for making you believe for thirty-one years of your life that Curtis was your father when all along I knew the truth. Nasir, baby, I'm sorry for the way I lashed out on you when all you were trying to do was help me because you knew something had stirred my spirit. I just continue to pray every day that y'all will forgive me, and I cannot stress that enough. Listen to me when I say this though. There's no need for y'all to go and question and be nasty with your grandmother at this point. I've already accepted the past and the distance between us. I don't wish her any harm nor any negativity, but at the end of the day, she knows what the fuck it is between me and her. And this is just between us. I promise to make this right, y'all. Momma promises...I love you each so much, and I just thank God that we can all get through this storm together now."

Catori broke down with a mixture of joyful and saddened tears. She was reverent to tell her truths but still felt like shit for the things she'd held away from them. They didn't deserve the affliction she'd caused in their lives, especially her baby boy, and she'd carry that burden to the grave.

Steelo's mind was running a mile a minute. He'd spent all of his life trying to heal wounds that no one other than Catori could ever mend. Everything made so much sense now. It made so much fucking sense, and here he was harboring such brutal vengeance for this woman when Hezekiah had been the one rolling the dice to keep them all apart.

Silence consumed them for a while. For minutes to an hour as they all sat there huddled up with their mother who they all loved to the moon and back. And yes, that includes her youngest and crazy ass son as well. Steelo no longer hated her on account of the satanic hell that she'd been dragged through. It truly wasn't her fault. His vibe could feel it. His instincts led him to firmly believe that evil didn't rest within her like he always felt it had, and for that he could throw in the towel so easily. Just as he'd done that night when Tiri's face should've been on an obituary back when they'd first met. Ali didn't love Catori any less for keeping his real father away from him because that bitch ass nigga wasn't even worth the strain. Nasir didn't hold it against their mother for snapping after learning about the demons that she could never purge from her system. Her slate was finally clean, and Catori deserved that shit tenfold after thirty plus years of carrying such a heavy load of baggage.

Sadly though surely, this was only the beginning for Catori. She would need daily counseling; excessive prayer. Relentless strength to walk tall and with her head held high following this day. She was so mentally construed to the point that her children feared for her wellbeing; only because they loved her, and she'd come too far to relapse. And although this blow might've been the hardest hit she'd ever stomached compared to all of her pains of the past, just knowing that she now had all three of her children by her side, nothing could come in the way of her healing process. They were her motivation. The push she needed. That little quote in the morning that everyone cherished before beginning their day. Her six A.M. caffeine. Her fix. An addiction that she wasn't afraid of having when God and their love had always been her saving grace.

"We have so much catching up to do, Nuri."

Steelo looked his mother in the eye as she rubbed his back, offering her a warm smile. God, she was beautiful.

"So much, baby. I don't ever want you feeling like an outcast because of the things your father's done. That's behind us now, and I just want you to give me the opportunity to fix this, son. *Please*."

He may have been verbally speechless, but Catori could feel his spirits. They were in cahoots. Their minds were on the same page, and that's all that she could ever pray for.

"We will. In due time. We still got some loose ends to tie up before the rejoicing can begin though. Don't take that the wrong way. I'm just wired to work like that. I'm just sitting here wondering what made that nigga pop up on you so all of a sudden? Ain't no way he just gon' show his face after all these years without it being a motive behind it."

That was the crime lord in her son talking. A bitch ass nigga Jamie-O might've been, but Steelo had inherited that nigga's street credibility from the nut sack. The killer in him wouldn't have a lick of mercy for that nigga once he got his hands on his father. Fuck blood. That shit never mattered before this very moment and it sure as hell wouldn't go into consideration when it was time for Steelo to decapitate his every body part from his fingers to down his toes. Jamie-O was a dead man walking. Mark his fucking words.

"Looking for his mother's lockbox key and the 16.5 million dollar fortune of his that he stashed away in her basement before he left. He knew she'd never sell the house until she died, but he didn't expect her to leave anything to me of all people. When that old bitch came to America, she was just as vile and as grimy as him. Apple didn't fall too far from the damn tree. Before I sold the house, I discovered this cellar underneath the basement, and once I saw what was inside, I just knew he'd be back... That key you found, Nas, is what that was for, and I thank God that something told you to bring it with you that day after our little tussle because as you can see, he trashed my apartment." Catori's eyes dilated twice their normal size in panic remembering her and Jamie-O's conversation from that night he popped up. "Oh my God. Nas. Nuri."

"What?" they all questioned in sync.

"He-he-he said something about going after y'all because Nuri had things locked down on the west coast and you, Nas, were an asset because of your connections to the Platinum Cartel. We've gotta—"

"Slow yo' role, ma. Don't worry yo' self about that, a'ight?" Seth's voice startled them all as he entered the door to the den, catching the last bit of her spiel. "I got something I think y'all would like to see," he expressed with a condescending tone.

Catori swallowed the lump in her throat as Seth led them down to their own cellar. After descending the steps, they all were face to face with the brutally beaten, black-eyed, and fractured skull having Hezekiah "Jamie-O" Valentine. The mastermind behind all of their turmoil. Boy, look at how the fucking tables have turned.

"When we found out it was him behind the shit with us getting hit and two of our soldiers being murdered, my team ain't stop until they killed his wife and children, then brought him back alive. He was planning on bringing back some company in search for that lil' measly ass 16 M's he couldn't find. Shit was short lived though. And for the record, y'all had two lil' twin brothers. That's my fault."

Seth's face was blank, and his eyes were filled with the same tenacious glare that he wore on a daily. Was he supposed to be moved? Or maybe even feel some type of way about that shit? Nah, he didn't think so either.

"Fuck 'em. Ain't shit relevant to him outside of Catori Rutger. Fuck his family." Nasir's words were like ice, causing her husband to grin. His lil' wife had some thug rooted within the pit of her soul. He'd always loved her bark and bite when the time was right.

Reprisal was written on Catori's face as her chest rose and fell while she stared at her husband. She and Jamie-O were only separated according to the United States marriage bureau. His current status in Missouri was missing. Legally, they were still one. She was still a Valentine no matter what her signature said. He could change his identity a million damn times for all she cared. Compensation for everything he owned would only suffice as a band-aid for all the shit he'd put her through. And no, she wasn't a killer, but the adrenaline surging through her blood gave her the idea that she'd have to make an exception for this one special case.

Jamie-O was so horribly beaten that he kept going in an out of conscious, and even though both of his eyelids were swollen shut, but he could feel her. He knew when she was around. Ironically, after all of the years that may have passed them by, he still felt a connection to the only person in this world he'd loved him through and through, no matter how good his island beauty was to him before her untimely death. The energy

323

in the room was brooding. Death was infiltrating throughout his lungs and bloodstream, teasing him of the afterlife that he was moments away from being cast in once the people surrounding him were finished. His young wife begged him to take his stash as a loss since he'd been compensated by Geni already. Fifty compared to the loss of sixteen million was a greater reward in her eyes, but Jamie-O insisted. And now, his time had come. He'd been coined as the foolish digger of his own grave, causing him to exhale in defeat. Sure enough, karma had caught up to him, and the ransom could only be paid with his life.

"Aye, yo', Steelo. You might wanna check on ya boy, Marius. Word is this nigga had linked up with the Irish Mob in attempt to take y'all out. He staged the Rich and Gunna scene to make it look like we got hit from y'all's team. Had an army out on the west coast on the outskirts of the city's perimeter ready to rock any day now. I took care of that already, but ain't no telling what the fuck that nigga Geni on. That's all my peoples could find out about y'all's situation. Geni MIA right now. Whatever you might need just let me know and we'll step in further if need be."

That fucking email.

Seth's explanation sent a shock of rage throughout Steelo's body, forcing him to reach into his pants pocket and pull out his phone to dial Marius' number. If that nigga had already known that the Irish Mob was after him before forcing Steelo to leave town, then that meant he was preparing to go to war alone. Blood couldn't make them any closer. Marius was his fucking brother, and no matter what the hell was going on with Steelo and his personal issues, it was a dishonor; hell, an unfit act of disloyalty that he wasn't there to be by his side. The mere possibility of his dawg not making it out alive from taking on a war that they were supposed to ride out as a team would rot his soul to the core, and Steelo prayed to God that he made it out to Trinity before it was too late.

Taug Jaye

HUFR

12 Noon
One Hour until Marius' meeting with the City Council

It's not that Marius didn't believe KD when she said she was gonna be somewhere whenever they were apart. It's not that he didn't trust her. It simply made him sleep better at night seeing it with his own two eyes that she was at that specific location considering the life he lived.

With that being the case, the moment Marius activated the locator beacon on her phone and engagement ring, and he couldn't pull up her or the kids' whereabouts, at first, it shocked him. Was it his reception? Was his phone broken? Was there a malfunction with hers? Had she left her engagement ring somewhere by mistake because she was so busy messing around with the kiddos and simply forgot it? Oh, there were so many different scenarios running through his head before he automatically jumped the gun and assumed the worse. But one thing was certain; something out of the ordinary was wrong here. Or, maybe he had too much on his mind right now and couldn't view things clearly.

Taking a deep breath, Marius rubbed the insides of his sleepy eyes that he hadn't shut in over twenty-four hours, before he hit the locator button for a second time. But once again, he was stammered and pissed off after receiving the same bullshit ass results: location not found. With his heart now surging blood beyond its capacity, Marius stood to his feet and called her. Twenty redials later, and no, this isn't an exaggeration; it truly did appear in his call log that he'd dialed her number twenty damn times, just for it to continue to ring until her voicemail picked up. With the worse in mind, he started to get dressed and headed down to his ammunition chamber until an unrecognizable phone call came through on his phone, starling him.

He wouldn't typically answer a number he didn't know off rip, **except** for the simple fact that he always knew who was calling, and the average Joe couldn't just pick up the fucking phone and start a got damn conversation with him. It had to be his wife.

"Where you at, KD?" his voice was eerily calm as he took a seat along the top of the stairwell that led to the basement.

"We safe. Wassup?"

Marius chuckled out of frustration while scratching his bushy beard. She was with the shits right now, and he didn't have time for the silly ass cat and mouse games she wanted to play.

"What's wrong now, KD? What the fuck is you on, and I want a straight answer?"

"Marius, handle yo' business, alright? You wasn't that damn worried about me and the kids when you took your ass out to Ireland not too long ago to keep playing games with them niggas, and I shouldn't have to explain that shit no further for you. You did this shit. You kept on testing me, thinking this shit was a game, and I wasn't letting anyone else get caught up in the middle of your crossfire. This family ain't taking no more bullets for yo' ass. *Especially* not my damn kids. Me, GG, and the Koi's are straight. Call me once you done with this shit for good, and if not, then don't ever bother calling back. But if you do change your mind, don't take too long to hit me up because the number to reach me at might not be of service by then either."

Did she just?

Y'all...He snapped.

"DON'T FUCKING PLAY WIT' ME, KOVU! WHERE THE FUCK IS Y'ALL AT!"

"AIN'T NOBODY PLAYING WIT' YO' ASS, MARIUS! *YOU* THOUGHT THIS SHIT WAS A GAME! *YOU* TOOK ADVANTAGE OF THE TIME YOU THOUGHT YOU HAD TO GET THIS SHIT TOGETHER, SO *YOU* AIN'T GOT NOBODY ELSE TO THANK BUT YO' SELF! NOW TELL THE KIDS YOU LOVE THEM SO THEY CAN TAKE THEIR AFTERNOON NAP! THEY MISS YOU!"

Ooooooh, she was hitting him in the jugular with this shit. KD knew that her and their children were his ultimate weaknesses, and then she had the nerve to bring Louise into this shit too? She was serious. This was no bullshit, and Marius' anxiety was through the fucking roof as he paced the hallway, feeling as if he couldn't breathe. His lungs felt like they'd collapsed in the pit of his stomach. A lump was caught in his throat so thick that it hurt even with the slightest attempt to swallow. The room was spinning, his panting was audible, and his chest felt like someone had knocked all of the wind out of him in one bop. This wasn't life right now.

"KD, li-li-listen to me, a'ight? Mama, please, just..."

Marius tried to plead his case. The desperation was on the tip of his tongue. Hell, this man was two tears away from crying. I ain't lying. Because he knew that KD wasn't backing down from him this time. He knew that there was no talking her back against the floor with his sweet nothings as an attempt to temporarily persuade her that this was truly the last round. She'd brutally forced him to choose between his family and Trinity, but to **his** dismay, she'd already made the decision for him. He was crumbling.

"Come on, kids. Say hi to daddy so y'all can lay down."

His heart just...it shattered.

Marius dropped down to his knees before he could mentally realize what was really happening. He couldn't think. Everything was falling apart at a lightning speed that it took a minute for it all to register in his head, like damn: *she fucking left me...*

Kovu was murdering him. She was burying him. She'd literally ripped his fucking heart out of socket with her bare damn hands, and from the looks of it, Lady Monster gave no fucks about do so either...just as he'd shamelessly done in the past to so many innocent and lost souls him damn self. Marius created that monster inside of her, and now she was using it to manipulate his regality. He was conquered.

"Love you, daddy!" little Aubrey sang into the phone with a wide smile across her face. He could hear her blowing miniature kisses into the receiver.

"De-de! De-de!"

That was Jayce's way of saying *daddy* into the phone with his three teeth showing from him wearing a wide grin too.

Marius was subdued by the intricate engineering Kovu had used to belittle and break him. Only she knew how to do that. Only she had the ability to do such a cruel thing to get him to bite that sentimental bait, and the lump in his throat ceased him from replying.

"Daddy?" Aubrey questioned with concern when she didn't get a response from her father.

"I'm-I'm here, baby girl." The forced smile he made felt as if someone had taken a sharp razor blade to each corner of his mouth and sliced the permanent admiration on his face. It hurt so much to stand solid for his little princess. The angst was almost too hard to bear. "I-I-I love y'all too, you hear me?"

"Yaaaaaaay! Love you too, daddy! We go sleep now. C'mon, Jay-Jay! We go sleep. I tired, daddy. Hmm, mommy."

He could hear Aubrey hand her mother back over the phone, but Kovu rudely hung up in his face not wanting to hear another word out of his ass. Marius had chose where he wanted to be, and it was obvious that with his family wasn't it.

𝔥𝔲𝔣𝔯

City Hall

Tom Ford was his guilty pleasure. Tailored to perfection, the brown Prime of Wales Atticus jacket and black cashmere crewneck sweater gave Marius a wealthy though evenly swagged out appearance as his loafers glided down the hard floors of City Hall. With one hand in his left pants pocket and the other down at his side, casually swaying back and forth with his stride, he wore his signature poker face with his thick left brow raised from a hint of uneasiness. It wasn't the move he was making that left him eternally bothered; his wife had pushed his back up against the wall and Marius was feeling that shit.

To the twelfth power.

He was surrounded by a diamond formation of bodyguards. One leading the front, two men catty-cornered on either side of him, two catty-cornered behind their boss, and a monstrous soldier with a seven-foot height and three hundred pounds of mass tailing the back.

Marius "The Monstrosity" Usher gave off *007* vibes with his suave though deadly appearance and intimidating aura. He was a dangerous man. A very dangerous man. A vengeful monster who would give Trinity a run for their fucking money for the rest of his unnatural born life if his family wasn't the ultimate collateral.

So now all bets were off.

The police force was tight as Marius and his crew continued to stride throughout the hall in unison until they reached their designated conference area. Six SWAT team soldiers equipped with deadly army guns stood war-ready with bulletproof vest and helmets on as protection for their legislators as he entered the room. Normally, Marius would be a wise guy; you know, crack a corny ass joke, greet them with a sinister smile, or wait on them niggas to serve him a drink to lighten up the mood, but today was a different ball game.

The tension in the room was so thick it made it hard to breathe. Men pulled at their collars, the judge had to continuously fan herself, not sure as to whether it was just hot in that bitch or if she were having a damn heat flash. The inquietude set the mood just right, serving as a forewarning that Marius didn't come here today to fuck with them.

I mean, check out the size of the balls on this man to not only coerce them into abiding by his regulations, but to cockily show up like he truly owned this town was just sickening. They allowed this man to become this way, and once Marius realized that he truly did have the power in the palms of his hands? Nothing was the same, dawg.

Nada.

In silence, he took a seat across from the state judge, comfortably resting his left elbow amongst the surface of the cherrywood conference table with his hand lazily lying against his mouth. Marius respected the respect that was present in the room. All of the people surrounding him feared him to such a degree that they were obviously willing to cut him loose with his freedom. Knowing damn well that he needed to be: A., strapped down for lethal injections, B., bolted to an electric chair and have the fucking currency run until his ass burst into flames, C., have his sculpted arms and legs tied to four different horses and let that shit run its course (get it?), or D., to have a noose strapped around his neck.

Shit, how about all of the fucking above? He'd rightfully earned each selection in the grimiest way that they could possibly present it.

And yet, a proud and unapologetic villain posed as such a threat to these niggas that they were willing to emancipate this man. As long as they had a legal agreement signed, stamped, and dated agreeing that as long as he stayed away from their city (continuing to live his life with the illegal currency that he'd cleansed them of) with no legal action taken against him to settle the peace, then they were willing to put that shit in motion.

Today was a day of days.

"Mr. Usher."

"Judge Caldwell."

She'd taken Judge Raymond's place over the last few years following Marius' case back in December of 2016. Judge Raymond tried everything in his power to make sure Marius was convicted before he retired in the Spring of 2017, but catching him slipping hadn't been the easiest thing to do until they received an inside tip that led them here. She'd go down in history for his disappearance.

"You know, I should have them take your Black ass in right this moment, you cocky son of a bitch."

Judge Caldwell was seething with anger. Her hairy top lip curled with rage as she sat across from him in a too little navy-blue skirt and suit set that the jacket was only moments away from bursting open. That damn button was holding on for dear life.

"And I should hop up from this table and slit your fucking throat after cutting your tongue out for trying me like I'm not a man of my word; just before I have my men slaughter your sick and obese husband who's stationed out in Seattle on nine liters of oxygen with COPD. If anything they're already killing him for me, but guess what? We're here now. The papers have been drawn up, and now that you're not wasting any more of my fucking time with your repulsive ass mouth, I'm just as ready to get this shit over with as you are. So butch up, bitch, slide me the iPad, and I'll be on my way."

Judge Caldwell's face changed from a retributive shade of red to a *Casper* hue of white. His bite was wantonly vicious, causing fear to simultaneously pump through her veins as her old, dry pussy started to get moist. Her comrades all stared her on, waiting for her to reply. Mr. Samuels sat next to her in excruciating pain due to the third-degree burns igniting a thrombosis of heat along with an imperative shock of affliction to evade his body. All of their signatures were already inscribed amongst the document that Marius was able to tap into their file system and alter to ensure that it wouldn't be used against him in the future, prior to his arrival. All that was missing now was his John Hancock. Aye, he'd be a fucking criminal until the day he died.

A fugly smug emerged on the judge's face as the officer nearest to her retrieved the tablet and handed it over to Marius. He hesitated at first, getting a thrill from the sight of them each holding their breaths until he signed his name. A copy was automatically sent and saved to his hard drive since he was still tapped into their system.

Winning wasn't something he actively did; it's who he was.

"That's game, lady, and gentlemen. I'm out."

The moment Marius stood to his feet, the conference room door was kicked in, and a blow from the shotgun in Geni's hand instantly killed one of the guards who was blocking him.

"You ain't the only man in this city with connections in legislation, you piece of shit!"

The melody of tenacious gunshots swarmed the atmosphere as Marius pulled a strap from the back of the nearest goon's waistline and ducked for cover. He'd been waiting on this wannabe hard ass nigga to show up on his retaliating bullshit, and he came right on time. You can only tame a wild dog for so long until it finally got loose, and now, they were celebrating Independence Day a few seasons too early. Trinity PD tried their best to protect their legislators from the chaos, but the Irish Mob had infested City Hall like a plague.

Marius held his arm around one of the SWAT team members he was using as a shield and busted rounds at them niggas' heads, knocking 'em all off until his clip expired. Just as he tossed the empty weapon to reach back into his waistline for something heavier to work with, Geni shot in Marius' direction. He splattered the officer's dome on impact, barely missing Marius by seconds had it been too late when he quickly reacted and blocked his path of the flying bullet.

Leaving out the door was not a fucking option in this battle, so now with a Draco in his hand, The Monstrosity's bullets thumped like firecrackers as he made his way over to a shattered window. Geni was on to him but managed to miss his chance when Marius leapt out of the aperture with bullets ringing behind him.

Hanging four stories from the ground, The Monstrosity tried his best to get his footing as his fingertips gripped the cemented ledge for dear life. But once he saw Geni stick his head out the window, he didn't hesitate to extend his gun and shoot a few rounds until he was forced to focus back on his balance.

Missing the shots by seconds, Geni retreated inside of the office until the coast was clear, prompting him to hang his automatic out the window and relentlessly fire, but just like that, his target was gone. Marius' body wasn't splattered or injured along the pavement below them, so the only possible solution was that he'd reentered the building through another window on some sly shit, and now the game had changed from a face-off to finding a lost mouse in a maze. Marius wanted to test Geni's gangsta, so let's do it. He had all fucking day to make this shit happen, and best believe he wasn't stopping until he walked out the door with The Monstrosity's bloody detached head in his hands, coining his victory. He owed it to his father and his family all looking down at him right this very minute from the gates of heaven. Geni had to make them proud.

𝕳𝖀𝕱𝕽

Kovu felt like a total heartless bitch after the shit she pulled with her husband about six hours ago. She hated to cross that line and turn into a monster in order for him to, not only hear her this time around, but to understand where she was coming from. Sometimes she felt like the things she said to him nonchalantly went into one ear and out of the other. There was no reason why she should've had to yell, curse, and scream at Marius to make him realize that he'd been wrong. But using their children as middlemen to sabotage and hurt him, even though leaving was geared towards their safety above all, was just below the belt. And at the end of the day, no matter how right she was, things still shouldn't have gotten to that point of retaliation.

Lines had certainly been crossed.

It took a lot to hurt Marius; fifty percent being Aubrey and the other fifty percent to be Jayce, and Kovu knew she was doing just that the moment she forced him to tell them that he loved them as if he'd never see them again. Proving a point to Marius was one thing, but somewhere along the line, her anger began to outweigh the love they shared, and Kovu found herself pushing to break him just to make herself feel better; if, that made any sense at all.

332

And now she was drowning in guilt...

The kids were sleeping. Their five hours traveling overseas had her babies jet-lagged, and after giving them a bath to wash away the grime of the flight, ten minutes into watching cartoons they'd finally called it quits. Aubrey and Jayce got on jets and ironically loved what it felt like to fly versus being triggered or frightened, so the of them ran around playing, getting into all kinds of mess with energy that KD had never seen before. After they slept the first couple of hours it was on like Donkey Kong. They chased their mother from one end of the plane to the other and she was wore the fuck out. Hell, on the entire way out to Honolulu, Kovu couldn't help but to think, *Lord, how did I end up with two kids back to back?*

Hawaii had always been a beautiful state to KD, but the city of Honolulu, specifically, held a special place in her heart. It was majestic, the air was clear, and the town low key in some parts of the city. Being surrounded by the clear blue waters was simply breathtaking, the atmosphere was welcoming, and she could see herself growing to love it there.

They needed something different. Something new. One hell of an adventure that was sure to force them to come out of their comfort zones, and what better choice was there than to dive headfirst into the luxuries of one of their favorite vacation spots? And they had good weed just a delivery away from their connects in Columbia? Shiiiiiiid, it got no better than that.

Her favorite luxury was their year around mid-seventies weather. She'd get used to waking up to translucent blue skies and the pleasant salty fumes from the ocean shore in no time.

The sun was high in the sky right this very moment. With her phone, a baby monitor, and her mini essential oil mist machine in hand, KD stepped foot out on the patio and headed to the sandy beach that was a good twenty feet away from their new backyard. Marius had no clue that she'd purchased their one hundred million dollar vacation home and had been crowned as the owner for about six months now. He stayed so busy fucking shit up and terrorizing Trinity that one hundred mil was like a twenty dollar bill with the way his illegal charades had a boatload of residual cash steadily flowing in.

Nevertheless, she'd been putting the money back into their savings with all of her royalty checks that were coming in since she grossed around 100k a month considering all of the projects she had her foot in. That's not even including the money she made from her Netflix contracts, the new television show she was writing for BET, endorsements, her stock investments, or the money accumulating from her book tours. One thing KD learned from Marius was how to get a muthafucking bag from numerous sources of income.

So, it's not like she stole it from him. What's his is hers, and Kovu knew damn well that she didn't have to ask for Marius' permission to do anything. He trusted her, and that was one of the strongest dynamics in their relationship.

She sat alone in silence on her pallet soaking up some sun as she allowed the eucalyptus mint to soothe her tension. Her conscious kept telling her to grow the fuck up and at least check on her husband after the low blow she'd hit him with. Kovu knew she wasn't leaving him; she knew that for an absolute fact, but if she didn't put some fire up under his ass then Marius would've continued to ignore her, and she was growing tired of that shit.

Clicking the side button on her phone, she instantly smiled at her screensaver. It was a picture of Marius sleeping on his back with Jayce lying on his chest and Aubrey at his side, all snuggled up in his arm; each of them knocked the fuck out with their mouths wide open. Dottie and Rayman were even snuggled up with them down by her husband's feet too. She exhaled with defeat allowing her face ID to unlock her phone, but just before she could dial his number, her father approached her, opened a lawn chair, and took a seat.

"Wassup, Mr. Daniels. So, what you think? Is Hawaii a fair trade, or would you rather stay home in St. Louis?"

Ernest popped a few honey roasted cashews into his mouth and sipped on his chilled D'USSÉ before lighting the blunt that was tucked behind his ear.

"It's a long way from home, I tell you that. Are *you* sure about this though, boo?"

KD swallowed a lump in her throat after her father's hard inquiry but found herself smiling brightly at the feeling of a million butterflies fluttering around in her stomach.

"I'm a hunnid, daddy. I mean, yeah it's a bit scary, but you only get one life to live, and home gon' always be there. We can always sell the house and move back if push comes to shove."

He nodded his head in agreement.

"True 'nuff, baby. I guess I better make myself comfortable then. You must be out yo' got damn mind if you think I'mma let you and my grandkids move away from me."

Kovu giggled as she eyed her father wearing a white undershirt and Nike shorts with his bare feet sinking into the sand. He never went anywhere without the pic in his mini afro or his gold Jesus piece around his neck like it was till 2003. God love 'em.

"Pick you out a dope ass loft or something, pimp. Just front me the bill once you done. I know you like yo' space, and it's plenty of women around here to keep you busy."

"You know that's why you always been my favorite oldest daughter, right?" he cheesed like a Cheshire cat.

"Daddy, I'm your only oldest daughter."

"That's why you my favorite. Nah but, we do have to stick together though. You and the grand kids are all I've got after what happened with your sister; *and* with Gerald pleading guilty now serving a twenty year sentence. It ain't been easy, I tell you that. Especially once we lost your mother too. Tammy wasn't always wrapped too tight, but once she got them demons out of her, she was cool people."

Kovu might not have been in touch with her mother for the past two years, but Ernest always kept in touch, having a special bond with his ex-wife. One that he always prayed would rekindle with her and her daughter, but…

"I know right." Kovu's voice was low as she redirected her attention to the waves crashing along the shore. "I don't know why Gerald wouldn't just let me help him out of that situation though. Like, daddy, that's fucked up." She couldn't help it when she croaked.

"What he did was fucked up. Yo' brother knew he shouldn't have been drinking like that. He killed four people. The guilt's eating away at him. He couldn't allow you to step in when he knew the truth. Gerald is aware that you gon' ride for him through whatever, but this ain't the first nor the third at fault drunk accident he'd gotten into. And now, a family is grieving over people they'll never get back because your brother wouldn't go get help when he knew he needed it."

Kovu sighed as she sat up on her knees. It was a hard pill to swallow, accepting her brother's conviction. She knew what Gerald did was wrong, but damn. Twenty years? On top of the two he'd already served prior to his trial that finally happened only a month ago? It hurt her like no other to lose so much of her family like a domino effect. That's why she held her babies so close; she wouldn't know what to so if she ever lost them...or her husband.

Looking over her shoulder, she could make out an image heading in their direction. The top knot instantly gave his identity away, forcing her to hop up to her feet and meet him in the middle.

"Steelo, what are you doing here? How did you find us? Where's Tiri? Are y'all okay? Is Marius here with you?" KD tried her best to catch her breath after running so fast. That light jog had her winded as hell.

She was so busy trying to replenish her lungs with air that the look in Steelo's eyes went over her head. She couldn't see how hard it was for him to keep it together in front of her. His orbs were red. His energy was depleted. Shoulders were hunched over...

His mind was fucking gone.

She'd finally peeped his demeanor once she stood up from resting her hands on her knees, the acknowledgment forcing her stomach drop and trigger an onset of discomfort that made her body quake with terror.

"Steelo," she expressed with authority, not feeling his disposition. "What the fuck is wrong! Where is Marius!"

Steelo stopped her from running past him and gently pulled her back. He could hardly make eye contact with his sister as he unlocked his phone and handed it over to her.

Kovu's bottom lip quivered as she looked down at the device in her hands.

"Is this some kind of a fucking joke, Steelo?! Where the fuck is my damn husband?!"

"Wa-watch the video, KD."

The fact that his voice was hardly above a whisper...The fact that he too was trembling and lowered his head to hide his emotions made KD fall down to her knees in peril as she pushed play.

Trinity PD had all exits leaving the city blocked. Patrol cars infested the streets with red and blue lights flashing like fireworks as they tried their best to hold up against the Irish Mob while also attempting to bring in The Monstrosity and Geni. They were roaming the town like terrorists.

With his arm extended, Marius let off the clip of his Desert Eagle as he hid behind a black Tahoe truck. Shit was moving so fast he could hardly remember breaking free from the building, thanking God that he'd made it out alive before it exploded. The Trinity bridge was located a block across from City Hall, and it was currently blocked off as well on both ends, trapping him from making another escape. Glass was shattering from flying bullets, there was a shell lodged into his side, and he was out of ammo. Sirens were ringing, pedestrians were screaming, and on top of him trying to dodge Geni's crazy ass, 5-0 was nothing but another army that he had to steer clear of too if he wanted to make it to see another day.

His chest heaved up and down with pressure so heavy that his heart hurt. Where could he turn? Where could he go? Who else was there to come to his rescue even if it got him out of the smallest jam? He was surrounded.

Geni sat squatting behind an abandoned car on the bridge as well, reloading the AK-47 in his hands. He could give a fuck about Trinity PD surrounding them. While his men continued to hold them off, his main focus was putting a round between Marius' eyes before he met his own fate, knowing this wasn't a battle that either of them would see it through. From the bullets in close range that previously danced in his direction, he could make out that Marius was hiding behind the Tahoe truck that was one car ahead of him. Using his teeth, Geni detached the safety pin after depressing the striker level, then threw the last grenade that he retrieved from his Kevlar vest that was saved for this moment, into the air.

Swoosh!

"DUCK FOR COVER!"

The police officer's trembling voice projecting through the bullhorn forced Marius to look up into the sky. Lo and behold, a grenade with his name on it was falling in his direction.

Time moved in slow motion.

He could hear his heart beating through his ears as he watched the explosive slowly linger in the air while he caught an eighteen wheeler semi-truck passing underneath the bridge out the corner of his eye.

BOOM!

The Tahoe rose in flames as Marius jumped over the bridge and plummeted on top of the moving vehicle. He tried to gather his bearings and stand up while wrapping his mind around the crazy shit he kept getting himself into as the fight continued on. He thought he was seeing shit when he caught a glimpse of Geni soaring in the air after him, hopping over on the truck he was riding from the one on the side of him.

He had to admit that Geni had given him the toughest challenge he'd ever faced throughout this entire career. The nigga had heart.

The truck driver had to be traveling around seventy miles per hour at the very least, so gathering a proper footing with blood staining his clothing and the surface of the cargo bed was the least bit easy.

Geni had dropped the machine gun that was in his hand as he jumped over to reach Marius, so now pissed off beyond measure, he charged at him in rage. Geni brought nothing but heat implementing uppercuts, a combination of jabs, and horse-powered blows until he knocked Marius back off of his feet. They scuffled around the hood, their hands around each other's throats as the truck driver swerved in and out of the treacherous traffic on one of California's most dangerous freeways.

The end was near.

"Say, mate!" There was laughter in Geni's voice as he held his hands around Marius' neck, cutting off his circulation. "I'll be sure to fuck your bitch real good before she and those pretty little children of yours are met with the same demise as my family, 'if' I manage to make it out alive after killing you! This one's for you, Papa!"

The moment he reached into his waistline for the .22 that was tucked away for backup, Marius removed a switchblade from out the breast pocket of his jacket. He drove it right into the center of Geni's neck before he kicked him off of the cargo bed, and his body was splattered by a speeding truck before he could hit the ground.

Marius grit his teeth together as the pain from his gunshot wound sent a burning sensation throughout his body. He laid there trying to figure out what his next move on the board was. Trinity PD had their cameras on him via a chopper that had been following the truck from the moment he *jumped off the bridge. Harsh horns began to ring in the air, forcing Marius to look up and realize that they were heading underneath the low built Trinity Tunnel. They approached the bridge so quick he found himself leaping off of the truck once again, not sure if he'd given himself enough leverage to make it.*

The Trinity shore was located on the left side of the highway, so when he jumped...he took a hard fall, crashing into the water just meters away from a charter yacht that instantly rose in flames due to the rocket that was shot from a gunman on the helicopter. A gulf of fire and smoke filled the air with no remnants of Marius' body in sight.

The Monstrosity had been slain as a direct order from the Trinity Police Department, no matter what it took to get the job done.

"MARIUS!!! NOOOOOO!!!"

The screams soaring from Kovu's lips were horrifying as she tossed Steelo's phone across the yard. She hopped up to her feet with tears running down her cheeks ready to kill some got damn body. Infuriated, heartbroken, and left in shambles, she fought against Steelo with all of her might trying to break away from him so she could go do something. She had to go look for him. She had to go back to Trinity. She couldn't believe the image her eyes had just seen even if someone paid her to do so. This was a freaking nightmare, and she was begging God to open up her irises and wake her up from her sleep.

"Steelo, let me go! I have to go find him! I have to—"

"KD, he's dead! I already sent out a team! They couldn't...find the body..."

His words were like a slap to her face that stopped everything around her from moving. Steelo's tears matched her own. His eyes were just as swollen. His heart was just as broken; an indication that Marius' death hadn't been staged...It was true...Her husband wasn't coming back...

A dizziness swept over Kovu as her heart rate increased well above its normal capacity from the shock of the aftermath until she blacked out and collapsed into her father's arms before she could hit the ground.

Heart Up For Ransom

Taug Jaye

Alexa, play "Officially Missing You" by Tamia

Heart Up For Ransom

Chapter
17

The bags underneath her puffy and swollen eyes were dark as night and as deep as the undiscovered Mariana Trenches, sluggishly hanging just inches away from her high cheekbones. Her hair was thinning, her skin was flushed in a lifeless, dry sand color, and her body had shed fifteen inches in all of two months' time. Kovu could never be herself again. Ever. Foolish it may have been. Delusional and mentally off her rocker she may have become, but with the absence of her husband, life just wasn't the same.

KD was being selfish as if she didn't have two beautiful children to continue to live for, but everyone grieved differently. Month two felt more like minute two after Steelo dropped the atomic bomb on her that made her brain completely shut down. At first, she didn't want to believe it. Couldn't believe it. Wouldn't dare let such an ugly confession be thrown out into the universe because karma was the only bitch on this earth who was badder than she was. And baby, we all know that Kovu Corletta Usher was the baddest of them all.

But seeing Marius jump overboard and the Trinity chopper shooting after him, which caused his demise with her own eyes, it sunk her further into a world of darkness and isolation that she couldn't see herself climbing from out of anytime soon.

Her heart ached; as well her malnutrition body.

She could feel her empty stomach in the pit of her abdominal cavity since eating and drinking hadn't been much of a thing she'd done these days.

No one could get a word out of her. No one but her precious little Aubrey and Jayce, who triggered an endless onset of tears each and every time her irises landed upon their smiling faces.

This had to be what hell felt like.

What it looked like.

There was no way that she could get through life without her husband along her side. Not with how numb she felt. Not with how dark and cloudy her days were despite the clear blue skies of Hawaii that hovered over their family as if such a tragedy had never occurred.

The taste of bile had permanently taken over her throat as she continued to dry heave into the grey bucket until it made her dizzy. The task had her exhausted. Fatigue had utterly swept over her body and gained control over her every ounce of muscular movement. KD could hardly take two steps without feeling a gust of excursion trampling her like a ton of bricks; or, from getting winded because the news had also physically impaired her.

Her family was a Godsend. If it weren't for her father, Reba and Chef Koi, Tiri and Steelo, she probably would've killed herself. Nor, would she even had attempted to get out of bed to tend to her children.

They all gave Kovu their condolences, and this might've just been all in her head, but she could see the disgust hidden behind their eyes. The scornful thoughts and sentiments emerging from her treating Aubrey and Jayce as if they were nothing because she was hurting.

Took her nine months in two separate years to bear the fruit of her husband's labor, yet in less than one funky ass trimester worth of time, she'd transformed into a weak and unstable mother; a weak and unstable woman because she'd mentally fucked herself into a sulking and depressing coma.

She didn't know that the very words *Until death do us part* would hit like a wrecking ball. Never in a million years would she ever fathom Marius sacrificing himself for the welfare of their family as if he weren't the fucking Monstrosity. As if he couldn't have pulled off anything else other than suicide to ensure their safety. It was sickening. This shit was a nightmare. Like a tumultuous migraine that wouldn't cease to quit throbbing against her temples no matter what she did or took to alleviate the pain.

It haunted her from sunup to sundown the way she forced him to tell their babies he loved them. She crumbled knowing the last conversation she had with her husband could've been avoided or steered in another direction if she weren't being such a bitch and selfish about it.

None of that shit she was once disgusted about didn't even matter anymore. Marius had killed himself...for the welfare of them...right after that meeting. Right after signing those papers. Just moments after finally calling it quits and removing himself from that life like he'd promised.

Oh, God if only she'd heard him out.

If only she could've made a way to have another team on standby to get her husband out of that city and safely. If only she'd come to his rescue so swift and smoothly as she'd done once before knowing he needed her. Marius was so got damn cocky. Why in the entire fuck would he show up to such an imperative meeting like that with one fucking team? Why wouldn't he allow Steelo to be by his side? Why wouldn't he have asked for help? Why the fuck did he take it so lightly?

Had this been the plan all along? To sacrifice himself so his family wouldn't suffer from the ramifications of the hell he'd caused knowing they'd always be targets if he were alive? KD needed answers! Because the ones in her head simply weren't adding up. She didn't want to accept the truth no matter what the case may have been. No matter what her husband had done in the past.

Then she had to turn around and make their last moments together so bleak and revolting...

Kovu's heart was in limbo. She was uncertain of her beliefs. Disappointed in herself for deceiving those around her and losing her grasp on faith. She had no clue what to do. A part of her kept trying to listen to that little voice of reason in the back of her head; the one that kept trying to assure her that this stage she was drowning in was only temporary. A transitioning echelon in which she prayed to the very God that she'd strayed away from, would be done and over with hopefully sooner than later.

She wasn't sure if she could make it through the storm this time around. The rain was pouring down like cats and dogs, her vision was hazy, the roads were slick with oily debris coating the very streets that were interfering with her traction. Her wipers wear shot, the tank read five miles 'til empty on top of needing an oil change so she wouldn't fuck up her motor. Her steering wheel was locking up, transmission was slipping, she couldn't switch gears, her brakes were diminished...what the hell was she to do in times like these when the storm wouldn't seem to fade away?

It had been three long, sweaty and musty days since she last showered or zenned her body. Been months since she'd had her pussy waxed or shaved her legs. Her underarm hair was getting thick and musky. The heels of her feet had totally been neglected. Her hair was atrocious.

She could hardly stand to look at herself in the mirror until she finally peeled her crunchy clothes from off her body, washed her spicy crotch, and parted ways with all of the access hair she could no longer allow to accumulate another day.

Her wet and curly tresses hung down her shoulders as she exited the master bathroom over an hour later, smelling like her calming bottle of Aveeno body wash and the all-natural Summer's Eve for *down there.* Her fresh face was less pale and now rich with a darker shade of life after intensely scrubbing with a charcoal mask. Her teeth were brushed and flossed, skin now lathered in Nivea Shae Butter body lotion, and with the hot water opening her pores, her nose was no longer congested, making it that much easier to breathe.

She felt childish rushing past the crystal chest of drawers to avoid peering at the photo of she and Marius framed from her twenty-fifth birthday in Dubai. A shower and shave still couldn't evoke the turmoil rotting away inside of her heart, but she promised God if he gave her just a spoonful of energy so she could get cleaned up and hug and kiss her babies, that she'd put her selfless actions behind her for the day and try to be on her best behavior.

Spring in Honolulu was absolutely gorgeous.

Kovu took in the welcoming fragrance from the lemon verbena candles that lit up the hallway on her route to the patio as her newly painted and pedicured feet graced their glistening hardwood flooring. Her father was over; thank God he'd decided to relocate to the islands with her and her family or else she'd really go nuts. He was holding his smiling grandson in his hands, tossing him in the air while Aubrey ran around with her partner in crime, Steelo; inevitably forcing a smile to appear on Kovu's face.

The men all succeeded at getting the big screen programmed with *Jumanji: The Next Level* for them to enjoy as a family on their weekly movie night. Hues of oranges and yellows were mixed in the clouds above them as the sun continued to set. She knew that Aubrey and Jayce weren't tripping on the picture being too clear right at this moment because they were too busy having fun being outside. Her kids had a thing for technology for sure but planting their little feet in the cool ocean shore water, making sandcastles, and going on picnics so they could play with bubbles and water guns put smiles on their faces that KD absolutely enjoyed and would forever cherish.

The pleasant smell of burning marshmallows filled the air as Tiri, a toothless Louise, and Reba Koi sat back chit-chatting on comfortable lounge chairs surrounding the cobblestone fire pit, fresh popcorn was popping in the Red Matinee Movie Theater style maker, and the snack table was loaded with a nice spread of appetizers, all prepared by the best chef in the entire world.

Dressed in a baggy white Champion t-shirt that *used* to belong to Marius and a pair of her matching shorts, her bare feet climbed down the soothingly warm, cobblestone walking ramp as she inhaled the pleasant fumes from the burning wood. Kovu smiled when her family all recognized her; her arms crossed over her midsection with a shy look plastered on her face. She was choking back mind-numbing tears with anxiety plummeting her like an angry crashing wave, but the heartening sound of her two little peanuts calling her mommy forced her to kneel and welcome them into the comfort of her loving arms. She kissed their heads repeatedly until she scooped them up in her grasp and took a seat next to Ernest, who also kissed her head too.

The individuals surrounding her breathed the life she swore she couldn't live without Marius, back into her hoarse lungs. The days to come would surely be a battle, but Kovu had two little babies...and a third one cooking whom all needed their mother to be on her A game. If she wasn't in her right mind, then her offspring wouldn't flourish to their full potential. It was time for Kovu to get back into her good spirits. To reach out for the helping hand of her Lord and Savior who'd never let her down before so she could not only make her children proud, but her husband too...

Her appetite picked up out of nowhere once she'd gotten a whiff of Chef Koi's buffalo shredded chicken sliders on Hawaiian rolls. Kovu inhaled a good three of those bad boys until the urge for a bottle of sparkling wine salivated her mouth, causing her to head back towards the house and into the kitchen.

With her hands along the marble countertop, KD inhaled deeply, blinking back tears. That little spoonful of energy she prayed for was burning out and thoughts of Marius holding her, telling her how much he loved her and the smile she knew that would be plastered on his face after hearing that they were having another child, were violently starting to flood her with no remorse.

Sweeping her tears away, she went into the fridge in search of her drink until she came across a pan of fresh banana pudding. Chef Koi couldn't put his foot in her exact recipe like she could, but it was a close second! Weary or not, she couldn't resist it. Like a kid sneaking for a bowl of cereal at 2 A.M., she hid behind the refrigerator door and stuffed her face with spoonful after spoonful. That is, until her conscious kicked in and she literally had to force herself to refrain from being a fat ass.

After wiping the corners of her mouth to hide any evidence, Kovu finally grabbed the unopened bottle of sparkling Rosé. She closed the door prepared to rejoin her family...just to jump out of her skin when the six-foot-two, vanilla toned, classic, Tuscan Leather by Tom Ford wearing husband of hers stood hovering over her.

The glass bottle shattered at her feet.

Her heart stopped.

Her lungs collapsed.

The earth paused; suddenly sitting paralyzed, no longer rotating on its axis as she stared deeply into his eyes. Those same whiskey brown eyes of his that palmed and snatched her soul the very night they'd met.

He casually stood there.

The guava colored, quarter length sleeve, Dolce & Gabbana linen top that complimented his flourishing and even toned skin, triggered the juices in her vagina to effortlessly drip and saturate the bed of her thong. Negro even had the nerve to have his shirt unbuttoned so that the portrait of the mole above her lip to accentuate her beautiful smile was peering through on the left side of his chest.

KD didn't give a damn how good this nigga appeared to be. The fact that he was standing before her alive, well, and fucking breathing when they all were convinced he was dead caused her to snap once her spell was broken.

Screams began to emit from her trembling lips from an uncontrollable rate, and before Marius could manage to explain himself, she started throwing everything in sight at him. Including the trays of food from off of the island counter. Kovu lashed out like a madwoman.

"Noooooo! Marius! Fucking, noooooooo!"

Kovu's screams filled the vicinity of the kitchen with such intensity that each glass window and cabinet rattled from the aftermath. The fact that he stood there before her chuckling; just laughing his happy little ass off while bobbing and weaving each item she continued to throw, did nothing but piss her off to the next level. She felt like the devil was holding her heart and lungs in a vice grip as she rushed him with her adrenaline pumping at rates that should've caused her to blackout.

She swung blows that mushed the top of his head, his chin, his nose, his ears, his chest, and stomach until she started running low on steam. And Marius just let her. He gave her the green light to release the pent-up energy, negativity, sorrow, hurt and pain that he knew he'd casted upon her for pulling such a low and dirty hoax over their eyes. He could only imagine how crushed she was. The devastation. The onset of affliction he never wanted to intentionally force her to endure, but if his wife nor Steelo wasn't sold on his death then his disappearance never would've worked.

Marius hated to put Terrell in the middle of such a sticky situation and ask for his help to fake his death, but who else could he trust other than his day one? As stated before, Marius knew Geni would use that meeting as his opportunity to bury him. That's why he staged it to look foolish on his end for taking it lightly. He *did* have a team stationed to successfully carry him out of harm's way no matter how fatal it looked on camera. Marius may have been a lot of things, but foolish wasn't one of them. Sometimes you had the test the waters when it came to the welfare of the people you loved.

He encouraged Steelo to make amends with his mother not only because he knew his brother needed that, but to also keep him, and Tiri out of harm's ways. Steelo showed him loyalty in ways that were unnatural to the human eye, unnatural to the human understanding, and for that, he'd be damn if he let his dawg lose anyone or his own life due to his selfish desires either.

Marius had a feeling that Kovu was up to something with the way she'd been a little distant from him lately, but he couldn't quite put his finger on it because he'd been so busy preparing for his grand finale. You think he would've just let her leave? Just let her hang up in his face and not react? It would've been fuck that got damn meeting, and he'd been a fugitive for the rest of his life **if** there was no other way out. You see, if he couldn't find a location on Kovu right then and there, that meant that the enemy couldn't, so Marius had to play it on faith knowing she and the kids were also out of harm's way.

And she took his sweet little Louise with her too? That shit touched his heart. Made him realize that a love like theirs was rare, that a love like theirs was hard to come by, and if faking his death had the power to save that love so that they could continue to bask in that ambiance forever, he'd do it again with no questions asked.

So missing her was an understatement. Not hearing her voice? Not being able to wrap his arms around her for two whole months? Not being able to kiss her lips? To see her smile? Hell, he even missed her famous mean mug and the sound of her cussing his big-headed ass out because she was so got damn sexy when she was mad. Marius wasn't living in paradise when he was hiding out. The same sickness and confusion plagued his heart too, and his vacancy inside of his own hell without his wife and kids by his side was the hardest blow he'd ever taken.

That's why he had to wipe himself from off the map. No judicial system in existence nor a man alive would ever rob him of the most precious gifts that God could've ever blessed him with as a collateral for his horrific childhood. To his dismay, it was do or die at the sacrifice of his wife's sanity, and he prayed that she would forgive him.

"Bitch, I hate you! I fucking hate you! You'd really put me through that shit! Our kids?! Do you know what I've been through! I'm on the verge of losing this baby, and you pop up—"

Marius grabbed his wife in a bear hug, muffling her harsh words and screams while rocking her back and forth. Enough was enough, but Kovu wouldn't call it quits. She fought against him, trying her best to pry her way out of his arms. She wanted to spit in this man's face she was got damn disgusted with him.

Food was covering the surface of the kitchen floor surrounding them, so mixed with the way KD was shoving and scuffling against him, Marius inevitably slipped on the sweet and spicy shredded chicken with his left foot and hit the floor with his wife landing on top of him.

With his gun withdrawn and Ernest right behind him holding a bigger strap ready to kill some shit from the sounds of Kovu's screams shocking and frightening them all, Steelo bucked towards the house with speed like no other.

Their new lives on the island wasn't nearly as dangerous or threatened as it was while living in urban streets of the States, so housing a huge army of goons on standby wasn't as necessary. It still raised a red flag in Steelo's head how someone could possibly get past the security gate. That is, until they entered the kitchen and were stopped dead in their tracks by the sight of Marius rocking his hysterical wife back and forth with his shirt now ripped down the middle.

It wasn't long when the rest of the family arrived after realizing that no shots had been fired and the commotion had come to a halt sooner than they expected so. Tiri walked over to her man and wrapped her arms around him, her head resting along his chest with tears in her eyes from the sight of seeing both his best friend and the love of her girl's life, alive. Reba, Chef Koi, and GG stood with the kiddos as tears welled all in their orbs as well.

It hit everyone like an earthquake when his "death" hit the surface. The days were clearly over when Marius thought he didn't have a family or loved ones who wouldn't suffer, mourn, or be affected if the slightest thing happened to him. Marius was loved. More than he'd ever received in his lifetime. More than he'd ever expected or anticipated, so to look up and catch a quick glimpse of the glazy eyes and warm smiles; the eagerness of his babies who were elated to see him, each screaming his name wanting to jump into his arms, had evoked any sorrow or hate that had once resonated in his heart.

Kovu's muffled cries drew his attention away from them for a second; his orbs landed on the most perfect woman in the world in awe. The only woman he'd ever crossed paths with who had the remedy to mend the aches and pains from his past that he swore he'd never heal from. She was the greatest asset he'd ever poured into and wouldn't trade her for the world.

"I love you," he whispered with a kiss to her cheek.

"Bitch, I hate you."

Her tone was so nonchalant, calm, and collected that it forced a chuckle to seep through everyone's lips.

Marius held her tighter while placing his hand on her stomach. Shorty was pregnant with another seed to the Usher lineage. What more could he possibly ask for in this life of sin? Besides this.

"You still gon' re-marry me, mama? Suit and tie like we planned?"

It was silent for a moment before Kovu sat up and looked her man in the eye. She wanted to snatch the assault rifle from out of her father's hands and blow this nigga back into the grave that he had them all convinced he was rotting away in, but...

"Under one condition," she whispered.

"Name it. Anything you want and I got you, love."

Kovu forcefully wrapped her hand around his neck, staring him in the eye while her irises flushed into killer mode.

"If you *ev-er*," she clenched her teeth while squeezing tighter on his throat, pressing her thumb against the artery in his neck that could make him faint had she not let up on it the next sixty seconds **or less**. "Do that shit again, Marius...I swear to God I'll torture you for a week and feed your every last body part to all them got damn animals back in Trinity. You feel me?"

Marius chuckled, grateful that she was still willing to put up with his ass after her whole entire world had been rocked.

"Yes, ma'am."

Taug Jaye

"You're all I need
You're more than just a friend to me
You're everything
'Cause you're my better half"

-Ginuwine, Betta Half

Heart Up For Ransom

New Year's Eve

Nervousness is being easily agitated or alarmed; tending to be anxious; highly strung.

And y'all, Kovu was a nervous fucking wreck. She and Marius had been arguing so excessively lately that she was having major doubts about their future together on their wedding day. It's not like they weren't already "married," but a ceremony, a preacher, a wedding gown, her man in a tux waiting for her at the altar, and all of their families sitting in the crowd cheering for their union in holy matrimony was a different story.

Kovu was sick. She held the bottle of Ace of Spades champagne up to her lips and chugged it like she wasn't an hour away from squeezing into a damn wedding dress. Homegirl needed something to calm her anxiety.

"KD! I know you not that damn nervous!"

Kovu jumped from the sound of Ahni's voice startling her, causing her to spit the champagne out all over the floor. Of course her very best friend in the whole wide world would be there for her special day. Her and Korsika both. Life kept both of her mamacitas busy due to their families, but when the time came for them to support one another, any of them would stop what they were doing to be present. Their friendship was a forever thing.

"Eeeeww! Gross!" Korsika teased as she and Tiri followed behind Ahni.

They were absolutely beautiful in their pearl white, thin-strapped, floor-length gowns with a mermaid styled court train that hid their open toe, Rene Caovilla sandals. Each of their bouquets were handcrafted with white and magenta pink peonies, tied together by a white silk bedding and a shimmer magenta bow in the center.

The sight brought tears to Kovu's eyes. She was getting married for real this time around and it honestly terrified her.

"Why are you crying, yuck mouth?" Ahni teased as she handed her a couple of napkins.

"Y'all. I don't know if I can do this," Kovu confessed as she held her face in her hands.

"What the hell do you mean, you don't know if you can do this? After you pushed us around these last eight months and terrorized the hell out of everybody, including your damn man, who I'm surprised hasn't left your ass by now, you don't think you can do this? You're joking right?"

"Korsi. For reeeeeal," she whined like the big baby she truly was.

"What now? You're so overdramatic. Its New Year's Eve, and I'll punch yo' ass dead in your shit if you cancel this wedding when I could be at home with my man popping this good ole' pussy for him."

"Shut the hell up, Ahni! You already pregnant again. What more could you possibly want? At least they flew us out to the Canary Islands and paid for damn near everything."

"Okay," Tiri chimed in, agreeing with Korsika. "Shit, I think this bish dun' topped Keisha Kaior's and Gucci Mane's wedding budget."

"Oh my God. How did I end up with y'all three crazy asses for best friends?" Kovu laughed as she now stood in front of the floor-length mirror scanning her body.

She'd been on a strict vegan diet the last two months to keep her waist snatched after having she and Marius' second son, Marcel. But with all the nerves from her long lost husband, who she hadn't seen nor talked to in the last three days, eating away at her sanity, the anxiety forced her to get some lemon pepper wings delivered to the hall where they were getting married at. Not only was she off her damn rocker, but now, her stomach was terribly aching from one damn bite of her food, and she was regretting the shit like it was no one's business.

The silk Kimono house robe hung off of her shoulders while the nude, no show panties and tape bra looked painted on her healthy frame. Despite how snatched and beautiful she may have been, Kovu was sad. She felt empty. Her heart was hollow, and it was beginning to be too much for her to bear.

"Do y'all know that me and Marius haven't spoken to each other in three days? *And* I haven't even seen him." Her voice was low as she dropped her face trying to hide her tears.

KD knew she'd been acting ridiculous ever since he popped back up after faking his death, and she knows that she'd also been getting on his damn nerves, but when he went silent on her ass, it fucked with her psyche. Marius finally figured it out how to really check her stubborn ass. He started pulling that silent treatment shit on her as a firm demonstration of retaliation. And not only that, but the nigga even had the nerve to leave her and the kids alone in their Air BnB like he didn't have a damn family that he too was responsible for. It got up underneath her damn skin. She'd been calling him nonstop for the last three days they'd been on the island, but there was no luck. Steelo wouldn't even tell her where he was, and that really sent her head through the damn roof.

"Do y'all think I pushed him away? Has anyone seen him?" She sobbed.

"No. I've been calling him, but I get nothing. He wouldn't even answer for Steelo when I had him call him before we went in to get our makeup done," Tiri expressed.

"Y'all, Steelo, Terrell, and Válo ain't even here. I haven't seen either of them for like, the last hour," Korsika informed.

"What the fuck do you mean they ain't here! Where the fuck are my babies!" Kovu panicked.

"Now hold on. Just chill. Aubrey, big man, and Marcel are out there with your dad and GG. They're just fine. I just kissed their little cheeks right before we walked up here. And **Ceas** and Asia are getting their makeup done now. They should be up in a minute, but them other niggas? That puzzle I cannot solve for you."

Kovu threw her hands up in the air following Ahni's comment. Just fuck it. She sparked up the Backwoods that she had rolled and ready, sitting on a crystal tray next to her champagne bottle and called it quits.

"Ain't no damn wedding. Fuck this shit. Tell everybody they can go," she demanded as the smoke released through her nose.

"Now you're just being extra. You gon' have us out there smelling like weed! You trippin'! Give me this!"

Kovu didn't even try to fight Ahni off when she snatched the blunt from her hand and put it out. She was so disgruntled it simply just made her heart shatter.

Looking over her shoulder at her wedding gown, she could feel as the tears began to race to the surface of her weary irises once again. The off-shoulder, long sleeve, white and sparkly shimmer dress designed by Artisha Cole-Rodgers was breathtaking. The addition of over one hundred thousand magenta pink Swarovski crystals beaded into gorgeous flower designs accentuated her fitted and mermaid styled ensemble with perfection. The sides were cut out where a thin layer of white mesh would barely hide her caramel skin, and the deep slit in the back that stopped right above her butt gave it that splash of sexy that she'd always possessed, no matter how formal the event was. Hell, it was *her* wedding for crying out loud. Who gave a fuck about following a dress code in this day and age anyway?

Accompanying her gown was a beautiful six-foot court train that would linger behind her as she walked down the aisle. Kovu was fit to be the most beautiful bride that anyone in their crowd had yet to see.

The sudden ringing of the alarm going off on her cell was an indication that it was now time for her to slide into that very ensemble that she couldn't remove her eyes from and shut the scene down. They were now forty-five minutes away from showtime, and she still needed her hair finished, plus help with getting her shoes on.

But how could she get ready if the man she were supposed to be marrying wouldn't be there for her to meet him at the altar? The thought crushed her spirits.

Kovu was being a big ass spoiled brat right about now, but if she had to be honest, she was more than ready to officially marry Marius. She was. It was all she'd dreamed of ever since he slid the ring on her finger when they were in Dubai three years ago. But when she felt a disconnection between them, especially after all that's happened within this last year or so, it was like the end of the world in her eyes, and it threw her entire state of mind out of whack.

Their souls were one, so to know that he was still absent and she'd yet to hear his voice had put her in a dark place. Hell, it was tough enough trying to slap a smile on her face and force herself to enjoy what was supposed to be one of the happiest days of their lives, when she and her man weren't even on speaking terms.

What a way to be feeling on her own damn wedding day.

"Aye, yo'! Marius, man!"

Irritated, he pulled the ear buds out of his ears once Steelo called his name for the umpteenth time during his 21's. He just couldn't ignore his ass anymore, so with an attitude very similar to the one his wife's had for the last three days herself, Marius sat the weights in his hands down and reached for a towel to dry his face.

Steelo, Válo, and Terrell were this close to getting their asses popped. They'd been aggravating him for the last hour, damn near begging him to go down to the hall and get ready for his wedding.

"This nigga," Terrell groaned before he took the shot of whiskey that was in his hand.

Marius was now leaning up against the patio railing and was enjoying the ocean view surrounding the Air BnB he'd been residing at alone. His nonchalance was driving them all crazy; they couldn't believe this boisterous as nigga was standing there acting as if he wasn't about to get married in less than an hour.

"Yo', bruh. KD gon' kill you for real if you don't show up at that wedding in forty-five minutes."

Marius ignored Válo's comment as he pulled the cap off the Virginia Black and threw that shit back. He wouldn't dare admit it to them niggas that he was straight up scared as hell to marry this girl for real. Of course, he wasn't gonna "divorce" her after that shit went down in court a couple years back. Marius loved the hell out of Kovu. She was his queen, but this wedding shit was blowing his damn mind. He'd put it off for as long as he possibly could without her turning up on his ass due to his own fears, and now there was no running away from it.

"Would yo' ass just admit that you scared and come the fuck on? Nigga, I'm stressed and it ain't even my damn wedding!" Terrell threw his hands up.

Whenever Marius got to playing these damn games with Kovu's feelings, someway somehow, he still ended up in the middle of the shit. Whether he was on the road or in town with his brothers, it never failed, and never had Kovu been afraid of giving his ass a piece of her damn mind either. Anyone could catch this fade no matter who they were, and Terrell knew it.

"Aw shit. Three page text message from the Mrs.," Steelo chuckled as he opened their thread on his phone. He'd been sent a nice little memo that was typed in all caps of Kovu cussing his ass clean the fuck out.

Marius ran his hand down his face as Steelo showed him the screen but soon let a comforting gust of laughter escape his lips.

"That girl crazy, man."

It was the first time he'd smiled all day.

"Bruh, get yo' shit, finish that drink, and *let's go*. I ain't playing wit' yo' ass today."

"See this shit right here? That's that, 'my wife runs this shit,' attitude right there. I ain't ready for this shit, man." Marius waved him off.

Asia had Terrell wrapped around her damn finger since the day they'd met, and Steelo wasn't exempt either. Tiri had that ass right where she wanted him after three months tops, so his sap ass had fallen underneath that same damn spell. It made Marius shake his head because they all were whipped. And Válo might've been keeping his lil' timid ass quiet, but he was goofy as shit for Salt too, so none of them niggas had the room to talk.

KD often had him tripping *just like* these clown ass niggas; his brothers, his A1's, the only men he'd ever trust with his life. His ohana. Note to his actions right about now.

"Look, man. Y'all ain't spoke in three days. You ain't seen her. You ain't seen yo' kids. All bullshit aside, man. Me, T, and V know how you feel about KD. If you wasn't with it, then we wouldn't even be here. I'mma just be honest, we all know sus runs shit, so let's take this last shot and get to it."

Steelo *had* to be the voice of reason here because with the way Terrell was spazzing out mixed along with Marius' untamed emotions and Válo's goof troop ass recording everything with endless laughter, who knows what the fuck they'd get into if they all were tripping.

"In a minute, I'm about to knock his ass out, and we gon' drag this nigga to the altar. He gon' be standing there with a damn ice pack up to his head when KD come down the aisle if it's left up to me."

Marius couldn't hold his laughter back. Terrell was a damn fool. He was the most anxious of them all like it was his damn wedding!

When the text message notification went off on Marius' phone though, his heart started racing when the name **WIFE** appeared on his screen. Seeing it honestly slapped an inevitable smile across his face.

Marius was acting just as spoiled and obnoxious as his woman was. Boy, were they two peas in a got damn pod.

WIFE: If you don't want to marry me, it's okay. Can I just see you? I miss you. *sad face emoji*

𝔥𝔘𝔍ℜ

It was twenty minutes to show time and Marius had left her text message on *read*. KD sat along the luminescent, white gold ottoman crying her eyes out with thoughts of his emotional, ole' mean ass leaving the island and going back home. Marius *would* pull some shit like that; and yes, even on their wedding day. She knew him like the back of her damn hand and wouldn't put anything past him after he'd faked his damn death like that.

Her cries filled the air as the door to her suite quietly opened. Kovu sat with her back to the entrance, so she paid it no mind when the person had walked through the door. She was going through too many emotions to pay attention to her surroundings. Not when this turmoil and sorrow was drowning her beyond all means. Shorty was just through.

"I'm supposed to be happy...nothing about this fucking day is happy. I just want my husband. God, we don't even have to do this anymore. I just want him to hold me. I'm sorry..."

Kovu's heavy tears trickled onto her lap like little lost falling stars, staining her bare thighs since she still hadn't gotten dressed yet. She wouldn't dare remove that damn gown from off of the mannequin. If anything, she was two seconds away from sliding her jeans on and leaving this damn island with her little munchkins in tow in a minute. How's that for a grand entrance?

"Straighten up your face, KD. You know I hate to see you like this."

Quicker than she could process his voice consuming the crevices of her ears, Kovu spun around on the seat to be face to face with her stubborn ass man.

Damn.

Marius uttered in pure astonishment at the sight before him. His wife was...absolutely beautiful and flawlessly divine to every sense of the English word. Her makeup was styled with a light natural beat with hues of magenta eyeshadow and silver shimmery eyeliner enhancing her look.

362

Her hair was pinned up with long, silver clamps to help her deep waves retain their body and volume. And even though she wasn't fully dressed nor near ready to make an appearance, Marius felt his chest tighten knowing that the angel sitting before him was all his with no strings attached. He honestly wanted to shed a few tears... to this day, Kovu Corletta *Usher* was one of the rarest diamonds he couldn't believe he'd been blessed to find.

Something so precious and historically monarchical that he'd do anything to sacrifice or die for. Hell, to Jodeci cry for...

A feeling of relinquishment overcame his weary wife, forcing her to exhale and crack a genuine smile for the first time in the last thirty minutes. Just knowing they were in the same room, despite tradition, gave Kovu such a relishing sense of peace.

So fuck that it's bad luck to see your groom before the wedding bullshit. Legally, that ass was already hers! Usher had been slapped on her name for three years now, so to hell with a punk ass superstition.

She too was captivated by the appearance of her knight in shining armor. He was clean as a fucking whistle in the white custom made, Mandarin collar tuxedo suit specially designed by Tom Ford. Along with a pair of complimentary black straight leg slacks and men's twist-front leather loafers, his attire was tailored to underline his frame with precision. And how could we forget the magenta hanker

chief peeking out of his jacket pocket to match his bride's gown?

His hair was tapered, lined, and cut to perfection with his deep, silky waves spiraling out of control. A diamond encrusted Richard Millie clung around his right wrist as two matching diamond encrusted Cuban cuff links donned his left. His thick and full beard flawlessly outlined his full pink lips, coining him with her favorite look of his of all time. Marius was pissed when she made him cut his hair after growing it back out to his curly fade, but it was whatever to put a smile on her face no matter how much he wanted to give her aggravating ass a damn swirly.

Without hesitating, Kovu hopped up to her feet and jumped into her man's arms before she could even begin to second guess it. Instantly she was hypnotized by the smell of his cologne drifting from his clothing as he reached down and gripped her juicy ass that was spilling out of her thong.

"Marius, I'm sorry! I'm sorry! I'm sorry! I'm so, so sorry, babe!"

Kovu sobbed with agony as she wrapped her arms tightly around his neck. It felt like they hadn't seen each other in ages all due to her bratty behavior.

Marius chuckled as he pulled his head back and stared her beautiful ass in the eyes before he placed a kiss to her lips.

"I'm sorry too, mama. It's not just on you. Papi should've kept it real wit' you from the jump. I swear everyday with you is like the first time when I got the chance to hold you in my arms...This shit is scary, KD. I'mma be honest."

Kovu got lost in his copper-brown eyes, remembering those very words from the day when they made up at the hotel following their first dispute. She hung her head over to the side, admiring his facial features while rubbing the back of his head. My God, she'd missed this man to infinity and beyond. She didn't understand why he continued to play with her heart, knowing she was bat-shit crazy for his love.

"Then you have to communicate that with me, babe. Not just walk away. We're better that..." her voice was soft as she lightly pressed her forehead against his, their lips only meters apart. "And I know I'm a handful. Planning a wedding is not easy at all; especially when I just wanted our day to be perfect, but I wouldn't be me if I wasn't this way, Marius. Nobody told you to ever love me the way you have since the day you picked me up from the police station. Babe, I feign for you. I need you. Sometimes I think I'm so fucking hooked and crazy for the rush you give me that I need to be weaned from off of you."

"Ain't no weaning from off of shit, mama. I crave you just as much as you crave me. More than I've craved roaming the streets, or anything else in this world for that matter. That's why we're now, right...right?"

The desire burning between them should've triggered the fire alarms to disengage; oh, they were in so deep. A groan escaped between Kovu's lips when her husband slid his wanting tongue into her mouth. A ravishing spell consumed her yearning body with mounds of intensity as the bulge in Marius' pants continued to grow and press against the sacred apex between her thighs.

Kovu was panting; their lips hungrily smacking against one another's as their caress projected nothing but fiery, passionate sounds.

"Marius...fuck me...fuck me now," she demanded with her words releasing each and every time she broke their kiss to somewhat breathe.

KD didn't give a damn how many minutes were closing in on them until the ceremony was set to begin. She needed to feel his thick dick tattooing the pits of her feminine cave with permanent traces of his fucking name.

His majestic tongue driving even deeper into her sweet folds until her pussy flooded along the hood of it so he could feed her the remnants. Right before he reentered her moist fortress and worked her middle with tantalizing thrusts that would continue to concur more of her buried treasure.

Kovu wanted to submerge his pulsating cock so deep inside of her that she could taste the saltiness from his shaft, mixed with the velvet bliss produced by her juicy pussy amongst the taste buds embedded into her mouth. She wanted him so fucking nastily that the smile on her face as she walked down the aisle would be a dead giveaway to the attendees that it was, indeed, dick induced.

Marius held himself over Kovu's body panting, gasping for air while their bodies moved as one until they couldn't go another inch. KD wrapped her arms around his back as he collapsed on top of her. The sound of the bells ringing in the air indicated that the pianist had begun with the first song in preparation for their wedding party to begin with their entrance into the ballroom. They looked into one another's eyes and laughed at the thought of them wrapped up within the sheets and laying in each other's arms when a crowd of over two hundred people were waiting on them to be wedded.

"You promise not leave me this time, Mr. Usher? Once I put that dress on, you know there's no turning back, right?"

He looked into her eyes while holding up her left hand to kiss her ring before he leaned over and kissed her lips.

"I do...I love you, Lady Monster."

Kovu smiled bright as day as he laid his head along her chest, now ready to get with the program, thankful that they were finally on the same page.

"I love you too, babe. Now, come on. Let's go do this thingy."

"You mean our wedding?"

Laughter escaped her lips as he gracefully planted wet kisses amongst her neckline.

"Yes, babe. Let's get dressed so we won't be late to our own wedding."

𝕳𝖀𝕱𝕽

Marius had the entire audience in tears from the way he wept the moment Kovu turned the corner and appeared at the back of the Cabana. It was elegantly decorated with an eight-foot tall arch consisting of freshly picked white begonias, magenta orchids, and nearly one hundred silver-studded pearl bead stems, giving it the perfect splash of color to match their wedding theme. A smile covered her face witnessing Steelo and Terrell by his side, their hands on each of his shoulders as he cried into the handkerchief. It wasn't one of those cries that made you question a man's masculinity. It was a cry deep from his soul proving to everyone in attendance that KD was the love of his life. He gave his heart to Kovu when he knew nothing about love. When he had no hope in women. When his fears were haunting, and his heart was primitive, yet she walked with him through every single trial and tribulation.

Even at his worse, KD saw the man in the mirror. Even when he fought teeth and nails against the love and affection that she had to offer; she never gave up on him. On most days he swore he didn't deserve her. Dripping in insecurity, before his retirement, he'd been waiting on the day when she packed up her shit, took their kids, sold him out to the feds, and walked away because she knew that she deserved better than a Marius Lionel "The Monstrosity" Usher. And although KD did have to take some of those things to that measure to show him that there wasn't room for both; for his selfishness and selfless acts, Marius manned the fuck up and did what he had to do instead of seeing her as a threat; as an enemy.

Falling in love with the beautiful soul making her way down the aisle to him was like a rebirth.

A second chance.

A restart button.

A double roll of the dice.

A do-over.

The opportunity to exit the cold world he'd been drowning in so he could enter the gates of heaven that he never believed awaited him.

Marius loved Kovu's spirit. Her smile. Her drive. The way she'd always had his back through wrong or right. The woman whose chest he could nestle upon in the wee hours of the night and not feel judged or less of a man when he needed that extra love and affection. She'd taught him everything he'd known about love. It's purity. How it was altruistic. It's difficulties; the complexities that could easily tear them apart if they weren't willing to do the work and water one another when they needed the strength. He'd love this woman and their children beyond the grave; beyond this lifetime. Their love was like an infinite oasis that would never dry out, and even if he had to go heads up against mother nature herself, then that was a risk he was willing to take to keep them afloat.

Marius got himself together as Kovu kissed her father's cheek, who too had tears in his eyes. He was officially giving his daughter away to the only man he'd ever see fit for his princess; one who had treated her like nothing less than royalty since the day he'd met her, and for that, they would always have his blessings.

The crowd reacted in awe when Marius wrapped his arms around Kovu's waist and buried his face in the crook of her neck. Their love hovered over them all like a nexus as they then pulled apart and stood before the preacher, giving him the ground to take the ceremony from there.

Kovu's 40's styled, deep and wavy long tresses slightly blew in the wind as she held her hands in the palms of her man's; never breaking eye contact as the preacher continued with his spiel. A smile covered her tearful face as Marius continued to reach up and thumb them away, careful to leave her makeup intact. She was so beautiful. An angel who restored his faith. A cherub who rekindled and reconstructed his magnanimous bond with the Lord who they were soon to be united in holy matrimony under.

He wished Lena could be there as a witness. To observe his growth and be proud of how far he'd come from such a harsh beginning. Through all of their hardships, one promise he'd never broken was to always love and cherish his mother despite her demons. Marius believed that the love he retained for Lena was the exact sentiment that he needed for the day when he laid eyes upon his KD. A black soul wouldn't have saved her. A Monstrosity he may have been, but even a single grain of rice could tip the scale. After all of these years, he'd finally accepted his lack of hate towards his mother. Marius was no longer ashamed of feeling such a way because it symbolized that seed of faith that Louise had always warned him about. It was the faith that he needed to surpass the demons and insecurities that have always held him back from evolving into his greatest potential as a man, and that was being this woman's husband.

The light winds blowing caused the beautifully custom made, Bohemian crystal wind chimes to sing a melodious beat in the air as the preacher began to wrap up before the exchange of rings. It gave them both the jitters to know that they were only moments away from being joined as one, and as Marius continued to look Kovu in the eyes, he thanked God repeatedly that tearing up Trinity was a tribulation in life that he had to experience. In all honesty, if it weren't for him raiding that club, he never would've crossed paths with her, nor be blessed with the opportunity to bask in her love until they grew old together.

His life was now complete.

Opting out of vows like a traditional wedding, once the preacher was finished with the opening and the reading, Kovu turned around and smiled brightly at Ahni, her maid of honor, when she handed over the velvet ring box. She then smiled brightly at her husband once she flashed the custom made Patek Philippe diamond encrusted wedding ring of his. It was designed with a thin band of rose gold diamonds in the middle to match the same rose gold center around the ring of her very own.

Kovu was articulate and down to the wire with every last detail when it came to their ceremony, and little did she know, her husband appreciated her time and dedication. Not only given towards the physical aspects of this very day, but towards the dynamics of their relationship as a whole.

He too slid a wedding band around her ring finger to accentuate the diamond glistening on her engagement ring before they held their hands together and followed along with the reverend by cues.

"Do you, Kovu Corletta Daniels, take Marius Lionel Usher to be your lawfully wedded husband, promising to love and cherish, through joy and sorrow, sickness and health, and whatever challenges you may face, for as long as you both shall live?"

Two solitary tears slid down her cheeks as she trembled a bit before bashfully smiling and nodding her head in agreement.

"I do."

"And do you, Marius Lionel Usher, take Kovu Corletta Daniels to be your lawfully wedded wife, promising to love and cherish, through joy and sorrow, sickness and health, and whatever challenges you may face for as long as you both shall live?"

"I do."

"And now, by the power vested in me, I hereby pronounce you husband and wife. You may kiss your bride."

The crowd went wild once Marius flipped Kovu's veil back, grabbed her by her precious face, and kissed her lips as the music from the band began to play. As of December 31, they were officially united together, under God, as Mr. and Mrs. Marius Usher.

𝕳𝖀𝕱𝕽

Her happiness made his heart swell with pride. That beautiful woman standing in the middle of the dance floor holding their newborn son in her arms with their daughter and Mr. Big Man, Jayce, down by her side, was all he needed in this life of sin. Family once was a word that Marius used so lightly that it honestly didn't exist in his vocabulary outside of his brothers and great-grandmother. Now, he wouldn't know what to do without that unity.

"Aye, congratulations, bro. That nigga, married. For real, for real this time, Touché. This ain't the same lil' nigga that used to hit the streets with us in Louisiana all summer; nigga who swore he'd never get tired of fucking hoes."

Marius chuckled as she slapped hands with his childhood friends Redd and Touché. Back when he explained to KD how he became The Monstrosity during their car ride throughout Compton three years ago, the OG's he was referring to was BTG and Touché's father, Magnus. They would come down south to visit Redd's family in New Orleans, and since Marius was living with GG during their teenaged years, him and his St. Louis potnas did nothing but spend the summers getting into a shitload of the same havoc that him and Terrell cast upon the streets of Trinity.

It was only right to incorporate his brothers in his wedding while their families enjoyed the ceremony from the crowd. They'd all come a long way; transformed into powerful men who owned the largest pharmaceutical companies, in *and* associated with the United States. Had their hands in the worldwide oil distribution, and now that Marius was making residual income without having to get his hands dirty, the game of golf would be his new niche and gambling enterprise. Hey, he wouldn't be himself if he didn't have his foot in something illegal. His picture was next to the word criminal in the dictionary for crying out loud. Y'all know what the fuck it is when it comes to Mr. Usher. He was a real life savage.

370

"On me. I'm happy for you, man. Never thought I'd see the day. Her court shit was one thing, but to see this nigga in a suit and tie with a wedding band on is another story. Lil' Kovu got yo' ass right. Congratulations."

Marius laughed at Touché's comment before they each took a sip of their drinks.

"Y'all know KD run this shit. Ain't no point in fighting against it now. Shorty got me bagged and tagged to say the least."

"Aye, we married too, bro. Trust me, we feel you on that shit."

Redd still wore his wedding ring after burying his wife in September. He continued to refer to himself as a husband no matter what Lala's current circumstance may have been, and Marius respected that. He knew his brother was hurting. Even when Redd smiled, the traces of his mind-numbing pain lingered with evidence in his eyes. And the days sure as hell weren't easy for him to get through, but slowly yet surely, he was fighting to keep going while hanging onto his faith. Hell, it scared Marius half to death knowing he'd *presumed* his demise to his wife, so having to deal with the aftermath of actually losing a spouse was a battle that he knew wasn't easy to fight. His heart went out to Redd. He prayed for his strength on the daily. Lord knows he needed it.

Marius chopped it up with his potnas for a little while longer before Touché's wife, Jenneda, and her sister, Sweetie, came over and pulled the men onto the dance floor. Everyone was live, vibing to the old school rap that was blaring through the speakers until that "Notorious Thugs" started playing next.

His eyes searched for his bride immediately. Ernest was now holding it down with their toddlers while GG sat with baby Marcel in her arms feeding him a bottle, so that left the newlyweds with the opportunity to do their thing out on the dance floor to their favorite cut. Kovu knew she shouldn't have been drinking since she was breast feeding, but with the amount of milk she'd pumped in the last week alone, Marcel would be well off until she was able to detox and get back on with the schedule. Today was her wedding day, and there was no way in hell that she and Marius weren't making love gone off that brown liquor. There was no-fucking-way.

"NOOOO-TORI-OUS THUUUUUGS! (NOTHING BUT THE USHERS! NOTHING BUT THE USHERS-USHERS!)"

Marius doubled over in laughter at everyone in the crowd chanting him and KD's remix to the iconic track. The support and happiness for their union was mad real, so he swallowed the rest of his drink and put the glass down on the table nearest to him before he proceeded to join her in the center of the dance floor, but first, he had to make one stop.

Steelo was making his way back to the party after pulling his little chocolate drop to the side to eat her pussy for a good five or six minutes because drunk him just had to have her when his tongue wanted it. She'd already made her way back to the crowd and was dancing with KD and the other women. That gave him the opportunity to pop a piece of gum in his mouth and straighten out his collar as Marius approached him. They slapped hands and embraced like good potnas normally do, but when Marius held him secure for a little while longer than usual, Steelo understood that Marius was taking this moment out to appreciate him and their brotherhood.

So he hugged his dawg back, showing the same love and respect before they pulled away. Marius had a pleasant message for him.

"Luh' ya, boy. Straight up. From your undeniable loyalty to the way you've always held KD down; along with my kids. You my brother. I always got you and that's word. I appreciate all you've done throughout the years for me, youngin'. I'm proud of you, and I wish you and young Tiri the best. You continue to treat her right and next thing we know; we'll be back at this shit for y'all's union, a'ight?"

Steelo chuckled as they shook hands one last time.

"Death before dishonor. That's what we live for. That's what you instilled within me, and I'mma hold onto that for show. Be my best man and we'll call it even."

"That's a word, bro. Now come on before KD have them start the song over. You know she a lil' special in the head."

Their laughter filled the air as they headed to the dance floor.

Once he was in range, Steelo snuck up on Tiri and wrapped his arms around her waist from behind before planting a kiss to her cheek. As Marius predicted, Kovu had surely cued the DJ to start the track over from the beginning now that her husband was present. The crowd all surrounded the happy couple and gave them their space as KD draped her arms around her man's neck and kissed him passionately before it was time to chant their lyrics a second go around. The party had just begun. With the way the liquor was being passed around, they'd be outside all night until the countdown for the New Year began, and the after party with a few strippers kicked in.

Wearing a drunken smile on her face, Tiri looked back at her man, not only with blazing, love-filled eyes for him present, but she also had a serious question formulating in her head, triggered from the sight before her. Steelo had already known what she was thinking, so beating her to the punch, he kissed her lips and whispered in her ear, "You already know that's gon' be us one day. I ain't letting you go, shorty. Real shit, so be ready so we don't have to get ready when the time comes. You bagged and tagged."

Heart Up For Ransom

Taug Jaye

"Cause baby in a world full of cancer
When everyone needs a ransom
My momma said love is the answer..."

-Jhene Aiko

Heart Up For Ransom

Epilogue

"Bae, I don't see it!"

"Well, look again, Steelo! I know I put a new bottle in the closet because I grabbed some when me and KD were just at Target yesterday!"

"I said it ain't in here, woman!"

Rolling her eyes, Tiri got up from comfortably relaxing on the lower level of their quilted, soft-gold, tri-level platform bed and followed his whining ass cries into the bathroom. Pushing him out of the way, it took her all of three seconds before her irises landed on the clear bottle of coconut oil that was literally in his face.

"Just like a nigga," she mumbled while sealing her blunt with one hand and grabbing it with the other. "Steelo, are you low-key blind or something? It was right here."

"Maybe if you wouldn't have put all this shit on my face then I could've focused. You know I get a lil' ADD from time to time."

"Boy, shut up. You ain't got no damn, ADD. You'll say anything to justify you doing something dumb."

Yet he constantly called *her* the ditsy one. Tiri took the tip of her index finger and fiddled with the Mimi Luzon 24k pure gold facial mask that he wore, matching the one she was donning too. It worked magic for their skin.

"How much longer I gotta wear this shit?" he griped, tired already of doing the girly shit she'd planned for them to do today. Sundays were her days to call all of the shots unless it was football season and she ran with that shit from one end of the playing field to the other.

"Until I tell you to take it off," she mouthed with a raised brow. "Now come on, Stevie Wonder. I've still gotta do your hair. You want the plaits or a bun?"

"Tiri, I'm a man. It's called a top knot, a'ight?"

Tiri giggled when he picked her up and threw her over his shoulder while smacking her bare butt along the walk back. All she wore was skin and a white Chanel G-string with her hair styled in a high, forty inch extended ponytail.

"Yeah, yeah. You just wanted to see me naked."

Steelo gently sat her down along the sofa section, where she was previously seated before planting a deep kiss to her lips. Tiri could feel the gears in her tender pussy turning as their tongues swiveled back and forth. Her man stood over her with his hands planted on either side of her body for stability, trying his hardest to keep his dick from reaching a peak. He'd been blowing her back out nonstop since five that morning and was sure that juicy thang of hers needed a mini vacay along with some prayer for healing after the hurting he'd put on her.

"I get the pleasure of seeing you naked every day, love. Don't hate the playa, hate the game, a'ight?"

"Shut up," she smiled between their last few kisses before he took a seat on the floor between her legs.

"Tiri, we watching *Matilda*, again?"

"You know I love this movie!"

Steelo shook his head and took the blunt from her hands to bind the seal with the lighter as she got started on oiling his scalp. They'd been laying around the house for hours as if today weren't the debut for her edible café that the citizens of Honolulu and a slew of tourists were eager to attend. Tiri couldn't believe the permanent decision she made to leave California with Steelo and start their lives over with a new journey on the island. She'd be lying if she said she missed the urban streets of the big cities like Trinity and St. Louis because she surely didn't. Hawaii bore a sense of tranquility that neither of her previous homes emitted, but what else was a G6 private jet good for besides putting that purchase to good use?

Traveling wasn't a worry of theirs, and money would never be an issue either. She not only owned a multimillion dollar marijuana segment located in Trinity, St. Louis, and her new hometown, but each location also had its own dispensary, an edible shop, and now, her third and biggest café was going up after all of one year in the game. Not only was Tiri flourishing beyond anything she could've ever imagined, but most importantly, besides being blessed and highly favored in the Lord, she was happy. Standing on her own two feet. Living out dreams that she'd been crowned as the creator for, and beside her along this life-long adventure was her partner in crime: Mr. Valentine.

It was two hours left until they'd have to start getting ready for the big event, so Steelo rolled up another couple blunts and they went through a three-pack of Backwoods to chillax while Tiri got his "top knot" together. High out of their damn minds, they both sat there staring at the television wondering how the fuck Ms. Trunchbull got her position as an elementary school principal in the first damn place. Like they hadn't seen this shit a million times before.

"Babe?"

"Wassup, mama?"

Tiri leaned over and rested her smooth and clean face against his while rubbing her soft hands up and down his bare chest. She took the time out to inhale the natural scent from his skin and the eccentric way it merged with the Aveeno body wash he religiously used. Steelo would always be a sight for sore eyes. From his beautiful face to his mountain height, cocky though lean stature, thick dick, and magical tongue, she could get lost in the sheer excitement that her man candy inevitably exuded.

"Okay. I'm gonna ask another question. Promise you won't get mad."

Tiri and her damn inquiries. She'd do no credit report on this earth any sort of justice. Steelo inhaled, surprised that he was as unbothered this time around by his motor mouth of a fiancé. He'd honestly grown to be thankful that her mouth was so big. Not only was it the perfect place for him to shove his thick dick, but her curiosity kept him from being boxed off and secluded. Via Tiri, he'd learned to express himself in ways he'd hardly done in his past until their worlds collided, and he owed that elevation all to his shorty.

"Wassup, love?"

Her goofy ass giggled before replying.

"Okay, soooo. This might sound weird, and I know you're gonna turn your face up at me for asking such a silly ass question as if we haven't been dating for like, almost two years come the fall."

"Ask your question, Acela Express."

"Who the hell is that?"

"It means you talk too damn much."

"You're so rude," she played like she was choking him with of both her hands wrapped around his neck before kissing his cheek. "No, real shit though. Like, how did you properly know how to date me when we first met?"

"Shit, I didn't. I wasn't the nicest nigga on the block if I let you tell the story."

Tiri took a sip of her ice water before she continued.

"Okay, I worded that wrong. More so like, around the time when we started to progress in our relationship, yet before our intervention in Bali happened. It's like, I just always thought it was weird how open you were with me. A lot of men don't have the ability tooooooo..." she let her brain contemplate for a few seconds, making sure she gathered her words correctly. "To be so evasive and expressive like you were. Especially after all that you've been through. Not saying nothing bad about it. I honestly admired it but always wondered like, how? Am I making sense?"

Steelo chuckled. He knew exactly what she was saying, which is why he laughed. It did come off quite questionable how someone as dark as he used to be, had the heart and initiative to love and care for her and not destroy her outlook on relationships. So he didn't reply right away, being sure to conjure up his words correctly to present young Tiri with one hell of an answer that she didn't expect from him.

"Truth be told, shorty, I learned a lot from watching the way Marius had courted Kovu when they got together. I don't date, Tiri. I fuck. Let me correct that before you get to going in on my ass. I *wasn't* dating. I *only* fucked. I mean, it's not rocket science. Just because I was out of touch with my emotions at one point in time, doesn't mean that I didn't have any. Keeping it one hunnid, bro has always treated KD with respect. Like a queen. I mean, the way he looked up to her as a woman and the way he respected her in correspondence to the way niggas in Trinity respected him? That shit broke barriers for me. Bro adored my sister and he still does. That ain't a secret.

But watching him give her the world without questioning those actions or the dark places he'd come from, honestly prepared me for the day when I met you. I learned more than how to survive and orchestrate crime from that nigga, ma. Had it not been for our brotherhood and me protecting sus, this *Love Jones* shit with me and you would've never worked. Once the seed was planted and my love for you started to expand, I was selflessly willing to put you before my insecurities, the ones I was willing to break away from at the moment of course, and not because I was shown to do that, but because I genuinely wanted to. I'll always want to because I'll always want you...Does that answer your question?"

When he turned to face her, the look plastered across Tiri's perplexing face had said it all, causing him to laugh before he kissed her lips. Shutting her up was one of his greatest specialties.

"Nigga, you just tryna get yo' dick sucked," she sassed while rolling her neck.

"I'mma get my dick sucked regardless; might as well tell the truth."

If she had a quarter for each time this man of hers made her smile, she'd be coined as the richest woman in the world.

The sudden ringing of their doorbell cut what was getting ready to be yet another steamy round of mind-numbing sex, short, before they could proceed any further. Steelo slid into a pair of shorts and an undershirt while Tiri slipped on a casual little tube dress that she wore around the house before they walked hand and hand down to the front door. The moment Steelo opened it, Tiri screamed at the top of her lungs before she jumped into the open and welcoming arms of her best friend, hugging her with all of her might.

"Ceeeeeeeeeeas! Hiiiiiiiiiii, best friend!"

"What's up, girlfriend! Did you think I would miss your grand opening or this opportunity to leave Trinity again? Bitch, you are stuck with me! I've missed you soooo much! Hey, Steelo! Sorry to be so rude."

"None taken, ma. Do ya thing."

Steelo took in their greeting with ease, reverent that his girl had some solid people in her life who would support her at all cost. Behind Caesar and Glen was the rest of him and Tiri's family as well. For the first couple of nights, the crew would be staying with them in their twelve bedroom, twelve bathroom palace before Seth, his sister, and the babies went to spend the last few nights with Meme Aruba and her husband in the Platinum mansion on the other side of town.

The old him wouldn't know what to do with having so many people lodging in his damn house no matter how many square feet or acres of land it consisted of. But the fact that he had a "family"; one who undoubtedly loved him in return, one who had the room in their hearts to shift around for his fit, one who was eager to make up for lost time and create new memories with him now in the picture... it was something he'd always prayed for. And to his surprise, God had taken his loneliness and multiplied the family he never had into two dynasties that Steelo continued to thank Him for every night before he closed his eyes for bed.

The prodigal son was no longer in existence.

"Hi, Uncle Steelo!"

Steelo squatted down low and caught his beautiful niece, Ariel, in his arms, who was the spitting image of his sister.

"Wassup, boo. Missed you."

"Missed you more! Oooooh, is this your house? This mug slaps!"

"Aerie, stop saying that," Nasir laughed as she walked up on the porch with a sleeping Asim on her hip. Seth Jr. was too busy clinging to his father's side, who was still over by the limo.

"But it does, mommy! Looky!"

"You're three. What do you know about anything slapping, young lady? I see I'mma have to slap y'all damn daddy because that's where you get it from."

"I'm almost four, mommy!"

"Our crib do slap though, sus."

"Shut up, Nuri. You're not making it any better," Nas teased as they embraced. "Hey, baby brother." She kissed his cheek. "How's it going? Is Tiri pregnant yet?"

Steelo chuckled.

"You gon' be the first to know when it happens, sus. I promise."

"Mommy, I have to pee-pee," Ariel whined while reaching for her mother's arm.

"This child has the bladder the size of a peanut. You just used the bathroom before we got off the plane. Come on, little diva. Where's the nearest bathroom, brother?"

"To the left, third door down on the right."

"Okay, thanks."

Glancing across the yard after Nasir disappeared inside of the house, Steelo could see that Tiri was pretty busy conversing with her brother, Riley, Seth, and the rest of them as they unloaded their limousine too. Her smile was contagious, and that was the main thing that he lived for these days.

"Wassup, lil' bruh."

"What up." Steelo slapped hands with Ali before they embraced with a traditional one-arm hug. "How you holding up?"

"I'm straight. Them stock numbers so mu'fucking high I can't keep up. I'mma need me a secretary in a minute fucking wit' you, man."

His little brother chuckled.

"On me. That's the power of supply and demand, mane. Finessing niggas at they own game. We gon' always eat."

"Aw, fasho."

"Awwww. Look at my boys."

They each turned around at the loving sound of their mother's cooing voice. She was holding a sleeping Boo in her arms before Ali grabbed his princess so she and Steelo could embrace. He wrapped his arms around his mother's shoulders as if he'd been doing it all of his life and held her close. A chill ran up his spine each time she was near. Each time he heard her voice, it was infectious and provided him with mounds of gratitude, honored to call this woman his mother. He was truly blessed.

Steelo placed a kiss to her forehead before they pulled back and looked one another in the eye. One year later and Catori still found her green irises tearing up from the mere sight of him. Mr. Nuri Princeton Valentine: ex-assassin and crime lord, present-day stock owner/investor who was worth millions of dollars, owner of one of the two pharmaceutical companies in Ireland that once belonged to the O'Sullivan heritage, a free man to live his life as he pleased, and most of all, Catori was just thankful that she was now a part of it.

Her life was complete.

"How's life on the islands been treating you? In a minute I'm gonna have to get a place out here, myself. Love the new house by the way. This one has your taste written all over it."

Between the ocean-front view, the vineyard, the black granite accenting rooftop paired with the white pillar structure, the floor-ceiling open windows, the twenty foot long fountain that decorated the front yard, and a homegrown farm, her son and Tiri were surely living in paradise.

"It's been fulfilling; a lot better than I could I ever tell you though. I'mma have to show you. How was your flight?"

"Now that sounds like a plan," she smiled. "And it wasn't bad. Just a little jet lagged. An old lady is surely gonna need to take a little nap before the event."

"Bet. Let me show you to your room."

"Hi, Ms. Catori! Sorry I took so long getting back over here; it's so many of y'all all at once! You look good as always!" Tiri exclaimed as she ambled towards Catori wearing a *Colgate* smile with her family in tow.

"Hey, lil' bit. Congratulations! I'm so proud of you!"

"Thank you!"

After greeting everyone else and exchanging a number of hellos, wassups, hand slaps and hugs, Tiri and Steelo led their family inside and gave them a tour of their beautiful home before everyone got situated in their rooms and prepared for their outing.

Of course, Tiri would be the last one to exit the house preceding their departure. Steelo stood from leaning against the hood of the Aston Martin that he gifted her for Christmas last year when she finally exited the front door.

A white, long sleeve button-down crop with a v-cut bust and the back cut completely out showcasing her flawless mahogany toned skin was paired with low-rise denim jeggings that hugged those wide hips and bouncy booty of hers perfectly. Gold, snaked skinned, Tom Ford pointy-toe pumps adorned her feet. The white-gold, diamond chain fashionably worn around her slim waist matched her extravagant 19th birthday gift that glistened around her neck. Tiri's long ponytail swayed from side to side with the sashay of her hips as she carefully descended the stairwell while hiding her face.

She blushed in embarrassment and covered her eyes as Steelo cat called after her with his camera recording her every move. The sunlight was hitting her velvet melanin with perfection through the iPhone lens. If their families wouldn't have been present, he'd bend her over the hood for a couple of minutes and eat that pussy one last time since she had the audacity to get his dick so damn hard. She was fucking gorgeous.

"Let me see that booty, girl. Yo' family know you a freak," Steelo teased as he zoned in on her curves.

Tiri tugged on the waist of her jeans and shimmied inside of them a bit, turning even redder by the second from his comments.

"Yeah, that's all me right there. You see the ring? You see the name, mane? Nuri P on the beat. Tell 'em, ma. That's all me."

She used the tip of her American painted, almond shaped nail to underline his name that was tattooed along her ribcage for the camera, flashing the thirty-karat diamond engagement ring on her wedding finger.

"Signed and sealed, baby."

"That's that shit I like to hear, mama."

After snapping a few more pictures of his chocolate goddess, they began their thirty minute commute to the city since they lived on the outskirts of the capital on a private terrain.

Tiri's eyes began to water when they arrived at their destination just to see the line wrapped around the building and down the block. The elation from witnessing hundreds of waving and cheering customers who were beyond excited to see and soon meet one of the richest African American women who made the Forbes List last year was such a surreal adulation.

As they approached the entrance, Tiri could see Marius and Kovu standing front and center with the kiddos, along with the Koi's, Mr. Daniels, Louise, Terrell and his family, and her roll dog, Válo, with his boo, Salt, too. The support from all of her family and friends was so overwhelming she had to take in a few deep breaths of air to calm her nerves.

The applause was tumultuous when Steelo opened the car door and held her by the hand as she stepped out. Kovu rushed up to her bestie with a bouquet of peonies in hand, Tiri's absolute favorite, before anyone else could do so and hugged her tight. She congratulated her girl on such a big move and her unwavering success as she told her she was proud of her over a million times in twenty seconds.

Treets & Sweets was doing immaculate numbers at her first two locations, so there was no doubt that the one in Honolulu wouldn't be just as successful. Considering the amount of tourist that visited Hawaii throughout the year, she'd bet her bottom dollar on making Forbes a second year in the row.

Cameras were flicking in overtime as young Tiri stood in front of the red bow with a giant pair of scissors in her shaky hands. The crowd was counting down until the moment she was finally able to snip the bow in half, now jumping up and down in jubilance as if it were Christmas in the spring. She couldn't wait for them all to get a taste of what she continued to work her ass off for each and every day, staying up into the wee hours of the morning until she was satisfied with her results.

Dusk purple sofa sectionals aligned the walls of the left side of the café with round marble tables to sit, eat, and socialize at accentuating the extravaganza throughout the building. Recliners, fancy hardwood chairs, oversized bean bags, and smaller marble tables were also stationed in the center of that side of the eatery while the right half was decorated with both personalized and two-seater swing sets that hung from the ceiling. A floor-to-ceiling bookshelf with the greatest African American Urban fiction/Urban Romance novels aligned a wall of its own for customers to enjoy during their stay. And best believe that there was a shelf dedicated to the oh so famous and talented Kovu Usher with her fifty book collection available as well. She even went as far as having a section specifically reserved for the artistic authors that Kovu had signed to her company such as Erin-Gray, their girl Ahni, and even Redd's youngest daughter, Cali.

There was a huge diversity of people in attendance buying their Sweet *Treets* and soul food plates, and to top it all off, she managed to book and fly out Tonya Poynter and The Melvin Turnage band for light entertainment. They were her brother's favorite band that played at *Gold Horns* back home in St. Louis every weekend, and Tiri just had to have them after Tonya sung at Kovu's and Marius' wedding.

Everything was perfect.

Tiri was taking a picture with a few teenaged girls from the city when Messiah approached her. After hugging her happy customers goodbye and encouraging them to enjoy their visit, she turned around and hugged her big brother around his waist.

"Ma and pops would've been proud of you, girl. Congratulations."

"Thank you, big brother. I'm so glad you came."

Her words were slightly above a whisper as she soothingly rubbed his back. They were missing each other more and more these days with her being even further away now, but Messiah was reverent that his baby sister was living her life with no fears, no boundaries, nor limitations. She wasn't the same little Tiri who hid behind athletic clothing anymore. Being bashful was a thing in the past. Uncertainty of who she was, what she wanted, and what direction she was traveling in no longer existed. Tiri Nyree Stallion, soon-to-be Valentine in the future that was sure to come, was finally walking in her purpose and she thanked God for the journey she wouldn't have traded for the world.

"Christmas in Honolulu this year, right?" she beamed as they pulled back and looked each other in the eye.

"You already know it. The girls excited already. Well, Shanti is. You know Jayla still getting her feet wet now that she walking, so she just gon' go with the flow. Yo' nephew will be here before then too, so you know we really gon' be lit."

"OMG! Riley's pregnant again?! *What*?! She did not tell me! Where she at, I'mma get her!"

Messiah chuckled.

"Just found out the gender last week. Lil' skinny ass just started showing. Put some extra *treets* in her to-go bag. I gotta get my woman back stacked out here."

"Siah!" Tiri playfully slapped his arm. "Congratulations! I know you're excited; it's your first boy. You're a great husband, a phenomenal dad—"

"And a loving big brother who gon' always have yo' back, Ny. Living in Hawaii ain't changed shit, you hear me? You know for a fact that I'll pop out under **any** circumstance. I still go crazy out here; especially for my favorite girl."

She couldn't help it, but two solitary tears slid down her cheeks as he kissed her on the forehead. What would she do without their bond?

"I hear you. Malama Pono, Siah."

"Malama Pono, sus. Can't believe you gon' be a married woman one of these days, girl. Steelo takes care of you. I respect that man. Perfect fit for you. And I mean that. Sincerely."

Messiah's emotional ass was gonna have Tiri messing up her makeup in a minute. Her brother could honestly say that he wholeheartedly trusted her no matter how hard it was for him to let her go and live her life. His wife was right. Tiri turned out to be a lot stronger than any of them could've ever imagined, and he was truly proud of the woman she'd become.

"Speaking of Steelo." Messiah raised his hand as his sister's fiancé approached them. They dapped each other up and firmly embraced before Steelo wrapped his arm around his girl's waist.

"Appreciate you, man. Even after all that's popped off, you still standing solid on the frontline for her. That's all I could ever ask for. Thank you for protecting my baby sister. I sleep better at night knowing she's with a man of yo' caliber, and that's real talk. So welcome to the family, again. You stuck wit' us now, mane."

Steelo chuckled as he nodded his head in Siah's direction.

"Appreciate that, man. As long as there's a breath in me," he looked Tiri in the eyes getting lost in that loving gaze of hers that's always held him captive. "Then she gon' be straight."

Messiah took that as his cue to excuse himself and go check on his family while the two love birds enjoyed some alone time.

Jhene Aiko's "Moments" featuring Big Sean began serenading in the air as Tiri wrapped her arms around her man's neck. She'd just known the shit was a joke when she woke up one morning with her fat ass engagement ring around her finger until Steelo got down on one knee and proposed, swearing up to God that he wanted to make her smile for the rest of her life. No, they weren't in a rush to get married nor have children anytime soon, but accepting his hand in marriage and knowing that the love they shared was sacred, unmatched, and on some days, surreal, how could she turn down his offer when on his arm is the only place she'd rather be?

"Five months shy of twenty-one and you made the Forbes List, young Black girl. That's iconic. That's historic. And I'm proud of you. You stayed focus, and you birthed a movement that inspired so many others like yourself to never think that dreams are too big to make anything happen. That the hustle may be sold separately, but things *will* grow into fruition as long as you keep grinding. How I got so blessed to be able to one day call you my wife? How I got so blessed to cross paths with you? Not knowing that you'd be the key and the answer to everything in my life that I'd been missing?

Nothing but God. I'll always be indebted to you, shorty. The fact that you've always been positive and sure enough to tell me that things would be alright, and how that's always been true...I'll always love you, Tiri. If anybody deserves the applause and thanks, it's you. Thank you for rescuing a broken man's heart from out of a ransom that was too high for me to pay on my own. I wouldn't know what to do without you, girl. This shit between me and you is a forever thing, and I'mma stand ten toes behind that."

"You put that on everything?"

Steelo leaned in and planted a deep kiss to her lips before nodding his head in agreement.

"I do."

"Everything you need to be contended is right here
Right in this minute
You can have it when you understand
That all that matters is right here."

-Jhene Aiko

The End.

Taug Jaye

Heart Up For Ransom

Introduction to

Welcome to the Dahlhouse

𝔄 𝔡𝔬𝔭𝔢 𝔞𝔰𝔰 𝔠𝔯𝔦𝔪𝔢 𝔰𝔢𝔯𝔦𝔢𝔰 𝔟𝔶

Taug Jaye

Taug Jaye

Heart Up For Ransom

Warning:

Salt and Válo's story is linked to the Welcome to the Dahlhouse series. The series will be introduced to show you how Salt fits in, then it will give you the prelude to her and Válo's book. Hope you enjoy.

-Author TaugJaye

Taug Jaye

Heart Up For Ransom

Doll /dal/ noun:
A small model of a human figure, typically one of a baby girl, used as a child's toy

Dollhouse /dal hous/ noun:
A miniature toy house used for playing with dolls

Taug Jaye

Heart Up For Ransom

Ever since 1959, Ruth Handler had the world believing that the Barbie doll was the perfect emblem of a woman. Her tiny waist and precise measurements. Her ravishing and "fair" beauty; her wardrobe. God, that bitch's closet was every woman's greatest fantasy. Even greater than a ten-inch dick that could satanically stretch her pussy out into a different dimension.

Yeah, the access to countless Gucci and Fendi, a collection of Chanel bags, lipsticks in twenty-six vibrant and lusterless, though, whimsical colors, and multiple pairs of pumps to match each and every shade...had certainly trumped the presence of a man for sure. Dick would always be a close second because fashion would always reign supreme.

At face value, a doll was nothing more than her hair or her appearance. No one had ever taken her ability to morph beyond a physical puppet seriously. Not when she was crowned as the first female President of the United States of America. Or, when she was an astronaut who'd just touched base on the moon. Not even when she won a Nobel prize for discovering the cure to one of the numerous infectious diseases that the Whites infected our people with many years ago.

Under-fucking-rated.

Only when she was a debutante or a physically unattainable sex mogul; one that birthed the ridiculously high standards that these niggas continued to use against us and demand that we uphold...was a "doll" ever appreciated.

Yet, in today's day and age, when you hear the word "dahl," a masquerade or a night of temporary forever's isn't what instantly pops up into mind. The six women who made up the Dahlhouse in Chamberlain, California, were more than just a figment of the imagination.

More than a piece of pussy.

More than a man's plaything...

A dahl was simply more than a fucking woman.

She was saturated in regality and ran the world ten times as dexterous than her male counterpart because her brain sufficiently focused on more than just a wet ass and a warm mouth.

A dahl under Dahlshay Blaze's command, the founder of their exquisite and flawless syndicate, is more than the clique of bad bitches that are getting ready to take you along a journey in this series that you're not quite ready to indulge in.

Danger is only the beginning of the journey to come. Risks were held to a height to where it was either do or die when it came time to getting money, and the laws that they'd created of their own were equivalent to the very curse that controlled each of their wellbeing.

Each day those very laws were dared to be broken, and although such a sacrificial token…somewhere along the lines, things mistakenly got sloppy, and it soon was the ignition of the Dahlhouse's inevitable demise.

Prelude

"Aht-Aht! No! Who the fuck is this bitch?! When did we even agree on *ever* adding someone else to the fucking mix? Was Dahl's funeral *not* just two days ago? Like, what the fuck are you on, Fox? You smoking glass dicks around this mu'fucka or something? 'Cause I know you fucking lying!"

Honey was furious. As if they already weren't dealing with enough bullshit, this little pleasant surprise had surely taken the cake. With loads of attitude and her neatly manicured hands decorated with bedazzled nails resting upon her curvaceous hips, Honey continued to snake her neck not giving a fuck how her opposition made Fox feel. Hell, she cockily stood there mugging her quote-unquote "sister" up and down as if she were the fucking ops.

"Bitch, have you lost your got damn mind?! You forgot who the fuck you was talking to just that muthafucking quick?!"

Now, Fox was steaming, pipping muthafucking hot as she gripped the handle on her custom made, chrome Desert Eagle, now aiming it right between the center of Honey's American Whiskey brown irises. Those two have always had a love-hate relationship. Fox was mean with a mouthpiece and Honey had a chopper of her own too. She backed down to no bitch—well, not anymore...so if Fox's cocky ass was talking about spitting shells, then why not draw her steel too? She'd waited years to make this bitch eat her clip, and the muthafucking day had finally arrived.

"Look, would y'all quit it? Grow the fuck up. This lil' petty shit is stupid."

Sincere had always been the voice of reason. The mediator. The dahl with the most sense and structure opposed to her wild ass comrades who always stood war ready.

"Nah, fuck all that. Let her bold ass step. Ho, you got a problem, then let's handle it. Trust me, I got yo' bitch right here."

Salt's voice spun sexy and smooth like newly threaded silk as she stood next to her cousin, Fox, with her extended clip aimed at Honey's boisterous ass too. No bitch alive was still around to tell the story of them disrespecting her due to the simple fact that Salt took care of that shit before a war could even begin to brew. Salenthia Santana didn't play with bitches, and if Fox hadn't assured her that joining their crew would make her a billionaire overnight, then little Ms. Honey would've already had three holes in her head like a bowling ball. This bitch had her fucked up.

"Fox...Honey...Just...please. Y'all taking this too damn far. Put the guns away."

"Nah, fuck that shit, Willow! I'm tired of this shit with her!" Honey countered, now standing with both her arms outstretched and both of her burners off safety. One or both of these bitches was gon' die today, and she'd see to it to prepare both of their eulogies her damn self.

Willow, on the other hand, was terrified. Both of her sisters were deranged from the capitol "D" all the way to the lowercase, and if she or, well, more so Sincere, didn't quickly intervene, then their poolside would be lit up and thumping like it was the Fourth of July.

"Pull the trigger, bitch. You mad? Oh, you *mad-mad*, huh? Lil' petunia, don't let these new circumstances get yo' fat ass fucked up around here, you hear me?! I'm seconds off yo' ass; on God I am! And you know can't none of y'all bitches out finesse some heat better than me, so now what?"

Fox's neck was rolling so hard with each word she spat that her oversized, gold door knockers flew in opposite directions, landing on the cemented ground at her feet. Her flawless MCM leather toned skin was glowing in the blazing hot sun that was beaming down on this warm summer day. Her Ferrari red, pixie cut styled in finger waves shaped her face perfectly. The white t-shirt tied in a knot at her breasts, paired with skintight YSL jeans and Jeffry Campbell stilettos complimented her five-foot-seven frame like no other. Her split resemblance to Teyanna Taylor should've painted the perfect visual for your mind to fabricate how buck she was acting as if she were on set for a film audition in this moment.

"Smugga puss, please. You were so quick to withdraw that shit because *you know* that *you* can't beat my ass! And guess what, you can ask your nigga how good this fat ass tastes since you thought that lil' punk ass comment was really gonna move me! Talk shit now, ho!"

"Look, Fox, you want me to smoke this bitch or what? She's mad disrespectful, yo', and I don't have time for this shit."

"Bitch, the exit is right there! You were never invited to the got damn cookout anyway!"

Clink-clink-POW!!

"E-FUCKING-NOUGH! I'M SO FUCKING SICK OF Y'ALL! LIKE, GOT DAMN!"

Silence engulfed the atmosphere while smoke emitted from the Remington in Sincere's hand that she'd just let off into the air. She hardly ever raised her voice, so knowing that she of all dahls was now provoked, in any minute now, it was really about to get ugly.

"Y'all, please. I'm just as shocked about this shit as y'all are too, but like Honey said. Dahl is gone. We just buried her, and in a matter of two days, things have gone from sugar to shit. We're better than this and y'all know it. Y'all really need to chill."

Willow's voice was like the burning sage that omitted the tension and negative frequencies that kept nitpicking at them each, desperately trying to start a civil riot. She was soft-spoken. Sweet as pie. Innocent and almost childlike on most days due to her bashful nature. Each of her sisters, along with Salt, eyed her standing there, beautiful as ever with a peach, pleated bodycon maxi dress hugging her slim frame and wide hips. Long, jet black tresses hung down her back in soft curls while a floppy sun hat shielded her face from the overbearing heat. She looked more like Vanessa Simmons than Vanessa Simmons looked like herself.

And although Willow wasn't the baby of the click, her sisters all felt the need to shower her with a little more love and protection. Willow was more book smart than gangsta, but don't let the apprehension swindle you. In order to even be considered a dahl, you had to be a dog ass bitch. Weak bitches couldn't even make the cut. That was law.

"Well, she started it!" Fox challenged, reverting her attention back to Miss Honey.

"Didn't I say grow up? If y'all low key like each other then that's one thing, but don't be coming up in here on all of this goofy shit. Y'all both starting to look real clownish these days."

"Shut up, White girl."

Honey rolled her eyes following her comment towards Sincere while tucking her hands underneath her arms. She shifted her weight to her right hip, never removing her fingers from off the triggers in case somebody decided to jump stupid.

"Honey, that was low. You know Sincere hates being called that," Willow expressed. Sincere was honestly her favorite dahl, and she hated when people said or did anything out of pocket towards her.

"Mother Theresa, *bye*, okay? Why am I the only one who don't think that this shit is sketchy? This ain't some fly by night operation. We don't even know this bitch, and she's in our dahlhouse? Like, get real."

"You're not the only one blindsided by this shit, alright? How the fuck do you think we feel? We're all mad as fuck about this shit too, but you don't see us pulling out guns on each other either? Do you, *Fox*? Do you, *biggie*?"

"Fuck you, Sincere," Honey snorted with hurt in her eyes. "Y'all got one more time to call me fat. I am pleasurably plump, I don't like women, and y'all gon' stop it with that shit."

"And that's what the fuck I thought. Did all this extra shit for nothing. Crybaby ass."

Sincere sucked her teeth pissed beyond the max. She'd never picked at Honey about her frame, not even in a joking matter, but calling her White girl was a slap in the damn face. She was one hundred percent Black just like the rest of them, and they all knew that shit ignited a demon in the pit of her dark sided soul trying to call her out for her complexion.

"Look, whether y'all like it or not, I'm next on the chain of command, so feel however the fuck you wanna feel about it. If I say Salt running with this crew now, then that's what the fuck it's gon' be," Fox reiterated with a roll of her neck.

She may have spoken with finality, but the other dahls honestly weren't tryna hear that shit. No Sincere nor Willow didn't agree with the way she was going about this, but who the hell had the energy to argue with her right now except for Honey? The dirt on top of Dahl's grave was still fresh, and they just didn't have it in them to be confrontational with all of the emotions that were already killing them softly as an aftermath.

"Who's Salt? What I miss? And, why are y'all so got damn loud? Cere out here shooting big boy shells, y'all all holding guns. Like, what the fuck is up?"

Their attention changed to the confused and late, Trey, who exited from out of the backdoor of their home. She wore pastel pink, Versace pajamas with a matching cami that her C-cup breasts and pointy nipples peered through. Her choppy bob was wild and all over her head from her well rested night before, and an avocado facial mask covered her luminescent, white gold skin tone.

"Well, it's nice of you to finally join us, Su Young. Sorry to disturb your fucking peace."

Fox was snappy beyond all measure, but just like the rest of them, Trey wasn't about to put up with her shit this early in the got damn morning either.

"Who the fuck put salt in your sandwich, ho? Don't be coming at me like that because you're feeling a way. And I'm mixed with Korean for the millionth time. Stop disrespecting me like that. Like, for real."

"Whatever, Trey. I called this meeting last night right after dinner, so tell me why you just now moseying yo' way down here twenty-three minutes after seven? You wouldn't dare disrespect Dahl like that, so keep that same fucking energy now that we up under new management."

"You couldn't wait to take her place, could you? Sounds fishy to me, bitch. Did we even vote on you stepping up? Hell, you never even discussed the possibility of adding someone else to our mix, but mad because we peeped you moving funny. Did you even discuss this shit with Dahl before she died? Does *she* even know Dahl? Has she even met her?" Honey challenged.

You see, Dahl had this sixth sense that made her an Alpha and Omega. She could read people like an open book from a mile away; deciphering the real from the fake like a psychic. Once upon a time, the six of them, minus Salt, of course, were complete strangers. Dahl was the mastermind behind their syndicate; behind their entire organization. It was her who crossed paths with the each of them: Fox Givenchy, Sincere McCausland, Yumi "Trey" Braxton, Willow Sigel, and Honey Farrar, before she introduced them each to one another.

Over the last ten years, they'd all grown close, were still thuggin', and held the Dahlhouse down with nothing but strength and loyalty. Dahl saw something in the each of them that she knew they could bring to the table and help her rake up millions, hell now *billions* of dollars in the dirty money that they all were surrounded by. They formed a dynamic sisterhood that couldn't easily be broken or tarnished. Of course, they argued. Six bleeding bitches in one household? That shit was *gonna* happen, but despite any of that shit, they were rock solid.

So Fox was dead ass wrong for the silly shit she was tryna pull. No one had anything against Salt, let's make that clear. But then again, they didn't know her as Honey so heavily protested. The Dahlhouse was home to a discreet crime organization; one so low key that they'd all been living double lives for years now as if the shit were a formal normality. So why did Fox think they'd be cool and willing about such an abrupt, dangerous, and risky proposition that she tried to force upon them as an ultimatum? It was uncanny and fucking suspect.

"You mean, murdered."

Their attention shifted back to Willow following her comment.

"What the fuck are you talking about?" Fox shot with a contorted face. She was so irritated with all of them.

"Honey said Dahl *died*. She was *murdered*; there's a difference."

Trey lovingly slid her arm between Willow's before intertwining their fingers and kissed her cheek. The sorrow in her verbiage was highly evident, forcing them all to take a moment of silence out of respect for Dahl's absence.

"How about this," Sincere began while running her fingers through her hair. "Let's get an early brunch going and calm down over some fried green tomatoes and mimosas so we can discuss this in peace."

"I—"

"Enough, Fox." Sincere interrupted. "You know you fucked up by not discussing bringing someone else over here, and no disrespect to you, Salt, but this just ain't how we operate. Yeah, Fox, you are the new face of us due to your seniority, but we still working on this transition, so blinding us from out of nowhere wasn't cool. Just say you were wrong and let's get all of this figured out as a team. Agreed?"

"Agreed."

Sincere smiled. Willow was the only one to reply right away, and the most beautiful thing about her personality was her ability to be willing and flexible while also holding herself down. That was her girl.

"Agreed," Trey co-signed.

Honey wore a pissed off look on her face until she gave in and relaxed, finally eliminating her previous grimace.

"Fine, but that still don't mean shit. I got the right to feel how I feel and not be so willing to move forward with this shit either."

Fox smacked her lips as Honey walked off and back into their one hundred million dollar slice of paradise.

The rest of the group followed suit and retreated inside, leaving Fox and her cousin alone to ventilate.

"Aye, love. I love you and all, but don't ever have me walking into no BS like this again. The disrespect I let them bitches get away with almost cost you your life. You know how I rock. I'm only doing you this one solid by overlooking this little situation because I know you loved Dahl and you're out of touch right now with her being killed. But do yourself a favor though and get it together real quick because I'm already not feeling this."

"Look, I know my fuck up, alright?" While resting her hands on her hips, Fox paced the poolside, sauntering with her stilettos pitter-pattering in a sound pitch until she gathered her thoughts correctly. "Listen, mama. I need you. I love all my dahls with everything in me, even that got damn Honey. I'mma ride for they asses tenfold, but me and you? We gotta special bond, and it's crucial that we link up. You making a high rise in this opioid shit, and I know you got connects in Trinity. Check it. Before she died, Dahl was coming for any crew pushing pharm meds in her Terrain.

Bitch was so bananas she wanted to go heads up with that nigga Monstrosity herself until she realized he was an asset and not a threat. You'd rather link up with me than be in my way when I hit the ground running. I'm about to help you make so much fucking money it'll blow ya damn mind. You a whole connect out here, Salt. Take advantage of that shit. I'll smooth shit out with my sisters, trust me, but do you only wanna make pennies in three punk ass cities, or do you wanna go international with this shit like me and the dahls are doing? Look, we addicted to dirty money. We live for this shit. So what about you?"

Salt contemplated over her cousin's spiel, quickly trying to weigh all of her options here. Paper was one of the only things that got her pussy wet these days after all the bullshit she'd been through.

But Fox never knew her girl to hesitate, so it made her wonder what had her cousin's mind boggled.

An image of Trey walking through the backdoor and over to them just five minutes ago appeared in Salt's head before she quickly shook the flashback and looked Fox in the eye. What more did she possibly have to lose besides opportunity?

"I've always been addicted to dirty money, baby. Way before you became accustomed to this life of hustling."

Fox deviously smiled to match the look plastered across her girl's face.

"Alright then. So, *Welcome to the Dahlhouse*, ma. Let's get this money."

Taug Jaye

Heart Up For Ransom

Taug Jaye

Book 11 in the *Welcome to the Dahlhouse* crime Series

Addicted To Dirty Money

Salt & Válo's Story

Taug Jaye

Heart Up For Ransom

Prelude

Police sirens were almost...therapeutic to Válo's spirit at the age of twenty-three. The fumes of boiling baking soda and crack-cocaine sometimes even made his stomach grumble knowing that the scent was associated with a phase in his life when he was the hungriest and most willing to do anything to survive in the streets of Trinity.

There was point in his life where shit wasn't always hand-painted in solid gold for him. Those dark days when he hustled and engaged in police chases to ensure that he'd see another sunrise. Days when his sixteen year old self was running in and out of the projects, robbing and blowing nigga's brains out, then covering his tracks before the Ops arrived.

In times like those, there were days when Válo couldn't see the light lit at the end of the tunnel. God knows there were moments when he'd ran out of faith and let these hard times humble him because persistence almost seemed impossible.

Once upon a time, the strength he now harbored was nonexistent. A time where niggas had him laid out, curled up into a human ball; crying, weak, and terrified while he sat there and got his ass kicked because so much pussy was harvested within his weary heart.

Your spirit was broken in a completely different manner when your own mother turned around and sold you for a fix. Just for the Latina who bought you to introduce you to your first wet dream at the tender age of ten and was sucking your dick before she made you please both her and her woman. Válo was young. Didn't know cat shit from apple butter. Was oblivious to the fact that he'd been getting molested and was being manipulated until he could no longer handle the nightmares mixed with the pressure that ultimately gave him the strength to pack up what little he did have and flee.

Or, at least he tried to.

Malina wasn't a woman who you could easily escape from. She had eyes and ears on every corner of the projects in Trinity because she sold crack in the wide terrain of South-East County. So when her little bundle of Black boy joy was safely returned to her requisition, Válo was faced with his first lesson in physical abuse followed by sexual atonement due to his attempt to leave her. It wasn't until three years later when her apartment was raided for drug trafficking, and he was then thrown into the foster system to begin a new life, had shit changed.

But that was a long time ago. A time that Válo honestly thanked God for. Recovering from those trenches molded him into an isolated, freak of nature that he was one hundred percent proud of being, and now that he'd been blessed with the keys to the streets of Trinity after Marius' and Steelo's retirement, he'd never need for a thing. The great had trusted him with his territory. With the lead in the game. With ownership to one of his most prized possessions before he met a woman who was worth more than his supremacy over a dark terrain.

Y'all, Válo was the muthafucking man in charge now, and he didn't wanna sound too cocky about it, but with the way he was planning to hit the ground running, Trinity wasn't ready for the reign of man like Mr. Santiago. Shit was about to change like they'd never seen it done before.

Válo: You fucking me tonight?
Salt: You eating this pussy tonight?
Válo: I'd eat that fat ass pussy from each and every angle, every fucking day of the week if you quit playing wit' me. I ain't the nigga that hurt you.
Salt: *three floating dots lingering into space yet no reply*
Válo: That's what I thought. HMU when you get yo' mind right. You know where to find me.

𝔄𝔗𝔇𝔐

The city of Trinity had been quiet lately.

Peaceful you could say.

Joyous.

Its citizens were thankful and forever grateful that The Monstrosity was no longer in existence and that his mob had "fled the city." According to legislation, them niggas knew that the consequences would be lethal if they dared to stick around after the brutal attack happened with the Irish Mob some odd months back.

Niggas could revert back to moving pounds and key's without the hood tax evasions burning their profits. Business owners could sleep at night, not in fear of the possibility of losing their wives and children, or worse, coming up dead or missing because a nut shit ass nigga was no longer robbing them of their revenues either.

Hell, people were inhaling the air differently, swearing that industrialization had never been birthed. Not with the way ventilation had been deemed to be so crystal clear. You see, shit moved differently when you didn't have a noose around your neck or a bounty on your head...but how long would the peace last until the right force came along and triggered a new reign of turbulence?

Válo sat in the backseat of the Maybach limousine cool as a fan with a blunt hanging out the side of his mouth. Being chauffeured around had its pleasantries. Just know off rip if he was behind the wheel of a vehicle these days, either Válo was on some late night tip shit or he was on a mission that usually involved gunfire, roaring engines, and high-speed chases. That dangerous shit, you feel me?

When the vehicle began to slow down upon their arrival to their destination, Válo grabbed the lint roller from off of the seat next to him and ran it over his black cotton, button-down by Givenchy before hopping out once his door was swung ajar. Depending on the caliber of the meeting, he'd either stick to his swag and don a fit that was more comfortable versus pulling out the ole' faithful Tom Ford three piece suit if he knew he wasn't getting his hands dirty. Yet he'd known for a fact that bloodshed would be the aftermath preceding his current visit, so Balmain denim jeans and Givenchy Black Jaw High Sneakers to complement his top was more suiting for the hour.

Standing six-foot-two in height with a slim yet lean build, Válo wore a grim look plastered across his face as a squad of five men strode in uniform behind him dressed in all black. A gold, diamond encrusted pinky ring and Patek Philippe 18k diamond watch to match the Herringbone chain swaying around his neck, reflected in the sun as he removed the blunt from mouth. After taking that last deep toke which caused his high to elevate to the next level, Mr. Santiago was officially war ready.

Silky, tsunami thick waves and a precise fade crowned his face with perfection. His dark-fawn colored, clear skin graced in a mural of black ink from his brows to his ankles; his piercing hazel eyes, full pink lips, and fine mustache hairs to accentuate the hair on his chin inevitably put you in the perspective of musical artist, Bandhunta Izzy. Fine as hell with murder in his veins and 94 inches of thick dick swanging between his legs that only the right bitch could take... and hell, she needed to get her muthafucking act right and quit fucking wit' him like his time was free or like he wasn't feeling their vibe, but that's another story for a different chapter.

When murder was on his mind, the rest would have to wait. Válo had an insatiable desire to make niggas remember his name after paying lucky contestant number one a pleasant visit. He'd deal with Salt's wishy-washy ass later on tonight, no matter how tripped up she was after his last couple of text messages. The city of Trinity had a new ambassador in place who was ready to make his debut, and he swore with his right hand up to God that them niggas weren't ready.

His palm and his trigger finger was itching, meaning anybody could get it, and they'd all learn soon that there was never a promise made that Mr. Santiago didn't keep. He'd learned from the best and was born a different breed...

Coming Summer of 2020

Other titles by
TaugJaye

Sweet Like Rosé 1-2
Boss Bitches Need Love Too
Love From A Boss
Boo'd Up with A St. Louis Goon
Do It For The Kulture: Love In The Lou
Rich Sex (Collab c/ AJ Write) 1-2
Christmas With My Westside Hitta
Power of the P: Love, Sex, & Thugs 1-2
Your Love Keeps Pulling Me Back
All These Kisses: Love From A Young Thug
Falling For A Young Baller (Collab c/ AJ Write)
Down To My Last Breath
Lovers Until the Grave 1-3
Behind Closed Doors

Taug Jaye

Heart Up For Ransom